SCAR
ISLAND

DAN GEMEINHART

SCHOLASTIC INC.

For all the librarians, teachers, and parents who
dedicate themselves to getting books into the
hands and hearts of our children.
Heroes, one and all.
—Dan

Copyright © 2017 by Dan Gemeinhart

This book was originally published in hardcover by Scholastic Press in 2017.

All rights reserved. Published by Scholastic Inc., *Publishers since 1920*. SCHOLASTIC and associated logos are trademarks and/or registered trademarks of Scholastic Inc.

The publisher does not have any control over and does not assume any responsibility for author or third-party websites or their content.

This book is a work of fiction. Names, characters, places, and incidents are either the product of the author's imagination or are used fictitiously, and any resemblance to actual persons, living or dead, business establishments, events, or locales is entirely coincidental.

ISBN 978-1-338-05385-2

10 9 8 7 6 5 4 3 2 1   18 19 20 21 22

Printed in the U.S.A.   40
This edition first printing 2018

Book design by Nina Goffi

CHAPTER ONE
A DARK PLACE INDEED

It's no fun shivering when you're wearing handcuffs.

It doesn't help to be seasick, either.

Jonathan Grisby sat hunched over in the wildly rocking boat and tried not to throw up. And he tried not to let his teeth chatter together so hard that they shattered. And he tried, at the same time, to look like he didn't care.

It wasn't easy.

The little boat rocketed off of each wave and crashed into the next with a jolt that sent shots of pain into his rear from the metal bench. His clothes were wet from the salty spray. The wind kept blowing his straight black hair into his eyes, and with his hands cuffed he couldn't brush it away. The sun was already down and every second brought more darkness.

He noticed the boat's pilot grinning at him. It wasn't a nice grin. He was missing most of his teeth, and the few that he still had were brown and crooked. Tobacco juice dribbled out from his bottom lip into his scraggly gray beard.

"Ya look scared!" the pilot shouted over the whine of the outboard motor that he steered with one hand. Jonathan just blinked and looked away.

"'Tis all right to be scared, boy." The pilot eased back on the motor, slowing the boat so that he didn't have to yell. He was still smiling, and his eyes twinkled with a mean hunger.

"I'd be scared, too, if I was goin' where you be goin'." The pilot's smile widened, showing off even more stained teeth.

Jonathan threw back his head to clear the hair from his eyes and looked out over the white-capped ocean, ignoring the leering pilot. He was sitting with his back toward the front of the boat, facing the pilot and the dock they had left minutes before. Next to the pilot sat his partner. He was young, maybe seventeen or eighteen, with a kinder face. Not much more than a kid, really.

"Aw, leave 'im alone, Cyrus," the younger man said. "There's no need to tease 'im."

"I ain't teasin', Patrick. I'm warnin'." The grizzled pilot narrowed his eyes and nodded at Jonathan as he spoke. "Wouldn't be fair to toss him to the wolves with him thinkin' he's goin' on some seaside vacation! 'Tis a dark place yer goin', boy. A dark place indeed."

Jonathan, trying to ignore the old pilot, looked at the younger man, Patrick. Patrick's eyes slid away from his own. Like he felt bad. Like maybe the old man was telling the truth.

" 'Course, ye probably knew 'twas a dark place, though, didn't ya?" Cyrus continued. "That's why yer goin' there, after all. A dark place for dark youths such as yourself. Trouble-makers. Delinquents. Criminals." He savored each word in his mouth like a salty piece of bacon.

"How old are ye, boy? Twelve? Thirteen?"

Jonathan bit his lip. He didn't want to talk to Cyrus. But

he was feeling awfully lonely, handcuffed in a boat on the way to prison.

"Something like that," he said at last, with a shrug.

Cyrus's mouth widened into a wolf's grin. "Ah, yer right in the middle, then. Criminal boys, aged ten to fourteen. That's what Slabhenge is for, idn't it? Can't imagine what dark crime ya committed to get yourself sent *here,* boy. They'll have ya meek as a lamb in no time, I'd wager, beggin' to run back to yer mama's lap."

"Leave him alone, Cyrus." Patrick spoke again. "There's no point in taunting him so."

Cyrus's eyes widened innocently. "I ain't trying to taunt him, Patrick! I just feel the boy should know what he's gettin' into, is all."

Patrick frowned and looked out over the water.

"Ah, and there she is!" Cyrus crowed. "Go ahead, boy, turn around and take a look at yer new home!"

Jonathan twisted in his seat and craned his neck to get his first view of the Slabhenge Reformatory School for Troubled Boys over the rusted bow of the boat.

It was a hulking, jagged building of gray stone, surrounded on all sides by the foaming sea. The walls were high, rising up two or three stories from the crashing waves. Several towers stabbed up even higher into the gathering black clouds from each corner of the building. Each was flat-topped and crowned with a black iron railing. A few dark windows dotted the higher parts of the walls. Instead of glass, they all had thick metal bars. In a movie, it would be where the evil lord lived. Or where the good guy died.

There was no beach, no land, not even any rocks . . . The waves smashed and churned right up against the great square stone blocks of the walls. Jonathan gulped. It was worse than he'd heard—and what he'd heard had been terrible. He ground his teeth together and let the stiff ocean wind dry his angry tears before they could fall from his eyes. His hands, shackled together behind his back, squeezed into fists, then went loose.

"Pretty, ain't it?" Cyrus chuckled. His laugh turned into a cough and finished with a thick spit over the side of the boat. "It weren't always a school, ya know. 'Twas built first fer lunatics and madmen." Cyrus laughed again. "That there, for the first hundred or so years of its miserable existence, was an asylum. A madhouse. A prison fer the criminally insane."

Jonathan's eyes wandered over the moss-covered walls, the bars, the turrets and shadows. It didn't look like the kind of place where the sun would ever shine. Thunder rumbled in the dark clouds above them. He swallowed a salty ball of fear.

"Still is, I s'pose," Cyrus went on. "Only now, the psychos is just younger, is all." He finished with another throaty cackle.

He slowed the motor even more, dragging the ride out as long as he could. They were crawling now toward the stone prison, riding up and sliding down the green-black waves instead of bouncing along their tops.

"I wouldn't be thinking of escape, either, boy. Never been done. That's half a mile of ocean we be crossing, chocked with currents and undertows. Plenty of the crazies tried, of course. Threw themselves from the top of them walls there. But the sea is hungry here. It swallowed them all, without a trace. After it dashed their brains 'gainst those walls, of course. Aye, 'tis hungry water 'round here. You can feel it, can'tcha?" Cyrus was almost whispering now, his voice a hissy growl, like a bully telling a ghost story. "Why, it's eating at Slabhenge itself! See it there, chewing on them walls! Eating away at 'em, wave after wave! Did you know there used to be rocks 'round it? There did! And a pier! And a wee little sandy beach all the way around! But the sea, she's been nibbling away nigh on a century and a half. And she'll have it all 'fore she's through."

Cyrus punctuated his words with a good-riddance spit into the ocean. Then he cocked a smirking eyebrow at Jonathan. "You got yerself a cozy new home indeed, boy. A nuthouse full of delinquents, being swallowed by the sea. Ha! But don't you worry . . . if you get homesick, there's always the rats to keep you company!" Cyrus threw back his head and hollered out a laugh.

Jonathan looked to Patrick, who shrugged apologetically. "Yeah," he said. "There be plenty of rats."

They were right in the shadow of the massive walls now. The waves splashing against them were loud. He looked up to the top. There were stones missing, tumbled down into the ocean. The place was falling apart. They passed a window, two stories up. It was black and barred and shaped like a tombstone. For a moment, Jonathan was sure he saw a pale face looking out at him. He had to catch himself when the boat was rocked by a wave, and when he looked back, the face was gone. He shivered again, only partly because of the cold.

"And here we be," Cyrus said. He steered the boat up toward a darkened doorway in the wall, the same tombstone shape as the window. A heavy metal gate blocked the entry and, behind it, a huge wooden door. Stone stairs led down from the gate and disappeared into the black water.

The boat nudged up against the submerged stairs and Patrick leapt out onto the steps, a rope in his hands. He tied the boat off to a rusty metal ring jutting out from the prison wall.

"Enjoy yer stay!" Cyrus hollered as Patrick helped Jonathan step out of the boat.

"Don't let Cyrus scare ya," Patrick whispered as they climbed the steps toward the door. "Just stay quiet and keep on the Admiral's good side. Ya'll be fine."

"What makes you think I'm scared?"

Patrick looked at Jonathan with raised eyebrows, then up at the dark prison they were entering. "Well, good lord, ain't ya?"

Jonathan almost smiled. Almost. He looked up at the grim, crumbling walls of his new home. It looked bad. Just as bad as he deserved.

The wooden door creaked open. A giant stood in the doorway, wearing a dark blue uniform with shiny silver buttons. He was skinny as a skeleton but taller than any man Jonathan had seen in real life. His skin was pale, his black hair short, and he had great dark circles under his eyes. Other than one slow blink, nothing on the man's face moved.

"Is this the Jonathan Grisby?" the man asked in a deep, scratchy voice.

"Aye," Patrick answered. "'Tis." He pulled some papers out of his jacket pocket and handed them through the bars.

"How are you, Mr. Vander?" Patrick asked. His voice cracked nervously.

The man only looked at Patrick from under his dark eyebrows, then jangled a huge ring of keys and unlocked the gate. He swung it open just far enough for Jonathan to slip through. Patrick gave his elbow one last squeeze before letting go. The gate clanged shut.

Jonathan felt himself pulled a few steps forward into darkness. The door began closing behind him with a loud creak.

"Good-b—" Patrick started to say, before his voice was cut off by the slamming of the massive door.

A huge hand, hard and strong as iron, closed on Jonathan's shoulder just as the world turned black.

CHAPTER TWO
THE SINNER'S SORROW

The pain was burning up from Jonathan's knees like hot-white fire. Sweat crawled down his back and he bit his tongue to keep from crying out.

He was kneeling on a dark wood contraption in the Admiral's office, facing the Admiral's desk. He'd been ordered to kneel there as soon as he was ushered in, and the Admiral hadn't looked up from the papers on his desk since.

The Admiral's office smelled of waxy candles, sweat, chocolate, and a vague whiff of alcohol. It wasn't a pleasant mix, and combined with the heat of the room and the sharp ache in his knees, it was enough to make Jonathan want to throw up. His shoulders were burning from being twisted back into the handcuffs after he'd changed into a drab uniform, and his stomach clenched with hunger. He'd gone from shivering in the boat to sweating in the stuffy heat of the Admiral's office. The one-piece gray garment he'd been given was stained and threadbare, and it stretched from his neck to his ankles like a prison uniform. He blew his hair out of his eyes and tried to keep his arms from going numb.

The Admiral sat behind a huge desk made of dark, shiny wood. His thin hair was mostly gray and was slicked down across his head with some kind of oily grease. His nose was the size and shape of an eagle's beak, and above were two shiny eyes, black as olives, that looked too small for the rest of his face. His eyebrows looked like two monstrous, bushy cockroaches crouched on his forehead. A patchy shadow of stubbly whiskers grew on his cheeks and chin. He was wearing a dark blue uniform jacket with fancy brass buttons, like they wore in the navy. It might have fit him when he was younger, but now his neck fat squeezed over the top button of the collar, and his belly bulged out from under the bottom three buttons, which were undone. He sat shuffling through some papers, sipping from a glass of brown liquid, and stuffing chocolates into his mouth. A crinkly pile of shiny gold wrappers grew by his elbow with each chocolate he devoured.

A blond-haired boy, a little older than Jonathan and kind of chubby, stood in the corner with his hands crossed in front of him. He was watching the Admiral with eager eyes, and from time to time shot a smug smirk Jonathan's way. He looked like a teacher's pet, but the kind that bites.

The only light came from ten or eleven tall white candles, flickering here and there from brass holders around the room.

"Brandy," the Admiral said at last. His voice was deep and breathy. Like a dragon's.

The boy in the corner sprang forward. He pulled a bottle from a shelf and poured another splash of brown liquid into the Admiral's glass. The Admiral didn't move except to exhale and raise one of his cockroach eyebrows. The kid frantically reopened the bottle and sloshed more brandy into the glass. The Admiral scowled and smacked his lips but picked up the glass and took a loud, slurping sip. The kid returned the bottle to the shelf and scurried back to his corner.

"Jonathan Grisby," the Admiral finally said. He said Jonathan's name the way most people might say the word *diarrhea*.

Jonathan swallowed.

"Yeah."

The Admiral's glass froze halfway to his mouth. His eyes slid to the kid in the corner, then back to Jonathan. The kid practically ran over to Jonathan, then leaned down to hiss into his ear.

"*You gotta call him sir or Admiral, dummy!*"

"What?"

"*Sir! Call him sir!*"

The kid retreated back to his corner, and the Admiral set down his glass.

"Jonathan Grisby," he said again. The whole room seemed to wait.

"Yes," Jonathan replied. Then, "Sir."

The Admiral smiled with half his mouth. He tapped the papers with his finger.

"This is a terrible crime you've committed, Jonathan Grisby."

Jonathan didn't answer.

"I suppose you, like most criminals, insist you are innocent?"

"No," Jonathan replied quietly, his eyes downcast. "I did it. Sir."

"Hmmm. I see. Unapologetic. Unashamed. No lesson learned yet, then?" The Admiral's face twisted into another half smile. "It will be learned, though. It will. We have wonderful ways of teaching you lessons." He took another wet sip of his brandy and swished the alcohol around in his mouth.

Jonathan swallowed a dry breath. He felt a warm bead of sweat start down his forehead.

With a grunting sigh, the Admiral rose to his feet and slumped around the desk to where Jonathan knelt in misery.

"Take, for example, the ingenious piece of furniture you're currently enjoying. Are you comfortable?"

"No, sir."

"Of course you're not," the Admiral spat. "And nor do you deserve to be." He caressed the age-polished wood with chocolate-stained fingers. "This device is known as the Sinner's Sorrow. She was here even before myself, a lovely leftover from one of Slabhenge's former lives." The Sinner's Sorrow was made all of wood, and rose as high as the Admiral's bulging belly. At its base was a rail where Jonathan's knees rested, a long piece of stained wood that was sharpened to a vicious edge that was biting at his flesh like a dull saw blade. At its top was a slanted, flat desktop and an old inkwell. "Who knows how many lunatics and criminals have knelt here, paying the price for their evil." The Admiral's eyes, blurry from liquor, lapped hungrily at the wretched wood of the Sinner's Sorrow. His gray tongue licked at his dry lips. "How does that rail feel on your young knees? It burns, doesn't it?"

Jonathan looked up, straight into the Admiral's eyes for the first time. "No," he answered in a level voice. "It doesn't burn, sir. It just hurts."

The Admiral raised an eyebrow and sniffed. "Yes, well, *you* would know, wouldn't you, Jonathan Grisby?" Jonathan looked down quickly, stung by the man's words. The Admiral cleared his throat and took a step back. "You're just the latest degenerate to feel her bite. And she is just one of the tools we use at Slabhenge to educate and civilize and correct. And you will be corrected. A crime as wicked as yours will require quite severe correction." The Admiral leaned close so that Jonathan could feel as well as hear his next words in his ear. "You *have* done terrible things, haven't you, Jonathan Grisby?"

Jonathan lowered his head and didn't answer. The Admiral wheezed out a phlegmy sigh and took a step back.

"But all that begins tomorrow. You'll see. You've arrived late. It's nearly all-dark time. Only one little thing remains to be done."

He reached for something from his desk and slid it onto the Sinner's Sorrow's little writing surface: a pen, and a blank piece of paper.

"At Slabhenge, all of our boys write a letter home to Mommy and Daddy every day. To let them know that you are safe and sound and that their investment is paying off. The mail goes out in the morning, and yours is the last letter we need."

"What do you want me to say?"

The Admiral's eyebrows dropped. The corner kid shuffled over and squeezed the back of Jonathan's arm in a hard, vicious pinch. "*Sir!*" he spat into Jonathan's ear.

Jonathan tried to shift from knee to knee to ease the growing pain.

"What do you want me to say, *sir*?"

The Admiral turned his hands palm up and spread his fingers.

"Whatever you like."

Jonathan frowned at the paper and thought of all the things he'd like to say to his parents.

"I can't write with my hands cuffed, sir."

"Of course not." The Admiral tossed a heavy ring of keys to the chubby kid, who jangled and fumbled behind Jonathan until there was a click and Jonathan felt his hands finally swing free. He rubbed his sore wrists and wiggled his stiff shoulder sockets. With a quick glance at the Admiral, he picked up the pen and scribbled out a few sentences, then folded the paper and handed it to him.

The Admiral unfolded the paper.

"*Dear Mom and Dad,*" he read aloud. "*This place is just as terrible as I deserve. Give my love to Sophia. Jonathan.* Hmm." The Admiral shook his head and clicked his tongue. "No, no, this won't do. Try it again, Jonathan Grisby. You can say whatever you wish, of course, but you cannot speak poorly of our fine institution. We don't want them regretting the difficult decision they made to send you here. So, again, without the parts about Slabhenge." The Admiral slid another blank piece of paper across the desk.

"My parents didn't send me here. Sir." Jonathan knew that it wouldn't help him at all to argue, but he felt he had to say it. "A judge did."

The room hung in taut silence.

"Do you think I don't know that?" the Admiral asked, and his voice was darkly low and quiet. Jonathan didn't answer. "Yes. A judge sentenced you to a reformatory for your heinous crime. But he gave your parents several choices, did he not? And they chose Slabhenge, did they not?"

Jonathan swallowed. All of his trembling parts screamed at him to let it go. But he couldn't.

"Yes, sir. But . . . only because it was the cheapest. They had to . . . to pay for half, and we don't have—"

"Enough!" the Admiral interrupted. He bent down low so Jonathan could look into his shiny, bloodshot eyes. "Everything that I wish or need to know about you and your pathetic life, I have already read. You are here because they sent you. And, yes, we save money at the same time that we save souls here at Slabhenge—even souls not worth saving.

Since I now know how very frugal you are, I shall make extra certain that we don't waste a single unnecessary dime on your care, other than the discipline required to correct your corrupted character. Now, the letter!"

Jonathan resisted the urge to wipe the spittle off his face that had flown there from the Admiral's mouth. He blinked down at the paper through the sweat that was dripping into his eyes. His knees throbbed. He scrawled another message and handed it to the Admiral.

"No," the Admiral said after reading it. All the teasing was gone from his voice. "Longer. More pleasant. And mention our food."

"What food, sir?"

"Our delicious and nourishing food."

"But I haven't had any food, sir. And I'm starving." Jonathan's stomach growled as he spoke.

The Admiral ground his teeth and blinked his eyes slowly. "Write the letter, Jonathan Grisby. Then dinner."

It took Jonathan seven tries to write a letter that the Admiral would accept. By the time he was done, his stomach was rumbling loud enough for all three of them to hear, and the boy in the corner was glaring at him with open hatred. The Admiral had gone through three more gold-wrapped chocolates.

"There," the Admiral said, folding up the final letter and slipping it into an envelope. "It shouldn't have been that hard. Awful things happen to boys with awful attitudes."

Too late, Jonathan wanted to answer, but he bit his lip and kept his eyes on the cracks between the stone blocks of the floor. His hair dangled down in front of his eyes and he let it stay.

"Brandy," the Admiral said, and Jonathan heard the kid hurry to fill his glass. The Admiral walked to the door and opened it.

"Mr. Warwick. Show Jonathan Grisby to his quarters."

"Yes, sir, straight away."

Jonathan's head shot up.

"What about my dinner?"

A pair of rough hands pulled him up from the agony of the Sinner's Sorrow and yanked him toward the door. The Admiral yawned as Jonathan was paraded past. He held out his hand to stop them, his fingers pressing into Jonathan's chest. He smacked his lips and leaned down to speak into his face. The sour mix of chocolate and liquor on his hot breath made Jonathan's stomach curl.

"Do you really think a boy who wastes six pieces of paper to write a simple letter deserves to be spoiled with food? Hmmm?" Jonathan's heart sank into his aching belly. The Admiral's eyes slithered to the man who was pushing Jonathan from behind. "No pillow for this one, Mr. Warwick. He doesn't have a brain worth cushioning."

"Yes, sir."

"I will see you in the morning, Jonathan Grisby. Do try to get some sleep. Tomorrow will be a very hard day for you."

CHAPTER THREE
THE HATCH

"Got on the Admiral's bad side, did ye? Ya idiot." Mr. Warwick hawked up a mouthful of snot from his lungs and spit it onto the floor. He was guiding Jonathan through a twisting labyrinth of dark hallways and steep, shadowy stairwells. The whole place—floor, walls, stairs, and ceiling—was made of the same huge blocks of gray stone. Their way was lit only by a hissing lantern that swung from Mr. Warwick's outstretched hand.

"Ye all do, nearly. Bunch of scum, ye are. The Admiral knows ye fer what ye are, aye." Jonathan stumbled on a slippery step and Mr. Warwick jerked him roughly back up to his feet. "Still, ye got it better'n some. You get a blanket, at least. More than ye deserve, likely."

"Lucky me," Jonathan muttered.

Mr. Warwick spit again and flicked Jonathan in the ear hard enough to make his eyes burn.

"Don't ye be gettin' smart, now. Smart gets ye nowhere good 'round here."

"Look, Mr. . . . Warwick, or whatever," Jonathan started, rubbing his ear. "Could I get something to eat, something small, even? A biscuit or an apple or something? I haven't eaten since breakfast."

Mr. Warwick scratched between his legs and snorted. "Ah, me heart's just a-breakin'. Poor little criminal's got 'im an achin' tummy!" He coughed out a mean, small laugh.

Suddenly, he pulled to a stop and grabbed Jonathan's arm. "Ah, now look here, boy." His voice was tight and breathless. He held up the lantern to show a narrow stairway leading down from the corridor they were in. The stairs curved down and around a corner before they were lost in darkness. A low rumbling, gurgling sound and the salty, rotten smell of stale seawater wafted up to where Jonathan and his guard stood. A frayed rope stretched as a flimsy gate across the stairway opening.

"Don't ye never stumble down this wretched staircase, boy," Mr. Warwick whispered. He leaned close to Jonathan's face in the yellow lantern light. For the first time, Jonathan saw his wrinkled face and his one puckered, empty eye socket. He shivered and pulled back.

"Why? What's down there?"

Mr. Warwick's lips pulled back to show a toothless smile. "Why, the Hatch, me boy! A door, of sorts. And beyond it: death and despair and darkness! It be a door that holds back a *monster*. Ancient she is, and dark, and hungry, and just barely held back. She's there, though, knockin' and waitin' and bidin' her time! Not locked in, boy, but locked *out*—and not for long, I'd wager!"

Mr. Warwick stared into Jonathan's face with his one eye for a breathless moment before breaking into a wheezing cackle. "Aye," he said, running his tongue over his toothless gums. "Death himself is yer downstairs neighbor. Yer room be straight up here, with the other no-goods."

Mr. Warwick stumbled ahead with the swinging lantern. Jonathan stood for a second longer, his eyes peering past the rope and down the darkened stairs. He knew the morbid cyclops was just trying to scare him, the new kid, with his ghost stories. And Jonathan was past believing in most kinds of monsters. But up from the stairwell came a thump and a rattle, then a slurping growl. He shivered and hurried after the retreating yellow light.

They rounded a corner and then stopped before a large metal door. At eye level, just above Jonathan's head, was a small rectangular opening crossed with metal bars. Mr. Warwick rapped on the door with his knuckles. The knocking echoed in the cold hallway. Water dripped all around them in the darkness, and there was occasional scurrying, off in the shadows.

Through the opening in the door came the sound of shuffling footsteps punctuated by the steady *thwock* of a cane hitting the stone floor. A bald forehead and a glaring pair of eyes appeared in the little barred window.

"It's I, Mr. Mongley," Mr. Warwick said to the eyes. "I've got me the new one here. No pillow for 'im, either, so you know."

The half face disappeared and there was a jangling of keys and then the door swung open. Mr. Warwick pushed Jonathan through the doorway and stepped in behind him.

Beyond the door was nothing but darkness, but Jonathan could tell from the echoes and the movement of the air that the room was large, with a tall ceiling. Besides the smell of ocean and mold and wet stone, there was also here the smell of sweat and bodies and the unmistakable odor of an over-used bathroom.

The man who must be Mr. Mongley stood glaring at him sideways, one shoulder hunched over. He shielded his eyes from the light of the lamp.

"It's all-dark," he rasped. His voice was a scratchy hiss, like his throat was stuffed with cotton. He was wearing the same blue uniform that Mr. Warwick and Mr. Vander had. Without another word he turned and limped off, thumping away into the darkness on a crooked black cane.

"Go on, go on," Mr. Warwick grunted, poking Jonathan in the spine.

Jonathan's eyes darted around the shifting shadows as he followed the hunched form of Mr. Mongley. There were puddles on the floor here, too, big and small. He could just make out, on both sides of him, openings in the walls. Large rectangular doorways, each with a lightless room behind it, each blocked with the sturdy metal gate of a jail cell. They *were* jail cells, he realized. Or, he reminded himself, *madhouse cells*. They were cells built to hold the criminally insane of the previous century.

There were no windows. No torches. Not even a single, flickering candle. There was no light at all in the room, none except the shifting, swaying light of the lantern behind him. But in that unsteady light, Jonathan saw a silent face behind each black cell door as they passed it. A pair of hands, sometimes, gripping the iron bars. The light was too dim and the room too big for him to see any of them clearly, but he knew they could all see him, walking in the lantern light. He could feel all their eyes on him.

Mr. Mongley stopped at a cell door and rattled it open with his ring of keys. He stepped to the side and Mr. Warwick started to shove Jonathan in.

"Wait," he protested. "I can't sleep in here!"

Mr. Warwick gave him a final push and slammed the metal door. "Then don't," he said through the bars as Mr. Mongley turned the key in the lock.

"What about a bathroom?"

Mr. Warwick raised the lantern and held it through the bars. The cell was narrow—Jonathan could have almost touched both walls with a hand if he stood in the middle. A few feet from the cell door, against the side wall, was a single bed on a metal frame, covered with a thin, lumpy mattress and one ragged blanket. No pillow, of course. And no window. No chair. No desk. No sink. The only thing in the cell besides the bed was a rusty bucket sitting in the back corner.

Mr. Warwick swung the lantern toward the bucket. "That there's yer night bathroom, boy. Sleep tight. And Mr. Mongley don't take to no talkin' after all-dark, so I'd be keepin' yer mouth shut tight, if I was you. Which I ain't, thank the devil."

And with that the light jerked away and disappeared step by step, leaving Jonathan to stand in thickening, choking blackness. Mr. Mongley's cane tapped away with it. There was the creak of the metal door opening, then a final crashing clang as it slammed shut, taking the last of the light with it.

At first, there was nothing but silence and absolute darkness. Jonathan could hear his own desperate breathing, and the hammering of his heart. A cold draft blew through his cell door and goose bumps popped up on his neck. He wrapped his arms around his body.

Water dripped and dropped and dabbled all around, a crazy constant pattering and pittering. And then, all around the room, he heard a scraping and shuffling sound. He strained his ears and then realized that it was all the other boys, walking back from their cell doors to crawl into their skinny beds. Mixed in was the squinchy squeak of mattress springs as bodies lay down and curled up.

He cocked his ear and stepped toward the wall to his right. There had been a watching face in the cell next door, he remembered, but he didn't think he'd heard the sound of footsteps or mattress springs from that cell yet. His closest neighbor might still be standing at his cell door, only a few feet away.

Jonathan leaned one hand against the damp stone wall and pressed his face through the bars closest to the wall.

"Hey!" he whispered, as loudly as he dared. "Is anyone there?"

There was no response.

"Hey!" he tried again.

There was a sound, like a sigh or a breath. He screwed his eyes shut in the darkness and listened harder.

"What?" Jonathan asked.

There was the sigh again, just as faint, but this time Jonathan's ears picked up the sounds inside it.

"*Quieter,*" the voice whispered, almost impossibly quiet. "*Mongley hears everything.*"

"Mongley's gone!"

"*No. He always stays. All night. Quieter.*"

Jonathan shook his head. He couldn't possibly speak any quieter.

"What kind of place is this?" he asked.

"*A bad place. Quieter.*"

A chill shook Jonathan's body. His teeth were starting to chatter. It made the whispering harder.

"It can't be as bad as it seems."

The voice paused before answering. Like it wanted to say a lot more than it could in a smoke-thin whisper.

"*No. It's worse. You'll see tomorrow,*" the voice breathed at last. "*Quieter.*"

Jonathan gulped and took a few deep, shaky breaths. Behind him was a cold bed with no pillow and a bucket he didn't even want to think about. He changed the subject.

"I'm Jonathan. What's your name?"

"*Walter.*"

"Do you have any food?" Jonathan's hunger got the better of him, and his rumbling belly grabbed him by the throat when he asked the question, raising his voice above the whisper he'd intended. His question came out as a desperate plea. It echoed, just barely, in the dark cavern of the room.

Somewhere off in the darkness, Jonathan heard a grunt. Then, coming closer through the total blackness, the tap-tap-tapping of a cane. Beside him he heard Walter scuttle back to his bed. Jonathan held tight to the metal bars, eyes wide, his head rotating from side to side, seeing nothing. The tapping came closer, and closer, straight toward him.

Finally, it stopped. In the echoing stone chamber Jonathan couldn't tell where it had stopped—in the middle of the room, or inches away. He waited, breathless.

There was a whoosh and another grunt and then Jonathan was hit by a shocking surge of freezing water. It hit him full in the face and drenched his clothes. His breath was sucked from his lungs by the frigid water.

"*No talking,*" Mr. Mongley hissed like a dying rattlesnake. Jonathan gasped and coughed, his body racked by violent shivering. "*The next bucket won't be water.*"

The cane tapped away, quieter and quieter, and then fell silent. Jonathan stood shivering, his teeth rattling. Then he turned and felt his way back to his bed.

He eased down onto the mattress. It was about as thin as a folded-up newspaper and just about as soft. He pulled the scratchy blanket around his soggy self and curled into a shaking ball.

Something snuffled and squeaked under his bed.

He blinked into blackness and tried not to imagine a day that could be any worse than the one he'd just had. He bit his lip and ran his fingers over the skin of his arms. After a few moments, his thoughts were no longer for himself or his cold or his hunger. Shivering alone in the black, his thoughts were for Sophia. And his silent tears, when at last they came, were for her, too.

JONATHAN'S FIRST LETTER HOME

Dear Mother and Father,

I have arrived at the Slabhenge Reformatory School, safe and sound. The trip was pleasant. The school is quite impressive and the food is very good. I'm better fed here than I was at home! Although I am a little angry at you for making the difficult decision to send me here, I am sure that it will all be for the best. Give my love to Sophia.

Your loving son,
Jonathan Grisby

CHAPTER FOUR
A DARK TALE, TO BE SURE

Jonathan gripped the knife in his hand and fought back the tears that burned in his eyes.

"My god," he whispered to the boy next to him. "How long do we have to do this?"

The boy looked around to make sure no adults were within earshot. The dark brown skin of his head was shaved almost bald, and it glistened with sweat from working in the hot, crowded kitchen.

"Until they tell us to stop, man," he murmured, handing Jonathan another onion.

Jonathan had opened his eyes that morning to the same nightmare he'd fallen asleep in. Freezing cold. Ravenously hungry. Lost in hopeless darkness. They'd been roused from their sleep by Mr. Mongley's hoarse whisper-shout and the clang of his cane against cell bars, then lined up and marched to a huge, cluttered kitchen. With no welcome or instruction, he'd been handed a knife and a basket of onions and shoved over to a long counter. He was three onions in now, and his belly was howling for food.

He looked around as he worked. All around him, other boys were bustling and cooking and chopping, each wearing the same dingy gray one-piece uniform that he was. There seemed to be about fifteen of them. Some looked a little older than him, some a little younger. None of them looked happy.

"Don't they have, like . . . a cook, or something?"

The kid snorted and rolled his brown eyes.

"Yeah, right. Why pay a cook when they can make our sorry butts do it? The more we do, the more money goes in the Admiral's pockets." He wiped at his eyes, then nudged Jonathan and pointed with his chin at Mr. Warwick, glaring at them from the corner. "*Quieter*," he whispered.

Jonathan smiled. "You're Walter?"

The kid nodded. "You almost got me drenched, man. Jonathan, right?"

"Yeah."

"Well, welcome to Slabhenge. How long you here for?"

"Ten weeks," Jonathan answered. It hadn't sounded that terrible in the courtroom. He'd almost *wanted* to come, to get away from . . . everything. But standing there now, ten *hours* seemed like more than he could stand.

Walter whistled and his wide eyes shot up to Jonathan.

"*Ten*? Geez, man, what did you *do*?"

Jonathan looked into Walter's eyes for just a moment, then looked away again quickly.

"Why? How long are you here for?" he asked.

Walter snorted.

"Well, I was sent here for four weeks. But that was almost two months ago."

"Why are you still here?"

Walter rolled his eyes again.

"Everyone stays longer, man. Just when you're about done with your time, the Admiral sends a little letter. To your folks, to whatever judge or state sent you here. Tells how you're coming along fine, but there's still more work to do, that he's sure you'd come right around if he had just a little more time to educate you." Walter's voice dripped with scorn. "And he offers to extend your education. At a reduced rate." He finished chopping an onion and started on the next. "You're supposed to be here for ten weeks? Sorry, man, but I bet you don't get outta here in less than fifteen."

Jonathan chopped numbly, trying to digest what he'd been told.

"How do you know all this?"

"Benny," Walter answered. He almost spat the name out. He motioned with his chin across the kitchen to a kid standing at a sink, lazily splashing a scrub brush around a soapy bowl. Jonathan recognized him—he could still feel the painful pinch the kid had given him on his arm.

"I saw him last night," Jonathan said. "He works in the Admiral's office."

"Yeah. Little punk. He tells us all about those letters he stuffs into envelopes and addresses. Just loves to tease us, you know?"

Walter looked around the kitchen, pointing out kids with his knife.

"That big black kid there is Tony. He's cool. The guy grating cheese is Jason. He's super quiet, but seems all right. Stole a car, I heard. Next to him is David. Doesn't say much, but he's tough. Do *not* call him Chinese, okay? He's Japanese. Couple of kids made that mistake early on and had black eyes to show for it."

Jonathan's eyes darted around the room, trying to keep up with Walter's fast talk and chop onions at the same time without cutting off a finger.

"See those two meatheads working together to stir the oatmeal? That's Roger and Gregory. Dumb as catfish and just about as friendly. Miguel's the one making coffee. He's funny. Or thinks he is, anyway. That tall dude manning the toaster is Francis. Total jerk. But the *real* jerk is Sebastian. Him you gotta watch out for, man. He's out setting the table, I think."

Walter looked over and saw Jonathan fumbling with his onion. "It's easier if you pull your sleeves up, man." He reached over toward Jonathan's arms. "Here, let me show—"

"No," Jonathan snapped, pulling his arms away. "I mean, no, thanks. I'm still cold. It was a wet night."

Walter looked at him, then shrugged. "Yeah. Mongley got you good. I swear that guy can see in the dark."

"You guyth need help with the onionth?"

Jonathan looked up at a new kid who'd joined them at the cutting board. Or rather, down at him. He was a good foot shorter than Jonathan. He had blond hair trimmed in a bowl cut, green eyes, and skin as pale white as paper. His chin and his nose were kind of pointy.

"Hey, Colin. This here's Jonathan. First day."

"Of courth. I heard the thplath latht night."

"The what?" Jonathan asked.

"The thplath. From the bucket. Almotht everyone geth the bucket on their firtht night."

Walter looked up at Jonathan. "Colin and I got here on the same day. He talk*th* funny." Walter exaggerated the lisp, but he gave Colin a friendly dig with his elbow when he said it.

Colin nodded. He smiled, a fleeting little smile at the corners of his mouth that flashed like a bird and then vanished, but his eyes stayed down on the onion he was cutting. "Yeth," he said quietly. "I'm thure he notithed."

"It's all right," Jonathan said quickly, his voice as soft as Colin's. "My—I have—I used to know someone who talked different, too." Colin looked up, for just a second, at Jonathan and smiled. Then his eyes dropped back down.

"Well, welcome to Thlabhenge," he said softly.

All around them, savory smells grew stronger. Sizzling onion, greasy bacon, frying eggs, boiling potatoes. Across the kitchen the chubby kid who Walter had said was named Tony was flipping golden, round pancakes on a griddle. Jonathan almost had to lean on the cutting board to not collapse.

"At least the food here is good," he said. "I'm gonna eat 'til I puke."

Colin and Walter exchanged a glance.

"Thith food ithn't for uth," Colin whispered.

"What? Who's it for?"

"*Them*," Walter answered with a meaningful look over Jonathan's shoulder. Jonathan risked a backward glance. Behind him was a long, glassless window that looked out into a big room with two long tables. Sitting at the closest table were five or six adults, including two he recognized: Mr. Vander, the tall zombie who'd met his boat, and the hunched-over form of Mr. Mongley. As he watched, the Admiral came marching in the door, still wearing his blue navy jacket. A sword hung in a scabbard on his hip. He was wearing baggy blue pants that met his shiny black boots at his knees. A huge, old-fashioned wide-brimmed hat was held under one arm, the triangular kind you see in history books, being worn by ship captains or Napoleon Bonaparte. The Admiral flopped down in a heavy wooden high-backed chair at the empty table.

"They get all this?" Jonathan asked.

Colin and Walter nodded.

"What do we get?"

"Oatmeal, usually," Walter replied.

"Thometimth toatht."

Jonathan bit his lip and nodded.

"Great."

Eventually, all the food was ready on platters and in bowls lined up on the counter by the kitchen door. Jonathan licked his lips and watched the steam rising off the hash browns, pancakes, scrambled eggs. He saw the gooey cheese oozing out of the omelets, the salty grease pooling on the platter under the bacon, the butter melting on the flaky biscuits.

"When do *we* eat?"

"*When we tell ye to!*" a voice barked in his ear. Jonathan jumped and turned to see Mr. Warwick's one eye glistening at him. "*If* we tell ye to. Now grab a bowl, boy."

One by one the boys filed by and picked up a serving dish and carried it out through the door. Jonathan grabbed a butter dish and a little pitcher of syrup and followed. The table was already full when he got there, but he found a tight spot for his items. The men were all slurping and reaching and smacking their lips, piling their plates high with food and shoveling it by the forkload into their mouths.

The boys, once the food was delivered, stood back against the stone wall with their hands behind their backs.

"More coffee," the Admiral said through a mouthful of sausage, and a boy darted back to the kitchen.

"And salt!" a bearded man with gold earrings shouted after him.

When the boy returned with the salt and coffee, the Admiral swallowed his mouthful and glowered up at the boys against the wall.

"All right," he said, wiping some grease off his chin with the back of his hand. "Go clean and eat. That kitchen better be spotless or it'll be no lunch for the lot of you!"

The boys turned and filed toward the kitchen. Jonathan followed with them but was stopped in his tracks by the Admiral's foul voice.

"Jonathan Grisby! A word with ye."

Jonathan gulped and stepped out of line and walked over to where the Admiral sat.

The Admiral stabbed a piece of roasted potato. He slid the silver blade of the knife into his mouth and leaned back to look Jonathan in the face. Jonathan waited with downcast eyes as the Admiral chewed and swallowed.

"How was yer first night, Jonathan Grisby?"

Jonathan didn't want to do or say anything that would risk his breakfast getting taken away like his dinner had the night before.

"Fine, sir."

"Can be a long night with no pillow, I imagine. Neck a bit sore, eh?"

"No, sir. I'm fine, sir."

"Mmm. Good. I read your file last night. 'Twas fine bedtime reading. The sad history of Jonathan Grisby, boy delinquent. It is a dark little tale, isn't it?"

Jonathan blinked and breathed through his nose.

"Yes, sir. I guess so."

A rotten smile spread across the Admiral's face.

"Oh, it don't take any guessin'. 'Tis a dark tale, to be sure." The Admiral leaned forward and lowered his voice. "Between you and I, a lot of these boys don't really deserve to be here. A belt and a bellow would suffice for most of them, I'd say. But you, Jonathan Grisby. You *do* deserve to be here, don't you?"

Jonathan swallowed and sniffed. He shifted from foot to foot. Then he looked up into the Admiral's obsidian eyes. And nodded.

"Yes, sir," he said, his voice a hoarse whisper. "I do."

The Admiral slurped half a sausage into his mouth and nodded. His eyes narrowed to dark reptilian slits and his smile widened. He chewed slowly, his black eyes burrowing like beetles into Jonathan's.

"I'm going to take a personal interest in your education here, Jonathan Grisby. A boy like you will require more focused attention, I believe. So troubled. So . . . *evil*. We'll begin your education right after Morning Muster today." The Admiral swallowed and then gulped a mouthful of coffee. He waved his hand dismissively at Jonathan. "That'll be all. Don't just stand there like a dead chicken."

Jonathan retreated numbly to the kitchen, where all the other boys were busy sweeping and scrubbing and cleaning up. A great cauldron bubbled on one of the stoves, and his nose sniffed hungrily at the smell of oatmeal.

Jonathan's growling belly was interrupted by a sharp shove from behind. A tall kid with scalp-short black hair glared down at him. His nose was broad and flat, like a tiger's. It was bumpy, like it had been broken before. More than once.

"What do you think you're doing?" the kid demanded. "You don't help, you don't eat."

"Oh . . . I . . . what . . ." Jonathan stammered, panicked at the thought of missing breakfast. "What do you want me to do?"

The kid scowled and looked around. He pointed at a pile of logs by the wall.

"Add more wood to the stove. It's about burned down." He bent over and opened the iron door at the bottom of the stove. A wave of heat blasted out. Jonathan looked at the glowing red coals, the licking red flames, the flickering, hungry fingers of fire.

"No," he said, shaking his head.

"What?"

"No, I—I can't. I don't like fire."

"You don't *like* fire?" the kid snorted.

"God, Sebastian, leave him alone. It's his first day." The voice came from Tony, the kid who'd been flipping pancakes. He lifted his chin in greeting at Jonathan and then grabbed a couple of logs from the pile and tossed them into the stove. He kicked the door shut with his foot and brushed past the broken-nosed kid and back to the pot he'd been scrubbing.

"Name's Tony," he shouted over his shoulder. "Welcome to Slabhenge, kid."

Sebastian scrunched his broken nose at Jonathan before turning away.

As the cleanup got done, the boys lined up behind the cauldron of oatmeal. Walter pulled Jonathan and Colin into line with him.

"This place stinks, man," Walter said. "No joke. But you'll get used to it." He smirked and cocked his eyebrows at Colin. "If short stuff here can make it, I'm sure you'll be all right."

Colin smiled back, for just a flash. He pursed his lips and pulled on one ear, his eyebrows screwed up thoughtfully. "Yeah," he said. "There'th no bookth, though. That'th the wortht part. I mith bookth."

Colin looked so small and sad and quiet, standing there pinching his own ear. He looked nothing like a hardened delinquent in need of reform.

"What did you do?" The question blurted out of Jonathan's mouth. "Why are *you* here?"

Colin ducked his head further. His eyes flitted up to Jonathan's and then back down.

"I'm a klepto," he whispered. Then he kind of giggled.

"A what?"

"A kleptomaniac. I thteal thtuff. Loth of thtuff. I can't help it."

Walter shook his head.

"Man, why don't you just say 'thief'? It's what your mouth *wants* to say."

Colin smiled, just a little bit.

"I'm a thief. A thneaky, thneaky thief." Jonathan smiled back at him. "Why are you here?"

Jonathan opened his mouth and shut it. He swallowed. Then the line started moving.

They filed past the great pot of oatmeal, where Benny stood, dolloping a ladle of the steaming gray glop into each of their bowls.

Jonathan grabbed a bowl from a pile on the counter and held it out when he got to the front of the line. Benny scooped his ladle into the pot and held it out toward Jonathan's bowl.

"No, Benny," Sebastian's voice said from behind him. "No breakfast for the new kid. He didn't do a thing to help clean up."

Jonathan spun around. "I'm *starving*, please—"

"Keep talking." Sebastian cut him off, leaning in close. "And it'll be no lunch, either."

Tears sprang to Jonathan's eyes. If there'd been anything in his stomach, he would have thrown it up.

He felt a gentle hand grab his elbow.

"Come on," Colin's voice whispered. "It'th all right."

Jonathan turned and let Colin lead him out to the tables, his heart and stomach as empty as his bowl. He sat down on the hard wooden bench between Walter and Colin. The other boys were all gulping and swallowing their oatmeal, not bothering to let it cool down. Jonathan closed his eyes and tried not to pass out.

Colin's elbow nudged him in the side. He opened his eyes. Colin had slid his bowl full of oatmeal in front of Jonathan and put Jonathan's empty bowl in front of himself.

He grinned a secret little grin at Jonathan and darted his eyes around.

"Hurry and eat it," he whispered. "Morning Muthter ith in a few minuth."

"But . . . you need to eat, too!" Jonathan hissed.

Colin shook his head and his smile stretched. He almost showed his teeth.

"It'th okay. I dethpithe oatmeal."

"Aren't you hungry?"

Colin nodded, his eyes shining. He pointed with his eyes down to his lap, and Jonathan looked down to where Colin was hiding his hands under the table. In one hand he held a biscuit slathered with jam. In the other, a glistening sausage link.

"How did you—" Jonathan started to ask.

Colin winked and took a quick bite of the biscuit.

"I'm a thneaky thief, remember?"

CHAPTER FIVE
MORNING MUSTER

It was Morning Muster time. The boys were marched outside into the drizzly gray courtyard. A light rain was falling, and bunched-up piles of clouds blackened the sky. Thunder rumbled in the not too far distance.

The boys trudged over to a line of small stone blocks on the ground, each about the size of a brick and spaced a few steps apart from one another. Without a word, each boy stepped up and squeezed his feet onto one, found his balance, and then stood at shaky attention. Jonathan took a breath and did the same.

The block was just wide enough for both his feet to fit on it, pressed tight together. The tips of his toes and the backs of his heels hung over the front and back. He wobbled and steadied himself and then looked up.

The courtyard was the size of a basketball court. He'd walked through it briefly his first day, following Mr. Vander in his handcuffs, but he'd been too tired and scared then to look close or notice much. He could see, to his right, the steep arched doorway, closed and locked, that led to the watery stairs he'd come in on. There were doorways on each wall that he could see, all closed.

The floor and walls of the courtyard were made of the same big gray blocks of stone that the rest of the building was made of. Green moss grew between the cracks in places.

The walls stretched high above them, thirty or forty feet, blocking out most of the sky and a good deal of the light. The part of the sky that was visible was getting darker and more ominous by the second. There was a flash of lightning.

The courtyard's stone block ground was flat and covered with so many big puddles that it was nearly one shallow lake. The surface of the puddles were pocked and pecked by more falling rain. Shifting snaps of wind whistled around the courtyard, chilling the boys and blowing Jonathan's hair into and out of his eyes.

The door to their left swung open, and the whole group of men from breakfast slumped out with the Admiral at the front. The ridiculous wide hat, roughly triangular, sat on his head, and the sword still swung at his side. The last two men in line came out sideways, grunting and holding the Sinner's Sorrow between them. They plocked it down with a wet thud on the stones before the boys. Jonathan looked at the kneeler's sharp, hard edge and winced.

The men formed a line facing the boys. They stood in an oily black puddle with their boots and shoulders touching. Jonathan counted them—eight adults. The Admiral stood in the center of the line, his arms at his sides and his chin held regally high.

Mr. Warwick, standing on one end of the line, held the wooden handle of a big brass bell in his hand. When the two men who'd carried the Sinner's Sorrow joined the line, he rang the bell. The dull metal clanging bounced around the grim gray walls and up to the storm-choked sky.

"Morning Muster, November the fifth!" Mr. Warwick hollered. The man on the other end of the line pulled some papers out of his coat pocket and held them with both hands in the wet wind.

"James Amherst!" he shouted.

"Here, sir. Content and well cared for, sir!" a boy Jonathan hadn't met yet shouted back.

"David Okada!"

"Here, sir. Content and well cared for, sir!"

"Benedict Fellows!"

"Here, sir," the kid called Benny answered. His voice sounded greasy even when he was shouting through a rainstorm. "Content and well cared for, sir!"

"Jonathan Grisby!"

Jonathan gulped and looked around. He almost stumbled off the block but caught himself.

"Here, sir," he called. His voice sounded thin and meek and was nearly lost in the windblown rain. "Content and well cared for, sir!"

The Admiral smirked.

"Colin Kerrigan!"

"Here, thir." Colin didn't shout—Jonathan wasn't sure he even *could* shout—but he did speak at more than a shy whisper. "Content and well cared for, thir."

All the boys were called, sixteen in all, and each gave the same answer. When they were done, the man folded the papers and slipped them back into his coat. "Sixteen charges, sir, all present and all report being content and well cared for, sir."

The Admiral grimaced and wrinkled his nose.

"Thank you, Mr. Washburn. Put it in your report."

The Admiral stepped forward. He took a few soggy steps toward the line of boys, his eyes sliding like a snake from boy to boy. He poked at something between his teeth with his tongue.

He had just opened his foul mouth to speak when the boy to Jonathan's right wobbled. The boy pinwheeled his arms to catch his balance, but it was too late and he dropped a foot off his block to the ground.

The Admiral's mouth snapped shut and he raised one of his cockroach eyebrows. He shook his head and clucked his tongue.

"To the Sorrow, Miguel Vargas."

The boy's head dropped.

"Yes, sir," he mumbled and slouched to the Sinner's Sorrow, its black wood dotted now with raindrops. He knelt on the horrible device and squinched his eyes shut. Jonathan remembered well the bite of that sharp rail. He bit his lip and looked away from Miguel.

The Admiral watched him for a moment and then looked back to the boys still on the blocks.

"Boys, we have a new student among us. As I'm sure you know. A young Jonathan Grisby, twelve years old." As he talked, the Admiral strode slowly down the line of balancing boys. He stopped before Jonathan. "Ten weeks we are supposed to have him. But for a crime of his magnitude, I think we may need him longer." Jonathan met the Admiral's sinisterly gloating eyes for a second, then looked quickly away.

The Admiral resumed walking down the line. "I thought it a good idea this morning," he said, his voice booming so as to be heard over the rising wind and growing thunder, "to remind you all what you are and why you are here. For Jonathan Grisby's benefit."

At the end of the line, a boy's foot dropped to the ground. Without a word he shook his head and walked to the Sinner's Sorrow. Miguel jumped gratefully up from the kneeler and limped stiffly back to his stone block. The new boy scowled and took his place on his knees. The Admiral waited for them each to get into place before continuing. By now he was back at the center of the line, and he took a step back so he could throw his grisly gaze over all his charges.

"Bloody, disgusting little scabs, boys," he said. He enunciated each word clearly and precisely. "That is what you are. The very scabs of civilized society." He smiled an ugly, pinched smile, then let it drop from his face. "And why, you might ask, do I call you scabs?" He started walking again, his eyes up at the clouds and the occasional, quick flickers of lightning. His voice lilted and rose like a schoolteacher's.

"Scabs, as you know, are nasty little things. An otherwise healthy body gets a wound. A disfigurement. And it begins to bleed, that wound. And it forms a dirty little scab. Good for nothing. An unhealthy nastiness. An ugliness. Well, boys, it is our civilization itself that is sick. It is too tolerant. Too soft. It is . . . *wounded.* Bleeding from its rottenness. And you, lads, are the scabs. The bad little bits that nobody wants."

He stopped and cleared his throat. Scratched at his nose. Looked at the line of boys with distaste. "And so society sends you here. Society picks you off like the little scabs that you are and flicks you out here to my island. To try and turn you into something better. And if I can't?" The Admiral lowered his chin and looked at them from under his eyebrows. "Well, at least we keep you out of the way for a while. And we give you what you deserve."

He raised his head again and trudged deliberately through them, between two boys. His elbow bumped one— not too gently—and the boy stumbled to the ground. He kicked at a puddle and took the second boy's place on the kneeler.

When the Admiral's voice bellowed again, it was moving behind them.

"So what can we do with you? Why are you all such incorrigible delinquents? It's simple." The Admiral paused dramatically. "Weakness. And rot. You've been spoiled and now you are rotten and weak and it is up to me to fix you.

So, at Slabhenge, we do not do what other schools do. We do not read stories. We do not talk about your . . . *feelings*. We do not play with numbers or write tedious essays about what you did last summer. What you did last summer was get weak and rotten. What you do here is *work*. You work. And, yes, sometimes you suffer. That, I'm afraid, is the cost of improvement. That is where strength comes from, boys."

The Admiral's voice circled slowly around until he was once again standing before them. The rain had picked up and was now a bit more than sprinkling. It dripped down Jonathan's face and off the brim of the Admiral's hat. The puddles were growing, swallowing the few blocks left between them. It was almost as dark as night, and flashes of lightning splashed the courtyard with wild shadows.

"We will work the weakness out of you!" With a flourish the Admiral yanked his sword out of its scabbard. It flashed bright silver in the dim, stormy light. "We will cut all the rottenness out of your character, if we can. We will certainly try. Just as society cut the rottenness out of itself by sending your worthless hides to Slabhenge, Slabhenge will cut the rottenness out of you. We will bleed the infection right out of you."

The Admiral took a step backward toward the line of men, his eyes still on the boys. The boy on the Sinner's Sorrow whined piteously and rocked from one knee to the other. The Admiral looked at him and rolled his eyes.

"Oh, back to your block, you baby," he muttered, and the boy jumped up and scrambled back onto his stone block.

The Admiral backed up until he was again in line, shoulder to shoulder with the others in the puddle. He raised his sword and pointed it straight up at the coal-black clouds that rumbled and flashed overhead.

"Work!" he hollered, practically screaming now to be heard over the gusts and crashes and rain. There was a tingling in the air. A buzzing, a charge, a vibration. "Suffering! Discipline! You are dirty little scabs, you devils, and you've been sent to hell!"

As the Admiral spoke, the metal buttons on his jacket began to glow with a strange blue light. There was a crackling, like static all around. Then a great blinding flash.

A hot-white bolt of lightning shot down from the black clouds and through the upheld sword in the Admiral's hand. Spidery lines of electricity surged and cracked through the crowd of adults, and in one blink of a bit of a second, the puddle at their feet burned to a hissing white burst and the world was split by a deafening cannon crack.

The boys screamed and jumped and covered their faces, and Jonathan felt himself thrown off his block and onto his rear on the ground.

Then, all was still. Jonathan sat on the wet stone with his eyes squeezed shut and heard nothing.

Bit by bit, sounds came back. A fading rumble of thunder. The rain dripping on the walls and puddles of the prison. Gusts of wind whistling between the towers. Jonathan lowered his arms and blinked open his eyes.

Two boys still stood on their blocks. The rest were on the ground, like him. They were all looking at where the Admiral and his men had been standing a moment before.

The men were still there. But they all lay in a heap on the ground. Perfectly still. Rain pattered softly on their coats, their boots, their bare hands. The air reeked of steam and burning and electricity and lightning. No one moved.

Slowly—first one, then two, then all of them—the boys crept closer. Step by step they formed a cautious half circle around the pile of grown-ups. No one got too close. There was the Admiral, facedown, his hat on the ground and the sword still in his hand. There was Mr. Warwick, on his back, his one eye open and gaping up at the storm.

"Is he . . ." one of the boys started to say.

"Are they . . ." another began.

There was a crack of thunder and they all jumped, but no one stepped away. They hardly noticed the rain pouring down around them.

"Oh, man. Are they . . . dead?" It was Walter who finally managed to ask the question they were all wondering.

"We need to check," the big kid named Tony said.

"How?" Sebastian asked breathlessly.

Colin took one step closer to the steaming bodies.

"Thomeone needth to check for a pulth."

Sebastian nodded.

"Right. Do it, Colin."

"Me? I don't want—"

"Just do it, Colin. You're closest."

Colin stepped forward. He tiptoed between the bodies like he was afraid they'd wake up. He shied away from Mr. Warwick's staring eye and reached down toward the Admiral. His hand stopped inches from the Admiral's neck and he looked up at Sebastian with wide eyes.

"Do it," Sebastian snapped.

Colin tucked the corners of his mouth into a frown and stretched down the last bit. He felt with his fingers past the Admiral's collar, trying to find the neck. Jonathan cringed and braced himself, expecting the Admiral to leap up at any moment with a furious roar.

But there was no leaping. No fury. No roar.

Colin stood motionless for a moment, his eyes on the ground and his mouth still frowning and the fingers of one hand held to the soggy neck of the Admiral of Slabhenge. Then he blinked and looked up at the boys gathered at a fearful distance around him.

"He'th dead," Colin whispered. "Dead ath a doornail."

CHAPTER SIX
A DARK AND DASTARDLY SCHEME

There was a moment of silence. Jonathan heard someone gulp. Colin realized he was still touching the dead Admiral and yanked his hand back and stood up straight.

"Are they *all* dead?" Tony asked.

"Check 'em, Colin," Sebastian demanded.

"No way, Thebathtian. I did mine. Thomebody elth'th turn." Colin hopped out from between the bodies and rejoined the group.

Sebastian grunted in frustration.

"Fine. Tony, you check those two," he said, pointing at Mr. Warwick and another body. "Benny, those two. And . . . you, Johnny or whatever, you do those ones." He pointed at Jonathan and then at Mr. Mongley and the man who'd bellowed out their names during Muster.

"It's Jonathan, and I—"

"Whatever. Just do it. Now."

Jonathan could tell that arguing wasn't going to work. He wiped his hands on his pant legs and stepped forward.

He checked the roll caller first. The man's eyes were closed, but his mouth was open. Steam was rising off his jacket. Jonathan pressed two fingers against the man's neck. His fingers were half-numb from the cold. He pressed them in harder. It felt like touching a warm steak.

He felt nothing. He waited, quietly. Nothing.

He looked up. "Dead," he said, and stepped over to Mr. Mongley. He heard Tony and Benny reporting the same thing from their dead grown-ups.

Without thinking or pausing, he shoved his fingers into Mr. Mongley's throat. He remembered the man's raspy, haunting breath. Raindrops were running down the old man's bald, flaky scalp. His head was to the side, his eyes both open, staring at the distant gray wall. They were actually kind of a beautiful shade of blue. Jonathan gritted his teeth and tried not to throw up.

The man's neck was still and pulseless.

"Mr. Mongley's dead, too."

He remembered the night before and his whispered conversation with Walter, before the bucket. *Mongley hears everything*, Walter had said. He looked up at Walter.

"Well," Jonathan said hoarsely. "He's not hearing anything now."

Walter's Adam's apple bobbed in a dry swallow.

"Maybe he'th hearing the choirth of angelth thinging," Colin offered.

Walter's eyes were still on the dead man. He shook his head and frowned. "I seriously doubt that, man."

Jonathan straightened up and stepped back into the quiet, watching circle.

"All the grown-ups are dead," Tony said in a hollow, wondering voice.

"Is this *all* of them?" Jonathan asked, his voice rising.

"There's no one else inside? A janitor, or a guard, or something?"

Walter shook his head. "It was Morning Muster. This is all the grown-ups, man. The whole Slabhenge staff."

"Why'd they all die?" Miguel asked.

"The Admiral was holding that sword," Jonathan said.

"And they were all touching," Sebastian added.

"Thtanding in that puddle," Colin finished.

Tony sniffed and looked back at the stone blocks they'd been balancing on when the lightning struck.

"We were on the blocks, up out of the puddles," he said in a trembling voice. "We'd all be dead, too, if we'd-a been standing on the ground."

Jonathan looked at Mr. Warwick's one glassy, dead eye staring sightlessly up at the storm clouds. "Which we weren't, thank the devil," he whispered.

There was a sudden, gusting blast of wind that whipped their hair and clothes around. Thunder cracked and the somber scene of wet children looking at a pile of dead bodies was lit by a long flash of lightning. The rain doubled in strength, rolling up to a real downpour. Suddenly, they each seemed to realize that they themselves were now standing together in a puddle, with the lightning still flashing. One by one, and then all at once, without anyone saying anything, they scurried over to the cover of the big gated doorway that led out to the boat landing. It was cold in the shadows of the stone archway, but it was out of the wind and rain and, most important, the bolts of lightning that darted across the sky.

They huddled together in the near-darkness, looking out at the corpses getting soggy in the courtyard. A couple of the smaller kids were crying. Not because they were sad, Jonathan thought, just scared.

"We're in so much trouble," Benny said.

"What?" Sebastian's voice was harsh and scornful. "What for? We didn't do anything!"

"Still," Miguel said. "Here we are. You know, *us* . . . the 'scabs' and all that. And all the grown-ups end up dead? I mean, my folks sent me here just for skipping school a few times, you know? I'm definitely gonna get grounded for at least a week for this when I get home."

His last word hung in the air between them. The wind couldn't blow it away. *Home.* It dawned on them at the same time.

"We get to go home," Walter said quietly.

"We get to go home," another kid echoed.

"We get to go home!" two or three kids cried. Someone cheered. A few kids clapped. Jonathan bit his bottom lip and frowned. Sebastian cracked his knuckles and furrowed his brow.

"When do we go?" Tony asked. "Can we call now? The police?"

"There's no telephone, idiot," Sebastian said under his breath. He turned his head so that everyone could hear him.

"There's no telephone, remember? No one's going home yet." He looked out at the bodies, his eyes narrowed, and he said it again more quietly. "No one's going home yet."

"Well . . . when can we go?" Tony asked again. "When's the next boat coming?"

They all looked at Benny.

"You worked in his office, Benny. You know the schedule best," a tall, skinny kid with red hair said. Jonathan remembered from Morning Muster that his name was Gerald.

Benny still had his eyes glued to his boss's body. He shook his head.

"Uh, well, today's Tuesday, right? There's no food drop-off or garbage pickup 'til Thursday. No new students are registered to come that I know of. So today would just be Patrick coming on the mail run."

"When's that?"

"Just before lunch, usually. Like ten thirty."

"All right," Walter said. "A couple hours. That's it. Then we tell that mail guy what happened and he sends a bigger boat out and then we're all outta here." A couple boys clapped again.

There were a few seconds of nothing but the sound of rain. One kid leaned against the stone wall. Another coughed.

"So, like . . . what should we do?" Miguel asked.

"Thould we get them out of the rain?" Colin asked.

Jonathan's brain was working. He was looking at all the dead grown-ups and frowning and thinking of home and family and everything that had happened to bring him here to the island of Slabhenge. A small, ugly, beautiful idea was wiggling in his mind. His stomach rumbled, wanting more than a meager bowl of oatmeal. It was hard to hatch a dark and dastardly scheme on an empty stomach.

"I think we should eat," he said, just loud enough for everyone to hear. "I'm starving."

Sebastian's brow was still creased with dark, thoughtful lines.

"Yeah," he said. "I'm with the new kid. Let's go eat." Then his face smoothed into a grinning smile and he cocked an eyebrow back at the huddled boys. "Whatever we want."

One kid clapped. But just one. Most of the boys had probably lost their appetites when they watched all the adults get struck and killed by lightning.

But Sebastian started off across the rain-drenched courtyard toward the kitchen door.

Jonathan stepped out after him.

All the rest slowly followed close behind.

The straggly line of somber, soaked boys snaked right past the lifeless bodies staring up at the storm.

The kitchen was noisy with cooking, but there was not much talking. Mouths were too full for talking most of the time.

Tony stirred a pan of ten scrambled eggs. Jonathan didn't think he planned on sharing. Benny was eating jelly out of the jar with a spoon. Sebastian was shoving a banana in his mouth while frying up six pieces of bacon. The two big brutes—Gregory and Roger, Jonathan remembered—were eating pepperoni slices by the handful, greasy grins on their faces. The little black-haired kid named Jason sat on the floor in the walk-in fridge and gnawed on a brick-size block of cheddar cheese.

Most of the boys just stood around, eating in the kitchen, but some got what they wanted and picked a spot at a table. No one sat at the Admiral's table. Jonathan made himself two gooey peanut butter and jelly sandwiches and joined them, sitting across from Colin and Walter. Another kid sat down next to him, a little taller than him, with glasses and short, curly brown hair.

"Francis, right?" Jonathan asked through a mouthful of peanut butter and jelly.

"Yes. And you're Jonathan. Our newest arrival." Francis held out his hand and Jonathan blinked at him for a second before reaching out and shaking it. Francis had a slight accent, but not a foreign one. He pronounced all of his syllables very precisely. To Jonathan, he sounded like the rich people on TV. "Looks like your stay here has been cut quite short."

"Yeah," Jonathan said, chewing. "Guess so."

"And what terrible wrong did you commit to deserve being sent here?" Francis asked. He was being sarcastic, Jonathan could tell, but he still flinched. He swallowed his bite.

"What did *you* do?" he asked back. Across the table, Colin frowned and took another bite of his apple.

"Oh, hardly anything, really," Francis answered in a bored voice. "I pushed our gardener off the ladder. Honestly, if he hadn't broken his hip, there wouldn't even have been charges."

"Was it an accident?"

Francis shrugged. "No."

"Why did you do it?"

Francis rolled his eyes. "Does it really matter?"

"I guess not."

Francis sighed. "Yes. Well, my father got a top-notch attorney, really quite expensive, but the whole thing happened at our summer house and all the local townspeople were quite up in arms about it. Really screaming for blood. Tried to make it all into some ridiculous wealth-class issue. So . . . here I am. Eating white bread. The damned country judge sent me here."

"That'th a terrible thing to do," Colin said.

"Yes, well, the judge's hands were really quite tied, I'm afraid. It's an elected office. He had to give the people what they wanted."

"I meant it wath a terrible thing to do to the gardener."

"Oh," Francis sniffed. "Well. It didn't end well for me, either, as you see."

They all chewed in silence for a while.

"How does the refrigerator work?" Jonathan asked. Everyone stopped chewing and looked at him. "I mean, there doesn't seem to be electricity here. It's all torches and candles. What's running the fridge and freezer?"

Walter scraped a piece of jelly bean out from between his teeth and looked at it stuck to his finger.

"Oh, there's electricity. There's a coal generator downstairs that we all get to take turns shoveling coal into. Makes just enough juice to run the fridge, freezer, and the Admiral's TV."

"Oh." Jonathan swallowed the last bite of his second sandwich and considered going to make another one. "And the freezer's big, too, like the fridge?"

Walter nodded. "Yeah. A little smaller, I guess, but still a walk-in. Why, man?"

Jonathan shook his head. "No reason. Just wondering."

But Jonathan's head was still buzzing with dark dreams. And he *did* have a reason for asking about the freezer.

Eight reasons, in fact.

The sixteen students of the Slabhenge Reformatory School for Troubled Boys stood at the gate, looking out at the white-capped waves of the ocean. Somewhere out there across the sea was the mainland and home. Home. With meals, parents, beds. A happy place. For most of them.

Sebastian had crept up and unclipped the key ring from Mr. Vander's belt, and they'd opened the heavy wooden door to the outside. They stood in the shadow of the stone arch, looking out at the water and waiting for the boat. The eight bodies still lay in the drizzling rain behind them.

They leaned with their hands holding the rusty iron bars. Some of them still chewed on crusty bread or chunks of cheese.

"How much longer?" a kid asked.

"I told you, any minute," Benny answered.

"What should we say?"

"What do you mean, what should we say? All the grown-ups got killed by lightning and we want to go home. Dummy."

The rain was just a constant gentle tapping now. The thunder and lightning were gone, but the clouds were still night-black and the world was dim and dark.

Then, thin and lost somewhere beneath the sound of the waves smacking the stone walls, there came a low buzzing sound. Like a fly caught between the window and the screen.

"There!" Miguel called out, his voice excited. "There! I see it!" He pointed. Other fingers joined.

"Yeah! I see it!"

"There it is!"

The boat was a dot, still far distant, fighting its way through the wind and the waves. To bring them back to the real world. Jonathan chewed on the inside of his cheek. He looked at Sebastian, leaning in the corner where the gate met the stone wall. Sebastian was the only one besides him who wasn't smiling. His scowl was as grim as the deadly clouds, his eyes as full of dark thoughts as Jonathan's. Their eyes met. Jonathan thought he saw a wet glimmer of tears in Sebastian's eyes before they looked away from his.

All the boys' voices fell silent as they watched the little boat make its way toward their gloomy island.

Jonathan took one deep breath and then spoke his voice into the silence.

"Maybe we shouldn't go."

Heads snapped his way. Sebastian's sour face turned sharply toward him.

"What?" Walter asked.

"Maybe we shouldn't go," Jonathan repeated. "Maybe we shouldn't tell what happened. Yet." Sebastian's eyes stayed locked on his. His jaw clenched. Jonathan cocked a questioning eyebrow at him. And then Sebastian nodded.

"What are you talking about?" a kid asked.

Jonathan raised his voice and put some strength into it.

"I'm talking about staying. Without the grown-ups. Without *any* grown-ups. I'm talking about all of us staying here at Slabhenge. Alone."

CHAPTER SEVEN
DEAD MAN'S COAT

"Stay? Why would we do that?" Francis asked.

"Why shouldn't we?" Jonathan answered. "Were any of us really that happy out there? I mean, we've got a chance here. We can live here. Without grown-ups. Without *rules*. Not forever. Just for a while. We could live here—free. Doing whatever we want."

Eyes blinked at him.

"Think about it," Jonathan argued desperately, knowing the boat was getting closer by the second. "Out there we're just . . . troublemakers. Punks. Here we could be *kings*."

"You're crazy!"

"No, he's not." The voice was Sebastian's. He pushed himself off the wall and faced them all. "He's right. We've got a winning lotto ticket here. And we're just gonna throw it away? Without spending any of it?"

The boys looked back and forth among each other.

"Don't you see?" Sebastian demanded. "How long have we all been here, besides Jonathan? Four weeks? Six weeks? Ten? And all that time, we've been crapped on. Cleaning. Working. Eating garbage. Kneeling on that stupid Sinner's whatever. Sleeping with rats. All 'cause of those jerks. And now . . ." His eyes wandered out to the bodies behind them. "And now they're gone. And we can enjoy this. Eat whatever we want. Whenever we want. Eat the Admiral's chocolate. Watch his TV."

"Use his bathroom," Tony added thoughtfully. "I hear he's got actual toilet paper."

"Sleep in his big, fancy bed," Miguel said.

"Go to bed whenever we want," Walter chipped in.

"With a light on," Jason squeaked.

"Thith ith crathy," Colin interjected. "You're all nuth."

"Don't be such a wussy, Colin," Sebastian said.

"Just for a couple days," Jonathan argued. "Like a little . . . vacation. A vacation from grown-ups. No punishment. No problems."

The tall redhead, Gerald, looked up at the building around them.

"God," he said quietly. "This place *would* be amazing to play hide-and-seek in."

"There's plenty of food," Jonathan said.

They stood quietly, each boy wrestling with his own thoughts.

Colin shook his head and opened his mouth to speak, but Sebastian cut him off.

"We're doing it," he said, his voice hard and decisive. "Just for a little while."

"But . . . the boat's coming," Francis pointed out.

Sebastian scowled and looked out at the ocean.

"We've still got like five minutes," he said. "All he's

coming for is mail. Benny . . . do you know where the mail-bag is?"

"Sure. In the staff room."

"What about the guy, though? Won't he notice . . . something?"

Jonathan shook his head. "When I got dropped off, Mr. Vander didn't even talk to him. He stood in the shadows the whole time."

Sebastian rubbed his chin roughly with his hand.

"But still . . ."

"We have Mr. Vander's jacket and hat," Jonathan said. "Well, we could *get* his jacket and hat." Some kid in the shadows gasped, but Jonathan kept going. "And if Gerald stood on a stool or something, he'd be just as tall. Wearing that hat and jacket, back here in the shadows . . ."

"Let's do it." Sebastian's voice was quick and bossy. "Benny, run and grab the mailbag. Gerald, stay here. Every-one else get around the corner out of sight. New kid, come with me."

There was only a momentary pause and then everyone scrambled. Colin was the only one who stayed where he was.

"Thith ith tho thtupid," he said to no one in particular. Sebastian grabbed him roughly by his shirt and jerked him around the corner so hard his head snapped back on his neck. He slammed him up against the stone wall. He pressed his forearm hard into Colin's chest and leaned in close to his face.

"Don't mess this up for the rest of us, you little jerk," Sebastian growled. "You do, you're dead."

"Hey," Jonathan said. "Take it easy, man. He's cool."

Sebastian snorted. "There's *nothing* cool about this little dweeb," he said.

"Come on," Jonathan said. "Let him go. We gotta hurry."

Sebastian gave Colin one last glare, then followed Jonathan out toward the heap of bodies. They stood together for a second, looking at the corpse of Mr. Vander lying in the middle of the pile.

"You really think we can do this, Johnny?"

"Jonathan. And it's worth a try."

There was no time to be queasy or delicate. Sebastian knelt down next to the tall, still form and started pulling at his long, blue coat.

"Damn! It's buttoned! Help me, will you?"

Together they frantically yanked the buttons through their holes. Jonathan kept his eyes on his fingers and away from the dead man's face. They did wander once, though— he saw the mouth half-open, a bit of dry gray tongue poking out, saw a raindrop roll off the forehead, saw the swirling storm above reflected in the cloudy, unfocused eyes—and he almost lost it. His breath caught, his fingers fumbled . . . but he blinked and looked away and kept going.

With the buttons undone, the boys started pulling the arms out of the sleeves. Mr. Vander's arms were incredibly heavy and stiff. Sebastian and Jonathan tugged and wiggled and jerked. Mr. Vander's head lolled and rocked from side to side, loose and floppy. Jonathan clenched his stomach and kept his eyes on his work.

"God," Sebastian panted. "And I thought I hated this guy when he was *alive*!"

They got one arm loose and, with a grunting heave, they rolled Mr. Vander over onto his stomach to work on the other. His face smacked against the stone ground with a sickening thud. Sebastian grabbed the cuff of the second sleeve and gave it a swift yank like a magician whipping the tablecloth off a table full of dishes. The jacket pulled free and Sebastian fell back onto his butt in a puddle.

"Grab his hat, Johnny."

They raced back toward the gate, Jonathan holding the hat, and the coat stuffed under Sebastian's arm.

Gerald stood alone, scratching at his neck and looking uncomfortable.

"Put this on!" Sebastian hollered, tossing Mr. Vander's jacket to him. He ducked low and peered out the gate. "He's almost here!"

"Man, I don't know if I want to put on a dead guy's coat."

Sebastian shot him a dark look.

"Don't put it on and you'll *be* a dead guy. Do it. All you gotta do is stand here in the shadows. Big deal."

Benny ran up huffing and puffing, a canvas bag slung over his shoulder. He tossed it on the ground at Sebastian's feet.

Gerald grimaced and pulled the long coat on. He

pinched it between his fingers like a dirty diaper. The bottom of the coat piled on the ground. Jonathan gave him an apologetic look and handed him the hat. Gerald closed his eyes and plopped it on his head. It dropped down onto his ears.

Sebastian stepped back to take a look at him. Behind them the sound of the boat got louder.

"Shoot!" Sebastian exclaimed. "We forgot the stool! You're way too short!" He looked frantically around for something for Gerald to stand on.

Jonathan thought fast. He dropped to his hands and knees in the shadows just inside the gate.

"He can stand on me," he said. "But make sure the coat covers me up."

Sebastian pulled Gerald over and he stepped gingerly up onto Jonathan's back. He was a lot heavier than Jonathan had expected. The hard stone blocks ground into his knee-caps. He felt Sebastian adjusting the long trench coat as best he could to cover him.

"Wait!" Gerald protested. "How am I gonna get the mailbag? And give him ours?"

Outside, the motor got louder, then quieter as the gas was cut back.

"Sebastian!" Jonathan hissed from the ground. "You do the bags. And try to stand between him and us!"

"All right."

"What do I do if he talks to me?" Gerald asked, his voice high and fast.

66

"Just grunt," Jonathan answered.

"He's here," Sebastian said. "Showtime." Jonathan lowered his head and peeked out from beneath the coat.

The dingy metal boat was just pulling up to the algae-covered stone steps. It was the same boat that had dropped Jonathan off the day before, but this time, Patrick was alone.

"Hello, Mr. Vander!" Patrick shouted good-naturedly as the boat bumped up to the stairs. Gerald didn't reply. Patrick leapt expertly out of the boat onto the steps, a rope tied to the boat in one hand and a canvas bag over his shoulder. Sebastian stepped down to meet him, the mailbag in his hand.

"I'll trade ye," Patrick said with a smile. Sebastian just held the bag out. Patrick shrugged and took it, then handed his own to Sebastian. "What'd ye do to get the supreme honor of being Mr. Vander's little helper?" he asked with a wink.

Sebastian froze. "I . . . I . . . nothing."

Jonathan winced from underneath Gerald.

Patrick squinted at Sebastian. "Ah. Well. Bet ye won't be doin' that again, now, will ye?" He looked past Sebastian, up to where Gerald stood atop Jonathan.

"How are ye there today, Mr. Vander?"

Gerald grunted. It sounded a little high and nervous to Jonathan. But Patrick only nodded and smiled with half his mouth. "Good to hear it."

They all stood for a moment looking at each other.

Patrick cocked an eyebrow.

"Well," he said. "Guess I best be off. Can't stand here jabbering with ye all day, Mr. Vander." He raised one hand to his forehead in a little salute and then waved. "Give me best to the Admiral, won't ye?"

Gerald grunted again.

Patrick laughed and hopped into the boat. Looking back over his shoulder, he threw the boat into reverse and receded slowly away against the incoming waves.

All three boys watched him, holding their breath. When he was far enough out, Patrick whipped the boat around and gunned it, chugging toward the mainland. He didn't look back.

Sebastian turned and walked up the stairs, a triumphant sneer on his face. "Nothing to it," he said. Jonathan rolled his eyes.

Gerald hopped down from Jonathan's back and tore the coat off like it was crawling with spiders. He threw the hat down on top of it.

"I'm *never* doing that again!" he cried.

Sebastian snorted and swung the big wooden door closed. "Yeah, you are. Mail comes tomorrow, too, you know." Gerald's shoulders slumped.

All the other boys were gathering around them. The rain had mostly stopped.

Sebastian stood shoulder to shoulder with Jonathan. He still had the cocky smile on his face.

"Well, boys, here we are," he said. "Got the place all to ourselves. You're welcome."

They all stood looking at one another. A seagull shrieked from the top of the wall above them.

"Well, then," Francis said, clearing his throat. "What should we do now?"

Sebastian looked at Jonathan and smiled, then looked back at the circle of questioning faces.

"Whatever the hell we want," he said, and his grin widened even more. He cracked his knuckles and started walking through the circle, toward the door to the main building across the courtyard.

"Uh, Thebathtian?" Colin called after him, stopping him in mid-step. "What about the bodieth?"

CHAPTER EIGHT
DRAGGING THE DEAD

They all turned and looked at the pile of soggy corpses. Sebastian stood with his mouth open, his eyebrows frowning.

Jonathan had already thought that through.

"The freezer," he said. "Otherwise, they'll—" He stopped and grimaced, then shrugged. "We have to put them in the freezer."

Sebastian nodded at him. "That makes sense," he said.

"The freezer's a long ways away," Tony said.

Sebastian raised his eyebrows at him. "Then we better get started."

Sebastian did the math of eight bodies and sixteen boys and assigned each body to two boys. None of the pairs could get their body more than a few feet before dropping it with a stomach-twisting, meaty splash in a puddle, though.

Dead bodies are heavy, it turns out. When they're wearing rain-drenched coats and wool trousers, they're really heavy. And when they're rain-soaked bodies of men being carried by a bunch of kids who don't even really want to touch them, they're almost impossibly heavy.

"Okay," Sebastian barked, gasping for breath and still holding Mr. Warwick's feet in his hands. "Two trips. Four people per body. Someone take one of these legs."

The bodies were still heavy, but in teams of four, they at least managed to drag them toward the door. It was tough going, though. Curses and accusations echoed around the courtyard.

"Come on! You're only *pretending* to hold that arm!"

"Lift higher! It's hard to pull when his head's dragging like that!"

"I *am* trying, Jason! His ankle is just too slippery!"

"No, not by the elbow, dummy! Grab under the armpits! Like this!"

"Gross! His tongue touched me!"

But, step by step, they got the bodies out of the courtyard and through the door and down the dark hallway and into the room where they'd eaten breakfast. The groups were spread out by then, depending on how big a body they'd gotten stuck with. Jonathan was with Colin, Miguel, and the kid named David. They, unfortunately, had ended up with the Admiral, and they were at the very end of the morbid, sweating, swearing parade.

"Dang, man," Miguel panted, wrestling with a leg that was slippery with rain. "Why'd I get stuck with three of the littlest guys?"

David, who was trying to get a good grip on the Admiral's right arm, shot him a look.

"I ain't no weakling."

"Nah, nah, you know what I mean," Miguel said quickly. "We all know you tough. That's why you're here, right? For being all tough and stuff and, like, almost killing some guy or something?"

Jonathan glanced nervously at David, but David just rolled his eyes.

"No. Just for fighting."

"Yeah," Miguel said. "But, like, a *lot* of fighting, right?"

David shrugged. They struggled for a few more steps in silence, but then he spoke again, his quiet voice a rush of frustration.

"I'm the only Japanese kid at my school, right? And every day—*every day*—they make fun of me. They push. They throw things. Whisper things. And so, yes, I fight back. So I get lots of practice, right? So, after a while, I start to win. And what's wrong with that? So some . . . some . . . *moron* starts up again and ends up with a broken jaw and a concussion and I'm supposed to be sorry? The judge says"—David bitterly slipped into a deep, adult voice—" 'All these terrible fights, all these stitches and broken noses, and *you* are the common denominator.' Me? I laughed at the judge. 'Cause from where I was sitting, the common denominator was all those stupid white boys."

Miguel dropped the Admiral's leg and straightened up to catch his breath.

"Sure, man," he said. "Whatever you say. You're on top. You're the *numerator,* man. Just remember I ain't white next time you start swinging, okay, champ?"

David scowled.

"What about you?" he asked. "What are you in for?"

Miguel shrugged.

"Eh. Truancy. I'm not, like, super great at showing up to school, you know? My folks *chose* to send me here, to fix my attitude. Can you believe that?" A grin spread across his face. "But look at me now! *Choosing* to stay here, when we could go home! I'm reformed!"

He looked around at them, waiting for a laugh, but they were all too tired and out of breath. Jonathan gave him a little smile and wiped the sweat from his forehead.

"What about you, newbie?" Miguel asked. "What'd you do to get yourself sent here?"

Jonathan's smile flickered away. His eyes dropped away from Miguel's. The Admiral was looking up at him, his foul mouth open and his dead eyes gaping.

"Come on," Jonathan said. "Let's get this over with. This guy ain't getting any lighter."

The boys stooped and regained their holds and hoisted the Admiral up with a chorus of grunts and curses.

"Thith ith abtholutely inthane," Colin complained under his breath, changing his grip around the Admiral's left arm-pit. "We thould've told right away."

"I'd keep that to yourself," Jonathan murmured, looking up the hallway. "I think Sebastian'll actually kick your butt if you keep talking like that." Jonathan was holding the Admiral's other limp arm and dragging him backward. Walter and David each had a leg.

"Thebathian? Thith wath all *your* idea, Jonathan."

Jonathan frowned and cleared his throat. The Admiral's head rocked from side to side as they walked, looking back and forth from him to Colin like he was listening to the conversation. Jonathan tried to avoid the Admiral's glassy, staring eyes.

"Yeah, well, I was right. I didn't want to go home." The Admiral's head flopped over to Colin.

"Well, thome of uth *do*." The Admiral's head flopped back to Jonathan.

Jonathan didn't know what to say. He looked away from the Admiral's accusing eyes.

"It's just for a few days, Colin," he said through gritted teeth. His fingers were burning from the Admiral's weight. "Just relax. It'll be fun." The Admiral's corpse looked back to Colin. His tongue was starting to stick out.

"Fun? With *him* in charge? He'll be worth than the Admiral!" Colin looked down at the Admiral's empty stare. "No offenth."

"Sebastian's not in charge," Jonathan assured him. "No one is. It's just all of us. He's not taking over."

Colin looked up into Jonathan's eyes and frowned his little frown.

"Jutht wait and thee." He shook his head. "The inmateth are running the athylum."

"The inmates are running the asylum? What does that mean?"

Colin shrugged. "It'th jutht a thaying."

"Who says it?"

"People."

"When do they say it?" The Admiral's head rocked back over to look at Jonathan.

Colin sighed and put his shoulder under the Admiral's uncooperative arm.

"When everything thtarth to go wrong."

By then, some of the boys had already made it to the freezer and dropped their bodies off. They walked out of the kitchen, red-faced and sweaty. Sebastian was among them.

"Listen up," he called out, panting. "Once you get both your bodies put away, we're gonna meet at the big table. We need to decide some stuff. And hurry up."

Colin shot Jonathan a meaningful look that he pretended not to see.

Finally, they got the Admiral's bloated body to the freezer. Their breath puffed in frosty clouds as they dragged and pushed him up onto the pile of corpses.

Jonathan was the last to leave. He slipped gratefully out of the freezer but groaned when the door hit the Admiral's jutting boot, six inches shy of closing. Colin and the others were already out the freezer door and into the kitchen, heading back for the next corpse.

He kicked at the Admiral's boot but his leg was stiff and the boot wouldn't budge. He sighed and looked over his shoulder and reluctantly walked back into the freezer. He grabbed the Admiral under both armpits and heaved, trying to twist him over and higher up on the pile of bodies. As he did so, he heard a metallic clanging and looked down.

A key had fallen out of the Admiral's jacket pocket. It was a big key, rusty and old-fashioned. Jonathan glanced around and shivered. He picked up the key and slipped it into his pocket, then gave the Admiral one last push to clear the door and walked out to rejoin the rest of the boys.

CHAPTER NINE
SCAR ISLAND

"Okay," Sebastian began when they all met at the table, exhausted and limp from dragging dead bodies across a hundred yards of stone. "First things first. I'm in charge."

Colin turned his head to give Jonathan a *very* meaningful look. Jonathan bit his tongue and didn't look back.

Sebastian was sitting in the Admiral's big wooden chair, his feet up on the table. Benny was sitting next to him, with Roger and Gregory nearby.

"Why are you in charge?" Tony asked.

"Because I say so, Tony. We can't have *no one* in charge. It'd be dumb. And I've been here the longest. And I'm the oldest."

"I'm older than you are," Gerald protested.

"Shut up, Gerald. I'm in charge. Anyone have a problem with that?"

"Do we have another choith?"

"No."

"Could we have electionth?"

"No. And you better shut up right now, Colin."

"*Let it go,*" Jonathan whispered through clenched teeth, nudging Colin. "*It'll be fine.*"

Colin just shook his head and frowned. His hand flitted up to pinch nervously at his neck.

"Okay, now that's settled. First rule is . . ." Sebastian

smiled like a cat with a mouthful of feathers. He spread his hands wide. ". . . there are no rules."

There was a little scattered clapping among the group. Some nervous laughter. Sebastian looked around at them, a little frown on his face.

"Why do you guys look so scared?"

No one answered. Eyes dropped to the floor.

"What's wrong with you guys? This is the best thing that ever happened to us!"

There was still no answer except the sound of the rain still pattering in the courtyard outside the window.

Sebastian jumped to his feet.

"What? You think we can't do this? You think we can't take care of ourselves and have fun?" Sebastian shook his head.

"Come on! The stupid Admiral? He called us scabs, right?" Sebastian's face darkened. "Picked off and thrown away, he said. But now he's gone. And here *we* are. Still around. 'Cause you know what you get when you keep picking at a scab?"

He looked around at them, his eyes shining.

"Bloody fingers?" Miguel suggested.

"An infection?" Walter asked.

"No!" Sebastian spat. "You get a *scar*, idiots. A scar. And scars are tough. The Admiral was wrong. We ain't scabs. We're *scars.*"

"Yeah!" Benny piped up eagerly. "Scars, man!"

Jonathan's stomach suddenly twisted and tightened. He blinked quickly and rubbed at his sleeves with sweaty palms.

Sebastian's mouth spread into a grin and he opened his arms wide.

"Look around, guys! This whole place belongs to us. We're the kings. No one to boss us around. No one to get us in trouble. It's *our* island now. Ours. We don't need nobody. 'Cause we're Scars now. Scars with a capital *S*. The tough Scars that got left behind. It's *our* island."

"Hell yeah!" Roger cheered in his deep voice. "*Our* island!"

"Our island!" Gregory echoed.

Sebastian slammed his fist down on the table, his face glowing with triumph.

"This whole island belongs to the Scars now!"

"Scar Island!" Benny crowed.

Sebastian had them now. There were cheers and smiles and high fives. Even Walter was nodding his head and grinning.

"This ain't Slabhenge anymore!" Sebastian hollered. "It's Scar Island from now on! Say it!"

"Scar Island!" all the boys shouted.

All the boys except Colin, who just sat looking around, pale and frowning.

And all the boys except Jonathan, still rubbing his arms and blinking.

Sebastian sat back down, his face flushed.

"The jerks are gone," he said. "We can do. Whatever. We. Want."

There was more clapping, more cheering.

"Except . . . we should eat meals together, I think," Sebastian added. "To check in. Make sure we're all okay. That makes sense, right?" He looked at Jonathan. Jonathan dropped his hands quickly from his arms. He shrugged and nodded.

"So do whatever you want, guys. Run around. Eat some more. Whatever. But be back here for dinner. Have fun, Scars."

Everyone sat and looked at each other for a moment. Then Francis stood up and started toward the kitchen. David got up and headed for the door that led outside.

"Wait," Jonathan said. "What about the generator? We still need electricity, right? For the fridge and the . . . freezer?"

Sebastian pursed his lips. "Oh, yeah. Right. We'll, uh, take turns. It only has to get done, what, like three times a day?" He looked to Benny, who nodded eagerly. "We've all done it, we know how it works. So, first, how about . . . you and you," he said, pointing at Miguel and another kid Jonathan didn't know yet. "Head down and fill it up." They grumbled and trudged away together.

Slowly the rest of the boys wandered away in different directions, most in groups of two or three. Sebastian headed out into the courtyard. Benny followed like a puppy at his heels.

Colin and Walter and Jonathan were the last left at the tables. Colin still looked unhappy.

"Cheer up," Jonathan said to him. "Now the good times start." Colin just rolled his eyes.

"So . . . what is there to do around here?" Jonathan asked.

It was Walter's turn to roll his eyes. "Who knows? All we

ever did was work, man. Mop the floors, clean the kitchen, scrub the toilets. I've been here weeks and I bet I ain't seen any more of the place than you have."

"Well, then," Jonathan said, standing up. "Let's go exploring."

Walter hopped up to join him, and after a moment Colin did, too.

"We're gonna need lanternth," Colin said with a sigh. "I know where they keep them. Matcheth, too."

A few minutes later, the three of them were walking through one of the snaking, shadowy hallways that had been so confusing to Jonathan the night before. Jonathan and Walter each held a hissing lantern.

"This place is like a maze," Jonathan said, moving his lantern from side to side to banish suspicious shadows in the corners.

"It *is* a maze," Walter said. "I heard they built it that way on purpose, to confuse the crazies. So only the guards would know their way around, you know?"

Jonathan slipped on an especially slimy stair and, putting out his hand to catch himself, almost grabbed a huge brown rat. He jerked his hand back and the rat squeaked angrily and slithered into a hole between two blocks.

"Well," he said, standing up. "If they weren't crazy when they got here, I bet it didn't take too long to get that way."

Walter looked uneasily at the hole the rat had disappeared into.

"Yeah, man. You got that right." He shook his shoulders in an exaggerated shiver. "This place gives me the heebie-jeebies. Thinking about all them crazies that lived here. And died here." He dropped his voice to a whisper. It echoed in the corridor like turning pages. He looked from Jonathan to Colin. "You guys believe in ghosts?"

Colin shook his head, but he didn't look so sure.

"I don't know," Jonathan said, squinting into the blackness ahead of them. "But if there are ghosts, this sure seems like the kind of place they'd be."

"Yeah," Walter answered. "No lie." He looked at Jonathan. He had second thoughts written all over his face.

Jonathan put on a smile that was a lot braver than he felt.

"Well, let's go find 'em, then."

Walter shook his head and almost smiled.

"Fine. I'm following you, though."

They wandered up and down staircases and peeked into sinister-looking side passages. Jonathan was hopelessly lost within minutes. They found one room they were pretty sure used to be some sort of dungeon; rusted chains dangled from the walls. They took a quick look and then kept going.

Suddenly, the light of Jonathan's lantern fell on something familiar. It was a rope, stretched across a staircase spiraling down into darkness.

"Hey! I know where we are! Mr. Warwick showed this to me."

Colin and Walter stood shoulder to shoulder with him.

"Yeah," Colin whispered. "He loved to try and thcare uth with thith."

"The door to the deep, he called it," Walter said in a low voice.

"The Hatch." Jonathan nodded. "What's really down there?" He felt both Walter and Colin shrug beside him.

"No one knows, man," Walter whispered. "They'd never tell us. Some big, dark secret, I guess." From the stairs rose the same thumping and slurping Jonathan had heard the night before. He swallowed, then stepped forward and lifted the rope. He ducked his head beneath it and stepped down onto the top stair.

"What are you doing?" Colin hissed.

"I wanna see it," Jonathan answered.

He took another step down, then another, holding his lantern out before him. When he didn't hear any footsteps behind him, he looked back. Colin and Walter were still standing on the other side of the rope in the corridor.

"Come on," he whispered. His voice echoed eerily in the tight staircase. "Don't make me go alone. Things are always bigger and darker when they're secret. Let's find out how bad it really is."

Walter gulped. Then he ducked under the rope and followed Jonathan.

"No way," Colin said. "I'm thtaying here."

"Suit yourself," Jonathan said. "But we've got both lanterns."

Colin scooted under the rope and joined Walter. "Jerkth."

Jonathan reached back to pat Colin on the shoulder.

"Relax," he said. "Whatever's down here can't be worse than the dead Admiral, and we spent plenty of time with *him* today."

"Thut up and go."

The stairs were steep, and the boys held one hand against the slippery wall to steady themselves. The steps curved down around a corner and then stopped at a small, dark landing. The landing was a little bigger than a bed, and on the other side, another staircase climbed up and away from them, in the opposite direction of the one they'd come down. On one wall of the landing was another doorway, smaller and rounded on top.

The scraping, slurping, knocking sounds were coming from the smaller doorway. They were louder here, closer. Goose bumps popped out on Jonathan's arms. He held his lantern as far out in front of himself as he could toward the doorway.

Through the doorway was another staircase. It dropped down into even deeper darkness. The lantern's light couldn't reach the end of it.

He felt Colin breathing in one of his ears, and Walter in the other, looking over his shoulder.

"I ain't going any farther," Walter whispered. The darkness down the doorway sloshed and chunked.

"Me neither," Colin breathed.

"Fine," Jonathan said. "I'll go by myself."

"Why?" Colin asked. "Why don't we jutht go back, Jonathan?"

Jonathan stared down into the blackness. He answered without turning his head. His voice echoed back at him from the dark downward passageway, like he was talking to himself.

"It's this big, awful secret, right? The Hatch, down here in the dark? Well, maybe, once you know it, it's not all that terrible after all."

He looked back over his shoulder and locked eyes with Walter.

"Maybe it's the hiding that makes it horrible, you know?" Walter furrowed his brow.

"Uhh . . . not really, man. I think we should get outta here. Like, *fast*."

Jonathan turned back toward the rattling, grinding blackness. "Big, dark secrets can't stay that way forever," he murmured. His free hand rubbed absently at the wrist that was holding the lantern.

A dull, heavy thud echoed up the stairway toward them.

"Jonathan?" Walter's whisper was right in his ear. "I am really, really, really"—he paused—"hungry. When you're done playing with the monsters, you can find me in the kitchen, eating sausage."

"I'll be with him," Colin added.

"Thanks, guys," Jonathan said, and his only answer was the sound of their footsteps retreating back up the spiral staircase.

He held the lantern in a shaking hand and shuffled to the end of the landing, to the very edge of the final staircase. This one was narrower than the other corridors; the walls weren't much farther apart than Jonathan's shoulders.

Jonathan took a deep breath. Before him, there was another loud clunk, and a snuffling sound like a huge hissing nose. When he blew his breath out, it came out shaky.

He took the first step down. The steps were bigger drops down than the other staircase. He had to fall the last couple of inches. He took the next step down. He almost turned and ran when an especially loud metal rattling rang up from the darkness below. But he licked his lips and took a breath and dropped down another step. And another.

The darkness before him growled and crunched. The walls seemed to close in around him. He felt with his foot for the next step and realized that he was at the bottom. And that somewhere along the line, he had squeezed his eyes shut.

He opened his eyes.

He was in a tiny square room with a stone ceiling so low he could've reached up and touched it. It was freezing, and the walls were covered in dripping moisture as if they were sweating.

In front of him was a huge, round, metal door. Heavy iron bolts circled its outer edge. It was rusty and grimy and covered in shiny, green slime. It looked ancient. The door was big enough that, if it had been open (and he was extremely thankful that it wasn't), he could have stepped through it without ducking. It was a door like a submarine would have, with the large iron handle in the middle that Jonathan knew would open the door if he spun it around.

The door seemed to rattle rhythmically, like it was breathing.

"The Hatch," Jonathan whispered. He stepped toward it. He reached out with his empty hand. He could see the trembling in his fingers. They closed around the iron handle in the center of the door.

As his fingers touched the metal, his eyes dropped down to a round shadow at the foot of the door. The wavering light from his lantern flashed across it.

A human skull, white bone spotted with green slime, propped against the grimy stone doorway, black eye sockets gaping right at him, toothy mouth frozen in a silent scream.

The door suddenly rocked and banged against his shaking hand. There was a tremendous crack and a wet, sloshing thud, and a freezing mist sprayed Jonathan in the face.

He screamed and fell back, slipping on the wet stone. The lantern dropped from his hand and landed on the hard floor with a shattering crash.

The light went out, plunging Jonathan into absolute, eye-choking darkness.

CHAPTER TEN
A VOICE IN THE DARK

Jonathan crouched on his hands and knees, panting in the blackness. He'd never seen such darkness before, so total and suffocating. Down in the deepest dungeon, pinned beneath a prison of dark stone, there was hardly even the memory of light. His eyes gasped like the mouth of a fish yanked out of the water. They found no light to breathe.

He waited for arms to wrap around his waist, long scaly fingers to close around his throat, teeth to pierce his shaking flesh. But one panicked breath passed. Then another.

All there was was complete darkness and the sound of his fear-gasping lungs and the same rhythmic watery thuds and sloshes of the Hatch. The stone under his hands was moist and clammy. The frigid, hard floor began to hurt his knees. His racing heart began to slow down, just enough for him to start to think. He tried to slow his lungs down.

He felt with his hands and found the lantern. The glass was broken and he shook and tapped it, but he knew that restarting it in the dark was impossible.

He was lost. In the dungeon of an asylum. In total darkness. With a skull. He couldn't help but wonder where the rest of the body was.

"*Crap*," he whispered, and tried not to freak out. Still on his hands and knees, he turned around and started crawling up the stairs, away from the Hatch, his hands feeling through the inky black mystery in front of him.

He found the steep stairs and tumbled up them, bumping his knees and knocking his elbow on the stone wall. Behind him, the Hatch rumbled and chomped. He scrambled faster, climbing up the staircase to the landing. He tripped on the last step and fell, twisting onto his back. Something scrabbled away from him in the darkness on sharp claws. It sounded big.

Gasping, he jumped to his feet and felt around for the walls. His breaths came fast and shallow. His heartbeat drummed in his head. He staggered with his hands reaching out in front of him like a blind man, until his foot hit a stair and he fell again onto brutal stone. With the Hatch behind him thumping as loudly as his heart in his ears, he raced up them in a stumbling crawl. He got to the top and felt a corner, a turn, and he shuffled with feeling fingers around it. The noise of the Hatch got quieter. He kept one hand on the wall to his right and fumbled down a long corridor until he could no longer hear the Hatch at all. He was still in absolute blackness, his eyes blinking and rolling and seeing nothing.

He stopped for a moment to catch his breath and calm down, leaning against the wet stone wall. He dropped his head against the wall and sucked in great gasps of the musty air and blew it out through round lips until his lungs weren't heaving and his heart was merely pumping and not pounding.

Then he remembered: *the rope!* He'd never ducked under or run into the rope stretched across the top of the stairwell. Which could mean only one thing: He'd gone the wrong way. After his spinning fall on the landing, he must have stumbled up the wrong staircase, the one that had led in the opposite direction of the one he and Walter and Colin had come down.

He gulped and his breath started speeding up again. He'd have to backtrack, back down past the seething Hatch.

Or go forward. Into darkness and mystery and unexplored passages.

Behind him, dimly, he heard a sharp bang and grumble. The Hatch. It was just a door. A rusty, wet door of ancient iron that held something back. But for some reason, Jonathan felt like it was waiting for him. Hungry, in the dark.

He clenched his teeth and took a step forward.

The corridor was straight for a while, ten or fifteen steps. His fingers found one doorway, closed with a wooden door so rotten it crumbled under his fingertips, but he continued past it. At the end of the straightaway, the hall turned in a sharp L to the right, and Jonathan scooted around the corner. He stopped and listened, hoping to hear the voices of the other boys or even the sound of the ocean, which would mean a window or a door to the outside. But there was only the always-and-everywhere sound of water dripping, and his own echoey breaths, and the occasional distant scratching of claws in the dark.

He took a step forward and the world was gone. His foot found only air beneath it and he tried to catch himself on the wall, but there was no grip on the slimy surface and he fell forward with a scream.

Dank air whistled past his face. He thrust his arms desperately out in front of him and then he slammed with horrible force onto a down staircase, the edges of the stairs like sharpened fists hammering his body. He slid and rolled and bounced down the stairs, each stair yanking a grunt or a groan from him.

At the bottom, gasping in blackness, he lay with his cheek in a cold puddle and felt each pain and pulse in his body. He flexed his fingers. Wiggled his toes. Bent his knees and elbows.

"Nothing's broken," he said out loud. His voice sounded small and alone in all that empty darkness. There was the rusty taste of blood in his mouth.

He was just pushing himself up to his hands and knees when he saw it. He froze in mid-crouch and tried to blink it away—but it was still there.

Light.

A thin line of light, glowing somewhere off ahead of him. With nothing else in the blackness for his eyes to compare it to, he couldn't tell if it was just out of reach of his fingers or fifty feet away. But it was there, shining in the darkness.

He started crawling toward it, his knees and palms

splashing through grimy puddles. The light got clearer, more solid around the edges.

The line of light was coming from under a door.

As he watched, a shadow moved across it, then was gone. Someone or something was moving on the other side of the door. Jonathan strained his ears for a sound, a voice, a laugh. Was it the other boys, the Scars . . . Had he circled around in the darkness back to where he had started?

He couldn't hear anything. Except, maybe, a low humming. He rose to his feet and took a step closer, then two more. Water leaked into his shoes.

There it was again, a deep humming song. He didn't know the tune. But it definitely wasn't one of the Scars.

It was the voice of a grown-up.

He took one final step up to the door.

His foot came down on a teetering pile of something stacked just outside the door. They clattered and crashed to the floor, shattering and skittering on the stones.

The humming stopped. There was a grunt and a growl from behind the door.

Jonathan took one step back but then froze.

The door jerked inward, flooding the corridor with yellow light.

Jonathan's eyes burned and he threw his arm over his face.

A deep, rumbling voice like wet boulders scraping together rasped out of the blinding light.

"What are *you* doing here?"

CHAPTER ELEVEN
A BEAUTIFUL RAT

Jonathan stood pinned in the light. He blinked his eyes and squinted up at the looming shadow before him.

"I'm—I'm just—" He took another step back, but a hand reached out and grabbed hold of his sleeve.

"Get in here," the voice rumbled. "Otherwise *they* will."

Jonathan was pulled by his arm through the door. It slammed shut behind him and the hand released him. He shrank back against the closed door.

The light in the room wasn't as bright as it had first seemed, after his stumbling nightmare in the total darkness. It was just candles, eight or nine of them, and one sputtering lantern.

Jonathan blinked and looked around. The room was full of—*books*. Shelves lined the stone walls, each covered end to end with large, leather-bound books. Low bookshelves divided the middle of the room, also full of neatly lined volumes, with more books standing up on top between heavy iron bookends. Along one long wall were evenly spaced window wells, deep and arched, but their views were blocked by leaning rows of books standing on their sills.

Jonathan knew in an instant that he'd stumbled into Slabhenge's library. And it had a librarian.

He eyed the flickering candles nervously. A bunch of candles in a room full of books didn't seem like a great idea, even in a prison made entirely of stone. He resisted the urge to jump and blow them out.

"Come for a book, did ye? Come to see? What we have?"

Jonathan looked to the source of the voice. The man was old. Incredibly old. Impossibly old. His face was deeply lined with wrinkles and creases. He was thin, and must have once been very tall, before he'd gotten so stooped over. He peered at Jonathan from behind thick, smudged glasses that magnified his eyes to silver dollars, shiny blue. His hair was thin and pure white and long, draping over his shoulders and far down his back.

He held his head to the side and tilted down, so his eyes had to look up into Jonathan's. A shy smile snuck onto his lips, revealing small, crooked, yellow teeth, but the smile scurried quickly away into the shadows.

"Or else *who* will get in?" Jonathan finally managed to croak.

The man's eyebrows crinkled and he frowned.

"I'm sorry?"

"When you—pulled me in. You said to get in or else they would. Who?"

The man's smile returned and stayed. He leaned a little closer to Jonathan.

"Why, the rats. Of course. *They* will. Come in. And we don't like them to."

Jonathan licked his lips and looked away from the man's eerie smile and shining eyes.

"No. I guess not."

"It's been a long time," the man said. "A very long time. Since we've had a visitor. That wasn't a rat."

Jonathan just stood there, blinking stupidly. His mind was still wandering in the dark in a world where all the grown-ups were dead.

"Go ahead. Take a look. Around. Pick one out. Or two." The man's little smile came and went as he spoke, like a bobbing lantern on a boat lost in the fog. He took a step back and spread his arms. "Any book you like."

Jonathan took a breath, then stepped past him and into the shelves of Slabhenge's library.

The books were all old. Their spines were cracked and painted with the gold words of their titles. Some of them Jonathan recognized. Most he did not. Their pages were yellowed and worn. The smell of leather and ink and old paper mixed and mingled with the candlelight and filled the room. All the books, despite their age, shone with a well-cared-for light—there were no cobwebs in this forgotten library, no dust on these ancient books.

"What do ye like? To read?" The librarian's voice trailed along behind him as he scanned the shelves. "Adventure, is it? Jonathan Swift? Mysteries, perhaps? Sherlock Holmes?"

"I used to read a lot," Jonathan answered softly, his eyes exploring the titles of the books as his finger slid over their spines.

"Before? Coming here?"

"Not exactly. Just . . . before."

Jonathan's finger stopped on a dark, well-worn spine. The librarian leaned in to see where Jonathan was looking. He stayed there, his face close to Jonathan's.

"Ah. *Hamlet*. A play, that is. By Shakespeare, of course. A good one. Dark. A prince. A ghost. A murder in a castle. And poor Ophelia. Hamlet loved her. But he thought it was his fault. Her dying." The librarian sighed. "To be. Or not. To be."

Jonathan pursed his lips and kept walking. He suddenly didn't feel like any book at all. He felt like being back where all the grown-ups were dead.

"I've gotta go. Thanks."

"But ye've got no book!"

"It's all right. I don't need one."

The librarian gave him a long, steady look. "We want you to. Take a book. Don't worry about the Admiral. And his rules. These books are for reading."

Jonathan's mind raced. The old librarian didn't know about the Admiral. About the lightning.

"Are you always here, just — by yourself?"

The librarian smiled his fleeting smile again. "Oh, yes. Yes. We are always alone. We don't like them. The Admiral. The others. And they don't like us."

"When's the—last time you saw them?"

The old man shrugged and looked away, scanning the shelves. "Don't know. Three. Four, maybe."

"Four days? Without seeing anyone?"

The librarian smiled a wide, staying smile. He looked up at Jonathan in his strange, sideways way.

"No, no. Four *years*. Four years without seeing. Anyone. At least."

Jonathan's mouth dropped open.

"What . . . how . . . don't you get—lonely?"

The man cackled a dry, coughing laugh. "No. We have our books. We have our stories."

"What do you eat? I mean . . . how do you get food?"

"We go down. In the very dark middle of the night. And we bring back. What we need. The Admiral leaves us alone. And we leave him alone."

"Oh. Okay."

The librarian pulled a book from the shelf and pressed it into Jonathan's hands.

"Here. Start. With this one."

Jonathan looked down. The book was thick, with a red, pictureless cover. In plain gold script on the cover was the title: *Robinson Crusoe*.

"It's about getting stuck. On an island." The librarian winked at him. "With bloodthirsty natives."

"Uh. Thanks."

The old man just nodded.

As they walked back toward the door, the man stooped down to pick up a large cat off a chair. He held it in one arm and stroked it with his other.

"Read it. Bring it back. When you're done. And then you can have another. Book." He patted Jonathan on the shoulder and left his wrinkled hand resting there. "We'll be here."

"Okay. You and your cat?"

"No. Me and Ninety-Nine, here." The old man smiled and held the cat out toward him.

"Right," Jonathan said, reaching out to pet the cat. "You and your c—" Jonathan gasped and jerked his hand back. The animal he'd been reaching out to pet was not a cat at all. It was a rat. A beady-eyed, pink-tailed, black-coated rat that was bigger than most cats he'd seen. Its eyes glittered up at him above two huge top front teeth that poked sharply out of its mouth.

"God! It's a rat! It's huge!"

The librarian laughed, a deeper laugh than before. His eyes closed when he laughed.

"Yes. Yes," he giggled and stroked the rat gently from its head to its naked, ringed tail. "My big, beautiful boy. Ninety-Nine. Is his name."

"That's the biggest rat I've ever seen. By a long shot." Jonathan was backing toward the door.

The librarian giggled again and nodded. "Yes. Very big. Years and years. It took me. A lifetime. Always bigger." The monstrous rat leaned back into the librarian's scratching fingers.

"You . . . made him that big? How?"

"Oh, time. Patience. Attention. Years. I found the very biggest. Rats. One boy. One girl. And I put them together." The rat's tail curled lovingly around his arm. "I let the babies grow. Just a little. To find the biggest. And I let the others go. After I cut off their tails."

"You cut off their tails?"

Another smile spread across the librarian's lined face. "Of course. So I would know. Who they were. Brothers and sisters can't make babies. You know. And I would find another. Big one. *With* a tail. And make more babies. And again. And again. So many times. So many tails. And always bigger." A cloud passed over the old man's face, erasing his smile. "I almost lost it all. With Seventy-Six. She wouldn't. Have babies. *Couldn't*, I was afraid." His smile returned and the cloud lifted. "But then she did. And they were beautiful. And big."

Goose bumps rose on Jonathan's arms.

"You mean—this is your *ninety-ninth* rat?"

"Oh, no," the man chuckled. "Much more. Than that. I just stopped. Counting. One Hundred sounds so ugly. It's no kind of name. For a beautiful rat."

"Oh. Right." Jonathan put his hand on the doorknob and turned it.

"You'll come back? To us? And another book?"

"Yeah. Sure," he answered, opening the door to the inky blackness of the passageway.

"We hope so. How are things going? Out there?" The librarian's white eyebrows cocked out at the darkness looming past the doorway.

Jonathan licked his lips. He smelled lightning, saw bodies in a freezer, heard a monster rattling an iron door and a bully taking control.

"Fine, I guess."

"Oh. Well." The librarian sighed again, wearily. "It never stays fine. For long. Things always go bad. Out there. So much evil. And darkness. And so much more always coming. That is why we stay here. Keep your wits. About you."

Jonathan eyed the waiting corridor. At the edges of the light, furry shadows scrambled and hid. He wondered how many of them were missing tails. He licked his lips.

"Can I borrow a candle?"

CHAPTER TWELVE
"I KNOW WHAT YOU DID"

When Jonathan got back to the light and the world and the rest of the Scars, Sebastian was sitting in the Admiral's chair with his feet up on the table. In his hands was the Admiral's sword. The very one the Admiral had been holding high in the storm, the one that had brought down lightning and death for himself and all of the grown-ups (except one).

Most of the boys were hanging out in the dining room. Some were munching on great mouthfuls of food. A few had found a deck of cards and were playing at a table. Most were just sitting around or lying around or standing and looking out the windows into the courtyard, which was once again dripping with a drizzling rain.

Benny, Roger, Gregory, and some other kids were seated around Sebastian, looking eagerly to their leader's smirking face like baby birds hoping for a worm.

"Hey! Johnny! Come here," Sebastian called when he saw Jonathan enter the room with his candle in one hand and the book tucked under his arm. Walter and Colin had jumped up when they saw him and they followed him to Sebastian's table, their eyes full of questions.

There were crumpled-up candy wrappers on the table and little dark smears of chocolate in the corners of Sebastian's mouth. He licked at them like a cat. Sebastian looked Jonathan up and down with a frown.

"Where'd you get that book?"

Jonathan shrugged.

"Found it."

Sebastian sniffed and picked at something between his teeth.

"We're divying up the grown-up's rooms," he said. "I got dibs on the Admiral's. But there's four more. Which one do you want?"

Jonathan looked around at the other boys. Their eyes were wide, waiting. Benny's reptilian eyes were narrow, glaring.

"Five? There's sixteen of us. Why would I get one?"

Sebastian frowned and shrugged.

"Whatever. Maybe I like you. Who cares. Don't you want one? Or do you want to keep sleeping in your little cell?"

Jonathan eyed the other kids. There were seven, counting Benny, waiting on his answer. Most of the kids were older—and bigger—than he was.

"Uh, no, thanks. Someone else can have it, I guess."

Sebastian screwed up one eye thoughtfully, then scowled and snorted.

"Fine. Whatever. Suit yourself. I'll give it to someone else."

"Maybe we thould take turnth in the roomth, Thebathtian. To be fair," Colin suggested.

Sebastian's eyes dropped into angry slits.

"Maybe you should *th*ut up, Colin."

Colin furrowed his brow and looked down at his feet. Jonathan turned to walk away.

"Hey! *They* said you went to look at the Hatch." Sebastian pointed with his chin at Walter and Colin.

"Yeah."

"So? What is it?" Sebastian's voice still wore its bitter coat of "who the hell cares," but there was a sharp edge of real curiosity to it.

"It's . . . it's . . ." Jonathan's voice faltered. He almost spilled it all, almost spit out everything about the eerie door with its ominous sounds and freezing spray and moss-covered skull.

But he stopped.

If he told them everything, they might want to see it for themselves. And if they went to see it, they might continue up the other staircase, and they might find the librarian. He didn't want them to. He wanted to keep the library a secret, just for himself. Like the key in his pocket. And the reason he was sent to Slabhenge in the first place.

"It's just a door," he said, with a shrug and a roll of his eyes.

"A door?"

"Yeah, like an old metal door. It's locked, though." He shrugged again and turned to walk away. "No big deal."

Walter and Colin followed at his elbow as he walked away into the kitchen. He was starving. Once they were away from Sebastian's ears and safe in the empty kitchen, they peppered him with questions.

"Where were you, man?"

"What took you tho long?"

"We waited for you at the top of the stairs! Where did you go?"

Jonathan looked around and grabbed the end of a loaf of bread someone had left sitting out. He took a big bite and gnawed it on one side of his mouth.

"I got lost," he answered with a shrug. "Went the wrong way."

"Where'th your lantern? What'th with the candle?"

Jonathan shrugged again and looked away.

"I broke my lantern. Then I found this. No biggie. What have you guys been up to?"

Walter rolled his eyes. "King Sebastian out there is really living it up. He's claimed the Admiral's room, of course, and most of the best food. He's called some big meeting in a few minutes, before dinner. I don't like that guy, man."

Jonathan grabbed an apple that was sitting on the counter and bit into it.

"You thould have thaid yeth to the room, Jonathan."

Jonathan crunched an especially big bite and chewed it loudly.

"What? Why?"

Colin sighed and scratched at his arm.

"Becauth. Now Thebathtian ith mad at you."

"Why would he be mad? I said no to be nice."

Colin shrugged. "He gave you a room. It wathn't to be nithe. It wath to thow that he'th the bawth. You made him look bad."

"I did not!"

Colin looked up at Jonathan with worried eyes.

"I don't think that'th how he theeth it." Behind them, through the door, Sebastian hollered for everyone to gather for the meeting. Colin pinched at his neck and started for the door with his pigeon-toed walk. "He'th only the king if we let him be. And you didn't let him."

Jonathan swallowed his apple and gave Walter a questioning look. Walter shrugged.

"The kid's weird. But he's smart, you know?"

"Yeah. I think he is."

In the dining room, Sebastian was sitting on a table, the blade of the Admiral's sword resting on his shoulder.

"All right, boys," he said to the last few boys grabbing chairs or a spot on the floor. "Time to get some stuff squared away. Some of us are taking the rooms upstairs. The rest of you can sleep wherever you want. Whenever you want. There's no all-dark tonight." There was a low murmur of approval from the group.

"We're gonna meet together every day," Sebastian continued. "Like, every night and every morning. To make sure everything's still fine. We'll meet right here."

"Every day? But . . . when are we going to inform the

authorities?" Francis asked. "You said this was just for a couple of days, Sebastian."

Sebastian tucked the chocolate-stained corners of his mouth down. "Yeah. Or whatever. We'll see. There's no rush." Benny jumped up and hissed something in Sebastian's ear.

"Oh," he said. "This is important. Did anyone find a key lying around?"

No one answered. Jonathan's mouth went dry and he fingered the Admiral's key through his pocket.

"We can't find the key to the Admiral's office," Sebastian went on. "Benny says the Admiral always carried it with him, but I—checked, and he doesn't, uh, have it. And the door is too big to break down." Jonathan thought of his one time in the Admiral's dark office. He remembered the smell of alcohol and the papers and files that the Admiral had, the papers that held the secrets of the crimes the boys had committed to get sent to Slabhenge. His grip on the key tightened through the fabric.

"Why do you need to get in there?" Miguel asked.

Sebastian shrugged. "There's paperwork and stuff that Benny wants. Plus, a bunch more of the Admiral's chocolates. And"—Sebastian smiled and cocked his eyebrows—"the Admiral's booze, of course. That could be fun." Some of the boys giggled nervously. "Well, if you find an old key, hand it over. It's around here somewhere. Whoever finds it gets a room upstairs and a handful of chocolates."

Sebastian rose to his feet and pointed with the sword toward the kitchen. "Meeting's over. You know where the food is. Dinnertime is whenever you're hungry. Same with breakfast. Any questions?"

"What can we eat for dinner?" another kid asked.

"Whatever you want."

"What are we doing tomorrow?"

Sebastian shook his head in exasperation.

"Whatever you want," he repeated impatiently. "Look, no more questions. Do what you want. That's the point. *They're* not here anymore. *We* are. It's us. Just us. The Scars."

"We *thould* have thome ruleth."

Sebastian clenched his fists and gritted his teeth.

"We don't need any rules," he seethed. "We don't *want* any rules." He held his hands out to the group. "Do we?"

There were some shaking heads, some grumbles of agreement, a few loud shouts of *no!*

"What about food?" Colin persisted.

"What about it?"

"If we all jutht eat whatever we want, we'll run out. We need to plan it out."

Sebastian smoldered like a dynamite wick. He opened his mouth to spit out an answer, but Jonathan beat him to it.

"He's right, Sebastian. The Admiral probably didn't order enough food for us all to eat like this. We're gonna run out."

Sebastian's eyes clouded with doubt. His dynamite wick sputtered. He licked his lips.

"Well . . . fine, then. We should—be careful about eating too much, I guess. Don't go crazy. Hell . . . go back to eating oatmeal if you want. But I've eaten enough oatmeal." He popped another square of chocolate into his mouth and chewed it loudly to make his point. Benny murmured something to him and he grinned a sticky brown smile. "And the supply boat comes in two days. Then we'll have plenty of food."

A thought shot into Jonathan's head.

"What about the mail boat?" he asked.

"The mail boat, *Johnny*, comes every day."

"So it'll come tomorrow?"

"Yeah. So?"

Jonathan looked around. He didn't want to make Sebastian look bad in front of the group.

"Well . . . so . . . we'll need something to give to it, right? Wouldn't it be suspicious if we didn't?"

Sebastian stopped chewing with his mouth stuck open.

"Oh," he said after a moment. "Yeah. Right. I was gonna get to that." He chewed thoughtfully for a few seconds before continuing. "We all still need to write letters every day, just like we were. No one eats dinner until we have your letter." Benny jumped up again and whispered something to him. Sebastian nodded. "And I'm reading every one. No one says anything about the grown-ups or the lightning or anything. Everything's just A-okay here at Slabhenge, right? Walter, go grab a bunch of paper and pens."

They all sat in silence, writing their letters home.

Jonathan stalled, looking around at the other boys bent over their papers. Tongues poked out of mouths. Eyebrows crinkled. Pen tips scratched on paper. Out through the windows, the sky was darkening toward night. It was raining hard now, the afternoon's drizzle turned to a steady pour. The boys around him were squinting to see their own words.

When each boy finished, he walked up and handed it to Benny, who read it over. He'd nod and hand it back and the boy would address the envelope and it would go in the mailbag.

Jonathan stared at his blank sheet of paper, trying to find words in the darkness. Colin sat beside him. He'd already handed in his letter, but he'd gotten another piece of paper and his hands were fluttering busily around it.

"What are you doing?" Jonathan asked him in a whisper.

"Origami," Colin answered. He made a few more quick folds and then held up the paper, now folded into an intricate shape. "Thee? It'th a bird. A crane." His smile rose and then flitted away. He handed the paper bird to Jonathan.

"Cool. Thanks. Where'd you learn to do that?"

Colin shrugged. "I thtole a book." They grinned at each other. Jonathan took a breath and went back to his own blank piece of paper.

Benny sneered at Jonathan when he walked up with his letter. He was by himself at the end of a long table, a tall white candle lighting his face. His eyes skimmed over Jonathan's letter.

"Looks good enough, Johnny. I guess. Who's Sophia?" His eyes flashed up to Jonathan. In the candlelight, they looked hungry and black, like a cobra's. But less honest.

"She's . . . a friend."

A venomous smile rose like oil at the corners of Benny's mouth. The points of his teeth showed like fangs. He lowered his voice to a taunting hiss so the boys at the other tables couldn't hear.

"*No, she's not. I saw your paperwork, Johnny. In the Admiral's office, the day you got here.*" His foul smile widened. Jonathan's breaths got shallow and fast. His mouth went dry. "*I know what you did. I know. You better do everything Sebastian says. And everything I say. Or I'll tell. And you don't want me to tell, do you?*"

Jonathan shook his head, one small shake side to side.

Benny grinned. He handed Jonathan an envelope. When he spoke, his voice was loud again.

"Here you go, Johnny. Write Mommy and Daddy's address right there." He flashed a smile like a knife blade in the dark and turned back to his own letter.

Jonathan had to steady his shaking hand to write down his parents' address. The librarian's warning echoed in his mind: *Things always go bad. Out there.*

CHAPTER THIRTEEN
THE THECRET

Colin was right about Sebastian being angry at Jonathan. He showed his anger after dinner, in the flickering light of a dozen candles scattered throughout the dining room.

Sebastian swallowed a final bite of a shortbread and wiped the corners of his mouth, then stood up. He banged his metal plate on the table to get everyone's attention.

"All right. In the morning, we'll have to meet the mail boat again. You ready for that, Gerald?"

Gerald burped and nodded.

"Good. You all can drag your mattresses wherever. Even in here, if you want." The boys looked around. It was a big room, with plenty of floor space. But it was also a little close to the freezer.

"Now," Sebastian continued, "it's time to refill the coal furnace. We need two people. How about . . ."—his voice trailed off as he scanned the room—"Colin. And . . . let's see." His dark eyes glittered in the candlelight and flashed to Jonathan. He smiled. "Johnny. Oh, wait . . . you don't like fire, right?" Jonathan's eyes dropped to the floor. He rubbed his hands on his sleeves. "Well, sorry. Everyone has to take a turn. Be sure to fill it real full."

Sebastian grabbed a candle and stalked away with Benny and some others at his heels. They disappeared out the door that led up to the grown-ups' bedrooms.

Colin sighed and looked at Jonathan.

"Well," he said, "I geth we thould jutht go and get it over with. It'th not that bad."

Jonathan nodded. "Yeah. Okay. Let's do it."

The furnace was in a room beneath the kitchen, down a steep, short staircase. The room was hot and muggy and smelled like a wet ashtray. The ceiling was so low, Jonathan could have jumped and touched it. It, too, was made of stone blocks, held together with crumbling mortar and forming a steep arch, so that it curved down to meet the floor at both side walls. The furnace was a black iron monster the size of a car, squatting in the far darkness. It hissed and hummed and rumbled. The rest of the room was filled with waist-high heaps of lumpy black coal. A little trail wound between the coal piles to the furnace.

"That's a lot of coal," Jonathan said.

"Yeah," Colin answered, hanging his lantern from a hook on the ceiling. "Coal delivery day ith the wortht. Three hourth of wheelbarrow work. And for every little lump you drop, you get a minute on the Thinner'th Thorrow. I dropped ten latht time."

"Ouch."

They walked to where a couple of shovels were leaning against a wheelbarrow. They each grabbed one and started scooping coal into the wheelbarrow. The scraping of their shovels echoed on the low stone ceiling. Black dust from the coal sifted up and soon they were both coughing and clearing their throats as they shoveled.

"What wath really there?" Colin asked between breaths. "At the Hatch?"

"Just a door," Jonathan panted back. "I told you."

Colin shook his head. "You're keeping thomething. A thecret."

Jonathan stopped and leaned on his shovel. "How do you know that?"

Colin shrugged and kept on shoveling. "I watch. Clothely. And lithen. Almotht no one elth doth that. And I can tell you didn't tell everything."

Jonathan sighed and scraped another shovelful of coal into the wheelbarrow.

"You're good," he admitted, then told Colin about the sounds and the skull and the strange, ancient-looking door with the spinning handle. He didn't mention, though, the other staircase, or the librarian.

"A thkull. That'th tho weird. It'th like a . . . warning. Or a threat." He dropped his shovel and grabbed the handles of the full wheelbarrow. Maneuvering through the coal piles, he rolled it up to the growling furnace. Jonathan followed cautiously behind him.

At the furnace, Colin stepped forward and turned a few rusty bolts, then swung open a thick metal door. A blast of heat rippled out into the room. Jonathan took a step back and covered his face with one arm. He squinted out from under his elbow.

Inside the furnace was a burning hell of flames and fire, glowing in shifting hues of red and orange and blazing white. He couldn't look at it without narrowing his eyes to slits. The heat made the air waver and ripple.

Colin turned and saw Jonathan backing away. He blinked and then swung the furnace door mostly closed.

"You're thcared," he said, and Jonathan looked away. "Why?"

Jonathan just shook his head. Sweat beaded on his forehead and dripped down his face.

"You can trutht me," Colin said. His voice was soft, but insistent. Jonathan nodded and swallowed a ball of fear.

"Something . . . happened," he said, his voice shaky. "To me."

"What?"

Jonathan took two steps forward and undid the buttons on the sleeves of his shirt. One after the other, he pulled his sleeves up to his elbows and held out his arms to Colin.

Colin's coal-smeared face leaned closer to see. The lantern swung from its hook above them, making shadows writhe and twist around them. His eyebrows rose into the beads of sweat on his forehead. His mouth rounded in surprise.

He reached out and ran his fingers softly over the twisted grooves etched into Jonathan's skin. He brushed his fingernails gingerly over the toughened swirls of hard scar tissue that covered Jonathan's arms all the way from his wrists until they disappeared into his bunched-up sleeves. Jonathan's hands were shaking. With a gasp he pulled back suddenly and tugged his sleeves back down to cover his tortured arms.

"I . . . I don't like to show people," he stammered, desperately fumbling with his sleeve buttons. "I don't like to see them myself," he added more quietly. Colin grabbed Jonathan's trembling hands and held them still. Then he gently buttoned up the first of Jonathan's sleeves.

"They're burnth," he whispered. "Were you caught in a fire?"

"No." Jonathan shook his head. Tears sprang to his eyes and he looked away. "I was not in the fire."

Colin finished buttoning the second sleeve and looked up at Jonathan with eyes that were quiet and wide. He was watching. Closely. And listening.

"When? When did thith happen?"

Jonathan took a ragged breath. "A while back," he answered.

"What happened?"

Jonathan ground his teeth together. He blinked and shook his head.

"We should—finish the coal."

"Okay. Thure."

Colin turned and reopened the furnace door. The small, suffocating room once again filled with heat and angry light. Colin pushed the wheelbarrow right up to the furnace's open, red mouth.

"It'th okay," he called back over his shoulder. "I think I can do it mythelf." He grabbed both handles of the wheelbarrow and struggled to tilt it up into the furnace. He grunted and his feet slid and slipped on the coal-dusted floor.

Jonathan shook his head and winced. He watched Colin wrestling with the heavy wheelbarrow. His arms were crossed, the fingers of each hand rubbing through his sleeves at the burns on his arms. Colin looked so small, so helpless by the burning fire. So in need of help. Jonathan stepped forward, shoulder to shoulder with Colin, and took hold of one of the handles. Together they lifted it and dumped the load of coal into the waiting flames. There was a shower of sparks and a fresh wave of heat. Jonathan's arms burned. They let the wheelbarrow drop and Colin slammed the furnace door.

The boys stood panting, leaning on the wheelbarrow. Their hands were black, and sweat dripped muddy trails through the coal on their faces.

"Well," Jonathan said, pulling at his shirt where it stuck to the sweat on his body. "That wasn't so bad."

"Yeah," Colin responded between coughs. "That wath one. It taketh five to fill it."

Walter and Colin and Jonathan pulled their mattresses into a corner of the dining room by the kitchen, away from the windows to the courtyard, which let in moonlight and cold drafts and memories of lightning.

Other groups of boys had their mattresses together in clumps, too, here and there around the room. No one wanted to sleep alone.

They laid their mattresses like spokes on a wheel so their heads could be together. They'd each carried a candle when they'd gone together to the old sleeping quarters to claim their beds, and when they lay down, they put the three candles together on the floor in the space between them. Their faces were smooth in the candlelight, their hair dark, with cold blackness all around.

Walter lay on his stomach, watching the candle flames. Colin was on his elbows, quietly folding more paper animals. Jonathan opened the book the librarian had given him. The pages were yellow and fragile and they whispered in the quiet of the room when he turned them.

"What book is that?" Walter asked. Jonathan turned back to the cover.

"*Robinson Crusoe*," Jonathan read. "*By Daniel Defoe.*"

"I've heard of that," Colin said.

"Is it any good?" Walter asked.

Jonathan shrugged.

"I haven't started it yet."

"Could you?"

"I was going to."

"No, man. I mean, like, out loud?"

"Oh. Um, yeah, I guess. If you want." He licked his lips and cleared his throat and paged back to the first line. "*I was born in the Year 1632, in the City of York, of a good Family, tho' not of that Country, my Father being a Foreigner of Bremen, who settled first at Hull,*" Jonathan began. Reading was hard in the dim, flickering light; he followed the words he read with a fingertip.

"York? Like New York?" Walter asked.

"No. I think it meanth York in England," Colin explained.

"Oh."

Jonathan continued. "*He got a good Estate by Merchandise, and leaving off his Trade, lived afterward at York, from whence he had married my Mother, whose Relations were named Robinson, a very good Family in that Country, and from whom I was called Robinson Kreutznaer.*"

"I don't get it," Walter complained.

"It's an old book," Jonathan said. "It's written all kind of old-fashioned. Nothing important has happened yet, though, I don't think."

"Oh. Okay."

"And stop interrupting."

"Okay."

"*But by the usual Corruption of Words in England, we are now called, nay we call our selves, and write our Name, Crusoe, and so my Companions always call'd me.*"

"What is that?" a voice asked over Jonathan's shoulder. He craned his neck to see Miguel standing in the shadows, the candlelight playing on his curious face.

"Just a book. *Robinson Crusoe.*"

"You gonna read that whole thing?"

"I don't know. I'm gonna start, at least."

"Huh." Miguel stood in the darkness and hugged his shivering body.

"Do you—uh—wanna listen?" Jonathan asked.

"No," Miguel answered quickly. "But, whatever. I'll go grab my mattress."

A moment later, Miguel reappeared with another boy, both dragging their mattresses behind them. Walter and Jonathan and Colin spread theirs apart to make room.

"I'll start over," Jonathan said when everyone was settled in. "*He got a good Estate by Merchandise, and leaving off his Trade, lived afterward at York, from whence he had married my Mother—*"

"Can I listen, too?" Tony stood just outside the circle of light, a pillow under his arm.

"And me?" another voice asked. Jonathan looked up and saw David standing there.

"Sure."

The boys already there made room in the circle for two more. Soon, there were seven heads facing one another through the flames.

"I'll start over," Jonathan said again with a sigh.

And he did, with six pairs of ears listening to his whispered words. They all listened together to the story of a man trapped on an island, far from his family. The story held them together like the light from their candles, warm and close against the dark stone and shadows.

But out in the darkness that surrounded them, there was the scurrying of rats. And above them, he knew, Sebastian slept with a sharp sword in the Admiral's bed. And below them, a hungry menace knocked at an ancient door. And even then, surrounded by friendly faces, his dark fears whispered at him, and the flickering warmth of their candles' light seemed terribly small and fragile.

JONATHAN'S SECOND LETTER HOME

Dear Mother and Father,

I am still here at Slabhenge. Of course. The food has gotten even better. I hope that you are doing better. Give my love to Sophia.

Jonathan

CHAPTER FOURTEEN
CRIMES MUST BE PUNISHED

The mail drop went off without a hitch the next day.

Crusty old Cyrus was there instead of Patrick, and he didn't even bother talking to "Mr. Vander." The bags were traded without a word and the boat motored off into the waves and fog and was gone. The rest of the boys, who had been hiding safely around the corner, came out to peer through the arch at the disappearing boat. It looked so small, and the distance so great. A gust of wind blew a mist of salty spray into their faces.

"One more day," Sebastian said with satisfaction. "At least one more day." He held the Admiral's sword casually in one hand, its blade resting against one of his cheeks. "Hand out the mail, Benny," he said, before spinning and heading back across the courtyard.

Benny pulled the rumpled envelopes out of the mailbag one by one and called out the names written on them. Jonathan jumped when his own name was called.

"Grisby. Got one for you here, Johnny." Jonathan bit his lip and stepped forward to claim his letter. Benny held it out and Jonathan grabbed it, but Benny didn't let it go right away. Jonathan looked up at him and tugged a little harder, and Benny narrowed his eyes and smirked. "I wonder what Mommy and Daddy have to say to you, Johnny," he said in a quiet voice. "Nothing too nice, I bet, huh? After what you did?" Jonathan's heart clenched like a kicked puppy and he felt the red creep of shame rising on his face. Benny showed his wet teeth and then let go. He blinked a bored, slow blink and called the next name.

Jonathan walked across the courtyard and inside. He lay down on his mattress, still with the others in the corner of the dining room, and ripped open the envelope. One folded piece of paper was inside. Jonathan swallowed, then pulled it open and read the words written in his mother's familiar, neat cursive writing.

Dear Jonathan,

Your father and I hope this letter finds you well. You were taken away just moments ago, and we've sat right down to write it. We will mail it tomorrow and hope that you will receive it soon.

The house feels so terribly empty now. We don't know what to say to you. So much needs to be said, we know, but we don't know what it is yet. We miss you. We've missed you for a long time now. We will write you every day, Jonathan, and hope that maybe we can find what it is that needs to be said. We go every day, with the flowers, like you asked. Maybe having you gone, for a while, will help all of us.

With love,
Your mother and father
p.s. If they let you write, please do

Jonathan chewed his tongue thoughtfully and read the letter again. He whispered a line aloud. "*The house feels so terribly empty now.*" He licked his lips, then reread the last line. "*Maybe having you gone, for a while, will help all of us.*" He blinked his eyes hard and sniffed.

A door slamming open behind him made him jump. He rubbed at his eyes quickly and stuffed the letter under his pillow.

Sebastian stormed into the dining room, dragging another boy by his collar. It was the little kid named James, whom Jonathan didn't know well, but he knew he was one of the boys to whom Sebastian had given one of the grown-ups' rooms.

"Everybody gather around!" Sebastian hollered. Benny and Gerald were just walking in from the courtyard. Sebastian pointed at them with the sword. "Get everyone in here," he commanded.

Jonathan jumped up and joined the nervous crowd

assembling around Sebastian and a terrified-looking James. They kept a few safe paces back.

"I wanted you all to see this," Sebastian said, glowering around at the group. "I just caught James here, sneaking into my room."

"It'th not really *your* room," Colin murmured.

"Shut up, Colin." Sebastian's eyes flashed cold fire at Colin, standing beside Jonathan. "I caught him in *my* room, going through *my* stuff."

"I'm sorry, Sebastian, I didn't think—" James whined, but Sebastian cut him off.

"Shut up, James. I caught him red-handed, eating my chocolate."

"It'th not really *your* chocolate."

"Damn it, Colin, you better shut your mouth."

Jonathan nudged Colin sharply with his elbow.

"*Drop it, Colin,*" he hissed out of the corner of his mouth. Colin sighed angrily.

Sebastian scanned the crowd, looking for defiance. All the eyes dropped to the floor when Sebastian's met them, except Jonathan's.

"What are you going to do?" Jonathan asked.

Sebastian's dark eyes flickered with uncertainty. He chewed his lower lip and looked doubtfully at James, still trembling in his grip.

Benny slipped forward in the hanging silence and hissed

something into Sebastian's ear. Sebastian's brow furrowed and he whispered something back. Benny leaned even closer and put a hand on Sebastian's arm, whispering fiercely into his ear again.

Sebastian nodded after a moment and then raised his chin to the group. He pointed the sword at Gregory and Roger.

"Bring in the Sinner's Sorrow," he commanded. A murmur ran through the crowd. The two boys exchanged a glance, then ducked out into the courtyard, where the Sinner's Sorrow had sat since that final, fateful Morning Muster.

"No, Thebathtian," Colin said.

"Ye*th*, Colin," Sebastian spat. "Even with us in charge, crimes must be punished."

"You don't have the right."

Sebastian's face contorted in fury. "I have the *sword*, Colin! What are you going to do?"

Colin looked desperately to Jonathan.

"Do thomething!" he pleaded.

Sebastian looked expectantly at Jonathan, but Jonathan was looking at Benny. Benny's mouth was set in a small, grim smile and he shook his head at Jonathan just one time.

"Jonathan!" Colin begged.

Jonathan eyed Benny for one more moment, then dropped his eyes to the floor and shook his head.

Gregory and Roger grunted in, tugging the dreaded Sinner's Sorrow between them. They dragged more than carried it, and when they'd managed to pull it close enough to Sebastian, they leaned against it, gasping. The raindrops dripping down the dark wood looked like blood in the cloud-darkened light seeping through the windows.

Sebastian shoved James roughly toward the dripping Sinner's Sorrow.

"How many pieces did you eat?"

James gulped and looked out at the other boys. Again, all the eyes dropped.

"Um, like, one or two, Sebastian, but I—"

"One or two?" Sebastian reached in his pocket and pulled out a handful of shiny gold wrappers. One by one he let them drop to the ground. "One. Two. Three. Four." He cocked an eyebrow and raised the sword to point it at James. "One minute per piece for stealing. And one minute per piece for lying to me. Eight minutes on the Sorrow." Tears pooled in James's eyes. His bottom lip began to quiver.

"The watch, Benny," Sebastian said, holding out his hand. Benny handed over a tarnished silver pocket watch. Sebastian looked out again at the gathered boys. "Who wants a room? One just became available. It's got a window and everything. Doesn't it, James?" James sniffled and nodded miserably. "Okay, who wants it?"

There was a tense moment of silence. Finally, the kid named Reggie raised his hand.

"I'll take it."

Sebastian smiled like a snake and tossed Reggie the watch.

"Keep him on there for eight minutes, Reggie. I'm getting lunch. Make sure he doesn't cheat and make sure he stays on the whole time. If he gets up, the clock starts over. Then the room's yours."

Reggie nodded and stepped hesitantly forward.

"Get on there, James," Sebastian said, lowering his sword and turning toward the kitchen.

"Wait." Colin's voice stopped Sebastian cold.

"Thith ithn't right. We never voted on thith."

The muscles in Sebastian's jaw rippled and he took two slow steps toward Colin.

"Mind your own business, Colin." Sebastian's eyes flickered over to Jonathan, then quickly back to Colin. "This is fair. He stole from me."

"You thaid there were no ruleth."

"Well, Colin, I guess there's at least one. Don't mess with me." He gave Colin a long, steady glare. "Next time you talk back to me, you get the Sorrow, too."

Sebastian stalked off toward the kitchen. The rest of the boys stood for a moment, awkwardly watching James kneel down reluctantly on the awful device.

"I'll start the clock," Reggie said quietly. When James whimpered and sniffled, Benny and a couple of other kids laughed. They spun some chairs around and settled in to watch James wiggle and moan. Jonathan swallowed down a sour sickness and turned away. Most of the other boys did, too. A few wandered outside or into the kitchen, their eyes held carefully away from James's torment.

Colin stood beside Jonathan, pale and frowning.

"Thith ithn't right," he repeated.

"Just leave it alone," Jonathan whispered. "It's not a big deal. If you stop pissing him off, you'll be fine."

Colin looked back over his shoulder at James shaking on the Sinner's Sorrow, and the three vultures watching him from their chairs.

"I don't think tho, Jonathan. I don't think tho."

CHAPTER FIFTEEN
A DROWNED DUNGEON

Jonathan shuffled through the pitch-black corridors, his eyes on the uneven floor before him and his ears listening for the skittering sound of rat claws on stone. He held a tall white candle in one hand. He gripped the candle tight, his palm sweaty. His body didn't like being that close to the hot flicker of a flame. Neither did his heart, for that matter. He steadied his shaking as best he could and pressed on through the darkness.

He ducked under the now-familiar rope gate and descended the stairs, pausing for only a second to listen at the narrow passage that dropped down to the Hatch. Then he climbed the other staircase and retraced his steps to the closed door of the library.

Again, light showed from beneath it. And, again, low humming sounded behind it. He took a breath and then knocked on the door. The humming stopped, and the door creaked open.

"Ah," the librarian said, with a raise of his bushy eyebrows. "It's you. Again. Come in."

Jonathan entered the lighted warmth of the library and let the door close behind him.

"Back for another book?"

"Um, no. Just to look, I guess."

"Are you reading? *Robinson Crusoe?*"

"Yeah. A bunch of us are. It's pretty good."

"Yes. It is." The librarian turned and walked back among the shelves. Jonathan followed, the candle still in his hand. He stepped quickly away when he saw the giant rat, Ninety-Nine, atop a shelf at his shoulder, sniffing and stretching toward him with his nose. The librarian saw and smiled.

"Oh. Don't mind him. He just wants. To be petted." The librarian reached back an arm, and the rat scrambled up it, his claws catching in the woolen sleeve, and curled up around the librarian's neck.

"What is the Hatch?" Jonathan asked abruptly. The Hatch—the sound of its violent knocking and sloshing, how deeply it lurked in the darkness of the prison like a shameful secret, with the skull standing silent guard—had haunted his thoughts since he'd left it.

"The Hatch? Ah. Yes. Quite a curiosity. Isn't it?"

"Yeah. It looks so . . . old. And it makes all these weird sounds."

The librarian smiled a strange, knowing smile and shook his head.

"It is old. But it does not make any sounds. No. It's what's behind it. That makes the noise."

"Well, what's behind it, then?"

The librarian pursed his lips and leaned forward, cocking one sideways eye at Jonathan. Ninety-Nine's beady eyes sparkled at him.

"The sea, my boy. It is. The sea itself. Behind that ancient door."

"The sea? How?"

The librarian heaved a heavy breath and walked over to the closest window, mostly blocked by standing books. He pulled one of the books down and peered through the space where it had been. The gray light shone through the old man's wispy white hair.

"The water," the librarian whispered, looking out at the storm-tossed waves. "It is rising." He cocked one eye back over his shoulder toward Jonathan. "Or the island is sinking. Both. I think." He looked out again through the gap at the sea. When he spoke this time, his voice was different. Faster, smoother, less labored.

"Years ago, back in the asylum days, the water was not so high. There was a beach around Slabhenge then. A smooth stretch of sand. With shells, and logs, and pools. We had a pier, even. Big enough for large boats to dock at. I would sit on the pier, sometimes, and fish. Watch the sun set. Or rise. Look off at the distant mainland and wonder. Of course, I was a boy then. So long ago."

Jonathan stepped to stand behind him. He stood on his toes to see the white-capped ocean.

"You . . . were here when you were a kid?"

The old man's eyes were trained far off in the distance. His voice was feathery and far away.

"Oh, yes. I was born here. My mother and father were

both . . . patients here. She was a madwoman. He, a lunatic. The asylum was my home. My school. My playground. The guards were my aunts and uncles. My friends. My tormentors, sometimes." He brought one wrinkled hand up to stroke the rat perching on his shoulder. The gigantic animal twisted and stretched so that the old man's fingers could scratch his itchy places.

"They offered to send me away to the high school on the mainland when I was old enough. The head warden, I mean. He was a kind enough man, I suppose. But I refused. It all seemed too terrifying. Leaving the island. The walls. The water. So I stayed."

The librarian sighed. It was a weary sigh, tired and breathy and covered in the dust of years.

"I became the librarian's assistant. I did my learning from these books. And my traveling. My living, really, right here in these pages. When the old man died, the warden let me take his place. Not long after that, my mother died. And my father. And I just . . . stayed. When the asylum closed, they allowed me to stay, to care for the facility. Run the lighthouse. Keep it all from falling apart. And when it reopened as a school, the Admiral kept me on."

"So you've *never* left the island? You've always been here?" The librarian was still turned away, toward the sea, but Jonathan could tell from the old man's voice when he answered that he was smiling.

"Oh, yes. Always. I have never once left this island. This

beautiful, crumbling island. Not once. And I never will. Never."

Jonathan took a breath and a step back. The rat turned on the librarian's shoulders and narrowed his eyes at Jonathan, his pointy front teeth showing.

"And . . . the Hatch?"

"Yes. The beach, foot by foot, year by year, went away. Swallowed. Then, in a storm, the pier was washed away. Behind the Hatch is a staircase that leads down to the very bottom floor. The cellar, if you will. During the asylum days, it was a sort of special prison for the most troublesome." He returned the book to the shelf and half turned to look up at Jonathan in his queer way. "A dungeon, you would probably call it. My father was there, briefly. During his dark days. Eventually, as the water rose, it was too wet for people. There was standing water at high tide. It was a storeroom then. High shelves. Then the water got too high even for that. It filled the room, began to climb the stairs. During one bad storm, maybe, oh, twenty years ago, there was a surge and it came all the way up, up into the main floor. So many rats died that night." He scratched his yellow fingernails through Ninety-Nine's fur and nuzzled the rat's neck with his face.

"So they installed the Hatch. That's an iron door, solid through. Nine inches thick, bolted into the stone with foot-long bolts. Sealed with cement and mortar and soldered steel. Strong enough, they say, to hold the sea back. And those sounds you hear? That is the sea, crashing and surging beneath us. Sucking at forgotten windows. Opening and closing submerged doors. Tossing old furniture around. Rattling old chains. Chewing at the foundations. And always, always, knocking at the door."

He closed his eyes and sighed and stroked his monstrous rat.

"The sea is in the dungeon. Seething, beneath us. But it doesn't want to stay there." The old man's eyes opened and focused on Jonathan's. "It wants the whole island. It wants it all. And someday. It will. Get it."

Jonathan's mouth was dry. He blinked. His mouth was stuck open.

"Now," the librarian said, taking a step and brushing past him. "What book would you like?"

"I'm, um, still reading the first one," Jonathan said, shaking his head. "I don't need another one just yet."

The librarian stooped down and Ninety-Nine crawled down his arm and onto a shelf. The old man looked back at Jonathan and shook his head and smiled a crooked smile.

"No. You can't leave a library. Without a book." He scanned the nearest shelf with a finger and one sideways eye. Jonathan stood where he was and watched the hunched old man creak along the shelf, muttering to himself and shaking his head.

"Ah. Yes. This one. Is appropriate." He pulled a thick volume off the shelf. "Another island story. About a boy. And a crazy sea captain. And treasure found." He held the book to his nose and closed his eyes and took a deep breath, then handed it to Jonathan.

Treasure Island, the cover said in plain black letters on red leather. *By Robert Louis Stevenson.*

"Thanks. I better get back."

"Yes," the librarian said, walking with Jonathan to the door. "You should. Thank the Admiral. For letting you come. It has been so long." Jonathan stepped out into the dark corridor, holding the candle before him. The librarian closed the door nearly all the way, so that only his mouth and one eye were visible in the crack. "And say hello. To the ocean. For me. When you go past. The Hatch."

The door closed, leaving Jonathan with his feeble flame and the sound of rats and, in the darkness ahead of him, a rattling door to a watery dungeon.

CHAPTER SIXTEEN
SORROW'S SINNER

"You know the drill," Sebastian decreed from where he sat on the table, his shoes on the Admiral's great chair. "No dinner until we have your letter. Get it done." He was bent over, focused on the tip of the sword he was holding. He was using it to carve something into the surface of the table.

The boys each filed by to grab a pen and sheet of paper from where Benny sat frowning officiously at them, coiled up in a chair. Already out the windows the sun had set on their second day alone on the island. The room and its long tables were lit here and there by flickering candles.

Jonathan sat and looked at his paper. He remembered his mother's words from the letter that still waited under his pillow. *So much needs to be said,* she'd written. *But we don't know what it is yet.* His fingers balled into fists. His tongue was pinched between tight teeth. He looked up and saw Colin watching him from across the table. His flitting, hummingbird smile came and went and he looked down at his own paper. All around was the sound of pen points on paper. A thin mile of ink, measured in words. *I love you*s and *I miss you*s and *can't wait to see you*s. Messages from naughty boys, sent home to worried mothers. Jonathan blew a breath out through his nose and picked up his pen and began to write.

He scratched out a message, writing quick without thinking too much. He signed his name in a hasty scrawl and walked over to where Benny sat waiting to check their letters.

Benny looked his letter over with his usual sneer and then snorted.

"You really think that'll make them feel any better?" he asked. Jonathan looked down and didn't answer. "Fine," Benny said and handed the letter back. "Now the envelope."

Jonathan addressed the envelope and sealed his letter inside and slipped it into the mailbag.

He saw, lost in the shadows along the far wall, the Sinner's Sorrow standing in darkness. He looked at the rest of the boys. Their heads were down, their eyes away, the dim candlelight glinting off the shiny moving metal of their pens. With a last glance at the group, Jonathan ducked away and over to the Sinner's Sorrow.

In the darkness, the wood was black. He ran his fingers along the top rail, worn smooth by countless sweaty, tortured hands. He bent to touch the biting edge of the sharp kneeling ridge. Outside, rain tapped on the windows. His throat tightened, and his eyes watered. His words would never make his parents feel better, he knew. Benny was right. With trembling fingertips he felt the burns on his arms through his sleeves.

Then he bent down and knelt on the punishing edge.

The pain was immediate, and familiar. He remembered the Admiral's words from that first night: *You have done terrible things, haven't you, Jonathan Grisby?* Jonathan clenched his teeth and nodded and let the growing pain sharpen and fill his brain. His breaths were tight and jerky.

The letter had brought back memories. Memories that Jonathan kept quiet and locked away, down where they couldn't drown him. He let the pain push them back down, let it flood them away. His breathing eased. His jaw clenched even harder. His eyes closed.

"What are you doing?" The whisper snapped his eyes open. Colin was standing beside him, his eyes concerned, one hand fluttering at his neck, the other holding a half-folded paper crane.

"Leave me alone," Jonathan whispered back in a shaky voice. He closed his eyes again.

"Thith ith crazy. Why are you on that?"

"Go away, Colin."

"You thouldn't let the otherth thee you. You thouldn't let Thebathtian thee you." A nervous hand tugged softly on Jonathan's shoulder.

"What are you tho thad about?"

Jonathan screwed his eyes shut tighter and bit his lip until it hurt as much as his screaming knees.

"Jonathan! Come on, get off it! You're gonna hurt yourthelf!"

"I know."

"What? What do you—" Their hissed conversation was interrupted by a commotion behind them, at the tables.

"Sebastian! Sebastian, come look at this!" Benny's voice was triumphant and angry. There was an ugly delight in it.

Jonathan opened his eyes and looked over. Colin was still looking at him, his pale eyebrows knit together in worry. Jonathan jumped up and brushed past him to join the scene at the tables.

"I just barely caught it!" Benny was saying. He was handing a crumpled letter to Sebastian, who had stalked over with the sword in his hand. "Look! Look at what he wrote in the fold on the back!"

The rest of the boys had jumped up and were crowding around, wide-eyed in the candlelight, a few steps back. One of the older boys, skinny with black, curly hair and a twitchy face, was standing at the table in front of Benny, eyes darting back and forth between Benny and Sebastian. Jason was his name, Jonathan remembered. Walter had said he'd been sent to Slabhenge for stealing cars. He was frowning and chewing at the inside of one of his cheeks. He was one of the ones who had joined Jonathan's group the night before, to listen to *Robinson Crusoe*.

Sebastian snatched the letter and turned it over. His eyes scanned the paper and then his lips tightened into a thin, angry line. He glared up at the black-haired kid.

"Really, Jason? You?"

The kid shrugged and looked down.

"Sorry, Sebastian." His voice was a little shaky but

resigned. He wasn't crying. His eyes slid back up to Sebastian's. "I hate it here. I wanna go home."

Sebastian shook his head. He looked like he was going to spit. He held the letter closer to his face and read aloud.

"We're in trouble. All the grown-ups are gone. Please send help."

A whisper ran through the crowd.

Sebastian set the sword on the table and reached to pull a candle in a tall brass holder a little closer.

"We're not in trouble, Jason," he said, his voice cold and angry. "*You* are." He held the letter out so that its bottom corner dangled in the slowly dancing flame. It caught fire and the flames licked quickly up the letter, curling it and crackling. The light in the room grew brighter. Sebastian's face was washed in brighter shades of red and flickering orange. He held the letter as long as he could, until the hungry flames were right up to his hand, and then let it drop to the damp stone floor at his feet. He sucked on his fingers and looked at Jason.

"Mommy and Daddy can't help you." He picked up the sword and tilted his head back and looked down his nose at Jason. "We don't need their help. They're the ones who *sent* us here, man! Screw them! And you want to, what, go running back? So they can blame us for what happened and send us to some other craphole? And you wanna do that to *all* of us?"

"No. I just wanna go home. I'm sorry, Sebastian."

Sebastian shook his head. "Home? Home?" His face twisted, then darkened. "No," he snorted. "You're not sorry. But you're gonna be." He pointed with the sword to the shadows where Colin and Jonathan had just been. "Sinner's Sorrow. Twenty minutes."

The watching boys gasped. Jason's face went pale.

Jonathan's knees were still burning. And he'd spent only a couple of minutes on the Sinner's Sorrow.

"You can't do that! That'th too long," Colin protested.

"*Damn* it, Colin. I've warned you to shut up." Sebastian turned to face Colin squarely. His face was etched in hard lines of anger. His eyes bore black holes into Colin's. He pointed the sword at Jason. "He gets twenty." The sword swung until its point was inches from Colin's nose. "You get ten."

"You can't make me."

"The hell I can't."

"I won't."

"Really?" Sebastian's eyes roved wildly through the room. They found Jonathan, and his jaw clenched. His sword swung to point at Jonathan. "Then your little buddy Johnny gets twenty. Is that what you want?"

Colin looked back and forth between Sebastian and Jonathan. Jonathan's mouth went dry and he tried to shake his head, but his neck wouldn't move. Colin sniffed and pinched at his neck.

"Okay. I'll do the ten minuth."

Sebastian smiled. "I know you will. I'll be running the watch."

"No." Jonathan's voice finally croaked free of his throat. Sebastian's gaze swung to him. "I'll do it. I'll take the twenty."

Sebastian narrowed his eyes and shook his head.

"No. Not you. This is Colin's. And then he gets tonight's coal duty. And no dinner. Come on. Jason's first."

Jonathan took one look at Benny's hungry leer and swallowed his protests.

The windows showed pure night blackness when Colin and Jason limped up from the coal room. Sebastian and his favorites had already gone up to their rooms, and the only light in the dining room came from the three candles set on the floor in the middle of the circle of mattresses. Jonathan and the other boys were already in bed, lying awake and waiting.

Colin crawled into his bed with a little grunt. His face was smudged with black coal dust. Jason fell onto his own mattress and pulled the blanket over his face.

"Are you okay, Colin?" Walter asked in a hoarse whisper.

Colin was lying on his back with one arm thrown across his eyes.

"It wath bad," he answered. "But not ath bad ath it'th gonna get around here."

The other boys looked at one another through the wavering candlelight.

"Well," Colin said, "are you going to read the thtory, Jonathan?"

Jonathan bit his lip.

"Sure," he said, and opened the book to the page he'd bent down to mark his spot. "It's a new chapter, called 'I Travel Quite Across the Island.'" He took a breath and cleared his throat. The other boys rolled over onto their elbows to listen. The warmth of the candlelight caught their ready faces.

"*I mentioned before that I had a great mind to see the whole island*," he began to read, and if there was the drizzle of rain or the skittering of rats, the sounds were lost in the words of the story.

JONATHAN'S THIRD LETTER HOME

Dear Mom and Dad,

I got your letter. Thanks for sending it.

I have had time to think here. And there's a lot to think about. You do seem far away. Maybe distance is a good thing.

I don't know anything. I don't know what comes next.

But I know that I think about you. Kind of a lot, maybe.

I know you told me not to say sorry. You told me I wasn't allowed to say sorry anymore. For what happened to her. But I have to. It's all I can say. Over and over and over. Even if you don't want me to. I have to.

I'm sorry. I'm sorry. I'm sorry. I am so sorry. Please give my love to Sophia.

Your son,
Jonathan

CHAPTER SEVENTEEN
THE SINNER'S REVENGE

The next morning, a supply boat was scheduled to arrive, with mail and food and anything else the Admiral had ordered. Sebastian had them all drilled and practiced and ready to go, waiting by the gates nearly an hour before the boat was supposed to get there.

Gerald was standing ready in the dead Mr. Vander's uniform.

"Remember," Sebastian was saying to them. "This ain't no big deal. It was always us that unloaded all the stuff anyway. Mr. Vander's gonna just be standing a little farther back this time, is all. I'll do *all* the talking, if we have to do any. We do it quick, we do it quiet, and we get them out of here."

The boys all nodded, Jonathan included. He looked back over his shoulder. Across the courtyard, Benny stood by the closed doors that led to the dining room. Jason and Colin were locked inside. The key was in Sebastian's pocket.

"I don't trust either one of you," Sebastian had told them in front of the whole group that morning after breakfast. "And we can't have you doing something stupid and messing this up for everyone." The last Jonathan had seen of Colin, he was standing, pinching at his neck and frowning thoughtfully as he watched Sebastian stalk out into the courtyard, brandishing the Admiral's sword. He also had the Admiral's hat on his head. It was a new touch Sebastian had added that morning when he'd come down for breakfast. Either he had a huge head or the Admiral had had a small one. The hat fit him perfectly.

Jonathan squinted out over the green and white of the tossing waves. Somewhere, just beyond his eye's reach, was the real world. Waiting. He breathed in, then out, and shivered. He wasn't ready yet.

The mailbag was heavy over his shoulder. That was his job, to hand over their letters. Polite little lies scrawled in childish writing to keep their kidnapped ship afloat. In the bag was his own letter. And Jason's new one, written that morning with Benny peering over his shoulder. Everyone's letter was in the bag. Except Sebastian's. Jonathan had noticed that: Sebastian never wrote a letter.

"Hey! I hear it!" Tony called out, and everyone snapped to attention. They waited.

"Aw, no, you didn't," Miguel said.

"I did!" Tony repeated. "I still do! There it is!"

All the eyes followed his pointing finger.

The boat was bigger than Cyrus and Patrick's little mail boat. Its noise was a deeper one, more rumble than whine, more easily lost in the constant low roar of the waves clawing at Slabhenge's walls. It pushed through the waves instead of rising and falling and hopping between them.

Gerald jumped up on his stool in the shadows by the gate opening and pulled the long coat tighter around him.

"Okay, boys," Sebastian said. "Here we go."

The boat rolled up sideways to where the staircase

dropped into the depths. Sebastian and David ran down to the water's edge, and a bearded man puffing a pipe threw a rope to them. Sebastian tied it off to the metal ring and the man slid a long wooden ramp over the rail of the boat.

The two men in the boat began sliding bags, crates, and boxes down the ramp, where they were grabbed by a boy or two and dragged or carried up the stairs and through the gate into the courtyard.

The boat rocked in the waves, and the ramp knocked and jostled, but it was all done in a matter of minutes. When the last crate was being hauled up the stairs, the bearded man waved to the fake Mr. Vander to come down to the boat.

The boys still on the stairs looked at each other.

"What do you need?" Sebastian asked the man.

"What do you mean? I need someone to sign that the order was delivered, boy!" The man waved a clipboard up toward Gerald.

"Oh," Sebastian said, looking back at Gerald standing in the shadows. "I'll bring it to him," he added quickly, snatching the clipboard before the man could object. He dashed away up the stairs.

Jonathan watched him talking with Gerald in the darkened archway. The man was watching, too, a frown on his bushy face.

"Here," Jonathan said to distract him. He shrugged the mailbag off his shoulder and handed it up to the boatman. The boatman coughed and spit. He took the mailbag from

Jonathan's outstretched hands and disappeared over the boat's side for a moment, then reappeared with a different one.

"Here's your incoming," he growled, handing it to Jonathan. Sebastian ran back to the boat and handed over the clipboard.

"Mr. Vander signed it," he panted.

The man looked it over.

"All right. And what about the next one?"

"The next what?"

The man pulled the pipe out of his mouth and shot Sebastian a withering look.

"The next order, boy. I assume ye all will still be wanting to eat next week, aye?"

Sebastian looked desperately up at Gerald, then over to Jonathan. Jonathan's stomach twisted into a nervous tangle.

"Oh, yeah, about that," Jonathan said, licking his lips. "The Admiral's a little behind. He's kinda sick, see. Most of us are. Bad flu going around. He told us to tell you that he'll be sending you next week's order in the mail in a couple days."

The man squinted and looked back and forth between Jonathan and the overcoated figure in the gateway. He popped the pipe back into his mouth and blew out a few little clouds of thick smoke.

"All right. Tell him to see that he does, then. I ain't coming all the way out to this damned rock to ask him what he wants."

"Yes, sir."

With a grunt the man heaved on the ramp, and Jonathan and Sebastian helped him pull it back on board the boat. The boat's motor roared and gurgled and the boat throttled away through the waves toward the mainland. Sebastian and Jonathan stood shoulder to shoulder, watching it go.

"Nice save, Johnny," Sebastian said.

"No problem," Jonathan replied, hefting the new mail-bag onto his shoulder. "And it's Jonathan."

They turned and walked up the stairs. The rest of the boys fell in behind them. In the courtyard, they swung the gate closed. The boat was already out of earshot, nothing more than a receding white-trailed dot in the green sea.

The shipment was piled just inside the gate. A few big burlap sacks of flour and oatmeal and rice. A dozen or so big crates, and some smaller boxes.

"Okay, everyone grab something," Sebastian ordered. He picked up the sword where he'd left it leaning against the wall. "We'll move everything into—"

"Sebastian! Sebastian!" It was Benny's frantic voice, screaming from across the courtyard. He was ramming the door to the dining room with one shoulder and calling back over the other. Sebastian sprinted across the courtyard with Jonathan, the rest of the boys following close behind.

"It's Colin!" Benny shouted as they ran up. "He's going nuts!"

They all crowded around the big windows that looked into the dining room.

Colin stood panting in the middle of the room, by the Sinner's Sorrow. In his hands he was holding the ax they used to chop the wood for the kitchen stove. Jonathan wasn't sure what he was doing until another boy gasped, "Look at the Sinner's Sorrow!"

The wooden monster was nearly in ruin. Its top rail was completely gone, smashed and shredded. The dreaded kneeling rail was almost as bad, torn up and splintered by the sharp blade of the ax. Jason stood in the distant doorway to the kitchen, peeking timidly out.

"Stop!" Sebastian shouted, his voice choked with fury.

Colin's sneaky smile came and went, and he raised the ax high above his head.

"Don't!" Sebastian roared, but the ax came rushing down and bit again into the Sorrow's bottom rail. Through the window they heard the heavy *thwock* as it hit home, taking another bite out of the dark wood.

Sebastian dug through his pockets and pulled out the ring of keys and fumbled with them, stepping to the door. Colin raised the ax and again brought it down.

"You're dead, Colin!" Sebastian screamed, jingling the keys and trying to find the right one. "Dead!"

The ax flashed again and with a final crack the kneeling rail split and broke in half. Colin dropped the ax and looked toward the window where they all stood watching. His smile flitted to and from his face, shadowy and sad.

Then Colin walked quickly over to the doorway that

led into the depths of Slabhenge's dark labyrinth. By the doorway sat an unlit lantern and a lumpy sack and the Admiral's fancy hat. He picked up the lantern and the sack, then pulled the hat onto his head and looked back over his shoulder.

"Stop!" Sebastian shouted, finally jamming the right key in the door and swinging it furiously open. But Colin just threw the sack over his shoulder, tossed a two-fingered salute at the crowd from the brim of the Admiral's hat, and disappeared through the doorway.

All the others came rushing in. Sebastian sprinted to the doorway but stopped at the edge of the windowless darkness.

"Come back, you little jerk!" he hollered into the hallway, but the only answer was his own hollowly echoing voice. His lungs were heaving. He wiped at the corners of his mouth with his arm. "Bring me a lantern," he barked over his shoulder.

"No," Jonathan said. "Let him go."

Sebastian spun around.

"Let him go?! Why?"

Jonathan shrugged, thinking fast.

"What's the point? Where's he gonna go? We're in a prison on an island."

Sebastian's top lip snarled like a lion about to roar. He shook his head again, furious breaths hissing through his nose. The Scars all waited in silence.

"Should I get a lantern?" Benny whined.

Sebastian's jaw clenched. He shook his head and spit angrily onto the floor. "Don't bother," he finally seethed. "There's nowhere for him to run. He's dead." He turned his face back to the doorway and shouted at the top of his lungs. "You hear that, Colin? You're dead! Have fun living with the rats!"

He turned back to the staring crowd. He raised the sword and pointed it at them all.

"No one helps him. No one feeds him. You do, you're out, too. He's dead to us. Got it?"

His angry glare scoured the group. No one said a word. His eyes stopped at Jonathan, a scary kind of mad shining in them. Jonathan didn't lower his gaze, but he didn't raise his voice, either.

"All right," Sebastian yelled. "Get to work. Bring all that stuff in here."

Without a word, they turned and walked outside to bring in the supplies.

They walked past the ruined Sinner's Sorrow on their way to the door. Every pair of eyes secretly raced over the wrecked and ravaged torture device.

"*Way to go, Colin,*" Jonathan whispered under his breath.

CHAPTER EIGHTEEN
MOTHER'S DAY

Jonathan didn't dare go back to visit the library that day. If he was seen ducking off into the passageways, Sebastian would be sure to think that he was helping Colin.

Sebastian spent the rest of the morning sulking in his room or storming around the kitchen, chewing and slamming cupboard doors. With their leader so ill-tempered, all the boys laid low. Some played cards or hung out on the stairs watching the water, but the *Robinson Crusoe* group lay on their mattresses and listened to Jonathan read more of the story. By lunchtime, there was only a thin pinch of pages left of the book.

Jonathan was halfway through his peanut butter sandwich when a shadow fell across the table. He looked up to see Benny's sour face glowering at him.

"Sebastian wants to see you in his room," he said.

"Okay," Jonathan answered, taking another bite.

"Now," Benny said. Jonathan put his sandwich down and followed Benny up the passageway to the adults' rooms.

They walked past the door to the Admiral's office, still closed and locked. The next door in the hall stood open, and Benny led him through it.

Inside, Sebastian was lying on a huge, high bed. It was fancy and old-fashioned, with a tall pole at each corner and thick curtains that ran between them. All the curtains around the bed were pulled open and Sebastian lay propped up on a pile of pillows, watching a TV that was blaring on a little desk at the foot of the bed.

"Here he is," Benny announced proudly.

"Leave us alone, Benny," Sebastian said with a bored voice. Benny frowned and gave Jonathan a dirty look and then walked out, closing the door behind him.

Sebastian sat up and scowled at the TV.

"The reception sucks," he said. "You can't hardly see a thing."

Jonathan shifted uncomfortably from one foot to the other.

Sebastian blew out an impatient breath and slid off the bed. He sat down at the foot of the bed and clicked the TV off, then looked up at Jonathan.

"Where is he?" he asked.

Jonathan didn't have to ask who Sebastian was talking about.

"I don't know," he answered truthfully.

"You're his friend," Sebastian persisted. "And I know you've been creeping around this place."

"I don't know where he is," Jonathan repeated. "This place is huge. He never told me he was leaving."

"I want him back. I don't like him being out there. It's not . . . right. I'm supposed to be in charge, right? I'm supposed to be taking care of everybody. I should know where he is, right?" Sebastian's eyes were sharp and troubled.

Jonathan shrugged. "It's not your fault," he said at last. "He ran away. You didn't make him leave."

Sebastian looked away and nodded, then his eyebrows lowered and he looked back to Jonathan.

"If you do see him, would you tell me?"

Jonathan swallowed and looked away. He didn't answer.

Sebastian frowned and shook his head.

"It didn't have to be like this," he said. "We could be doing this together, you know."

Jonathan looked at him.

"Doing what?"

"Running this thing. Being in charge. You're smart. This was all *your* idea, remember. You didn't have to make me the bad guy."

"I didn't make you anything," Jonathan protested.

"Yeah?" Sebastian jumped to his feet. Jonathan took a step back. "Someone has to be the boss. Someone has to make it work. How else do you make everyone write a letter? How else do you make sure no one tells the boat guys? How else do you get people to feed the furnace? Huh? How do you make it all work otherwise?"

Jonathan didn't have an answer. "I don't know. But I don't want to be in charge. I just want . . . I just want . . ."

"What, Johnny? What do you want?"

Jonathan blinked hard and looked at the floor.

"I don't know. I don't know what I want. I don't want anything, I think. And that's the problem."

He could feel Sebastian still glaring at him, could hear his angry breathing.

"Why did you even suggest all this? Do you *like* it here?"

Jonathan shrugged and looked up into Sebastian's face.

"I don't like it out *there*," he replied. "I just didn't want to go back to—all that. Here I can just be . . . nothing."

Sebastian regarded him for a moment. Then he nodded one small nod.

"Yeah. I don't like it out there either."

They stood looking at each other for a second. Then Jonathan's eyes dropped away and Sebastian walked over to a low dresser. A basket full of the Admiral's chocolates was on top. All around it, and spilling onto the floor, were wadded-up empty gold wrappers.

Sebastian unwrapped a chocolate and popped it into his mouth.

"You want one?"

"No, thanks."

"They're almost gone, you know. The chocolates, I mean. And without the damned key, I can't get into the Admiral's office to get any more."

Jonathan looked up at him. "I'm glad we can't get in there," he said quietly.

Sebastian's brow furrowed. "Why?"

Jonathan didn't blink or hesitate. "Because our files are in there. All the lists of the bad things we've done. The bad things we are." His eyes dropped to the floor. "I like it better like this. We're just the Scars, together. Whatever we did out there doesn't matter." He looked at Sebastian. "If that door opens, we just become our crimes again."

For a moment, there was only the sound of Sebastian's noisy chewing. Then he asked a question, but his mouth was so full and sticky that Jonathan didn't understand it at first.

"What?"

Sebastian swallowed.

"I said, why are you so damned sad? I never seen a kid as sad-looking as you all the time."

Jonathan looked away, around the room, then over at the window. Through the thick glass, he could see gathering black storm clouds.

Instead of answering, he asked a question of his own.

"How come you never write a letter, Sebastian?"

There was no answer for a long time. The gold wrapper fell from Sebastian's hand and fluttered to the thick rug on the floor.

"Shut up, Johnny," he finally said. "Go on, get out of here."

Jonathan nodded and walked to the door. Sebastian followed him and stood in the doorway.

"It's funny," he said, just before he closed the door in Jonathan's face. "You wanna stay because here you get to be nothing. And I wanna stay because here I get to be *something*."

The door closed with a click, and Jonathan stood for a moment before finding his way back downstairs to join the others.

Jonathan's toes connected solidly with the ball, sending it bouncing across wet stone to Walter's waiting feet. The ball—an ancient leather soccer ball that someone had found in an old storeroom—was hard enough that it actually hurt a little to kick it. Walter loved it, though, and was always pleading with the other boys to come out and play soccer. Walter passed it back and forth between his feet a few times and then launched it to Jonathan.

It was almost dinnertime, and the sky was getting dark. The game Walter had tried to organize had been called off when the clouds started to sprinkle, and only Jonathan and Walter were left outside.

"How you think Colin's doing?" Walter asked.

Jonathan kicked the ball back to him.

"I don't know. Fine, probably. He's pretty smart."

"Pretty? That kid's *crazy* smart. He ain't, like, super tough, though, you know?"

Jonathan sighed.

"Yeah. I'm worried about him. He's, uh, not exactly the Slabhenge type."

Walter laughed.

"Slabhenge type? Is anybody? I mean, what's the 'Slabhenge type,' man?"

Jonathan pursed his lips thoughtfully. He thought of Miguel and his wicked grin. He thought of Tony, who always cooked up something crazy in the kitchen and tried to get other kids to try it. He thought of Jason, a kid who supposedly stole cars but tried to slip a note to his mom because he just wanted to go home. He thought of quiet David, busted and sent here for fighting back. He thought of Walter, laughing and begging kids to come outside and play. He even thought of Sebastian, who acted so tough but who had noticed Jonathan's sadness and asked about it.

"I don't know," he answered. Then he grinned and looked toward the dining room. "Roger and Gregory, I guess," he said in a low voice. "And Benny. Benny's definitely the Slabhenge type."

Walter returned the grin.

"Oh, yeah. He fits right in here with the rats, don't he?"

The ball tumbled back and forth between them.

"You know, you've never asked me," Walter said.

"Asked you what?"

"You've never asked what we all ask. Why we're here. Don't you wanna know what I did?"

Jonathan rubbed at his nose with his sleeve. He looked up at the clouds, black like coal smoke.

"I don't know," he answered. "It's not my business." The words came out sounding ruder and harsher than Jonathan had meant.

There was a low rumble of thunder. That and the muffled thuds of their feet kicking leather were the only sounds.

"Okay," Jonathan finally said. "Why are you here?"

Walter smiled, his teeth shining whitely in the growing gloom.

"I thought you'd never ask!" He slapped his hands together. "Mother's Day, man."

"Mother's Day?"

"Yeah. Check this out. Around the corner from our place is this shop that sells all this little fancy stuff. You know, gloves and watches and hats and stuff. It's my mama's favorite store. She's in there, like, every day. And she's always going on about this purse that's in the window, right? One of a kind, it says, custom-made. This big ugly pink thing. And I know Mother's Day is coming up. I don't got any money, but I wanna get my mama something nice, you know? Now, there's no chance of me affording it. And no chance of me just sticking it under my shirt, either, 'cause Mrs. Swanson who owns the place always has her stink eye glued to me whenever I'm in there. So the night before Mother's Day, I break in."

Jonathan stopped the ball with his foot and held it.

"Seriously?"

"Seriously. There's this high window in the alley, way at the back of the store, and I get on a garbage can and crawl up through it. Soon as I hit the floor, though, this alarm goes off. Crazy loud. And I freak out. But I run up to the front and I grab that purse and run to the back door, but I hear voices outside. So I go back to the window I came in through, right? And I manage to jump up and start to climb through, but then I freeze, halfway out."

"Why?"

"Cops, man. I see their flashing lights at the end of the alley. Then I hear 'em. *Behind me.* In the store. And I'm sitting there, half out the window, with my rear end hanging in the store, and this ugly pink purse in my hands."

"Oh, man! Did they handcuff you and everything?"

Walter's smile stretched across his whole face.

"Nope. 'Cause they didn't even *catch* me, man!"

"What? You ran away?"

"Uh-uh." Walter shook his head. "I just hung there. And those cops walked all around that store with their flashlights. All they had to do was look up and they'd-a seen my scared butt dangling there in the air. But they never looked up, man. And nothing was broken. And the doors weren't busted or nothing. And the cash register was just sitting there, full. So they thought it was a false alarm. I hung there in that window for half an hour and then they left."

"No way."

"Yeah, man. That's the truth."

"Then . . . why are you here?"

Walter shrugged and his smile faded.

"I guess it wasn't, like, a super-smart crime. Seeing as how it was a one-of-a-kind purse from my mama's favorite store and everything. Next time she went in, she was showing it off, bragging about how I'd saved up all my allowances to buy it for her. Of course, Mrs. Swanson knew I'd never bought it. So that was that. And here I am." Walter shook his head, a small smile on his lips. "You shoulda seen her, though. The morning I gave it to her? You shoulda seen how happy and proud she was, man."

Jonathan kicked the ball to him.

"So that's my story, man. What's yours? Why you here?"

Above them, a bolt of lightning stabbed across the sky. A sharp crack of thunder rattled the windows to the dining room. They both looked up.

"Come on," Jonathan said. "Let's go grab dinner."

Over dinner the boys hardly spoke. Their letters were written in silence. Even Benny kept his snorting and gloating to a quiet minimum. Jonathan wrote his letter with a fast hand.

In bed, under the shifting light of the candles, he held the newest letter from his parents, the one that had arrived that morning on the supply boat. He breathed slow, even breaths, and read it again. When the other boys were ready, he opened *Robinson Crusoe* and began to read. He read to the very end, looking up from time to time into the ring of faces listening around the flames.

When he closed the finished book and blew out the candles, he went to sleep, with his parents' letter lying open on the pillow beside his head.

When he blinked his eyes awake in the morning, the letter was still lying by his head.

But it was folded into a perfect, delicate crane.

JONATHAN'S FOURTH LETTER HOME

Dear Mom and Dad,

I got your second letter today. Thanks. I do remember that trip to the beach. You're right. It was a great trip. Maybe that's why I try not to remember it. Good memories only make everything else feel worse.

You don't have to keep telling me you love me. I think I know it's true. But I wouldn't blame you if it wasn't. I wouldn't love me.

Everything is fine here. We had steak for dinner tonight. I overcooked mine, but it was still pretty good.

Do you think there will ever be a day that I don't think about it? Do you think there even should be?

I hope you are feeling better with me gone. I'm sure it helps to not have me around. Reminding you. Please give my love to Sophia.

Jonathan

CHAPTER NINETEEN
A HOME

With *Robinson Crusoe* tucked under one arm, Jonathan made his way quickly toward the library. His scrambled egg lunch sat uneasily in his stomach.

He knew his way well now. He didn't have to slow down or try to remember which way to go, and he could walk fast with the lantern held out in front of him. He saw more rats this time, probably because he could move so much faster. They didn't have a chance to get out of the way. They were very big. And he was sure he saw at least a couple, scrabbling and squeaking away, that didn't have tails.

He kept expecting to turn a corner and see Colin, but besides the rats, the way before him was vacant and still. Soon he was knocking on the door of the library, and the librarian was letting him in.

"Finished *Crusoe*. I see," the librarian said as the door closed.

"Yeah. Thanks." He handed the book over.

"Did you enjoy the book? Very much?"

Jonathan shrugged.

"Sure. We thought it was pretty cool, I guess. Boring in places. Big words."

"Yes. And you're here. For another book."

"Well, we still have *Treasure Island*. We'll start that tonight."

"Excellent. But you can't leave a library."

"Without a book," Jonathan finished. "I know."

The librarian looked at him with one twinkling eye and smiled.

"Yes. My thoughts. Exactly. Let me find a book. That you'll like."

Jonathan wandered off among the shelves, browsing through the books, casually reading the titles embossed on the spines. He almost cried out when he was surprised by Ninety-Nine, curled up on a folded blanket between two stacks of books on a shelf. The gigantic rodent yawned a toothy yawn and sniffed his long, whiskered nose up at Jonathan.

"You can pick him up. If you want to," the librarian said, peering over the shelf behind him.

"Oh. No, thanks." Jonathan moved farther along the shelves, leaving the rat to return to his nap. He stopped by one of the windows, mostly blocked by neatly lined books. The storm outside was growing fiercer by the hour, rattling the glass with rainy gusts of wind.

"Last time I was here, you said something," Jonathan began. "About—running a lighthouse, or something. What did you mean?"

"Just what I said." The librarian's voice was distracted, his eyes still scanning the shelves to find a book for Jonathan. "I used to run the lighthouse. Years ago."

"What lighthouse?"

"Ours. Slabhenge's. The island was first a lighthouse. Even before the asylum. Going way back. Hundreds of years. That is its true identity, really. Before all the tragedy. It still *has* the lighthouse. Unused, of course. For years and years, unused."

"Where is it?"

"At the top. Of the middle tower. The one above the warden's quarters. The Admiral's now, of course. Keep going up the stairs. And you'll find it. Dusty and in disrepair. I'm sure."

"And you were in charge of it?"

The librarian sighed.

"Oh, for a while. Not much to it. Wash the windows. Check the wood. Polish the mirrors." The librarian's voice quickened and smoothed out, just as it had when he'd been talking on Jonathan's previous visit. "It's very outdated. Not electric. A place for a fire. Giant mirrors to magnify and reflect the light. The mirrors spin by hand crank. Had to make sure those were oiled and ready. I only had to light it a couple of times, during big storms. Don't know if I ever saved any ships or not." He coughed a scratchy, jagged cough and then chuckled. "Probably still a stack of wood in the bin up there. Rotten, I'm sure, and dusty, like everything else on this island."

"Oh."

Jonathan read a few more book titles. Some of them were so worn with age that they were unreadable. Some weren't even in English.

"Can I ask you something?" Jonathan asked.

"Of course."

"Not to be . . . rude or anything, but . . . how come you talk so much easier when you talk about stuff from a long time ago?"

The librarian straightened up to look over the shelf at Jonathan.

"Do I?"

"Yeah. You normally talk kind of . . . slow. Like it's hard. But when you talk about, like, the old days, you smooth right out."

"Hmm." The librarian cocked his head even more sideways than usual. It was almost all the way to the side. His neck looked painfully twisted. "I don't know. I wasn't aware. That I did." His mouth screwed into a tight, thoughtful frown. "Well, the past is easier. It's done. It's there for me. To look at. I can live there. And know where I am."

His eyes drifted away from Jonathan, up toward the ceiling. As he spoke, they shifted slowly around the room and down to the floor at his feet. His voice got a little quieter with each limping sentence.

"It's the present. That is so hard. Working at it. Finding your way. Forward. Picking your path. Having to leave the past. Behind." His voice was barely a hoarse whisper. "It's so hard. Easier, I think, to stay in the past."

"What about the . . . future?"

The old man shrugged.

"I don't need a future. I have a past. Instead. You can really only have one. Or the other. I think. And I like my island."

"But it's a prison."

The librarian smiled. "It's a home."

Goose bumps broke out on Jonathan's neck. He tugged nervously at his sleeves.

The librarian's head slowly untwisted until it sat at a more natural angle. His voice rose back above a whisper.

"Here you go," he said, handing a book over the shelf to Jonathan. "This one. Is perfect. I think. One of our newest books."

Jonathan took the green-and-black book from the librarian's trembling hand.

"One of your newest ones?" he asked. The book looked like an antique.

"Yes. We got it. Just before the asylum closed. For good."

Jonathan traced the letters of the title on the cover.

"*Lord of the Flies*?"

"Mmm. Quite modern. That one. Also has an island. As a matter of fact. And a group. Of abandoned boys."

"Abandoned?"

"Mmm. Left to fend. For themselves."

Jonathan gulped and looked up at the librarian, then quickly away.

"Really."

"Yes. Doesn't go very well. I'm afraid."

Jonathan squeezed the book into the crook of his arm and picked up his lantern.

"Off?" asked the librarian. "So soon?"

"Yeah. They'll be wondering."

"Yes. I imagine."

Jonathan opened the door and stepped a foot into the corridor. He turned in the doorway and spoke one last question to the man's curved back.

"What's your name?"

"My name?"

"Yes. What's your name?"

The librarian turned with shuffling steps to face him. Ninety-Nine was nestled in the crook of his arm, leaning into the old man's scratching fingers. The old man blinked once, then twice. He closed one eye and reached up from the rat to scratch his own nose. His gray tongue licked his chapped, powdery lips, and then his hand dropped back to pet the rat once more.

"My name." The scratching slowed, and then stopped. "Why, I'm not sure." His voice was tinged with wonder, but not worry. He seemed only mildly curious. "It's been so long since anyone has called me anything at all. I used to be a son.

Then an assistant. An employee. A lighthouse keeper. A librarian. But now . . . well, I suppose I'm—nothing." He smiled, an unsteady, slightly troubled smile. "Ninety-Nine has a name. But it isn't really his. I suppose. He's just borrowing it. I guess you could call me that. Ninety-Nine. If you wanted."

Jonathan pursed his lips and held the book tighter to his body.

"No, thanks," he said. "I'll just call you sir, if that's all right."

The librarian smiled. The smile was as crooked as his hunched shoulders. "Of course. It is. Come back. Soon."

Jonathan hurried through the lightless hallways, the lantern swinging from his leading hand. He didn't slow to look down other halls for Colin. He was ready to be back to normal voices, to daylight and people.

He was almost jogging when he turned the last corner and stumbled, blinking, into the light of the dining room, so bright after the blackness of twisting stone and shadow.

"There he is!" he heard Sebastian's voice bark. He squinted and saw the older boy standing on a chair with the sword pointed right at him. "Grab him!"

CHAPTER TWENTY
THE FREAK AND THE RAT

Rough hands grabbed him by both arms and dragged him over to a chair in the middle of the dining room. Sebastian stood before him, his face white with anger. His eyes glittered like twin flames.

"Where were you, Johnny? His hideout?"

"What are you talking about?"

"What were you two doing? Giggling and shoving them in your mouth as fast as you could?"

Jonathan looked desperately around at the other faces. They all looked nervous. Walter held his hands up in a little shrug and crinkled his eyebrows sympathetically.

"I don't know what you're talking about, Sebastian, really—"

"Oh, cut the crap, Johnny. I know you were with him. Tell us where he is. Or it's gonna get ugly."

Jonathan opened his mouth to argue. Then closed it. He looked steadily into Sebastian's eyes. "What happened?"

"Like you don't know!"

Jonathan kept his voice calm. "What happened?"

"Fine. Let's all play a little game of pretend with Johnny." A rotten, ugly half smile rose to Sebastian's face. "We're all eating lunch. You, too. And somehow, while we're all down here, all the chocolates just—disappear! All *my* chocolates. And I find *this* in the basket." Sebastian fished in his pocket and pulled something out and threw it on the ground at Jonathan's feet.

It was a little paper crane. Carefully folded. And all crumpled up.

"And I come back down here and, *surprise*, Johnny's gone! And what do we find under his pillow?" Sebastian rummaged through his other pocket and threw something else to the floor. Without looking, Jonathan knew it was his parents' letter, folded neatly into a perfect bird.

"So, Johnny, you tell me . . . how stupid do you think I am?"

Jonathan looked back and forth between the two paper cranes, then back up at Sebastian.

"I don't think you're stupid. I think you're mad. And I think you're right. Colin took your chocolates. I *know* you're right. But I don't know where he is. That's the truth."

"You already told me that if you *did* know, you wouldn't tell me."

Jonathan nodded and pinched his top lip between his teeth. He looked away, out the window at the storm clouds piled atop one another above Slabhenge's crumbling walls.

"Yeah. And I wouldn't." Then he looked at Sebastian. "I *won't*. But I haven't seen him. I promise."

Sebastian licked the angry spittle from his lips. He blinked and blew out a breath and looked away. He opened his mouth to say something, but Benny butted in first.

"You can't trust him, Sebastian."

Jonathan's hands balled into anxious fists. He didn't like the eager edge to Benny's voice. The way his eyes were shining and his mouth opened and closed. Like a snake coiled and about to strike.

"Shut up, Benny, I—" Sebastian started to say.

"You can't trust him," Benny said again. "I know why he's here."

Sebastian's head turned slowly to look at Benny. His eyebrows scrunched together.

"What do you mean?"

"Don't," Jonathan said quietly, his eyes locked on Benny's.

"I peeked at his papers. In the Admiral's office, when he first got here," Benny said. His eyes stayed with Jonathan. The corners of his pudgy mouth teased toward a smile. "You can't trust him, Sebastian. Do you know what he did?"

"Don't," Jonathan pleaded again. He rubbed at his arms with his hands.

"What?" Sebastian asked. The whole room hung in waiting silence. Only the windows shook and spoke, straining to hold back the storm that fought to rush inside.

"I know why he doesn't like fire," Benny said, his smile ripening into a sickening sneer.

Jonathan shook his head.

"Little Johnny here," Benny said, savoring every bloody word like a vampire, "is a *murderer*."

Jonathan's jaw clenched down to steel.

"No," he said through his teeth.

"Oh, yes. A murderer. And do you know who he killed?"

Jonathan tried to stand up, but hard hands on his shoulders held him down.

"You shut up," he said, his voice cracking. Already, Benny was blurred, standing before him.

"He murdered his little sister. Sophia. Set a fire and burned their house down, with her trapped inside."

"Shut up!" Jonathan screamed, fighting at the hands that held him down.

"It's true!" Benny shouted back, stepping toward him. "Show them your arms!"

"No!" Jonathan howled. "Don't!"

"Pull back his sleeves! Look at his arms!" Benny crowed.

Jonathan, totally blinded now by his tears, felt his sleeves yanked back to his elbows. The room gasped, then hushed. The hands let him go. He closed his eyes, his body racked by sobs.

"God," Sebastian said. His voice was hollow, shocked.

"No," Jonathan tried to say, but he wasn't sure his voice made it through his choked throat.

He rubbed at his sightless eyes with his arms, forgetting that his sleeves were pulled up. The scarred and hardened tissue of his burns and scars scraped roughly on his face.

"Leave me alone," he managed to gasp, his voice echoing in the still chamber. "You don't know how much I loved her. How much I *love* her." But he couldn't tell anymore what he was saying from what he was merely feeling. It could have been that the words he meant to say only echoed, unheard, in the dank dungeon of his harrowed heart.

"I saw," Benny said, his voice low and stained with a stinking smile. "I saw the psychiatrist's report about your therapy. About your guilt over the burning death of your sister. I saw the doctor's report about your burns. And I saw your sentencing papers. For arson."

Jonathan just shook his head and kept his eyes closed.

"God," Sebastian said again, his voice dripping with disgust. "You're a freak. No wonder you want to stay here."

The windows shivered in their panes. The cold and endless dripping of water filled the edges of the silence.

"You better tell us," Sebastian said. "I want him back. He's a rat."

"I don't know where he is," Jonathan sniffed.

"Fine. Whatever. But you'll find out. He'll try to talk to you. And then you'll hand him over."

Sebastian turned and walked back toward the stairs that led to his room. His feet sloshed slowly from one puddle to the next. The tip of the sword dragged with a jagged scrape along the stone floor. He stopped at the bottom stair.

"You have until tomorrow night. If you don't give him to us by then, you have to go after him. And you can't come back without him. You can starve out there with him and the other rats." Sebastian coughed out a nasty little laugh. "The freak and the rat. Best friends in the nuthouse."

His steps receded up the staircase.

Everyone else stood in damp quiet.

Then, one by one, they turned and walked away. Walter was the last to go. He took a small step toward Jonathan, his eyes wide, and then stopped. He opened his mouth like he was going to say something. But then he shook his head and turned away, leaving Jonathan sitting alone in the hard chair, tears running unwiped down his face like the rain on the dark windows, his horrible scars exposed.

CHAPTER TWENTY-ONE
FIRES AND FLOWERS

Jonathan didn't take the turn that would bring him down past the Hatch and up to the library. He walked right by it, moving slow to protect his candle's fragile flame. He didn't have any matches. There hadn't been a chance to grab a lantern. The thin white candle was the only light he had.

He pressed forward through the darkness, stopping from time to time to listen. All he ever heard, besides his breathing and the ever-present dripping, was the papery scrape of tiny claws on wet stone.

"Colin?" he whisper-shouted. His voice came back to him in damp echoes. There was no answer.

He climbed a short staircase, then descended a longer, spiral one. He passed a narrow window set high in the wall. There was no glass—just a narrow, tombstone-shaped opening in the wall, a couple of feet tall. The wind blew spatters of icy rain into the passageway. Jonathan had to stand on the tips of his toes to peer out at the ocean that surrounded them. Dark clouds were stacked and heaped to the horizon, just as they had been since he arrived. They looked grimmer now, though, more threatening. Like they were coming for him. The waves jostled and crowded one another like an angry mob storming Slabhenge Castle.

He kept going, leaving the gray light of the window

behind, returning to the world of claw scrapes and candlelight.

"Colin?"

He turned a sharp corner into a hallway that was narrower, tight. He passed one door, closed and silent. Then another. Then one that hung open, the door dangling from a single broken hinge; the room behind it was small and dark and empty. Inside was only a broken chair and some empty bottles littered on the floor.

The fourth door was closed and Jonathan was just past it when something caught his eye. Something small and white on the floor, barely within the reach of his candle's wavering light. He stopped and bent down.

It was a paper crane. Tiny. Not much bigger than a marble.

Jonathan smiled and stood up. He pushed the door open with an echoing creak.

Beyond was a steep, skinny staircase that circled up into shadows. Jonathan walked up it, letting the door swing closed behind him.

It was a long staircase, rising in a tight spiral. Up and up and up until Jonathan knew that he wasn't just climbing a staircase; he was climbing one of Slabhenge's towers.

At the top was another door, open just an inch. He pressed his hand against the knotty wood and pushed the door open.

The room was perfectly round, with a high, coned ceiling. In the middle was a thin mattress covered in a rumpled pile of blankets. On the far side of the room, Colin sat in a straight-backed chair, looking out a round window.

He turned and gave Jonathan one of his short-lived smiles.

"You found my little bird," he said.

"Yeah." Jonathan stepped into the room. It had four circular windows, one looking in each direction. The glass was broken out of one of them. There was a puddle of rainwater on the floor beneath it. A chilled wet breeze spun through the room.

Colin shivered.

"There'th a thtorm coming."

"Probably."

"Definitely."

Jonathan crossed over to one of the windows. It looked inward to Slabhenge, down onto the courtyard. He could see Tony and Miguel halfheartedly kicking the ball back and forth. They looked small and far away. They looked like little kids.

"Do you want a chocolate?" Colin asked.

Jonathan looked at him and smiled. Colin smiled back.

"No, thanks. He'll probably check my breath when I get back."

Colin's smile widened.

"He'th pretty mad, huh?"

Jonathan's smile dropped away.

"More than pretty mad, Colin. You need to be careful. You shouldn't sneak down anymore. I—don't know what he'll do to you."

Colin shrugged.

"I'm careful. Everyone is athleep when I come down. Or eating. And I know all the wayth to ethcape now."

"What do you mean?"

Colin's eyes widened and an excited smile spread across his face.

"Thith plathe ith really amathing. All the hallth and stairth and roomth are connected. There are almotht no dead endth. It'th like an anthill. All turnth and loopth and thircleth. And I know it. Or motht of it. He'd never catch me."

Jonathan shook his head.

"Don't risk it, Colin. You can't let him catch you. He's kind of . . . losing it, I think. And I can't . . ." Jonathan's voice broke off. He frowned and bit his lip. "I can't protect you anymore. He won't listen to me now."

Colin tilted his head and blinked.

"What happened?" he asked. Jonathan looked away, out the window, then back to Colin.

"They think I know where you are. Well, they thought I knew where you were. And Benny . . . Benny told them some stuff."

"What? What did he thay?"

Jonathan swallowed and took a deep breath.

"He said that he'd looked through my paperwork. He showed them my—my scars." Jonathan rubbed at his arms. "He told them I was sent here for . . . for . . . murdering my little sister. Sophia." Jonathan's voice caught when he said the name. His breaths were fast and shallow and they burned in his throat. His voice scratched down into a whisper. "He told them I started a fire. And that she died. He told them I killed my little sister." Tears, as hot as the rain was cold, dropped from his eyes and down his cheeks.

Colin frowned. His eyes squinted into Jonathan's face.

"It ithn't true, though," he said.

Jonathan's throat tightened like a punch-ready fist. His eyes burned like deadly fire. He ripped a ragged breath from his lungs and looked away.

"Oh," Colin said, his voice a breathless whisper. "It *ith* true."

Jonathan rubbed at his tears with his wrist. He looked away, through his tears, out the window at the storm.

"Tell me, Jonathan," Colin said softly. "Tell me what happened."

Jonathan wiped at his face with a sleeve. "It doesn't matter."

Colin stood up and walked over to where Jonathan stood.

"It doth. It *doth* matter. Tell me."

Jonathan took a shuddering lungful of air. His teeth chattered when he exhaled.

"I . . . I . . . used to start fires. I don't know why. I don't even remember how it started. I liked to . . . watch the flames. Watch them grow. See something that I'd built get hot and bright and alive. I don't know." He looked up, for just a second, into Colin's eyes, then away again quickly.

"Little ones at first, then bigger. Then I set one at school. In the bathroom. But I got caught running away. I got in big trouble. Parents called in, kicked out of school, the whole thing. It was awful. I didn't start a fire for a while. And then . . . and then . . ." He stopped, the words stuck in his throat like ash. His teeth clenched hard and with one deep breath through his nose, he plunged forward.

"And then I started again. Small ones. In wastebaskets. At night, when everyone was sleeping. Sophia caught me. She was so mad. She was afraid I was gonna get in trouble again. She made me promise not to do it ever again. She . . . she even took the matches I had." Jonathan's voice got smaller and smaller as he spoke. He wanted to walk away, to slam the door, to retreat to the shadows with his raging. But Colin still stood there with his listening eyes before the storm-darkened window, and Jonathan's words stumbled on.

"And then. That night. It was . . . like a nightmare. The smoke. The flames climbing up the walls. So much smoke. I wanted to run. And then I heard her. Downstairs. Screaming my name. And the fire was just so hot. Growing so fast." He looked up through burning, blurry eyes. "It was like a monster, Colin. It was *roaring*." His voice was cut off by a choking sob. "I could hear her. But I couldn't save her. And she died in the fire. Screaming for me to save her."

Colin swallowed, his own eyes full, his fingers tugging at the skin of his neck.

"That'th why. Why you were on the Thinner'th Thorrow. You think it'th your fault."

"It *is* my fault!" Jonathan shouted, his voice hoarse and raw. "I killed my sister! I let her die!"

Colin took a step closer.

"Jonathan," he said. "It wath an acthident. Jutht a terrible acthident."

Jonathan shook his head angrily and wiped the tears out of his eyes with his wrist.

"My parents say the same thing. That it was an accident. That it wasn't my fault. How much they love me." He looked up into Colin's eyes. "But I can still hear her screaming, Colin. Screaming for *me*. It shouldn't be me at home with them. It should be Sophia." He took a shaky, broken breath. "I'm probably the only one of all of us that actually deserves to be here."

There was a moment of nothing but wind and the smell of rain and, somewhere out on the darkness of the sea, a low rumble of thunder.

Then Colin's thoughtful eyes narrowed.

"But . . . how did you get the thcars?" he asked.

Jonathan sniffed and cleared his throat and took a step away.

"I better go. Sebastian'll be getting suspicious. And you need to stay out of the way, Colin. Don't let him catch you."

Colin squinted and bit his lip. He seemed about to say something, then stopped. He nodded, once. Then he asked, "Are you going to be okay?"

"I'll be fine."

Jonathan opened the door and put his foot on the top step.

"Don't you think they mith you?"

Jonathan stopped. He didn't have to ask who Colin was talking about.

"You're the only one who geth a letter every thingle day. Don't you think they mith you? Don't you think lothing *one* of their children wath enough?"

Jonathan's eyebrows frowned. He chewed on his lip.

"Don't you mith them? Don't you mith home?"

Jonathan didn't turn around. When he answered, his voice echoed down the winding staircase.

"I do," he said, incredibly softly. Like a secret he was keeping from himself. "I do." He focused his eyes on the flame clutched in his hand.

"I went every day to Sophia's grave and put a flower on it. Every single day. She loved flowers. My parents promised that they'd do it for me while I was gone."

He closed his eyes, then opened them and looked back at Colin. His eyes took in the stone floor, the stone walls, the puddle and the shadows.

"There's no flowers here."

When the door closed on the round room, Colin was still standing pinching his neck, a thoughtful frown on his face.

When Jonathan returned to the dining room, they were just starting their nightly letter home. No one spoke to him. The dining room was again awash in candlelight and the whispers of pens on paper. Jonathan's letter was short. But he was the last one done. Benny read it and rolled his eyes and said, "Fine. Night-night, Johnny." Jonathan didn't reply, or even look Benny in the face. He supposed that he should have glared at him. Stared him down. He supposed that he should hate Benny. But Jonathan didn't have any hate left. He'd already used it all on himself.

When Jonathan went to his mattress to go to sleep, he found that the ring of seven mattresses had shrunk to three. Most of the other boys had dragged theirs away into a different corner. Away from him. Only Walter and David had stayed.

The two boys looked at him from around the slowly dancing candle flame between them.

Jonathan put his head down and closed his eyes.

"Aren't you gonna read, man?" Walter asked.

"You still want me to?"

"Yeah. Don't you have another book?"

"Um-hmm." Jonathan rolled over and fished *Treasure Island* out from where he'd stowed it under his pillow. He looked up at the faces of Walter and David, waiting in the yellow glow of the candles.

"You sure?" he asked. They both nodded.

He cleared his throat.

"*Chapter One*," he began, his voice still a wounded whisper. It gained strength as he read. "*The Old Sea Dog at the Admiral Benbow*."

In the morning, when he awoke, there was a new piece of paper lying on the pillow beside his head. It was not a crane.

The paper on his pillow was folded into the shape of a perfect flower. The flower had a shiny gold center.

A dark brown square of chocolate sat beside it.

JONATHAN'S FIFTH LETTER HOME

Dear Mom and Dad,

I miss you. Thank you for the letters.

I'm sorry. Not for what you think. For everything else. I really am.

Please give my love to Sophia.

Love,
Jonathan

CHAPTER TWENTY-TWO
CAUGHT

"Last chance, Johnny boy." Sebastian's voice was a snarl. Outside, the wind howled with fierce strength between the crumbling towers of Slabhenge. Lightning flashed on puddles growing and spreading across the courtyard stones. Thunder scared the window glass into shaking.

The storm had been growing all day. Jonathan had watched it rage and strengthen through the windows. He'd been locked inside during the mail exchange. He hadn't bothered going to see the librarian or Colin. He knew he'd have plenty of time for that when Sebastian banished him. It had been a long day. He'd read most of *Treasure Island*.

But now the sun had set. The day was over. His deadline had expired. All the world was dropping into storm and darkness.

"I don't know where he is," Jonathan lied.

"Liar."

Jonathan looked away. He was seated at one of the long dining room tables. Benny and Francis stood on either side of him. All the other boys were standing around, watching nervously.

"Fine. It's your funeral." Sebastian pushed a paper and pen across the table to him. "Write what I say. *Exactly* what I say. Benny, check his work."

Jonathan pursed his lips, then picked up the pen. There was no use fighting. It would only make things worse.

"Dear Mom and Dad," Sebastian started, and Jonathan rolled his eyes and copied the words onto the paper. "Everything is going fine. The food is good and I'm learning a lot." Sebastian lowered his voice. "Add an exclamation point to that. Make it look cheerful." His eyes rose to the ceiling in concentration. "I won't be able to write for a while. We are . . ." Sebastian paused and squinted one eye, drumming his lips with his fingers. "We are getting ready for a big test. I love you and miss you lots. Love, Johnny."

"You really want me to sign it 'Johnny'?"

Sebastian lowered his eyes and glared across the table.

"Love, Jonathan."

Jonathan's pen scratched across the paper and then he set it down.

"How'd he do, Benny?"

"Fine. He wrote just what you said."

Sebastian rose to his feet.

"That's your last letter home, Johnny." He looked past Jonathan to the kids standing behind him. "Give him a couple candles. And a book of matches." His eyes dropped back down to Jonathan and he smiled. "Although I don't know if we can really trust him with matches."

With an echoing crash, the door to the courtyard swung open and smashed into the stone wall. They all jumped and turned. Rain blew through the open door, splattering the dark stone wall. Some of the candles they'd lit blew out in the wind that blustered in among them.

"Damn it, close that door, Reggie!" Sebastian shouted. Lightning flashed, and a rumble of thunder cracked, sounding unnaturally loud through the open door. "And make sure it's closed *all the way* this time!"

When the storm was once again locked mostly outside, Sebastian turned back to Jonathan.

"Say hi to the little rat for me. I hope you two have lots of fun."

Jonathan was jerked to his feet. Candles and matches were pressed into his hand. Sebastian stalked around the table and poked him with the sword.

"Go on," he said, prodding Jonathan toward the door that led into Slabhenge's dark interior. "Go ahead and find your friend. And don't come crawling back here. You two made your choice."

He was pushed through the doorway, into the familiar musty shadows of the corridor.

"Good night," Sebastian's voice echoed after him. "Sleep tight."

With trembling fingers, Jonathan struck a match. He held the sputtering flame to a candle wick, then quickly dropped it with a hiss into a puddle at his feet. The rain was falling even harder now than it had been the morning the Admiral and his men were struck down. Slabhenge, inside and out, was all dripping and puddles.

Jonathan bit his teeth together hard and started off into the darkness.

It took him a while to find Colin's tower hideout. He'd been wandering the first time he'd found it and this time he had to circle and peer and look for landmarks. He remembered what Colin had said about everything in Slabhenge being connected, and kept walking. He stopped from time to time to listen; the rats seemed more than normally large and active, especially behind him. Maybe it was the storm, which was howling and thundering loud enough to be heard even through the thick stone walls.

At one point as he wandered he passed one of the staircases that he knew led down to the Hatch. It was wild tonight, knocking and rocking and echoing up from the darkness. Like a demon thrashing against chains ready to break. He swallowed and pressed on, looking for Colin's refuge.

And then, there it was. The long hallway with the four doors, the little paper bird hiding in the darkness. Jonathan slipped through the door and up the stairs.

Colin was sitting on his bed. Paper, some folded and some not, lay scattered and piled on the bed and floor around him. Four candles sat around the bed on the floor. Startling splashes of white light flashed through the windows from the storm outside. Colin was facing the door, chewing on a bright red apple.

"Hey," he said with a smile as brief and bright as the lightning. "I wath hoping that wath you."

A ferocious blast of wind whistled in through the broken window, shuffling the loose leaves of paper into a swirl of scattered white. One of the candles flickered out. When the gust had died down, Colin calmly relit the smoking wick with one of the other candles.

"You're here late," Colin said.

Jonathan took a couple of steps into the room.

"I'm here for good."

"What do you mean?"

"Sebastian. He said I had to leave. I'm, like, kicked out."

Colin's brow furrowed and he pinched at his neck with one hand.

"I thought he wanted to catch me."

"Yeah. He does."

Colin squinted one eye and cocked his head.

"Well . . . don't you think he'd jutht follow you?"

Jonathan opened his mouth. But before he could say anything, he heard the distant creak of a door from behind him, and then the rumble of footsteps running up the stairs.

CHAPTER TWENTY-THREE
AN INTRUDER

The lightning was constant and explosive and spectacular. It provided more light to the dining room than the candles that were lit on every table. Colin sat in a chair in the middle of the room, flanked by Roger and Francis.

Rain pelted the huge windows. Thunder booms like cannon shots rattled the glass. The courtyard was a rain-lashed lake, reflecting the violent white cracks of lightning above. The wind shrieked between Slabhenge's tall towers like an army of furious ghosts.

The sword glowed red and yellow in Sebastian's hand, from the candlelight. Except when it gleamed white in the lightning. The Admiral's hat was back on his head, retrieved from Colin's room. His sneering mouth was busy chewing one of the reclaimed gold-wrapped chocolates.

Jonathan stood off to one side with the others. Benny was holding him roughly with one hand, pinching harder than he needed to, his fingers like fangs in Jonathan's shoulder. Jonathan sniffed from time to time and rubbed at his nose with his arm. His sleeve was smeared with dark blood. When the boys had reached the top of the stairs to Colin's room, he'd tried quickly to slam the door, but it was too late; they'd burst in and Sebastian had knocked him to the ground with one vicious punch. Colin was bleeding, too, from a cut above his eye that Sebastian had given him when he'd tried to dash to the broken window and toss the Admiral's hat out.

"Admit it, Colin, you're the one who stole my chocolates."

"Of courth I am. You found them in my room, Thebathtian."

"Shut up. So you admit it, then, trespassing and theft."

"Yeth. I went into the Admiral'th room and took the Admiral'th chocolateth."

"*It's my room!*" Sebastian shouted, getting right in Colin's face. "*The Admiral is dead! I'm in charge! When are you going to get that?*"

"Oh, I get it, Thebathtian." Colin's voice was calm. Soft. Sad. "I abtholutely get it."

Sebastian straightened back up. His face was eerily pale in the shifting light.

"And we all saw what you did to the Sinner's Sorrow. That's destruction of property. You have to be punished."

There was an especially loud crack of thunder at the same moment as a particularly forceful gale of wind. One of the large windows shattered, sending shards of glass flying into the group of boys. They screamed and ducked and dove under tables. Rain blew in through the broken window. Wind whipped through the room, blowing out most of the candles.

"Hold that little thief!" Sebastian hollered. "Relight those candles!" The boys stood frozen, their eyes wide and scared. "Oh, Jesus, guys, it's just a little thunderstorm. Relight those candles. We'll cover the window in the morning."

They got the candles relit and moved to tables farther from the broken window. They all shivered wetly in the storm that was now in the room with them.

"Punishment," Sebastian continued. His black hair was plastered to his forehead with rain. Water dripped down his face. He had to almost shout to be heard above the wind and the thunder and the pouring rain. "The Sinner's Sorrow is ruined. So what could we do? What could we do to a thief and a criminal?"

The group blinked at him in silence. Teeth chattered.

"In some places, they cut a thief's hand off," Sebastian said. He held the sword up and looked at it, turning the blade to catch the light. His mouth widened into a grim smile. The tips of his teeth showed whitely. The group tensed. "But that would be too messy." He stepped slowly closer to Colin and his captors. "In other places, they just mark a thief. They carve a *T* into his forehead. Or his arm. Or his chest." The smile disappeared. "Put him on the table," he said. "Hold him down."

"No!" Jonathan cried, and Benny's arm jerked around his neck, holding him in a headlock.

Colin wiggled and fought, but he was too small. The older boys wrestled him onto a table on his back and pinned him down.

The lightning flashed. Thunder cracked so loudly the boys could feel it in their chests. It sounded like the thunder was coming from inside the prison.

"Come on, Sebastian! This is messed up!" Tony argued.

"Shut up!" Sebastian's voice was wild and furious. His face was twisted in anger. It was all white and black in the flashing light. It looked like a mask. "Open him up! Bare his chest!" he commanded, and the goons obeyed. Buttons popped and Colin's skin shone white in the twisted light. Sebastian stepped forward, brandishing the sword.

Jonathan twisted with a surge of energy and broke loose from Benny's hold. He ran toward Sebastian.

Sebastian turned to face him just as Jonathan slipped in a puddle on the floor. He hit the stone floor with a hard splash. He pulled himself quickly up to his hands and knees, but then Sebastian's booted foot swung into his side like a sledgehammer. All the breath was kicked out of his lungs with a piercing whoosh of pain and he rolled over onto his back.

Sebastian stepped forward and pressed a foot onto Jonathan's neck. It was wet and cold and hard. Jonathan blinked and gasped for breath. His feet kicked in the puddle. His hands tugged at Sebastian's leg, but Sebastian just pressed down harder.

The sword blade swung slowly around until it was inches from Jonathan's face, sharp and silver and dripping rain onto his nose.

"You're next, Johnny," Sebastian said.

Behind them, the door crashed open, letting in another mighty gust of wind.

"Damn it, Reggie, I told you—" Sebastian started, before he turned and looked and stopped.

They all did.

Someone was standing in the doorway.

A stranger. On Slabhenge. Looking at them all standing there in the storm-drenched dining room.

"I came to warn ye about the storm!" he shouted. It was Patrick, the guy from the boat. He was wearing a yellow rain slicker and he was out of breath.

The boys all stood, frozen, in the lightning and the flickering candlelight.

Patrick's eyes seemed to focus. He saw Colin, bloody and pinned down on top of the table. He saw the Sinner's Sorrow standing in splinters. He saw Sebastian, soaked and furious and wearing the Admiral's hat. He saw Jonathan, lying on the floor with a bloody nose and a boot on his throat and sword to his face.

"Where is everybody? What in the world is going on here?" he asked, taking a step back.

Sebastian raised his sword and pointed it at Patrick.

"Grab him," he said.

CHAPTER TWENTY-FOUR
ALL THE GROWN-UPS ARE DEAD AND GONE

After a few minutes, Patrick sat straining and panting, tied firmly to a chair. He'd been too surprised at first to run when the pack of wild boys had rushed him. They'd caught and tangled him in a tidal wave of arms and hands and pulled him to the ground.

Then he'd started fighting. At first, he'd gained ground. He'd wrestled and twisted and was almost free when he'd felt the tip of Sebastian's sword pressed against his neck. "Don't move an inch," Sebastian had warned. "Not an inch."

Patrick had frozen, an arm around his neck, others pinning his arms to his sides, his lungs heaving, and looked into Sebastian's eyes. He must not have seen any bluff there. He was tied up and walked to the chair where he sat, looking around with wide eyes at the savage boys.

Sebastian was pacing. He was grinding his teeth and idly swinging his sword. His eyes darted around the dark room. His shadow, thrown onto the wet stone walls by white flashes of lightning, loomed and jumped as he walked.

"Where is everybody?" Patrick asked again.

"We're all right here," Sebastian said with a sneer, holding his arms open.

"Yeah, but—what about the Admiral? Mr. Vander? Where are all the grown-ups?"

Benny, who was standing guard by Patrick's side, leaned in close to his face with a toothy sneer.

"All the grown-ups are dead and gone," he said. "And that's just how we like it."

Patrick looked at him like he was crazy.

"What d'ye mean? Ye mean . . . ye killed 'em?"

"No!" Sebastian shouted, spinning in a puddle. "We had nothing to do with it! It was lightning. They were all struck by lightning!"

Patrick gulped and looked around at the ring of frightened faces.

"What . . . *all* of them?"

"Yes, *all* of them!" Sebastian yelled, stamping his foot in the puddle. "We had nothing to do with it!"

Patrick licked his lips and shrugged.

"Okay. This *is* a crazy storm," he added, nodding with his chin at the raging tempest howling through the broken window.

"No, no," Sebastian said, resuming his pacing. "Not tonight. The last storm. What . . . five days ago?"

Patrick went pale. His eyes widened even farther.

"Five days? Ye've all been here by yerselves fer five days?"

Sebastian stopped his walking and glared at him.

"Yes. And we've been fine. Just fine."

Patrick's eyes darted to the shattered Sinner's Sorrow, to Colin's bloody head and Jonathan's bloody nose.

"Aye," he said carefully. "Sure ye have."

"But now we've got a new problem," Sebastian continued. "What to do with you?"

"I think ye should let me go," Patrick tried.

"No," Sebastian said with a small smile. "Then our game is over. And I'm not ready for that. I don't want to go back just yet. None of us do."

"I do."

"Shut up, Colin. Of course *you* do. We'll get to you in a second. First . . . what do we do with *him*?"

All eyes turned to Patrick. He looked nervously around.

"We could put him in the freezer with the grown-ups," someone suggested.

"Nah," Sebastian said. "That wouldn't be very nice. Anywhere out of the way will be fine. How about the coal room, for now?" He nodded to Roger and Gregory. "Take him down there. Leave a lantern on for him."

"Wait!" Patrick protested. "Ye never listened to why I came! There's a monstrous storm coming on. It be a hundred-year storm, they say. A hurricane. Class Five! Bringing a terrible storm surge with it, too, historic high tides. Why, it could wash this whole place away! They told me I was mad to even try and make it out here, but I couldn't leave ye all to drown."

Sebastian rolled his eyes.

"Take him away," he repeated.

"Ye've got to listen to me!"

"We're in a stone castle," Sebastian replied, his voice bored. "Built on a stone island. It's been here for hundreds of years. Islands don't sink."

"Yes, they do."

Everyone turned to Jonathan.

"It's true. This place is crumbling. The island is getting smaller. There used to be a beach and everything." He looked around at the silent faces. "It's true! Think of those stairs leading down into the water from the gate. The whole bottom floor is already under water—that's what the Hatch is!"

Sebastian blew his breath out through flapping lips.

"Uh-huh. Nice try. Shut up, Jonathan." He looked back to the kids standing around Patrick. "Take him away. Now."

The boys stumbled away, dragging Patrick roughly between them. Sebastian paced back and forth while they were gone, his feet splashing in storm-water puddles.

"Listen, man," Miguel said. "You gotta calm down and—"

"Shut up," Sebastian snarled with wild eyes. He shook the sword in his hand. "We're gonna be fine. All of us. As long as you keep your mouth shut, you'll be fine, too."

When the boys returned from the coal room, Sebastian turned and cocked an eyebrow at Colin.

"Now. Back to *you*. And your punishment."

Colin frantically shook his head. Gerald and Francis were holding him tight on top of the table, but now he was sitting up.

"Pleath don't cut me, Thebathtian."

Sebastian rolled his eyes again.

"I was never gonna cut you," he snorted. Colin's eyes narrowed doubtfully. "I *wasn't*. Jesus. I was just trying to scare you." Colin's body visibly relaxed. Until Sebastian continued talking. "Besides, I have something *better* planned for you."

The wind was an unending high howl now, as if the whole of the tortured sky was one great furious beast. It screamed through the broken window, bringing rain and chilling salty spray with it. The lightning was so constant that the moments of darkness between were more eerie and surprising than the flashes themselves.

"You two, bring him," Sebastian said to Roger and Gregory, lifting his chin toward Jonathan. They grabbed him roughly by his elbows. "And you guys bring him," he added to Francis and Gerald, still holding down Colin. He whispered something into Benny's ear, who nodded and ran off to the kitchen.

Sebastian stalked off toward the darkened doorway that led into the interior of Slabhenge. He paused at the exit. He gripped the sword in his teeth while he used both hands to light a candle, then looked at the crowd of boys waiting at the tables.

"All of you, follow me. Bring a candle." He smiled, a dangerous smile full of sharp, white teeth that glistened in the lightning. "It's time to find out what Colin's punishment is."

CHAPTER TWENTY-FIVE
A CRASH AND A BANG

They all followed Sebastian through the dark, winding tunnels of Slabhenge's twisting corridors and staircases. It wasn't clear where they were going, or even if Sebastian had a destination in mind. But whenever Sebastian came to a choice between two halls, he chose the darker and narrower one. Whenever he had to choose between staircases, he chose down.

In a winding, candlelit line they passed through the dip that went by the Hatch. It was only feet away, down that last cramped stairway and around a corner. It was a riot of violent, eerie noises, louder than Jonathan had ever heard it. Bangs and shudders and thirsty slurps and the high, pained squeaking of straining iron. Some boys slowed down on the landing that led down to the Hatch. Most shivered and sped up.

Finally, they came to a dark little windowless room, small and wet and cold at the bottom of a crumbling staircase. It was an especially desolate and forgotten corner of the madhouse island. Rats hurried out as the boys came in with their splashing feet and flickering flames, brushing past their feet, causing some boys to cry out and jump.

All together, the group nearly filled the room. The ceiling was low and dripping green slime. Even here, though, they could hear the storm raging away beyond the thick stone walls that surrounded them. It sounded far, and angry, and above them, like they were belowground.

"Here we are," Sebastian said with satisfaction. "It's perfect."

The last kids in were Benny and James. Benny had a rope over his shoulder and a sack in his hands. James was carrying a wooden chair. Sebastian took the chair and set it in the middle of the little floor. Its legs wobbled on the uneven stone. Colin was thunked down in the chair and tied firmly to it with the rope.

"Make sure it's good and tight," Sebastian said. When the knots were all tightened and Sebastian had checked them, he stood back and looked at Colin.

"You wanted to sneak around and steal like a little rat. Fine. Benny came up with the perfect punishment. You get to spend the night with the rats. All by yourself." Colin was panting, his forehead beaded with sweat. He pulled against the ropes binding him, but there was no give. "The bag, please, Benny," Sebastian said, holding out his hand. He reached inside and pulled out a handful of something. "We want to make sure the rats know their new roommate is here," he said, holding his hand up to the light. It was full of crackers and bits of cheese from the kitchen. Looking Colin in the eye, he scattered the food around Colin on the floor. He reached into the sack for another handful and tossed it on the floor leading to the stairs. Pulling out one more handful, he crumbled it together in his hand and sprinkled it onto Colin's lap.

The boys all stood in silence, watching wide-eyed.

"That should do it," Sebastian said, rubbing his hands on his pant legs. "You should have *lots* of little friends tonight. Come on, let's go."

"You're jutht gonna leave me here?"

"You got it. Not forever. One long night oughta be enough to teach you a lesson, I think. We can talk more in the morning, you and I."

The rest of the boys were already starting to plod back up the stairs. No one said a word. As each kid left with his candle, the room got darker and darker.

The last ones left were Sebastian, Benny, Jonathan, and the two goons holding him.

"Aren't you going to leave me a light, at leatht?"

"Oh. Sure, Colin. Here you go." Sebastian took a candle from one of the kids leaving and held it out toward Colin. His fingers opened, and the candle fell to the floor. It sputtered and hissed and went out in a puddle. "Oops. Sorry about that. Good night, Colin."

"Sebastian, seriously, you can't . . ." Jonathan began.

Sebastian's head swung like a hunting panther to Jonathan.

"I can, Johnny," he seethed. "I can. You had your chance. You picked your side. You'll get yours after dinner. Don't worry."

Jonathan struggled against the boys holding him, but it was no use. He was dragged up the stairs behind Sebastian and Benny and the last candle. The last he saw of Colin, he was sitting in the growing blackness, eyes wide and lips trembling, all alone.

Jonathan tried to pay attention as they made their way back to the dining room. At one point he thought they were close to where the library was, but they never saw it. The Hatch, when they passed it, was making an unholy racket. Like an army of watery demons on the other side, raging to get in. No boys paused to listen this time.

They all stopped cold when they got back to the dining room. There were no longer puddles in the room—the entire floor was under an inch of water. It was black and dappled by rain blowing in through the window. The light of the candles still burning on the tables was reflected eerily on its surface.

Lightning crackled, filling the windows with blinding light. There was a great boom of thunder that made them all jump.

"No letter writing tonight," Sebastian said, looking at the flooded room. "We can do it first thing in the morning, after the storm. Dinnertime."

"Uh, Sebastian, this isn't okay," David said cautiously.

"It's fine. A little water won't hurt us. It's just 'cause the window's broken."

"Where are we gonna sleep, man?" Walter asked, pointing at their waterlogged mattresses still lying on the floor.

"You can bring your beds upstairs for tonight. There's plenty of room."

"Sebastian," Jonathan said. "Remember what Patrick said about the storm and the surge and—"

"Shut up, Jonathan. No one cares what Patrick said. Don't piss me off—I'm still deciding what your punishment is." He looked at Gregory and Roger. "One of you keep your hands on him at all times. I know the little punk'll run away to save his little friend first chance he gets."

They ate dinner sitting on the tables, their feet on the chairs. The storm was so loud they couldn't talk over it. They kept having to relight their candles, blown out by the hard fists of gusting wind that hammered through the room. Jonathan sat where Sebastian had been carving with his sword a couple of days ago, flanked by a guard on either side. He fingered the crudely notched letters Sebastian had inscribed on the wooden tabletop: *S-C-A-R-S*. He looked around at the soggy boys glumly eating, shivering and soaked, sitting in near-darkness with rain blowing in the broken window. His mind kept circling around Colin, bound in blackness, swarmed by giant rats. He couldn't swallow a bite.

"We need to keep the furnace lit!" Sebastian shouted over the storm. "Jonathan—it's your turn! You two go with him!" He tossed a stale roll to Roger. "You can give that to our prisoner. Don't untie him, though!"

Jonathan managed to eat a dry bite of bread and slumped down to the coal room, Roger and Gregory right behind.

Patrick was tied to his chair in the middle of the room under a dangling lantern, surrounded by piles of coal. The furnace glowed and hissed behind him. His face was grim and he was drenched in sweat. Jonathan gasped and unbuttoned the top button of his own shirt. He'd forgotten how hot it was in the dark little cellar. There was a large puddle at the foot of the stairs. Jonathan frowned. He didn't remember the coal room having any puddles.

"Have ye come to yer senses, then?" Patrick asked.

"We're just here to feed the furnace," Roger said. "Here." He held out the roll.

Patrick looked at it, his hands tied behind his back.

"Uh, ye'll have to untie me."

"No way," Roger answered. He tore a chunk off the roll and shoved it into Patrick's mouth. "Get to work, Jonathan," he said over his shoulder. "I don't wanna be down here forever."

Jonathan was looking at the puddle on the ground. It was spreading and growing as he watched. He looked closer and saw the little rivulets of water running down the stairs along the wall.

"Water's getting down here," he said, pointing. "From upstairs."

"Who cares?"

"Well, that means—"

"Look, just get to work, okay? I'll help."

Jonathan and Gregory started shoveling coal into the wheelbarrow while Roger fed Patrick bites of roll.

"Ye boys are crazy," Patrick said when they stood gasping for breath after dumping the first load into the fiery furnace. "Ye can't keep going like this. Ye need to get outta here."

"Quiet," Roger said. "We're fine."

"What happened to yer nose?" he asked, looking at Jonathan. Jonathan sniffed and touched it gingerly with sooty fingers. It was still sore.

"Nothing. Just an accident."

"Aye," Patrick said quietly. "I bet plenty of accidents happen around that boy with the sword."

"Come on. Keep shoveling. I wanna go to bed."

They were just about to open the furnace doors for the second load of coal when they heard the crash from above them.

More than a crash. A shattering, shuddering explosion that echoed down the stairs. They froze in mid-motion, then turned to look at the staircase.

There was a moment of near-stillness. Then the water trickling down the sides of the stairs increased to a steady stream an inch deep from wall to wall, waterfalling into the coal room in dirty little cascades.

"What the hell?" Patrick breathed.

From upstairs came the sound of screaming.

Jonathan and Gregory dropped their shovels and all three boys tore up the stairs at a run.

"Wait!" Patrick called. "Don't leave me down here!"

But they were already gone, up the stairs and through the kitchen and into the dining room.

The room was in chaos. The storm, which had already seemed impossibly fierce, was doubled in strength and fury. All the windows had blown out, every single one, and the door was ripped off its hinges, leaving one whole wall open to the raging wind and rain. All the candles were out, leaving the room in darkness except when it was lit by flashes of lightning. The boys were all huddled behind tables.

Jonathan, Roger, and Gregory stopped in their tracks. The water in the room was no longer an inch deep—it was over their ankles, and rising.

"Look at that!" Miguel shouted over the thundering storm. "In the courtyard!"

Ducking heads peeked from behind the tables. Jonathan's eyes peered through the pelting rain into the darkness beyond the glassless windows. For a moment, there was only wet, howling blackness.

Then a bright white strobe of lightning lit the scene, and he saw it.

A boat, drifting in the courtyard. Sailing and bobbing right in the middle of the school.

Jonathan and Sebastian and a few others ran to the windows, standing a couple of cautious steps back and squinting into the darkness outside.

Lightning flashed again.

"It's empty!"

"That's the mail boat. The one the guy came in."

"The gate must have blown open!"

Jonathan looked down the row of terrified faces.

"It's floating out there," he said. "There's enough water inside for it to float."

They looked out at the boat, rocking its way through the storm toward them, rising and falling with the waves.

"It ain't just puddles out there," Walter said.

"It's flooded. The island's underwater."

They looked down at the water, now above their ankles.

From behind them came a wrenching, shrieking sound, followed by a thunderous bang. It rang out from the doorway that led into Slabhenge and for a moment overpowered even the sound of the storm raging around them.

Jonathan splashed through the water to the doorway. He took one step into the lightless corridor and listened. He heard echoes of banging, and rushing, and a wet slurping roar.

"It's the Hatch!" he screamed, the wind whipping the words out of his mouth. "It opened!"

CHAPTER TWENTY-SIX
GOING ALONE

The boys came out from behind and under the tables. They gathered in the middle of the room, feeling for each other in the darkness. A few were crying. Questions were shouted by shaking voices.

"Everyone settle down!" Sebastian's harsh command silenced the rising voices. "Just shut up, everyone! Let me think! We're all fine!"

His words shook Jonathan with a realization.

"All!? What about Colin! He's lower down than we are! We have to go save him!"

Sebastian shook his head.

"No way! We're not going past that Hatch if it's open!"

"We have to! He'll drown!"

"So will we if we go after him. We're staying right here until the storm stops. We can sit up on the tables."

"No, Sebastian, we have to—"

"No, Johnny. We can't save him." Sebastian's voice was as hard as the sword glinting in his hand. "We're not gonna die trying."

Jonathan swallowed. His whole body was trembling. With cold. With anger. With fear. He rubbed his arms with shivering hands, feeling the burns and scars through his wet sleeves. He imagined he could hear Colin crying for help. In his mind he saw soggy, water-ruined paper birds. Rain-soaked flowers.

"I'm going," he said, and his voice was soft but at least as hard as Sebastian's.

Sebastian blinked and breathed hard through his nose. His jaw muscles rippled.

"Fine. But you're going alone. And you can't save him."

"Yes, I can."

"Don't go!" Tony said.

"Don't do it, man," Walter pleaded.

"It's crazy!" Gerald yelled. The water was halfway up their calves now.

"Let me have a lantern," Jonathan said into Sebastian's eyes. Sebastian glanced quickly around.

"We only have three left." Sebastian said. Jonathan kept his eyes locked on Sebastian's, unblinking. After a moment, Sebastian blinked. "Fine. Take one. Better bring a candle, too."

Without another word, Jonathan jerked a lantern out of the nearest kid's hand. He yanked a candle out of the holder by the doorway. He was two steps into the corridor when a sudden thought stopped him.

"Patrick!" he exclaimed. "The coal room is flooding." He looked to Roger and Gregory. They didn't look tough at all. They looked soaking wet and scared. "Go get him and bring him up."

The two boys didn't move, except to look at Sebastian. After a moment, he nodded. They turned and jogged toward the coal room.

Jonathan adjusted his grip on the lantern's slippery handle and took off into the darkness as fast as he could through the rising water.

"Good luck!" Walter shouted after him. Then another kid shouted the same thing. As he sprinted around the first corner and out of earshot, Jonathan heard a chorus of scared voices shouting the same thing. Their voices echoed behind him, following him into the black, flooded maze of Slabhenge.

"Good luck!"

CHAPTER TWENTY-SEVEN
DARKNESS AND DROWNING

As he ran, Jonathan tried to retrace in his mind the path they'd taken when they'd returned from leaving Colin to the rats and shadows. Rising up was all he remembered clearly. And passing the Hatch. He made his way there, holding the lantern out in front of him.

He ducked under the rope and started down the stairs, then cried out and slid to a stop.

Three steps down, the stairs disappeared into black, bubbling water.

The lantern nearly slipped from his fingers. He caught it and fell against the stone wall, panting.

The Hatch *had* cracked open. And the ocean it had been holding back had broken out of the dungeon.

He held the lantern out. He could just see, through the water, where the ceiling flattened out above the landing, now lost under murky seawater.

"I can make it," he told himself. His voice sounded tiny and hollow in the echoing gurgles of the flooded stairwell. "Just a quick swim down, then up." There was an iron hook on the wall by his hand and he hung the lantern on it. He felt in his pockets and pulled out the book of matches that Sebastian had given him earlier, when he'd first sent him out to join Colin. It had been only a few hours before. It felt like forever.

He spit and blew, drying out his mouth. Then he tucked the book of matches into his mouth and closed his lips tight, holding the matches on his tongue. Clutching the candle in his hand, he dove into the dark water before his fear could get strong enough to stop him.

The water was freezing. His muscles tightened and shook and he almost turned around, but he shook his head and kept going. He kept his eyes open and the chilled, salty water burned. He swam with his arms and kicked with his legs and the light from his hanging lantern got dimmer and darker and more distant and then it was all the way gone. Jonathan swam through freezing blackness. He tried not to think of the skull that rolled and knocked somewhere in the dark water there with him.

Down he swam, under the ceiling ledge. He stayed near the top, bumping and scraping on the rough ceiling stones. The water wasn't still; it swelled and moved with currents and surges, no doubt coursing in and out through the Hatch with the rise and fall of the waves in the storm outside.

He swam along the level landing ceiling, his lungs beginning to burn. His lips were pressed together as hard as he could to keep the matches dry. A strong surge of water from below crushed him against the ceiling and pushed him back. He fought against it, digging his elbow into the corner where the wall and ceiling met, then kicked on desperately.

Finally, he felt the ceiling begin to slope upward. He was

swimming up the far staircase. It suddenly occurred to him that he had no guarantee that the far side was above water. Maybe the other side of Slabhenge was all already underwater. Maybe he would swim up and up without ever finding air and then drown in some dark and flooded corridor, a book of matches in his mouth.

But at last his head broke the surface and he gave a final kick and gasped a mouthful of cold, delicious air. His feet found the stairs beneath him and he stumbled up, out of the water. He staggered, dripping and shaking out of the stairwell and into the hallway.

He was in utter blackness. Just like the first time he'd come here, when he'd dropped his lantern by the Hatch. He shook the water off his hand and pulled the matches out of his mouth.

The hallway was filled with the wet sounds of storm and flood. His gasping lungs added their own noise. His hands shook as he struck the first match.

It lit, a beautiful yellow flame in all that looming darkness. He smiled and held it to the candle's wick.

Nothing happened. He kept holding it, waiting for the flame to grow and the wick to take light. But the match burned down to his fingers and then out.

"Damn it," he cursed, his voice tight with shivering. "Of course, idiot. The wick's wet."

He struck another one and held it to the wick. Eventually, he told himself, the flames would dry the wick. And then it would light. He had to believe that.

He didn't have time to wait. Colin could already be underwater. If he wasn't yet, he would be soon. He stepped cautiously forward, his eyes darting from his feet to the flame and wick in his hands.

The second match burned down. He held it until it singed his fingertips, then stopped to light another.

On the fourth match, the wick lit. Weakly at first, a bare little blue ball of flame clinging to the candle's tip. Then it grew and strengthened and stretched into a tall, bright finger of flame. He held his hand in front of it to keep it from blowing out and sped his steps to a jog.

The path came back to him. A familiar corner passed, then a stairwell he was pretty sure he remembered climbing up, then a twisting little passageway he was almost certain they'd filed through. He was close.

He dropped down a short staircase and stopped.

The water was here. Up to his knees. And he was pretty sure that Colin's room was another staircase lower. Up ahead, he heard a waterfall. No, he thought, not a waterfall. The sound of freezing water pouring down a stone staircase. He ran toward the sound, the deepening water pushing back at him.

"Colin!" he screamed. "Colin! Can you hear me?"

"Jonathan?"

Jonathan almost collapsed in relief when he heard the familiar voice answer him.

"Hurry! I'm almotht under!"

Jonathan ran to the staircase. Water was gushing over the edge, bubbling and frothing. He leapt down the stairs, pushed along by the river of water, and came to a splashing stop at the bottom, his head going under but his arm stretched high to keep the candle out of the water.

He quickly got his footing. The water came up to his waist.

Colin's head and neck were all that stuck up above the water. His eyes were wide and terrified. The water was rising fast enough to see it; even as Jonathan stood there, frozen with fear, it rose and lapped at Colin's chin.

"Untie me!" he begged, his voice high and panicked. "Hurry! Pleath!"

Jonathan hurried over, the water sloshing around his belly button. The ropes were underwater. He looked at his candle, then into Colin's eyes.

"We're gonna have to get out of here in the dark," he said.

Colin was stretching his neck up, the water now splashing against his mouth.

"Fine!" he gurgled. "Hurry!"

Jonathan dropped the candle and matches. The room was plunged into darkness.

His fingers fumbled under the water. They were cold and stiff. He found the ropes and pulled at them, jerking and tugging. They were tight and wet, swollen even tighter by the water. He worked his fingers into one of the loops and managed to pull it loose. He began tugging at another loop.

"Hurry u—" Colin started to beg, before his words were cut off by a wet gurgle.

"Colin?"

There was no answer, except a frantic moaning. Jonathan lifted one hand and felt in the darkness for Colin's face. The water was above his mouth now. His head was tilted back so that his nose just barely rose above the waterline.

Jonathan yanked and wrestled frantically with the knots. There was a surge of water. He felt the water level rise suddenly, up to his stooped shoulder. Colin's moans grew more desperate, but quieter. Jonathan felt with his hand again.

The water had risen over Colin's face.

He let go of the ropes and wrapped his arms around Colin's bound body. With all his strength he lifted him, chair and all, above the water. He heard Colin gasp and cough. The water was still rising. It was to Jonathan's ribs now.

"I'm gonna have to put you back down now," he said. "Take a deep breath." Colin sucked in a great gasping breath. Jonathan dropped him and reached for the ropes. Colin's whole head was underwater, and the ropes were too deep for Jonathan to reach without going under himself. He gulped a huge lungful of air and ducked beneath the surface.

He loosened another loop. Then another. He pulled a long stretch of rope through. The rope was mostly slack now, with one stubborn knot left tight against Colin's wrists. He pulled and tugged and got one loop loose before he ran out of air. He could feel Colin kicking and fighting in the water.

Jonathan wrapped his arms around Colin and picked him up again.

They both panted and gasped and choked. The water was to Jonathan's shoulders.

"This is it," he said. "I'll get it this time."

"You have to," Colin sputtered.

"I will." Jonathan readied himself for another drop into the water.

"Jonathan!" Colin said quickly, stopping him. "If you can't get it, jutht go. You can make it out yourthelf."

Jonathan took a couple more heaving breaths.

"Shut up, Colin. And take a deep breath."

They dropped together beneath the surface.

CHAPTER TWENTY-EIGHT
SAVED

The ropes were stubborn. The water was cold, and dark, and determined. Colin fought and thrashed against his ties. His closed-mouth screaming rang dull and frantic under the black water.

Jonathan's fingers and arms burned with exhaustion. His lungs screamed for air.

He felt the burning in his arms and gritted his teeth. His lungs begged him to swim to the surface, to air, but he held tight to the ropes and worked at the knots.

I can do it, he told himself. Even his mind's voice was breathless and terrified. *I can save her!* He shook his head and slid his fingers between the taut ropes. *I can save him*, he corrected himself. *I can.*

His fingers slid through. He hooked them around the last loop and pulled. It hung for a moment, stuck, then slid loose and the rope went slack and Colin shook his arms free and they both kicked up to the surface.

They tread water for a few ravenous breaths. He'd done it. He'd saved him. Tears were hot in Jonathan's eyes. He wasn't sure why. Relief, maybe.

His head bumped something hard and he jerked when he realized it was the ceiling.

"We've gotta get out of here!" he shouted. "Follow me."

They swam through the complete blackness toward the doorway. The water was still flowing down the staircase, pushing them back into the room, trapping them in the rising water.

"Grab the wall with your fingers!" he hollered over his shoulder. "You can hold on to the cracks between the blocks!"

He pulled himself block by block up the staircase, against the current, kicking with his legs. His fingers and arms ached but he made it, finally hooking his hands around the edge of the upper doorway. The water was only shoulder deep there and he was able to brace his feet against the doorway and help pull Colin into the corridor.

They stood for just a moment to catch their breath.

"Do you know how to get back?" Colin asked. "Without any light?"

"I think so." Jonathan started off, wading through the water, feeling the walls with his fingers.

"Hey," Colin said, reaching out to stop him. "Thankth for coming back for me. For thaving me."

"No problem." Jonathan thought about the swim still ahead, past the Hatch. The water was even higher now. "But I'd save your thanks. We're not out of the woods yet."

They made their way through the twisting blackness. Jonathan ran through the mental map in his mind, retracing the path he'd taken three times now, negotiating turns and stairwells and pitch-black hallways. As they rose, the water got more shallow. Eventually, they could move quickly, with the water only splashing around their ankles.

Jonathan led them confidently down a corridor and started to turn, then stopped. Colin bumped into his back.

"Wait," he said. "I need to warn him."

"Warn who?"

Jonathan chewed on his lip. The water was still rising. Time was running out. They needed to get back. But he knew he had to.

"Follow me," he said, and then turned and walked the other way. He knew exactly where he was now and he moved quickly, anticipating stairs before he got to them and turning corners confidently. Colin struggled to keep up.

"Where are we going?"

Jonathan stopped, gasping for breath. He could hear, all around him, rats splashing and flailing in the briny floodwaters.

"There," he answered, pointing up ahead at the thin line of light gleaming just below the water, shining from under a closed door.

They jogged forward and Jonathan knocked urgently on the door.

It swung open.

"Ah," the librarian said. "You've come back." His hair was wet, stuck down to his head and over his face in a stringy mess. Wind whistled in the room behind him, tossing a blizzard of pages and papers around in the air. Ninety-Nine shivered on his shoulder, his pink tail dangling down the old man's chest. Even soaking wet, the rat looked huge. Colin gasped and took a step back.

"Please. Come in. We can find you. Another book."

CHAPTER TWENTY-NINE
A LUNATIC (NOT AN IDIOT)

The library, always so neat and dry and dustless, was in shambles.

The storm had shattered the windows here, too. Rain and wind howled and blustered inside, soaking the books and ripping out pages and leaving puddles on the floor and bookshelves.

"We've gotta go," Jonathan blurted out, taking a step inside. "And you've got to come with us."

"Oh," the librarian answered calmly, turning and walking slowly into his wrecked library. "I don't. Think so. What kind of book. Would you like?"

"No, *really*, we've all gotta go. This is a hurricane. The whole place is flooded. The island's going under."

The librarian stopped. He turned and looked at Jonathan in his hunched, twisted way. A small smile rose, just barely, to his lips.

"Yes," he replied. "I know. It's the sea. Come at last. To claim her own."

"Then come on! We've got to get out! To higher ground!"

The librarian chuckled.

"Yes," he said. "You do. The sea. Is coming." He reached up and stroked Ninety-Nine's dripping fur. "But I. Am staying."

"You'll die," Jonathan insisted.

The librarian shrugged.

"I have lived. Long enough. I have never left. This island. Where else. Would I go?"

Jonathan shook his head and stammered.

"No . . . but . . . but . . ."

The librarian turned and looked out at the storm through his narrow, shattered windows.

"You must take the other boys. Higher. To the only part of Slabhenge. That will last."

"What? Where is that?"

"The old lighthouse. Up, up. Up. Above the Admiral's room. The lighthouse was here. First. Before the asylum. Before the school. It is built on the original stone. The true stone. Of the old island. The rest"—the librarian spread his arms to include the windswept stone structure around him—"the rest is all built on sand. But the lighthouse. Will stand."

"Come on, Jonathan," Colin whispered behind him. "We have to go."

Jonathan cocked his head. There was something the librarian had said that stuck in his mind. *You must take the other boys.*

"You know," he said, looking the librarian in the eyes. "You know about the Admiral. About the grown-ups."

The man's small smile grew just a bit.

"I am a lunatic. Not an idiot. I go at night. To the kitchen. It's been terribly messy." The librarian paused, working his fingers into Ninety-Nine's fur. Ninety-Nine closed his eyes and leaned back into the scratching finger. "And ice cream is my favorite food. It's kept. In the freezer. Of course."

"We didn't kill them. It was lightning. They were all outside, standing in a puddle. The Admiral had his sword in the air."

"Hmm," the librarian said thoughtfully. "The Admiral *was* a madman. Standing around in a puddle. Holding a metal sword in the air. During a lightning storm." He pursed his lips and shrugged. "Sounds about right. For him."

The librarian nodded, then looked to the nearest shelf. "Now. You must go. Quickly. So we need to choose. A book."

"No, I—can't really take one. We have to swim to get back. It'll get wet."

The librarian clucked his tongue, his eyes still on the books' spines.

"All of these books. Will be at the bottom of the sea. Very soon. And you cannot leave a library. Without a book. Ah. Here. This one."

The old man pulled a book off the shelf. It was thick and bound in soft black leather.

"*Moby-Dick*. The story of a madman. Lost at sea. He dies in a storm. The hero is the only one who lives." The librarian handed the book to Jonathan and squinted up sideways at him. "I don't think. That is what will happen here. No. You will save them, Jonathan. Now go. To the lighthouse."

Jonathan breathed quickly through his nose.

"Are you sure—"

"Oh. Yes. Go."

Jonathan looked into the librarian's eyes.

"Thank you," he said.

"Mmm."

Jonathan turned to go.

"Wait. There is one thing. You could do. For me."

"What?"

The librarian reached up and plucked the monstrous rat from his shoulder. He pressed his lips for a long moment into the rodent's neck, then held him out with two hands toward Jonathan.

"Take Ninety-Nine. With you. You could save him. Like the others."

Jonathan gulped. The rat looked at him with curious, shiny eyes. He didn't hiss or snarl.

Jonathan handed *Moby-Dick* to Colin and reached out reluctantly to take the offered animal. Ninety-Nine was surprisingly soft. And predictably heavy.

The rat sniffed for a second at Jonathan's hands, then scrambled gently up to perch on his shoulder.

The librarian watched. His eyes were wet and glowing.

"Yes," he said. "You can save him. And maybe. When you're home. Find him a wife."

Jonathan nodded.

"Sure. A nice big wife."

"Yes. That's right. Now. Off you go. Take a candle. I won't. Be needing them."

Colin grabbed a candle from atop the closest bookshelf and the two boys ran out into the corridor. Jonathan looked back once to see the librarian standing in the doorway with the door wide open. He was lit from behind by a few flickering candles, his hair whipped about by the wind. Rats were swarming through the open door by his feet, seeking the light and relative dryness of the library. Several of them had no tails. The old man made no move to stop them. He wouldn't die alone.

Jonathan followed the light of Colin's candle through the hallways. The water was above their ankles. They arrived panting at the stairs that led down past the Hatch. The water was much higher now than it had been when Jonathan came before. It was rising and falling and swirling, lapping at the very top step. It would be a longer swim this time. And now he had a rat.

"What do we do?"

"We swim, Colin. That's how I got through. Just a quick dip, down and then up again. No big deal."

"What about the candle?"

"Don't worry about it. There's a lit lantern on the other side. Just take a deep breath."

Jonathan handed Ninety-Nine over before Colin could think to push it away. He dropped *Moby-Dick* with a splash at his feet.

"I can't believe I'm doing this," Jonathan said. He tucked his shirt into his pants tightly, then unbuttoned the top two buttons. Taking the rat back from Colin, he slid him into his shirt against his bare skin. He rebuttoned his shirt. The rat scratched and writhed against his body, squeaking and squirming.

"Come on. Before he chews through my stomach."

Without thinking Jonathan dove headfirst, pushing off the top step as hard as he could to rocket himself through the water. As soon as the cold water hit them, Ninety-Nine went crazy. He tore and fought and twisted. Jonathan gritted his teeth and swam as hard as he could, pawing and kicking at the black water. He didn't slow down when an upwelling of water pressed him against the ceiling. He didn't slow when the rat's teeth sank into his skin. He didn't slow when he saw, through the salty murk, the glow of lantern light up ahead. He didn't slow until his feet found the far stairs and his head broke into air and he stepped up out of the water.

He climbed a few steps up. Ninety-Nine was shaking and coughing inside his shirt. He struggled weakly against the wet fabric. Jonathan unbuttoned his shirt and pulled the bedraggled rat out. Ninety-Nine coughed up some water and then slowly crawled back up to Jonathan's shoulder, his body shaking. Jonathan gave him a reassuring scratch.

Colin's head popped up into the stairwell, gasping for air. Jonathan helped him up the slippery stairs, pulling the lantern from the hook.

They stood panting, eyes on the dark water they'd emerged from.

232

"Well," Colin gasped. "That wathn't tho—"

His words were cut off by a wrenching, grating crack from below the water's surface. A great rush of huge bubbles rose to the surface, and with a sickening whoosh, the water began to rise more quickly. So quickly they could see it climbing and racing up the stairs in a rapid, steady surge.

"What happened?" Colin cried, stumbling backward up the stairs.

"I don't know! I think something else just broke open! We gotta go!"

The water rose up the stairs faster than they could climb, nearly overtaking them before they reached the top. By the time they broke out into the hallway, the water was a surging wave that came nearly to their waists.

Together they ran through the familiar hallways they both knew, winding back toward the dining room. The dark wall of water gurgled just behind them, slurping at the walls and sloshing around corners. Ninety-Nine clung to Jonathan's shoulders with a firm grip of his claws. His tail slapped on Jonathan's back as they ran.

They burst into the dining room just ahead of the wave.

They almost ran into Sebastian and the rest of the boys. They were all crowded around the door, holding lanterns and candles. Sebastian was at the front, his sword out in front of him and a coil of rope thrown over his shoulder, a dark look on his face.

CHAPTER THIRTY
HOME

The wave of water was slowed when it hit the narrow doorway. It crested and poured into the dining room, a frothy white head of bubbles at its top. Colin and Jonathan braced themselves as it hit their backs. Some of the boys who weren't ready were knocked off their feet and sent tumbling head over heels in the water.

The water pouring in from the doorway leveled out as the water in the room rose, until it all stood flat, above their knees. And still slowly rising. The boys regathered themselves, coughing and rubbing the water out of their eyes.

Sebastian had never lost his footing. He still stood with his sword, eyes on Jonathan.

"We were just about to leave," he said.

"Where were you guys going?"

Sebastian looked him in the eye.

"We were coming to find you."

"Really?"

Sebastian shrugged and nodded.

"Yeah."

"Oh. Thanks."

Sebastian shrugged again, then squinted and looked closer at Jonathan. "Jesus! What is that thing on your shoulder?"

"It's a rat. Don't worry about it. We gotta go. Quick. Or we're all gonna die."

"Go where?"

"To the lighthouse."

"What lighthouse?"

"I'll explain as we go. We've gotta move."

Jonathan started to brush past him, but Sebastian put a hand out and stopped him. Forcefully.

"Easy, Johnny. I didn't want to get blamed for you dying. Doesn't mean I want you in charge. We decided to stay here, where it's safe."

"It isn't safe here, Sebastian. This whole place is going under. The water's rising. And the island is sinking. We've got to go. Up."

"Up? It's safer down here," Sebastian insisted.

"What if the tower blows over?" Gerald asked.

"What if lightning hits it?" Francis demanded.

"Going up is our only choice!" Jonathan insisted. "It's the only way to save ourselves."

"You can't trust him!" Benny's voice was ugly and hissing. "You know what he's here for!"

Lightning flashed through the windows. The wind was a roar, swirling around them. Jonathan saw the boys' faces harden at Benny's words, saw the doubt flicker in their eyes.

"You're wrong, Benny!" Jonathan said, his voice rising with the pounding of his heart and the raging of the storm. "You *can* trust me! My sister . . . she . . . she *did* die in a fire, and . . . but . . ." Jonathan stopped, his voice choked by tears.

"But you didn't thtart it," Colin finished. "Did you?"

"Stop it, Colin," Jonathan said.

But Colin didn't stop.

"You told me, Jonathan. You told me she took your matcheth."

Jonathan swallowed. Took a choking breath. He looked into Colin's face. Colin's eyes widened.

"Oh," he breathed. "It wath *her*, wathn't it? Your thithter thtarted the fire."

"Shut up, Colin."

"And you took the blame. You let them think it wath you. Becauth—"

"Because it's my fault!" Jonathan interrupted, shouting. "They were my matches! She learned from me!" Jonathan's voice broke off, his shoulders shaking with sobs. Ninety-Nine's claws dug in harder to stay on. Jonathan closed his eyes against his tears and lowered his head. "It's my fault."

He heard, through the storm and his own sadness, the sound of someone splashing toward him. Two hands, gentle as birds, came to rest on his arm. They worked at the buttons of his sleeves, then pulled the fabric up to his elbows. Jonathan didn't fight.

"How did you get the thcars?" Colin asked.

Jonathan didn't answer.

"How did you get the thcars?" Colin asked again. Then, in a whisper so low only Jonathan could hear it, he added, "Tell them, Jonathan. If you tell them, they'll believe you. They'll follow you. You can thave them."

Jonathan took one breath. Then two. He opened his eyes. He lifted his head.

"I didn't start the fire," he said. The words came out scratchy and faint. He cleared his throat and started again, his voice ringing clear into the faces of the lost boys around him, and into his own ears. "I didn't start the fire. I woke up. And I heard her screaming. And I ran downstairs. But . . . the fire was too big. Too hot. I couldn't get to her. I tried. I tried so hard." He held up his arms. The scar tissue, twisted and tough, flashed whitely in the lightning. "I tried until the firefighters got there and dragged me away. I did everything I could to save her." He realized he was shouting, as much to himself as to the watching boys. "I did everything I could!"

Tears joined the seawater on his face. Warm tears, clean and true.

Walter walked up to him and put a hand on his shoulder.

"It's okay, man," he said. "It's okay."

Jonathan took a long, steadying breath. He nodded a thank-you to Walter, and to Colin. Then he looked up at all the other boys. The Scars.

"We've got to get to the only part of this place that's built on rock. The only part that isn't going to wash away. We've got to get to the old lighthouse."

His words hung like a tattered flag in the windswept room.

"He's telling the truth," a deep voice interjected. They all turned and looked to where Patrick sat, still tied to his chair but now atop one of the dining room tables. "About the lighthouse. There did used to be one here. Going way back now, to the old sailing days. It's built on the stones, indeed."

Jonathan looked at Sebastian.

"We need to go, Sebastian."

Sebastian's jaw was clenched. His chest was heaving with shallow breaths. He looked down to the water around his thighs, then up at Patrick.

"What about your boat?" he asked.

Patrick shook his head.

"No way. Too late for that. I barely made it out here, and the storm's only gotten stronger."

Sebastian bit at his lip. His eyes cut to Jonathan. He nodded.

Jonathan blew out a deep breath. He nodded back. Then he turned to Roger and Gregory.

"Cut him loose," he said. "And all of you, follow me."

Without waiting for an answer, Jonathan waded through the waist-deep water past Sebastian, past the waiting boys, toward the staircase that led up toward Sebastian's room. The Admiral's room. The lighthouse.

Colin followed him. Ninety-Nine clung to Jonathan's shoulder.

When he got to the stairwell, he stopped and turned. The boys were filing after him. All of them. They looked lost and frightened in the raging wind and the flashbulb lightning. They were drenched and exhausted and terrified. They needed to be saved.

Sebastian was up on the table. Sawing at Patrick's ropes with his sword. He didn't look terrifying. He looked like a confused kid, finding his way through the dark.

Jonathan felt something bump him, and looked down. It was a piece of the ruined Sinner's Sorrow, bobbing in the water. Several more pieces floated around him. He picked up a piece.

"Everyone grab a piece," he said. "We're gonna need the wood."

The storm was like a beast hammering at Slabhenge. Even running up the stone stairwell, they could hear it outside, through the walls, howling to be let in.

Jonathan ran past the doors to the grown-ups' rooms, past the locked door to the Admiral's office, to the far, dark end of the hall. The end of the hallway was a curved wall, crumbling with age. It was made of a different stone than the rest of Slabhenge. Bigger blocks of grayer rock, rock that looked even older than the rock Jonathan had grown used to being surrounded by.

In the curved wall of ancient stone was a door made of tremendously thick slats of dark wood bound together with rusty iron. The door looked like it hadn't been opened in years. Instead of a knob, it simply had a metal latch, like a pirate's treasure chest, that connected to a bolt on the stone wall. Jonathan yanked on the latch, and it opened with a protesting creak of rusty metal that had been wet and unused for too long. He pushed on the door and it swung slowly open.

Beyond the door was a round stairwell, leading up in one direction and down in the other. Its walls and stairs were made of the same gray rock. The air smelled stale. Dusty. Forgotten. It was even colder in the stairwell than it was in the rest of the school.

The boys piled up behind Jonathan.

"Up," he said. "We've got to go up."

They raced up the stairs, taking them two at a time. Round and round the stairwell spiraled, up and up through dank darkness, with all the dark world raging outside the walls.

Jonathan reached the top breathless. Colin was behind him, then the rest. Sebastian was the last, behind Patrick.

The top of the tower was a round room. On all sides were windows, sturdy double-paned glass crisscrossed by metal bars. The lightning filled the sky all around them. They were surrounded by the storm, teetering in the angry heavens. On all sides were windows to the black clouds and whipping wind and sideways rain.

In the middle of the room, on a raised stone landing, was a great black iron bowl, big enough for Jonathan to have stretched out and lain down in. A massive curved mirror stood on the far side of the bowl, mounted on a mechanism of gears and bars and wheels that circled the bowl. To Jonathan's right was a large metal handle.

"The lighthouse," Jonathan whispered. "Just like he said."

The boys stood in silence, looking out the windows at the hurricane that raged all around them, inches away. It was almost deafening.

They could see all of Slabhenge when the lightning flashed. The courtyard, flooded now halfway up the windows into the dining room. The boat still rocked between the walls.

They could see the roof that covered the rest of the school, rising and falling with the confusing ramblings of the mazelike building. They could see the other towers poking stubbornly up into the black skies.

"Look!" Miguel shouted over the storm. "Look at the towers!"

They all crowded to the windows.

"What?"

"What about them?"

"There's only three! One's missing!"

They all looked and saw it then. The far tower was gone. Simply gone. They could see where the stone walls led to the space that it should occupy, but the walls stopped in a jagged, sawtooth break. A loose pile of stones was all that remained of the tower, avalanching down into the white-capped sea.

Jonathan looked at Colin. Colin was staring at the pile of

rubble with wide eyes. It was Colin's tower. The tower with his mattress and his papers and his three lonely candlesticks. Somewhere among those waves bobbed dozens of white paper cranes. And a few shiny gold chocolate wrappers.

"There! Look at the gate!"

They all spun back to the courtyard with its ghostly boat. The far side, with the watery stairs and the gate through which they had all entered Slabhenge, was crumbling before their eyes. The arch above the gate crashed into the water with a massive splash. The gigantic waves poured relentlessly through the gap, pushing and pulling at the hundred-year-old walls. They fell apart, stone block by stone block, as the water coursed through. Soon the whole wall was gone, a heaped mound of stones just below the water's surface. The courtyard was left with walls on only three sides.

With the one wall gone, the waves rushed unhindered into the courtyard, rising above the level of the dining room windows. It wouldn't be long before the rest of the walls succumbed to the ravenous, storm-fueled waters of the sea.

"The whole dining room's under now," Walter said, his voice hollow with shock.

"The kitchen," Tony said.

"The freezer," David added. They all stood and stared.

"We should light the lighthouse," Jonathan said, watching Slabhenge fall apart. No one heard him over the wind and the thunder and their own openmouthed amazement.

"We should light the lighthouse!" Jonathan shouted, and stricken faces turned toward him.

"Why?"

"So they know we're here!" he answered. "So they send help!" He looked into Colin's eyes, then Walter's, then Patrick's. "I want to go home." His voice cracked at the end and got lost in the mad confusion of noise. He said it again, from the bottom of his lungs. "I want to go home!"

"If ye light it, they'll know to come!" Patrick yelled from behind them. "When they can, anyway! This old thing ain't been fired up since before I was born! They'll notice it for sure, and they'll know to come!"

Jonathan ran to a large wooden bin that lined one of the walls and threw open the lid with all his strength.

Inside, neatly stacked, were rows of split logs. Firewood. Stowed, dry and safe. By a man who began as a madhouse baby and ended as a forgotten librarian. In between, though, he was a lighthouse keeper.

"We need paper!" he shouted, turning to face the group.

"The school office is underwater by now!" Benny yelled back.

"What about the Admiral's room?"

They all looked at Sebastian. He shook his head.

"None in there! He didn't even have a book!"

Jonathan's mind flashed. "The Admiral's office!"

"It's locked, remember?"

Jonathan smiled. He reached into his pocket and pulled out the rusty metal key that had fallen out of the dead Admiral's jacket. Sebastian's mouth dropped open.

"Come on," Jonathan said to him, tossing his piece of the Sinner's Sorrow into the great iron bowl. "The rest of you, get the wood in the fire pit!" He took the lantern from Colin, then pulled Ninety-Nine gently from his shoulder and handed him to Colin. Colin grimaced and held him with two hands, out away from his body.

Jonathan and Sebastian ran back down the lighthouse stairs. When they got to the old door, Jonathan swore.

There was an inch of water running like a river down the stairwell, pouring in from the hallway. The water was even higher than he'd imagined. It was already to the second story.

"We've gotta hurry," he said to Sebastian. "This whole place is gonna fill up and fall down."

They bolted down the hall, their feet splashing through the rushing water. At the door to the Admiral's office, Jonathan held the lantern up and stabbed the key into the lock. It clicked into place. Then turned. He shouldered the door open and they ran inside. The water rushed in with them.

The office was lost in shadows, but Jonathan remembered it vividly from that first, awful night. The Admiral's sneering voice, his demonic eyebrows. The pain of the Sinner's Sorrow. The letter home, full of lies. The Admiral's acidic words as he'd read Jonathan's paperwork: *You have done terrible things, haven't you, Jonathan Grisby?*

Jonathan walked straight over to the standing file behind the desk where he'd seen the Admiral tuck his folder. He pulled it open. Inside were neatly ordered, identical manila folders, each stuffed with papers. He didn't have to count to know there were sixteen files. On the tab of the first folder was scrawled his own name. His eyes scanned the rest. *Colin Kerrigan. Sebastian Mortimer.* And thirteen more.

He set the lantern down and grabbed half of the folders, then handed them to Sebastian. He tucked the other half under his arm and picked up the lantern.

"This should be enough," he said, and they darted back out into the hallway. The water was even higher now. Jonathan winced and dodged a dead rat being washed down the hallway. Another one bobbed by, paws stuck out stiff into the air.

At the top of the lighthouse, the other boys and Patrick had half the wood piled in the big metal bowl with the ravaged remains of the Sinner's Sorrow. They stood waiting on the raised platform around it, looking out at the world gone mad. Jonathan glanced quickly and counted the towers. Another had fallen. Only two were still standing. And the lighthouse. Another of the courtyard's walls was mostly gone.

Jonathan looked at the name on the top file in his hands. *Walter Holcomb.* He handed the folder to Walter. *Reginald*

Miller the next one said, and he gave it to Reggie. Sebastian started to do the same.

Eventually, Jonathan was left with one folder in his hands. *Jonathan Grisby*, it said. He opened it and words from the top page jumped out at him. *Guilty. Criminal. Arson.* He ground his teeth together and crumpled the paper into a ball. He stepped forward and shoved it under the waiting pile of wood.

He looked at the second sheet. More words swam up through the darkness and lightning. *Death. Sophia. Injuries. Grief. Guilt.* Tears scalded his eyes. His lungs shivered as they breathed.

He wadded the paper up into a tight ball. As tight as his fists could manage. And he added it to the unlit fire.

Around him, other boys started to do the same. Amidst the roar of wind and storm came the sound of ripping paper, of crumpling files. And all around the circle, fuel was added to the lighthouse fire.

Eventually, they all stood, hands clean and empty. Beneath the ready logs was tucked a white mound of twisted paper. A crumpled pile of crimes. A bonfire's worth of guilt and punishment and dark history.

Sebastian took a candle from another boy's hand. He leaned forward. But he stopped, the candle's flame inches from the paper.

He frowned. He leaned back. He looked at Jonathan. Lightning flickered, showing his flooded eyes.

"I don't want to go," he said.

Jonathan blinked and didn't answer.

"You wanna know why I never wrote letters?" Sebastian asked. "Because there was no one to send them to. I got no parents. I got no family. I've spent my whole life in places like this. Or orphanages. Group homes. Foster homes." He looked out at the storm that was pressed in all around them, screaming and pounding the windows. "I don't have anyone to read my letters. No one cares. I got no one to write to."

Jonathan swallowed and took a step closer to Sebastian.

"You can write to me," he said.

Sebastian's eyebrows furrowed. His mouth opened, but he didn't say anything.

"You can write to me," Gerald said.

"You can write to me, man," Walter called out.

"You can write to me, Thebathtian," Colin said, just loud enough to be heard.

Sebastian sniffed. He nodded, looking around, then rubbed his eyes with his sleeve.

"Light the fire," Jonathan said. Sebastian nodded again, one more small nod, then stretched the candle out and touched it to the nearest paper. Other boys stepped forward then with their own candles, holding the flames to the papers closest to themselves.

Climbing fingers of flames crept up through the criss-crossed wood. The papers flared and burned into bright flashes of yellow. The boys stepped back and covered their eyes.

There was a crackle and a snap as a piece of wood caught fire. A couple of wisping sparks rose up and flickered out.

The sound of the fire grew louder, the light brighter, the flames higher, the heat hotter. The boys stepped down from the platform and back to the lower floor. The room grew warm. Their soaking clothes steamed in the heat.

With a final flurry of crackling, the whole pile caught fire. Flames arced and danced six feet high. The round room, hemmed in on all sides by the stormy world's fury, grew brighter than daylight. Jonathan stepped to the metal hand crank and muscled it into motion. With a shuddering, squeaking creak the gears and wheels attached to the mirror sprang to reluctant life. The mirror began to slowly rotate around the towering flames of their signal fire, magnifying and reflecting the light out into the clouds, the storm, the world.

Sebastian joined him at the crank and they worked together. The mirror moved faster, sending its spear of light out into the darkness.

After a while, Jonathan let go and stepped back, sweating and gasping. Another boy took his place.

He leaned back against a low wall beneath the windows. His arms were burning, the good burning of muscles put to good use. The room was filled with the vital heat of the fire he had built and lit, the fire that would save them all. A good heat, the kind that calms shivers and warms the chill from wet and tired bones. The fire felt good.

He closed his eyes and didn't try to stop the tears that seeped out between his eyelids, running in warm paths down his face. They ran down his cheeks and over his lips, which opened into a wide smile, tasting their saltiness. He laughed as the tears poured from his eyes.

Colin walked over and stood beside him. The giant rat still sat on his shoulder, sniffing at the smoky air.

"Why are you laughing like that?" he asked.

Jonathan laughed and sobbed and looked at the beautiful fire through the blur of his tears.

"Because I want to go home," he answered.

"Then why are you crying?"

Jonathan didn't wipe at the tears. He let them burn in his eyes until they were full and flooded out.

"Because I want to go home," he said. "Because I want to go home."

ACKNOWLEDGMENTS

As always, there are far too many people to thank and recognize. I feel so grateful and lucky to be surrounded, both professionally and personally, by so many many people who support, help, encourage, and inspire me.

My family, who cheers me on more than they probably ought to. Karen, Eva, Ella, Claire, Mom, Dad, Erin, Justin, Grandma, Noni, Bops, Brian, Linda, Michelle, and Michael. Love you all.

My friends, who lift me up but keep me grounded. Jabez, James, Carver, Andy, Tim, Kat, Jen, Pat, and Aubrey.

My agent, Pam Howell, and Bob DiForio, who always have my back.

My amazing editor, Nick, whose judgment and wisdom make all my stories better, and to all the tremendous folks at Scholastic: Jeffrey, David, Emily, Lizette, Reedy, Sheila Marie, and all the rest. I'm so over-the-top lucky to be with such an amazing team. And a special shout-out to Nina Goffi, the cover designer who has given my stories such beautiful faces to show to the world.

To the wonderful educators I'm so lucky to work with at Mission View Elementary and the Wenatchee School District. There are too many of you to name, but you are an inspiration and a force of incredible good in the world and I'm blessed to know you.

To all the fellow writers I've been fortunate to meet and connect with over the past couple years; it's been a thrill to get to know you, and the world is richer for having your stories. Your dedication to storytelling has inspired and strengthened my own.

To all the good folks at NaNoWriMo . . . *Scar Island* began as my first NaNo project several years ago, and look at it now! Thanks for supporting writers and writing, dreamers and dreaming, and a mad month of marvelous imaginings.

"It is incredibly rare and spectacular to find an author who possesses the literary talent to transport us so completely and persuasively to an utterly foreign realm. . . . Disturbing and provocative."   —*The Jewish Journal*

"Boianjiu is a writer who should be talked about for literary reasons, not the least of which is that her stories refuse to submit to moral clichés."   —*The Times of Israel*

"Carefully wrought, consciously structured, creatively imagined."   —*The New Republic*

"The term 'a distinct new voice in literature' had become a cliché long before Shani Boianjiu was born, but there is no better way to describe her unique, piercing tone. Reading it feels like having your heart sawn in two by a very dull knife. *The People of Forever Are Not Afraid* is one of those rare books that truly make you want to cry but at the same time doesn't allow you to."   —ETGAR KERET, author of *The Nimrod Flipout*

"This is big literature—the realism that nests inside the word surrealism."
     —RIVKA GALCHEN, author of *Atmospheric Disturbances*

"Shani Boianjiu is an enormous new talent. This is one of the boldest debuts I can think of—it reads like it was written in bullets, tear gas, road flares, and love."
     —ALEXANDER CHEE, author of *Edinburgh*

"I was hooked on Shani Boianjiu's remarkable voice from the first sentence of this book. It's urgent, funny, horrifying, fresh; the kind of thing I've been dying to read for ages."
     —MIRIAM TOEWS, author of *Irma Voth* and *A Complicated Kindness*

The People of Forever
Are Not Afraid

SHANI

BOIANJIU

HOGARTH
London New York

The People of Forever Are Not Afraid

A NOVEL

Copyright © 2012, 2013 by Shani Boianjiu
Reader's Guide copyright © 2013 by Random House, Inc.

All rights reserved.
Published in the United States by Hogarth, an imprint of the Crown Publishing Group, a division of Random House, Inc., New York.
www.crownpublishing.com

HOGARTH is a trademark of the Random House Group Limited, and the H colophon is a trademark of Random House, Inc.

"Extra Libris" and the accompanying colophon are trademarks of Random House, Inc.

Originally published in hardcover in the United States by Hogarth, an imprint of the Crown Publishing Group, a division of Random House, Inc., New York, in 2012.

Portions of this work were previously published in *The New Yorker, Vice* magazine, and *Zoetrope*.

Library of Congress Cataloging-in-Publication Data
Boianjiu, Shani, 1987–
    The people of forever are not afraid : a novel /
Shani Boianjiu.—1st ed.
        p. cm.
    1. Military education—Israel—Fiction. 2. Women
soldiers—Israel—Fiction. 3. Coming of age—Fiction.
4. Female friendship—Fiction. I. Title.
PR9510.9.B66P46 2012
823'.92—dc23   2012008962

ISBN 978-0-307-95597-5
eISBN 978-0-307-95596-8

Printed in the United States of America

BOOK DESIGN BY BARBARA STURMAN
COVER DESIGN BY ELENA GIAVALDI
COVER PHOTOGRAPHY: RACHEL PAPO

10 9 8 7 6 5 4 3 2 1

First Paperback Edition

The People of Forever
Are Not Afraid

I

Other
People's
Children

History Is Almost Over

There is dust in this caravan of a classroom, and Mira the teacher's hair is fake orange and scorched at the tips. We are seniors now, seventeen, and we have almost finished all of Israeli history. We finished the history of the world in tenth grade. In our textbook, the pages already speak to us of 1982, just a few years before we were born, just a year before this town was built, when there were only pine trees and garbage hills here by the Lebanese border. The words of Mira the teacher, who is also Avishag's mother, almost touch the secret ones of all our parents in their drunken evenings.

History is almost over.

"There are going to be eight definitions in the Peace of the Galilee War quiz next Friday, and there is nothing we haven't covered. PLO, SAM, IAF, RPG children," Mira says. I am pretty sure I know all the terms, except for maybe RPG children. I am not as good with definitions that have real words in them. They scare me a little.

But I don't care about this quiz. I will almost swear; I don't care one bit.

I still have my sandwich waiting for me in my backpack. It has tomatoes and mayo and mustard and salt and nothing more. The best part is that my mother puts it inside a plastic bag and then she wraps it in blue napkins and it takes about two minutes to unwrap it. That way even if it is a day when I am not hungry I can wait for something. That's something, and I can keep from screaming.

It has been eight years since I discovered mustard-mayo-tomato.

I snap my fingers under my jaw. I roll my eyes. I grind my teeth. I have been doing these things since I was little, sitting in class. I can't do this for much longer. My teeth hurt.

Forty minutes till recess, but I can't keep sitting here, and I can't and I won't and I—

How They Make Airplanes

"PLO, SAM, IAF, RPG children," Mira the teacher says. "Who wants to practice reading some definitions out loud before the quiz?"

SAM is some sort of Syrian submarine. And IAF is the Israeli Air Force. I know what children are, and that RPG children were children who tried to shoot RPGs at our soldiers and ended up burning each other because they were uninformed, and children. But that might be a repetitive definition. Last time the bitch took off five points because she said

I used the word "very" seven times in the same definition and that I used it in places where you can't really use "very."

She is looking at me, or at Avishag, who is sitting next to me, or at Lea, who is sitting next to her. She sighs. I think she needs to have very corrective eye surgery. Lea shoots a look right back, as if she is convinced Mira was looking at her. She always thinks everyone must be looking at her.

"Can you at least pretend to be writing this down, Yael?" Mira asks me and sits down behind her desk.

I pull my eyes away from Lea. I pick up the pen and write:

when are we going to stop thinking about things that don't matter and start thinking about things that do matter? fuck me raw

I have to go to the bathroom. Outside the classroom caravan there is the bathroom caravan. When I stand on top of the closed toilet and press my nose against the tiny window, I can see the end of the village and breathe the bleach they use to clean this forsaken window till I am dizzy. I can see houses and gardens and mothers of babies on benches, all scattered like Lego parts abandoned by a giant child at the side of the cement road leading to the brown mountains sleeping ahead. Right outside the gates of the school, I see a young man. He is wearing a brown shirt and his skin is light brown and he could almost disappear on this mountain if it weren't for his green eyes, two leaves in the middle of this nothing.

It's Dan. My Dan. Avishag's brother.

I am almost sure.

When I come back to class from the bathroom, I see that someone has written in the old, fat notebook, right below my question. Avishag and I have been writing in notebooks to each other since second grade. For a while we kept the stories we wrote with Lea when we all played Exquisite Corpse in a notebook too, but by seventh grade Lea had stopped playing with us, or with any of her old friends. She started collecting girls, pets, instead, to do as she said. Avishag said the two of us should still write in a notebook, even though two people can't play Exquisite Corpse. She said the notebooks are something we can keep around longer than notes on loose leaf and that this way, when we're eighteen, we'll be able to look back and remember all the people who loved us back then, back when we were young. And that way she'd also have a place for her sketches, and she could make sure I saw each of them. Also, she said when we were fourteen, we could have the word "fuck" in each sentence if we wanted to and not get caught, and we do want to, and we should, and we must. It is a rule.

fuck me rawer

Recently, it is like Avishag doesn't even exist. Everything I say she says a little louder. Then she grows quiet. She plays with the golden necklace on her dark chest. She fine-tunes her bra strap. She watches her hair grow longer and she grows silent. I guess I am growing in the same ways.

But the thing is, for the first time in the history of the world, someone other than Avishag wrote in the notebook while I was gone.

I am almost sure. There is another odd line, and no "fuck."

i am alone all the time. even right now,
i am alone

I close the notebook.
I want to ask Avishag if her brother Dan came into the

classroom when I was gone, but I don't. Avishag and Dan's mother, Mira, is special among mothers because she is a teacher. She is a teacher because she had to come and be a teacher in a village instead of in Jerusalem. Avishag's dad left them, so they didn't have enough money to stay in Jerusalem. My mother works in the company in the village that makes parts that go into machines that help make machines that can make airplanes. Lea's mother works in the company in the village that makes parts that go into machines that help make machines that can make airplanes. I am alone all the time.

I have this idea.

I am going to have a party even if it kills me, and I still don't know where the party is going to be, and I can't know, and I won't know anything more in the next twenty minutes because I am in class, but so help me God, Dan is going to come to this party. He will if I call to invite him, that's just manners, and it is this brilliant idea I just thought of, out of nowhere, a *party*, and if one more person tells me that sometimes it is Ok to be alone, I will scream and it is going to be awkward.

"Peace," I say and get up from my desk. I pick up my backpack. When Avishag gets up, her chair scratches the linoleum floor and makes Mira's lips pucker as if she just ate a whole lemon from the tree of the Levy family.

"There are still twenty minutes left in this class," she says. She might think we'll stay, but we leave.

"Fuck it. Peace," Avishag says. This is rare. Avishag hates it when swear words are said out loud. She only loves them written, so this is rare. Four boys get up as well. In fourth grade one of them ate a whole lemon from the Levy family's tree on a dare, but nothing happened after that.

You Can't Talk to Anyone

Avishag and I are walking up on the main dirt road leading up from the school. When I open my mouth, I can taste specks of the footsteps of our classmates before us and our own from the day before. I can barely speak there is so much in my mouth.

"I'm, like, dying. We have to have a party tonight. We have to make some calls," I say.

"Noam and Emuna told me that Yochai told them that his brother heard from Lea's sister Sarit where to get reception," Avishag says. Her black eyes squint.

All the cellular phones in the town don't work right now. At first there was no reception only at school. Then last Wednesday we didn't have reception even after we jumped behind the wooden gate and cut math. Avishag got two bars for, like, ten seconds, but it wasn't enough to call anyone. Then it became one bar and didn't change back.

We already walked to the grocery store, but there was no reception there, so we bought a pack of Marlboros and some gummy bears and walked to the ATM, but there was no reception there, so we walked to the small park, but there was no reception there, and someone had puked on the only swing big enough for two, so we didn't even stay, and then there was no other place in town we could go.

"It is actually not Noam or Yochai who told me," Avishag says. "Dan told me. He is speaking to me again. Or at least, enough to say that there is reception by the cellular tower."

I don't look at Avishag after she says that. I want to ask her if Dan came in and wrote in the notebook, but I know better.

The cellular tower. Of course. Sometimes I think that if

it weren't for people like Dan the whole village would die, we're that stupid.

What Is Love

In my whole entire life I only decided to love one boy, Avishag's brother, Dan. I have had the same boyfriend, Moshe, since I was twelve, but that's not really fair because I didn't really get to decide to love him. He was a family friend who threw apples at me, so I didn't really have a choice. Two weeks ago we broke up. We also broke up nine weeks ago. He has been in the army for about six months now, anyway. Dan is already done with all of that.

Dan used to have this test. That's why I decided to love him. It would drive him fucking crazy, this test.

Right at the end of Jerusalem Street, our town has a view. It has a view of the entire world and its sister. Really, it does. Standing there on top of that tiny hill you can see four mountains bursting with forever-green Mediterranean forest. You can see blankets of red anemones and pillows of purple anemones and circles of yellow daisies. And little caves protected by willows, and well, it hurts almost to look at it. Like seeing other people's children on the other side of the street.

And there are benches, of course, right there at the end of Jerusalem Street, and you would think you could sit and look out at this view, except you can't. Because if you did, your back would be to the view, and you would be staring at house number twenty-four on Jerusalem Street, and all you would notice are the underwear hanging to dry and an orphaned dog leash on the yellow grass and the recycling bin out on the porch.

And he would bring people there, Dan, and he would ask, *what is wrong with this picture what is wrong what is wrong*, and no one could tell him and he would grow mad, grow loud, and he would say that if it weren't for people like him the whole village would fucking die, we're that stupid. He can be arrogant. And then the person he would bring there from the town, his classmate, his mother's friend, his sister, his younger sister, would sit there staring at the yellow grass of house twenty-four for a while and say, "You said you wanted to hang out. I don't understand." But I understood.

In seventh grade, after I left Avishag's house, Dan jumped at me from behind an olive tree. Above him there were imported sycamore trees and birds, and the birds were invisible but swished around so quickly in circles they made spots of light dance around him, like in a discotheque. He moved one step closer. And then one more. He was so close I could see two eyelashes that had fallen off and were resting on his left cheek. I looked down, embarrassed, and noticed that his feet were bare and long. I snapped my fingers under my neck, nervous. He was so tall, just like Avishag. Or maybe I was short.

"Do you want to hang out?" he asked.

When I sat on that bench I just felt tired for a second. I turned my back around again and again to look away, so Dan wouldn't see how excited I was, so I would have something else beautiful to think about. And then it hit me.

"So a person comes and he has two benches and they tell him, 'Use cement and plant these benches in the ground,' and he, well," I said. I just wanted to have something to say, but Dan's green eyes were beaming, and his thick eyebrows were going up and down.

After that we sat there for a while on the ground, look-ing at the red blankets and caves ahead, and I told him all my secrets. That night I think I loved him a bit, but I don't know if it was true love because I only loved him because he loved me, or something I said. You could see that he did by the way he was rocking back and forth and also because when I showed him the notebook he promised he would write in it one day, something fucking smart.

I never spoke to him again after that night. Two months later he told Avishag one of my secrets. Two years after that he went into the army, and when he got back, instead of working in the company in the village that makes parts that go into machines that help make machines that make airplanes, or going to professional school so he could later be paid more to work in the company in the town that makes parts that go into machines that help make machines that make airplanes, he just stayed home and drew pictures of military boots. I know because my sister went there last week to play with his littlest sister, and when she came back she said there were sketches of boots and boots and boots. The entire kitchen wall was black with them, and heavy.

"Dan said he misses you," my sister said. "He said you don't hang out with him anymore," she added and made kiss-ing sounds, and then turned the volume of her *Bully the Snow Man* cartoon louder so I wouldn't be able to yell at her.

No House Is Empty

If you wrote something in someone's notebook, one thing you would also do is come to a party if they invited you.

By the time we reach the cellular tower I am almost sure

that it was Dan who wrote in the notebook. He wrote between my definitions of "RPG children" and "IAF." I guess I still care. I guess he must still care.

I know it sounds unlikely, but I just know he just waltzed right into the class like Superman and wrote in the notebook when I was in the bathroom and then stepped right out of the gates of the school. I would ask Avishag if he came when I was gone, and I wonder why she doesn't just tell me, but I also know she must have her reasons—people who have brothers have reasons—and besides, I am only almost sure and almost sure is better than risking knowing something you don't want to know.

I can't believe we haven't thought of trying to get reception by the cellular tower before. We are close enough to the cellular tower for it to shade us from the sun up on this rocky hill, and we are screaming, because even with the little reception it gives us it is still hard for people to hear us.

There are a lot of rare commodities in this village. Privacy, public transportation, 5 percent milk. But the rarest of all is an empty house. Every so often someone's parents go for a company-sponsored retreat in the next town over and get massages and swim in the hostel's pool. But that has never happened to my family, or to most of anyone we know. Most times parents go out for coffee at another house, agreeing to be out of the house until after eleven, and pesky siblings agree to have sleepovers. That's how an empty house is created, and then you can have beers and smoke and make out and not feel embarrassed.

But there seem to be no empty houses for our class to party in today, none.

We've called twelve people already, and there are wet

circles underneath our arms, but we can't go home because my sister is at home and Avishag's little sister is at home and we can't let them hear us planning this, just like in two years they won't let us hear them plan parties. Besides, I never go over to Avishag's house anymore now that Dan's back. She won't let me go there.

My sister would hear us if we went to my house, and she is the worst. You can hear anything on a landline. When my mother is on the landline, no matter how late at night, I can hear everything she says, even when she whispers, and I can hear it if she cries.

"ARE YOU SURE?" We are shouting into our cell phones.

Yes, Tali Feldman is sure. Her mother doesn't want to let her have a party when the house is empty because she is worried about her daughter's friends breaking more of her Romanian tea set, and Noam's mom doesn't want her daughter to have a party when the house is empty because she is worried about her daughter breaking her trust, and Nina's mom doesn't want her daughter to have a party when the house is empty because she is worried about her daughter's friends breaking her daughter's hymen, because she is a little on the religious side.

We also find out that Lea is having a party, that she has an empty house because her mom and dad are going to get a massage at the hostel in the next town over, but that her mother says I am not invited because last time I broke a chestnut pot and Lea told her it was me. The real reason is because Avishag and I are the only ones who are not super afraid of Lea, because we played with her before she was super popular, when she still played with people instead of just playing people.

I told Dan on the bench that day all my secrets. One of them was that Avishag and I still played with dolls. This is something we kept a secret even from Lea, ever since we were in fifth grade. It was actually better to play with dolls when we were in seventh grade, since we could think of things we couldn't when we were younger. The dolls could puke yellow Popsicles and then cover another doll in it, before burning it. They could invent a cure for cancer or pick up smoking or go to law school. It was a lot of fun.

When Avishag found out I had told her brother about us playing, she walked into class right at eight in the morning and opened my backpack and threw my sandwich on the floor, right there for everyone to see, and she stepped on it, and she was screaming. The tomatoes oozed yellow and red liquid on the floor when she jumped on them.

"Gross," she shouted. "He is my brother you sick, sick bitch. You have a boyfriend! Who do you think you are? I don't even know you." It was rare then too, that she cursed.

We acted for a while like we really didn't know each other, because really we didn't, I would agree on that, but I didn't know anymore if there was anyone I did know. Emuna took Avishag's seat next to me in class. Avishag switched to sitting next to Noam.

Then Dan went into the army. It was regular that he did, because he was eighteen, and it was regular that Avishag and I forgot about the words she said about him. But I know she thinks she doesn't even know me. I'll always know that.

"Are RPG children like those tiny RPGs that don't need a launcher?" she asks before we leave the cellular tower.

"No," I say. "You are thinking about the Soviet hand grenades that were also called RPGs, but no one used them by the time it was the Peace of the Galilee War. You are thinking about the past. I'll let you copy all the definitions later."

Inside My Room

We leave the hill with the cellular tower at around four in the afternoon and go home, unsuccessful at finding a place for a party. My mom usually gets in from work at five. I watch the national children's channel until she comes. *Chiquititas* and *Wonder Shoes* and *The Surprise Garden*. Shows even Avishag would think I am too old for. When I hear my mom's car outside I run into my room and lie on my bed and stare at the ceiling. She doesn't knock to ask how I am, and I am glad, because all I want is some quiet.

I can hear her whispering on the phone. I stare at the ceiling for about an hour, maybe two, trying to imagine what it would be like if I were forced to stare at this ceiling for my entire life. What type of details would I notice? I ask myself, and the voice in my head sounds suddenly like that of Mira the history teacher, Avishag's mom, and then it is my mom, and she is in my room. Her teeth are stained with nicotine and her back is hunched forward.

"I can't do this anymore," she says. "I need some help."

I don't answer. *I* need some help. If she wanted to, she could know that I want an empty house to have a party I can invite Dan to tonight. But she only wants to know what she wants to know.

Last Monday she asked me if I was sure I didn't want to try adding turkey to my sandwich.

"I have been screaming at you to pick up the phone for five minutes," she says, and hands me the phone. "I can't live in this house and be treated like a maid anymore."

"Are you there?" Avishag asks through the phone.

"Did Nina's mom finally give permission for a party?" I ask.

"Listen," she says. "Dan fell down and hit his head."

And They Say Russian Roulette

I was on the landline the whole night talking to Avishag. All of the other girls stayed at Lea's party. She made people stay, even after they heard something was up with Dan. I didn't care about that. And I didn't care that my mom could hear me or that my sister could hear me or that my dad could hear me. At first the thing that was up was that Dan hit his head so Avishag was worried, and then the thing was that he was badly injured in the head and in the hospital but Avishag's mom told her not to go, and then the thing was that he was accidentally shot in the head, and then the final thing was that he and a couple classmates went to the cellular tower hill and they called this girl, or that, but then they played Russian roulette because no one answered. I mean, no one but those in the town had cell reception and almost everyone was at Lea's party, and that was the thing. At six in the morning the thing was that Dan had died.

But I don't believe any of these rumors. I think he just went up that hill and blew his fucking brains out all by himself.

Mothers Disappeared

At seven in the morning I walk over to Avishag's. She lives in Jerusalem Street 3 and I live in 12, and that's why we became friends. I pass by one nearly identical house after another. I pass Lea's house, the olive grove, then the house of the British Miller family. The houses look exactly alike except Avishag's house has a red roof and the rest are green. Also, when you walk into her house there are seven bookshelves, because her mom, Mira, is an intellectual, because she is a teacher or because she is originally from Jerusalem the city, not the street.

Avishag's eyes are closed, so I hold her nose to make her wake up. That's how I always used to wake her up when we were little, but when I do it now I realize I can't wake her up like that anymore. Not now. Not ever. She doesn't shout at me when she wakes up; she doesn't say a word.

I remove the pillow from under her black, damp hair. I put it on the floor and I put my head on it and I close my eyes.

But after about an hour I wake up. I go downstairs to the kitchen expecting to find the chocolate milk and cereal waiting on the table, but there is nothing on the table at all. Even the chocolate milk and chocolate-spread sandwich Mira has out on the table for her youngest girl every morning are not there.

I expected them. I swear, of all things, this is the most shocking.

In my house my mother organizes a tomato and tea for me and tomato and bread and tea for my sister in the morning. When we wake up she is always gone because her work starts at seven. Work used to start at eight, so she used to be able to drive us to school, but in tenth grade the town started a bus service to ease morning traffic and make it so that moms can come to work an hour early. Now there is always just that same note. *Do your dishes after lunch.* She leaves lunch in the fridge, two plates covered by other plates, rice and lamb from Sunday to Tuesday and rice and okra the rest of the week. They taste fresh even though we have to microwave them.

I go back to Avishag's room.

"Avishag," I say, shaking her hard, "where's your mom?"

Avishag keeps her eyes closed. Still half sleeping, she arches her back and fine-tunes her bra. She passes her long fingers on her golden necklace, and she is so dark in between these white sheets, it is as if she is too present, and then she opens her eyes suddenly.

"I think she decided to go back home," she says. "She said she would before we even heard that Dan . . . before we knew everything."

"Go back home?" I ask. "But she is your mom."

"She said she is moving back in with her mom in Jerusalem. She said she is not going to raise kids all by herself if they are just going to go shoot themselves, and she said I never offer to do the dishes, and that I am a grown woman now and she—"

"She can't be gone," I say. "Wake up."

But Avishag closes her eyes and turns her back to me, pulling the white blanket above her head as if it were a cave.

Jewdifying the Galilee

I go to school alone. I don't know where else to go and I can't stare at Avishag sleeping any longer. The classroom has only three boys in it, sitting on their desks and looking at a magazine about Japanese cars. One of the chairs is flipped on its side, and someone has knocked over the trash can so there are orange peels and notebook pages on the floor.

"Lea's mom is gone too," one of the boys says. "She told Lea she decided she was just going to stay in that town that has the massages forever," he adds and bites one of his fingers. "But I don't think she can actually do that. And Mira the teacher will come back soon too."

"This is a whole town of crazy bitches," another boy adds. Then they turn their backs to me and huddle over the magazine.

I step outside and try to catch my breath, so I look down, but above me there are ravens and sycamores and the birds circle below the sun so there are dots on the asphalt underneath my feet, winking at me first here, then there, and I open my mouth and puke, until I am able to raise my head up again, and I keep it up.

I can't see a single person out in the streets. When they built this town less than thirty years ago, it was because people had this brilliant idea that they should Jewdify the Galilee, and in particular the Lebanese border. There is one empty brown hill after another in that region, the government said, and if we are a country, we can't all live in just one part of it. So they gave plots of land for barely any money to couples who promised to work in the factory they built in the village, and that way the couples had money and a home and then they had children.

The only thing they didn't think of is that money and houses create children and that children need buses, among other things. The only way to get out now is through hitch-hiking.

I stand by the old pay phone at the outskirts of town and stick out my thumb. I first think about calling someone, but I don't have any coins to use the pay phone.

When a red Subaru stops, I lean over and smell the aftershave of the bearded driver. He is listening to "Macarena," really, he is.

"Where are you going?" he asks.

On the ground, a snail is slowly making its way toward

me, leaving a trail of saliva behind it. Soon, there will be the first rain of the year. Soon, Avishag and I will graduate. Join the army. Everything. Even princess Lea will have to join the army. Everyone does.

And I realize I have no one I know outside the thousand houses of the town and that I am standing here on the luke-warm asphalt all alone.

I tell the driver I might as well stay where I am.

I Don't Go Up the Hill

And it is because I don't want to climb anymore just to get reception by the cellular tower, just to talk to someone. I go down the brick path and through the bike racks and the dump yard to the video machine, and I use a twenty-shekel bill to buy *Mean Girls*, since it is the only movie left in the machine that I have only seen once.

Now I have change, and I go back to the very end of town. The pay phone's receiver is so dusty it glistens, and when I pick it up I am almost surprised to hear a dial tone. This might be the very last pay phone in all of Israel. A few years ago the government uprooted them, one by one, and took them all away in a big truck.

I want to hear my mom's voice to make sure she didn't also leave.

But she is not the one I call.

Avishag only answers the third time I call. My mom is not the first one I call, not because I chose to call Avishag first but because almost sure is better than risking knowing something you don't want to know.

"Your mom is going to come back, you know," I say.

When I say it I know that she may not. When I say it I

know already that it was Avishag who wrote in the notebook that morning, not Dan.

"I am alone all the time, Yael," Avishag replies, and her voice is soupy. "Even right now."

Don't Call Us

I wait for a long time for Avishag to come get me. I sit on the sand by the pay phone and wait. I can taste sweat and salt and makeup trickling down from my nose to my lips. She said she'll come.

And she does. She comes, but she doesn't come and get me. We don't go home. We don't say anything. She walks right up to me and then changes direction. She knows that I will follow her wherever she goes today.

We walk up and up the hill. I hope we never get there, but I know we will.

There is no blood on the ground by the cellular tower. Not even a piece of clothing. Not even a boot.

Avishag takes a while to believe there is nothing there. She wants to see, at least something. Her neck is moving here then there frantically. She stands looking and looking in the shade of the tower, like she did when we were little, trying to find the last word on a word-search puzzle.

Then it is as if the tower is that word. Like she just notices that it is there, after staring right at it for minutes. She puts both her hands on it and pushes it and kicks it.

I join her, digging the dirt around the metal rods stuck in the ground with my shoes and shoving my entire weight on the tower.

We try to collapse the tower until it is dark. We try and we try and we try.

We don't talk. We won't talk. We've talked enough.
We don't need a cellular tower here.

RPG Children

RPG children were usually around nine or ten, so they were very small, and children. And the RPG launcher is this weapon that is very, very heavy, so you can't have just one child holding it, you have to have two, and the children took the weapons and they held them, two together, one from the front and one from the back. When you shoot an RPG, the front launches a missile so powerful it could even get through an Israeli tank, but the back releases fire, not a lot of fire, not fire that is necessary; it is just a part of how the weapon works, that there is fire at the back. So one RPG child held the launcher on his shoulder, and behind him stood another RPG child, on his toes, holding it from the back. And so when the RPG was launched, the child from the back's head caught fire, and then his shoulders, and soon his sandals too, if he had them. No one told the RPG children any better.

No one talked to them, no one told them anything, not the children who held it from the front and not the children who held it from the back, but one thing that is very, very interesting is that many times the child from the front would jump on his burning friend and hug him, and this increased the casualties in a very significant way, that one child didn't burn alone.

The
Sound
of All
Girls
Screaming

W e, the boot-camp girls, stand in a perfect square that lacks one of its four sides. Our commander stands in front of us, facing the noon sun. She squints. She screams.

"Raise your hand if you are wearing contact lenses."

Two girls raise their hands. The commander folds her arm to look at her watch. The two girls do the same.

"In two minutes and thirty seconds, I want to see you back here from the tents. Without your contact lenses. Understood?" the commander shouts.

"Yes, commander," the girls shout, and their watches beep. They run. Dusts of sand trail the quick steps of their boots.

"Raise your hand if you are asthmatic," the boot-camp commander shouts.

None of the girls raise their hands.

"Are you asthmatic?" the boot camp commander shouts.

"No, commander," all the girls shout.

I don't shout. I didn't get it that I was supposed to; I already didn't raise my hand.

"Are you asthmatic, Avishag?" the commander yells, looking at me.

"No, commander," I shout.

"Then answer next time," the commander says. "Speak up so I can hear you, just like everyone else."

In my IDF boot camp, the only combat-infantry boot camp for females, we can't tell what will become of us next based on what questions we raise our hands for. I know the least because I was the first of the girls in my class to be drafted, so I didn't have any friends to get info from, and my brother Dan never told me anything about the army, even when he was alive. I got so annoyed when people asked me if I was still planning to go into the army after he died, I decided to volunteer for combat just to make people stop assuming. I wanted to do something that would make people never assume, ever.

One can never assume in my boot camp. A week ago, we were asked to raise our hands if we weighed below fifty kilos. Then we were asked to raise our hands if we had ever shared needles or had unprotected sex shortly before we were drafted. It was hard to know what to assume from that. The army wanted our blood. Two liters, but you got strawberry Kool-Aid and white bread while the needle was inside you. The self-proclaimed sluts and druggies served it to the girls who were pumping their fists, trying to make the blood gush out quicker.

"Faster," the commander screamed.

"My hand feels like there is ice on it," one of the other soldiers said. "It feels frozen." She was lying on the field bed across from mine. I wanted to reach over and grab her hand, so that she would be less cold, so that I would be less alone. I couldn't. Because of the needle in my arm, because it would have been a mistake. Mom said that if I want to get a good posting after boot camp, I have to learn how to control my mouth. Mom was once an officer, and now she is a history teacher, and all. She left for Jerusalem a few weeks after Dan died, but in the end she had to come back and help me get ready for the army. Single moms have to come back always.

The girl on the field bed next to mine freaked out. She extended the arm with the needle away from her body, like it was cursed. Her face turned red. "I think it is taking too much blood. Can someone check? Can someone see if it is taking too much blood?"

I knew I should not say anything.

"I want to go home," she said. "I don't like this."

She looked very young. And eventually I spoke. "It's fine" was what I said.

That's when the commander intervened. "No one said you could talk," she shouted.

I was the only one who was punished. During shower hour, I had to dig a hole in the sand large enough to bury a boulder the size of five heads. The commander said the boulder represented my "shame." She smiled when she explained that. None of the girls helped. They just stood on the sand, waiting in line for the showers, and watched.

Now the army wants us to know what it is like to be suffocated. That's why they asked about contact lenses and asthma. It is ABC day. Atomic, biological, chemical. Every soldier has to go through that, not just girls in combat, they said. But it is especially important for us, because we will have to maintain functionality in the event of an unconventional attack.

We stand in two lines on top of a sandy hill. We help each other put the gas masks on.

"You are doing it all wrong, Avishag," the commander yells at me. "All wrong."

She stretches one of the black elastic bands tighter, and my hair is pulled so tightly it is as if someone had taken a handful of my hair and tried to pull it off my scalp. Except that someone doesn't let go. The mask is on my face to stay.

With our masks on, we all look like the bodies of soldiers with the heads of robotic dogs. The big gray filter stretches like a snout. The sun heats the black plastic of the mask, and the heat radiates inward. The sheer plastic above my eyes is stained, and wherever I turn the world looks framed and distant, a dirty, cheap painting of sand, then sand from another angle.

The commander goes down the line, breaking plastic miniatures of bananas. "Each one of your ABC kits has a few of these little bananas. If you break it and you still smell bananas, your mask is not sealed right."

I can feel the veins at the back of my head choking. When the commander passes by me, waving the tiny banana, I can smell it. Bananas. Bananas and sand.

"I can smell bananas and—" I say. My voice vibrates inside of the mask. My words, they fail me. I want to talk. All the time. About Dan. About things Yael said I still don't

understand. The banana fields by our village when they
burn. Everything. I am an idiot. Like it matters what I am
thinking.

"No one said you could speak," my commander shouts.
"Just get one of your friends to fix it," she says. They call the
other soldiers "your friends." I hate that. They are other soldiers. They are not my friends. Even Mom said, you don't go
into the army to make friends. Don't be fooled. Just look at
what happened to Dan.

The commander lets us into the tent two at a time. My
partner is a tall girl called Gali. We watch one of the girls who
entered before us lift the cover of the tent and run back outside as if she were on fire, her mouth dripping with saliva,
her eyes closed and wet, her nose running in green and yellow. She runs with her mouth open, her arms stretched to the
sides. She runs far, her small green body becoming a speck on
the empty horizon.

Gali laughs, and I do too. I did hear from Sarit, Lea's older
sister, that the tear-gas tent is the first place commanders can
get personal with their boot-camp soldiers. They ask them the
same four questions:

Do you love the army?

Do you love the country?

Who do you love more, your mother or father?

Are you afraid to die?

The commanders get a kick out of this because first they
ask these questions when the soldier has her mask on, but
then they get to ask them when the soldier is in the tear-gas
tent, without the mask, and watch her panic. That is the goal
of the exercise. To train you not to panic in the event of an

atomic, biological, or chemical attack. I fail to see the point of this. I told that to Sarit; I told her, "In that case, why don't they just shoot us so we know what that feels like?" but she said, "Don't get smart." We get to run out of the tent when we feel we are choking. Sarit said they expect you to stay as long as you can. I asked, "What's as long as you can?" and she asked, "How long can you breathe underwater?"

It is our turn.

Gali and I bend below the tent's folds and enter it. It is dark inside and so warm I feel as though the buttons of my uniform are burning my wrists. I can feel it. I can see it. The tent is full of poison. I know it, but the mask doesn't let it harm me. I feel like a cheater.

The commander, strangely, is just as identifiable with the mask on. The way she stands, with her arms behind her back, holding the handle of her gun. Her chin is raised high. She starts with Gali. Gali stands even taller, perking up her chin.

"How are you feeling with the mask, soldier?"

"Good."

"Do you love the army?"

"Yes. It is hard but it is a rewarding experience and I learn a lot."

"Do you love your country?"

"Yes."

"Who do you love more, your mother or your father?"

"I can't really answer that. I think I love them both the same amount, but in different ways."

"Are you afraid to die?"

"No."

"Take off your mask. You can run out when you feel you have to."

I watch Gali fumble to untie the elastic of her mask and then remove it. Immediately, her face crumbles inward like she is sucking on a punctured straw.

"Do you love the army?"

Gali opens her mouth to speak and then closes it quickly. She is drooling already. She opens her mouth again, smaller this time, and grunts out a sound. "Yeah."

"Do you love your country?"

Gali is flapping her arms near her throat, like a fish.

"Ahhh," she mumbles, and the mucus from her nose falls to her mouth. She runs out like a stork.

Now it is me.

"Do you love the army?" my commander asks.

"Yes and no. I mean, I definitely believe that it is important in a country like ours to serve in the army, but I hope for peace, and on a personal level of course boot camp presents its own hardships and also—"

"Enough. Are you afraid to die?" she asks. She skips two questions. She knows I am trouble, although I have barely caused any yet. Maybe trouble isn't something you do, it is something you are. I think Dan told me that once, but what do I know about what he said or meant?

"No, I am not afraid to *die*," I say. Short and concise. What she wants to hear, and also the truth.

"Take off your mask. You can run out when you feel you have to," my commander says. She sounds different than when she said it to Gali. More content.

I take off my mask and at first I feel nothing but the pain

in my scalp. Then I feel the fire, the burn. I cannot open my eyes. I stop taking air in through my nose. But I open my mouth, I do.

And I talk. I have been waiting for so long. This is my chance. As long as I am choking, I am allowed. Yael and Lea are not here to drown my words with their chatter. No one in my family is around to ignore me. My talking serves a purpose. My talking, my tears, are a matter of national security. A part of our training. I will be prepared for an attack by unconventional weapons. I could save the whole country, that's how prepared I'll be. My entire head is burning but my mouth rolls off words; they taste like bananas, and they go on and on and on.

My commander runs out of the original four questions. She has to make up a new one.

"What is your earliest memory?" she asks. It is a question they used to ask before someone was brilliant enough to come up with the mom and dad question.

I don't leave on my own. She tells me to.

I talk and I talk and I talk.

I think I stayed inside the tear-gas tent longer than any soldier has ever before.

Outside is when I cannot breathe. I cannot open my eyes and, although I do not want them to, my feet start running on their own, faster and faster. I can taste blood in my mouth coming from my nose, and my throat burns as though it is stuffed with boiling oil. The skin of my face is rubbed with sandpaper. I run and I run, until arms catch me midair and hold me for a very long time. When I can finally see again, through the water in my eyes, I see where I was heading: the cliff. It was my commander's arms that grabbed me. She held me, before I fell. My commander, this was her job.

They are sure I cheated, although they cannot for the life of them imagine how I did it. I am told I stayed in a tent full of tear gas for over two and a half minutes, and they say that is just not possible, that there must have been some funny business going on. It felt like I was talking longer. It felt like in that time I got to tell everything, almost.

After I change my uniform, I have to see the commander of the base. I enter the room, salute with my gun, and stare at him.

For a second, I think he is reaching for his gun. That the commander of the base is going to kill me. Sometimes I think things I know are not true. But he is just reaching for his cigarettes. His nostrils flare when he drags in the smoke. He gestures for me to sit across from him, and when I drop onto the office chair I can see that the hairs inside his nose are gray, like lifelines of spiders. He crushes his cigarette in an ashtray made of a green grenade shell and then reaches for another one.

It seems he is only interested in killing himself, and slowly. He doesn't care about killing me. It makes me sad that he cares about himself more than about me. Say I am just not being realistic, but it still makes me sad when people are like that. Most people are like that. Dan was like that, in the end. Only interested in killing himself.

The commander of the base says I need to get my act together. That don't I know people are dying? He hopes I will take some time to think of ways I can become a better soldier.

"And just a general point. Your commander says you keep

on speaking when you are not spoken to. Why do you do that?" he asks.

"I don't know. I guess I have all these thoughts," I say.

"One day soon you need to wake up and realize that your thoughts are interrupting everyone else."

My punishment is to sleep that night with my gas mask on. Creative and humiliating all at once. I am sort of impressed.

I wish I were a better soldier. At night, I think about everything except how to become a better soldier, no matter how hard I try. Dan, Mom, Yael. People who are not me and not soldiers. Even my dad; thoughts from when I was little and not a soldier.

All night long, I stare at the ceiling of the tent through the sheer plastic; it frames the thick green cloth, all this green, like an impressionist painting. The knobs at the back of the mask pierce into my scalp.

If I cry, it is not because I hope that one of the girls in the tent will hear me and wake up. We only get five hours of sleep each night. And we are not friends.

I cannot sleep, so I imagine one of two things could happen.

I could wake up after a night with my gas mask on and find out that Iran had bombed Israel and that I was the last living person in the whole country, that the mask had saved me. The other girls in the tent would be dead and blue faced, and I would march out of the gates of the base and into the Negev desert, where dehydration could kill me, or chemicals poisoning the skin of my body could kill me, but those things don't kill me. What kills me is that I have no one to talk to.

Another thing that could happen is that Iran doesn't bomb Israel, at least not on that day, and that I reach the place Yael says is the end of the world. I finish boot camp. I finish the army. I go to Panama and Guatemala and Argentina. There are Israelis, of course, swarms of them everywhere. But finally they all leave, and I am the last Israeli tourist left in Ushuaia, Argentina, the closest city to Antarctica, the end of the world. The bookstores are all in Spanish. The lakes are too cold for a swim. At the bars, all the clients are middle-aged Frenchmen, and I am alone.

My earliest memory. I open my eyes and see the small room through plastic. My father is wearing his mask, and my baby sister is on the carpet inside a gas-protective incubator, because she is too small for a mask of her own. Dan keeps on taking his mask off, and Dad slaps him. Dad takes off his own mask to take sips from his Araq bottle. It is 1991 and missiles are falling from Iraq. On the radio they say not to go into the underground shelters. They say to seal one room of the house with duct tape, wear the masks, drink a lot of water, and hope for the best. On the radio they say missiles are falling in region M, our region. We live in some town other than the village then. I don't know where. My parents are arguing. "Duct tape?" my mother asks. "This is silly."

I do not know all the details of this—I hear about it later, and it becomes my memory. That night, I do not yet have enough words to make a sentence. All I remember is my mother, her dark face bare, collecting me in her arms and running up the wooden steps onto the roof. Rain falls on the palm trees below, but my mother removes my mask and pulls my chin up, high up in the air. A ball of light rips through the night sky in pink and ember and blaze. My mother drowns her chin in my hair. We watch, and if I am alone I do not yet know it.

I stare at the ceiling of the tent through the sheer plastic into the night. The knobs at the back of the mask pierce into my scalp, still. I am crying, and not because I hope that one of the girls in the tent will wake up.

But then one does wake up. The blood one, the one who thought too much of her blood was being taken. She is awake, but she does not realize that I am a person, her fellow soldier, and in my field bed and crying inside a gas mask. My suffocated whines sound to her like the words of an animal.

"Is that a cat?" she whispers, a sound as spiky as a blade that pierces through the air and tent and ears. "Girls! There is a cat in the tent."

"A cat?" Gali asks. She does not bother whispering.

"Help me. I am allergic. I may die." The blood girl waits for the words of another person.

The mask protects me. They cannot see my face. They cannot see my mouth. They do not know that it was me who made the sound. If I scream, if I scream right now, a deafening and smashing and muted scream, there is a chance, there is always a small chance that no one will ever know it was me. It will be the sound of all girls screaming.

And so.

I scream. I scream as if this is the last time in my life I'll ever speak my voice, and maybe it is. It is as if no one hears me, hears me right now.

I scream the fear of blood, and ember, and blaze. I scream the terror of the beeping watches and boots treading the sand, and the panic brought upon by a reek that thinks it is bananas. The sound of the words I scream is the groan of my shame, my shame that is not a boulder, my shame that I never agreed to bury.

If you really want me to, I will tell you the words I scream, I will tell you all the sounds and words and letters. But first you have to, you have to swear that you really want to hear it from me.

Boys

I stretch my arms out, as if I am trying to push the darkness beyond the cement barricade. I braid my hair and then braid it tighter, even though I know no one will be able to see me for hours.

Eventually I allow myself to yawn and look down at the ammunition bunker hidden below the small hill where I stand. The eight-hour shift and the night broaden and spiral before me like my whole life ahead. When the wait is almost too much, I write my name on the ground in stones.

Yael.

I hate even my name when I am waiting, at least after I look at it and it looks at me for a while, at least when I see it written in stones. So I kick the stones.

I have been doing this since they stationed me in this

training base near Hidna after boot camp. At first I wrote other words, but then I felt bad about kicking them, even though I hated them, and I hated that I grew to hate each name and word.

After I am done kicking stones, I bend over and reach for the helmet, where I placed a plastic jar filled with chocolate spread. I jammed a plastic knife in it for me to lick when the night starts crowding in on me. I put it a few meters outside of the barricade so that I have to step out of it into the yellow weeds and dust of the hill. This makes time pass.

But the helmet and the chocolate are gone. The weeds where I dropped them are imprinted by the shape of the helmet, holding its absence. The night hums with silence and cold. I place my hand on the handle of my M-16 and click the safety once, then twice, then again.

The helmet should have been on my head, but none of the girls ever put theirs on. I had rested it outside the barricade, because the open chocolate spread has to be outside to make life interesting, and the helmet would make it harder for bugs to climb in.

I take out a flashlight from my ammunition vest. The light stretches in a giant triangle, exposing green shrubbery and fruit flies. I think I see movement on the mountain ahead, a movement methodical and curvy, like that of a giant mouse.

I close my eyes and hear giggles, or maybe it's just the radio coming from the houses of the Palestinian village nearby, or a car driving along Route 433.

I open my eyes. I take my hand off my gun. I turn off the flashlight. Then I see a flash of white, glistening on the ground straight ahead.

Whoever stole my helmet and chocolate crawled in silence all the way up the hill and right outside the guarding barricade. Then, before crawling away with the goods, he paused for a second, low on the ground and silent, took out the plastic knife from the jar, licked it clean, and left it right outside the barricade for me to find. That knife. Like a wink—I got you!

I know I'll get in trouble for losing the helmet, but I cannot help it. I can feel laughter growing in my stomach, then in my lungs, and then I am laughing so hard my eyes get wet and it is hard to breathe.

There is no doubt about it. This theft was the genius work of a boy. One of the boys from the Hidna village. And boys, well. I love everything about them.

I walk back crazed, confused, and knowing. I think I know something new after every shift. The thin metal fence around the base engulfs my body. The signs glued to the fence, reading CLOSED MILITARY AREA, blur. They've hung them up so that one glows in red, and the next is black, red, black, red. But with every step I take they become nothing more than letters in all the colors that there are.

א

IN THE middle of night, back in the caravan, after eight hours of laughter alone and staring, I call my boyfriend, Moshe, back in the village. He finished his service a year ago. I call him from under cover of a military blanket.

"We are breaking up," I say.

"Is it me?" he asks.

"Yes," I say. "It is you."

"But I just got a job in the next town over. It's not great, but by the time you're out of the army we'll have something to start with," he says. "How can it be me?"

"For sure you," I say.

א

THE VILLAGES around Hebron and even the youth in Hebron itself have grown restless and begun rioting. The entire unit of infantry boys we trained the week before has been called up. They could only spare four or five boys to help us guard the training base. The burden of guarding the base fell on our shoulders, the weaponry instructors, the girls. We had to do eight-eight. Eight hours of standing alone in the dark with nothing but your thoughts and full gear, your weapon loaded. Waiting for the minutes to crawl by like crippled snakes, waiting, waiting, waiting. Then eight hours of haunted sleep in the caravan, where I'd wonder what I had been waiting for all those hours. And again.

"One of the Hidna boys stole my helmet last night," I tell Dana in the morning. She sleeps in the bed across from mine.

"I don't get why we even have to guard," Dana says. She gets ready for her shift, sticking her thumb inside the five magazines in her vest to make sure there are exactly twenty-nine bullets in each. "These boys are like rats," she says. "I swear they'd steal the entire base if they could."

"I know," I say. "And it's like, they're kids. What are we going to do, arrest them?"

Dana rattles a water canteen by her ear, making sure it is filled all the way and makes no noise. "You're in trouble now," she says after listening to the silence. "That's for sure."

The door of the caravan of the more popular girls is open, and they have a clear view into our open door. Their leader, Hagar, the blonde, is looking right in at us. Her European face reminds me of Lea's. She is as mean as her, too.

"Aww," she says. "What did the new girl do?" she asks, smiling.

The other two girls burst out laughing, and I wish the joke wasn't on me, so that I could laugh too. The girls in my caravan never laugh.

ℵ

MY TROUBLE has a name. It's Boris. And he's great, he's great. Well, not great at everything. His unit chose to leave him behind at the training base because he can't shoot, really can't shoot. When I told my officer my helmet fell off the hill and I couldn't find it, he asked why it wasn't on my head. Then I said it fell off my head. Then he asked why it wasn't properly fastened. I wanted to scream at him that it wasn't properly fastened because there is nothing to be afraid of, because our only assailants are kids who would steal lollipop wrappers just so they can lick them, but instead I looked at the ground and waited to hear my punishment.

My punishment is to make Boris a better shooter. Boris's buzz cut is so blond it's almost white. He is exactly my height, a very short dude, but he is also bulky and firm and real. His blue eyes hide behind long lashes. He can't bear to look at me. "This is so humiliating, commander," he says as we walk on the sands leading to the shooting range. He is carrying a giant army radio on his back, a metal container of bullets in his right hand, and ten liters of water in his left. I have my weapon on my back, and a coat. Also, the carton of targets and wooden sticks. Chips of wood scratch my palms, like thrill. The cold pinches my nose, and walking by Boris's side I feel light. Lighter. Elated.

"You can call me Yael," I say. "I mean, we are the same age."

"I am eighteen," he says.

I am nineteen and two months. I was drafted late. It occurs to me that in a few years it will never again be accepted for me to even dream about the body of an eighteen-year-old boy. Then of any boy, really. I will only be allowed to dream of a man. There are nineteen-year-olds who are still boys. Twenty-year-olds too. I think it was after he turned twenty-one that I started noticing that Moshe was not a boy anymore.

We reach the shooting range that I booked with operations for us. The range is a small roof and a surface of cement. Boris lays down the equipment. He turns his shoulders in their sockets, and for a second it is as if the relief from the weight he was carrying has made him into a child, despite his embarrassment. I talk with operations on the radio, letting them know shots will be fired on range 11. When I turn back to face Boris, I see him lying down on the cement, holding his gun. His body is all wrong. I mean, his body is all right, but it is all wrong for shooting a weapon. The buttstock is not even in the dent between his shoulder and chest. It is resting, flying, somewhere above.

"Boris," I say. "Do I look like an ocean to you?"

He puts his gun down and sits on the cement. "No," he says.

"Then why are you getting carried away?" I ask. "There

is no need to start on the cement. I am sure you are not that bad."

Boris laughs. He laughs for a long time, his teeth showing and his nose twitching. "I really am that bad, though," he says.

We step ahead nonetheless, away from the cement and into the rocky sand of the shooting range. "I don't like practicing on cement," I say. "It is not realistic. Wars are not fought on cement."

I tell Boris to first show me what he can do on his own. I plant a stick in the ground and hang a fresh carton target, shaped like a green soldier, fifty meters ahead. Then I show him something small. I stand facing him, then take his hand in mine and place it at the dent between his shoulder and chest.

"Press around here," I say, "and pretend like you are swimming in strokes."

He doesn't argue. He does as he is told. My fingers are a little wet from the sweat of his body. I keep my hand on his, touching. "Now stop when you feel a dent or a hole," I say.

We move together until he says, "I can feel it! I can!"

"That's where you should put the buttstock when you shoot. It's is the best place for your body to absorb the recoil."

We spend a minute kicking away the copper bullet shells that litter the ground.

He lies down on the ground. Excited. "I'm gonna give it all I got, commander," he says in a voice nothing like the one he used before. That's how quickly, how physically, boys can flip.

"How about you give five bullets to the heart for now?" I say, and stick in my earplugs.

Boom, boom, boom. Boom. Boom.

I tell him to stay behind as I go and check his target. I run fast, aware that he is watching me, waiting, waiting but also watching me run.

There are no hits on the heart. I check the entire central mass area, but there are no hits there either. Nothing on the head. Nothing on the legs.

I run back, trying to hide the look of surprise on my face.

"Your weapon is just really not calibrated," I say.

Boris is sitting on the sand, holding his cheek in his big hand. "Oh, it's calibrated," he says, confident, gloriously confident, yet cheerless.

I bend over and lift his weapon off his back. I don't lie down. I put the weapon in the dent of my shoulder, standing. I tell Boris to step back and put his earplugs back in.

Boomboomboomboomboom.

I run ahead to check the target. Even though it is hard to be accurate with an M-16 while standing, I hit all the bullets right at the heart. They are less than ten centimeters apart. I contemplate calling Boris to see what I've done, to impress him, but then think better of it. This is not what he needs.

I run back to him and he looks at me, knowing, yet still somewhat hopeful.

"You are much smarter than me, actually," I say. "I changed my mind. Any good trainer knows that in order to achieve perfection, you have to start from the beginning."

"Cement?" he says.

"Cement and no bullets. We are gonna dry hump for a bit."

It's what practicing shooting a gun without bullets is commonly called, but I also said it to embarrass him, yet he is not embarrassed. He is not looking at me. The boy's eyes are on the goal, and he sees nothing but. As I unload his weapon, I notice that he is practicing his swim stroke, his eyes ahead, finding that dent again, making a mental note of it in his mind. He doesn't even see me or the sand or the hills in this moment, and his focused eyes are fantastic, unreal, not for me.

א

AT NIGHT, back in the caravan before another eight-hour shift, I call Moshe again. I call him upon waking, from under cover of a military blanket.

"We are back together now," I say.

"Is it me?" he asks.

"No," I say. "It's us again. Aren't you listening?"

"Good," he says. "Because I've already started looking for an apartment for us. The market these days. It takes years."

Once, he was fourteen and I was twelve. Once, I was afraid. He was not. Now we both are.

א

I SPEND two hours out of my next eight-hour shift thinking about Moshe, about how he is a man now, and how that is what nature is, or time, nature and time, and soon my thoughts loop.

Nature and him and him and nature and. On the third hour, I think I see boys running, glowing in red, on top of the hill. Small figures holding large squares. I blink, and they are gone.

When I get back to the caravan, I land my ammunition vest on the floor with a thump, and it wakes Dana.

"Haven't you noticed?" she asks.

"What?" I say.

"Hagar has been telling everyone the village boys have ripped the 'closed military area' signs off the fence."

"What do they need them for?"

"The officer said they sell the metal. That metal sells for melting. But listen to this—they only took the red ones. Isn't that weird?"

I cannot help but laugh. These little crawling boys have no qualms. They are not afraid. And now they have begun stealing our base.

"It's not funny!" Dana says, her whisper louder than a shout.

"It is sort of funny," I say. "I mean, I bet the boys stole only the red ones to be funny."

Dana doesn't get it. Her boyfriend is twenty-seven. They met when she was a senior in high school. She never knew him like I know Moshe; she never knew him as a boy. She is rubbing vanilla oil behind her ear, on her wrists and neck. This is because her boyfriend likes vanilla. He told her that once. She rubs it on her skin twice a day, even though he is so far away and cannot smell her.

She asks, "Why would they care about being funny?" but I don't even try to explain. I take off my military boots and climb onto the field bed with my uniform on, so I have more time to sleep before I wake up to train Boris. How could I explain to her that boys don't care about being funny, that they just are?

I don't explain it to her. Instead I wake up when she is still asleep and take the little glass bottle of vanilla oil and put it for safekeeping in the pocket of my pants.

ᔓ

BORIS HOPES we'll start the training with actual bullets this time, but after we set up, I take his weapon from him without a word and unload it. He lies down on the cement, and I hover about him, correcting his body.

I make sure that his left hand is at a ninety-degree angle and that his palm lets the gun rest on it without strain.

"We are working with bone here," I say. "If you work your muscles, they'll shake."

As I adjust the angle of his hand, I can feel his pulse and smell industrial soap.

"Don't break your wrist!" I shout, straightening his right hand, the one holding the handle. "We talked about this yesterday."

I kick his legs, hard, so that his left leg continues the exact line of the barrel and his right leg is spread apart, making a forty-five-degree angle. His butt clamps with every kick.

When I lean down and show him how to splatter his cheek on the buttstock, starting up then down until he is on target, I feel the softness of him, his pores with no hair.

I place a coin on the edge of his barrel and lie down right in front of it, holding my head up with my hands.

I tell him to look at me. "Aim for my eye," I say.

He slowly clicks the safety, then presses the trigger.

The coin falls, hitting the cement with a tiny rattle.

"Again," I say. "We'll do this until you are stable."

I place the coin back on the edge of the barrel. I lie back

down. He closes his left eye. His right eye looks into mine through gunpoint, circular and intending and blue. He presses the trigger.

The coin falls.

"Again," I say.

"Again," I say.

"Again."

I am going to do this all day. I'll do it until it's time for my shift. I'll do it even longer. The hell with the shift, the hell with everything, again, again, again, and then—

He presses the trigger and the coin stays on the barrel. The only part of him that moves is his left eyelid. Our eyes are staring right at each other, and we are silent.

"Again," he says, barely moving his chapped lips.

The coin falls, then stays, then falls, then stays, then stays, then stays.

I keep my eyes on his the whole time, but as soon as I let them wander I notice that his left elbow is wet, bleeding into his shirt from holding the gun for so long.

"You are ready to shoot," I say.

I put five bullets in his magazine. We shoot from the flat cement.

Three out of five! I swear! Two in the legs, but still, I swear!

I run back to the cement after checking his target and load five more bullets in his magazine.

"How did I do?" he asks.

"Again," I say, as calmly as I can, but I can almost feel the joy buzzing from my cheeks and into his blue eyes.

Boomboomboom.

"Stop!"

Boom.

"Stop!" I kick him.

Four boys have crawled onto the range, under Boris's fire. They are dark and small and elastic, moving faster and faster on the ground like lizards, collecting empty bullet shells in their plastic bags—fast, lit, their movements as exact as acrobats.

"What is that?" Boris asks, still lying on the ground.

"Boys," I say. "They are stealing our bullet shells. I mean, *actually* stealing bullet shells." Bullet shells are not even real metal. Even in Israel, they could probably only sell them for five shekels a kilo. I can't even imagine. It's brilliant. It is hysterical.

I know I should not smile, but I do, and with the smile I blink, and when I open my eyes again the boys are gone.

"Palestinian boys?" Boris asks. "How could we just let them go?"

"They are just boys," I say. "They steal things from our base all the time."

Boris gets up from the cement, and for a second we are standing very close. I smell the copper of his blood and his unwashed scalp.

"Tomorrow I'll teach you more things," I say. "Secrets, tricks."

Boris straightens his back and nods, like a gentleman, holding himself as tall as he can, the muscles of his neck shaking, loose.

א

AT NIGHT, back in the caravan, before another eight-hour shift, I call Moshe.

"We are broken up," I say.

"Now, I know it isn't me this time," he says.

"No," I say. "It *is* you. Aren't you listening?"

"Good," he says. "If it's me, then that's good. I never worry about me. I worry about you."

He is the only boy I ever kissed. Moshe. I have been kissing him since he was a very young boy, and I was even younger.

א

BORIS AND I move ahead to shooting from sand and rocks, an unsteady surface. Before we start, I tell him to give me his hand. Mine is more coarse. Though I am his height, my hand looks in his a lifetime smaller. I take his right index finger and explain.

"The lowest third of your finger is called the 'Indifferent.' It is not perceptive enough to accurately push the trigger. The top part of your finger is called the 'Sensitive.' It is too vulnerable to remain steady when you press the trigger." My breath releases fumes into the cold air. My nose drips a tiny drop into our hands, and when I look up Boris's white smile hits my eyes.

I look down again. "And this part," I say and pinch the middle part of his finger, "this part is called the 'Hammer,' and this is the part you should press the trigger with. This part is perfect."

"I never knew there was a part of me that's perfect," Boris says. His eyes are beaming at my words, just like Dan's did once when I was very young, when we both stood by a bench in Jerusalem Street. His hand moves in mine, and I cannot tell if it is the cold or intention. I hesitate.

"Well," I say. "Now you know."

We stand silent for a minute, until at once we both pull away. The hills of Hebron loom above us like monsters and the sky feels larger, further away when I look up at it, as if we are at the very bottom of an ocean.

"Hey Boris," I say. "Have you heard what they are doing behind the new mall in Jerusalem?"

"What are they doing?"

"Your mom," and with that I kick his leg, making him fall to the ground, hearing him laugh before he even hits it. A glorious laughter, deep and uncontrollable.

He shoots and hits two out of five. I run back from marking his target, and without a word I take the magazine out of his weapon and make sure it is unloaded.

"Get up," I shout. "Take your earplugs out."

I am sure the two bullets he hit are his first two. After that, he kept on moving out of position.

I point the gun in the sky and bring it close to Boris's ear. There are small yellow dots of dirt in his inner ear, and this makes me love him. Love him more.

I press the trigger, and then I don't let it go. One second, two seconds, three.

Clank.

"After each bullet you shoot, I want you to count to three. I want you to be able to hear this sound each time, the sound of a new bullet pressing into the chamber."

"What does it matter what I do after I already shot the bullet?" Boris asks.

It matters for tricking his brain. If he knows he has to wait after each bullet, he is less likely to jump the trigger and bend out of form. I don't tell him that, though. By now I know people only need to know what they need to know to do well.

"It matters because I said so, and you should do as you are told."

This time, he hits four out of five, three to the heart and one at the edge of the head.

א

DURING MY guarding shift, it starts as an idea, then it is a thought, soon a feeling, and then it is so real I can almost see it in front of my eyes, except I cannot; something is terribly off. Missing.

I reach the top of the hill overlooking the ammunition bunker, light my flashlight, and stare at the entire base below. Crickets bay away and close. I blink, then open my eyes.

It is the most ludicrous, charming thing I have ever seen.

The fence around the base, by the ammunition bunker; it is gone. Not there anymore. Vanished.

Those boys. Those devil boys. They have stolen it.

The metal buyer of their village could be melting it in these very moments.

This shift, like all others, is eight hours long, but the seconds and minutes and hours glide by like a child on a slide. I don't think of my boyfriend, or nature, or time, or boys even. All I can do is think:

The fence.

The fence.

They took. The fence.

Every few minutes, without planning, I find myself saying it out loud, and then, my laughter echoes, across mountains I cannot see in the dark.

א

AT NIGHT, back in the caravan, after eight hours of laughter alone and staring, I call Moshe. I call him from under the cover of a military blanket.

"You can't keep doing only the things I tell you to do," I say.

"But you told me to," he says. "I thought this was what you wanted."

"Yes," I say. "Exactly."

"I don't know what you want anymore," he says. "How come we only speak in code?"

Once, he was fourteen and I was twelve. Once, I was afraid. He was not. He climbed right up to the top of the German widow's apple tree and threw a shower of red apples on my head so fast and steady I thought I'd drown. All I could see between my winces was his crooked teeth between the highest branches, and all I could hear was him shouting: "Here's more, more, more, more, more."

"I don't want anymore!" I shouted from the ground.

"But this is fun!" he shouted back, and for a second I could catch his eyes as he reached for another apple; for a second I saw in them wanting, really wanting, nothing but that very thing.

"I am waiting for you to tell me what you want," I say now. "There is no code."

"Does this mean we are back together again?" he asks.

"What do you think?" I ask back, and I wait for a voice I still can't believe is long gone.

ℵ

I sit on top of Boris's back as I explain to him what Situation Zero is.

"Breathe in," I say, and I can feel his lungs swelling below me. "Now empty your lungs completely."

I explain about the things we can know for certain and the things we cannot. I explain that when you breathe, there is no way for you to know how much air is in your lungs. The only thing we can re-create is the situation in which our lungs are completely empty. In order for all of your bullets to hit at exactly the same spot, you must close your eyes before each shot and empty your lungs completely. This is how you know you are on target, right back where you were with the earlier bullet. Situation Zero.

His lungs rise up, then down, then up as I explain.

"I didn't say that you could breathe again, young lady," I say.

He stops, and even without looking I can tell that his mouthful of teeth is showing, that he is smiling.

"Do I look like a blender?" I ask.

"No," he says.

"Then why are you mixing things up?"

After we laugh, he shoots.

Two out of five, three out of five, three out of five, five out of five.

He doesn't lose his focus. Every time I run back from checking his hits with a marker, he gets back into position.

We don't even say, "Again."

He shoots as I sit by his side until our hair reeks of gunpowder, until our ears ring into our earplugs, until night begins to fall.

Soon his hits become consistent. A constellation of five stars around the heart.

As we walk back, passing one shooting range after another, I ask him what I've been wondering about.

"Boris, how the hell did you manage to pass boot camp without learning how to shoot?"

He stops walking, looks at me, and shrugs his wide shoulders.

I put a hand on his shoulder, from a distance. "Well, I am proud of you."

He is only a step away. I could step closer with ease and kiss him, but I don't.

He kisses me, then steps back and raises his arms, questioning.

I look at his eyes. His eyes to me are apples, just apples then. I think and smell apples, and I do not think of Moshe; I just hear his shouts. "More, more, more, more, more."

And then Boris. I see in his eyes wanting, wanting, nothing but that very thing.

Me.

Before I take off my uniform, I take out the glass bottle of vanilla oil I took from Dana and carefully rest it on the sand so that it does not break.

We don't go inside one of the ranges to do it. We are naked on the sand. Boris's movements are lumbering and hesitant and young and unknowing.

And he is not afraid.

Our bodies impress and dig and confuse the sand so much that when it is all over, I cannot find the glass bottle of vanilla oil. The truth is I spend little time searching.

After we have our uniforms arranged on our bodies again, I look at him, framing him with the sand behind him. This is how I want to remember him. Young, wide shouldered, victorious, very close and still a little far.

I put a hand on his shoulder, just as I did before.

Then he runs away, away under the roof of a shooting range near us. I can feel his shoulder slipping from under my hand, and for a while I leave it there, suspended in air.

Boom.

Boom.

Boom.

Boom.

The boys, I think. *The boys. Boris has shot them.*

And my breath halts at the entrance of the throat.

Then I run. I can run too.

"They are just kids," I shout at Boris as I kick him, then jump above him lying on the cement.

"When you see people without uniform in a base, you shoot them," he says. "It is protocol, no?"

His voice grows quieter as my steps widen ahead.

You don't shoot boys. Hasn't anyone taught him that? Was I supposed to teach him that?

The insides of my stomach tighten, and my chest hurts from jumping up and down with my unsteady scurry. I reach the foot of a hill and I stop, and I hear it. A suffocated laughter, just below my feet. The mousy sound of a tiny human. I press a button on my watch, and little rings of neon from my watch scatter on the sand.

Inside a dent in the earth, I notice, through the corner of my eye, the most beautiful boy I have ever seen. He is folded into himself, like a surprise ready to burst.

I notice details about him while I pretend I don't see him.

"Is there anyone here?" I shout into the air, and I notice.

I notice that his skin is dark, that his hair is jumbled, that his arms are longer than they should be. I notice that he is only a few years younger than me, below my feet, yet further away than anything I have ever before wanted. Boys when at their best are easy as life. They want what they want, and then they walk up and get it, their step balanced, self-assured, lovely, all the same.

I stand there, stretching my arms out as if they are searching, and the boy believes the impossibility that I have yet to spot him. He doesn't move; he is waiting for me to leave. He does not know I am there, watching him, pleased, my expectations all at once fulfilled.

The boy's elbows are poking the bushes of the prickly burnet. When I look above, the mountains blend with the sky behind us, as if eating or marrying each other. It could have been me who gave Boris the strength to kill the boy. My body still carries the smell of Boris, and the short minutes in which we confused the sand below us still hover above me as though they have yet to fade. But Boris could not kill the boy, he did not kill the boy, and now the boy is a surprise, my silent surprise inside a dent in the earth. If only I could, I would stare right at him forever, but I only get a fraction of a second to notice, and only out of the corner of my eye.

I blink.

When I open my eyes the boy is gone. I can hear his maddening laughter echoing across the mountains; *I got you, I got you, I did,* I imagine the echoes of his chuckles chanting. I take as much air as I can into my lungs, and then I smell it, a lingering smell of something that was just there but then was taken. Vanilla.

He took my glass bottle. That boy. I imagine his awe—*What is this good for?* he will ask his mom as she is chopping onions, onions he stole for her, on the kitchen counter. And he will hold the bottle open and stand and smell and think for a minute, until he knows in his eyes the only use in this world for the smell of vanilla inside a bottle. It is only he who will know, that boy. Not me. He took my glass bottle. He did! Before I laugh, I wait, hoping to catch the brief noises of his body brushing up against the leaves, the sound of bullet shells jangling in his plastic bag.

Checkpoint

I said no. That I was tired. Yaniv asked if I wanted to check cars instead of people, but I said no. He said he was sick of bending over. He said, "Lea, if you had a good woman's heart, you would say yes and take mercy on me because I have a bad back and problems at home," but I said no. No and that he was not supposed to be bending over and sticking his head in car windows anyway because that was against the rules. Then he called me a Russian whore, even though I am half Moroccan, half German.

It was four in the morning, and the line of Palestinian construction workers in front of the Hebron checkpoint curled further than I could see. There were hundreds of them, waiting for me and the other transitions unit soldiers to open the rotating metal doors and let them through. There was still an hour to go before we would be allowed to do that. The rules said that we opened at five. We closed at noon. It was not our decision.

It was just my luck that the first and only year of my service in the transitions unit was one of those years the government closed the sky for Filipino and Indian temporary workers, and so Israel started needing the Palestinian construction workers again. We needed them, but we were also a little afraid they'd kill us or, even worse, stay forever. These were both things the Palestinians were sometimes into doing. That's why I existed. I was responsible for checking to see that the workers owned a permit that assured they weren't the type likely to stay in Israel forever or try to kill us. The permit said they were only allowed to stay for the daytime. Then they had to leave Israel and go back to the territories. They got to see us every day, if they did what was right. And we got to see them too.

I also had to make sure they weren't carrying weapons or about to explode their bodies. We were there to notice what the government wanted us to, dangers, but I would still only notice what I happened to notice. This was because I couldn't realize I was a soldier. I thought I was still a person.

Fadi, the person I first noticed that day, was very close to the front of the line of workers. I noticed him because even though I could not see his face, even though they were all too far away to have faces, I could tell he was looking at me as though I had made a decision. A decision of horror. A future thing I had not yet done wrong yet nevertheless I could not undo. His curved chin was held up, as if destined never to budge, and pointing right at me, as if it were an eye. From that distance I must not have had much of a face for him to see, but I swear I knew he had already chosen me then.

On the asphalt road by the checkpoint, cars were lining up.

It was not my decision to be there, wearing that blue beret. I didn't want this. I said no.

ב

I DIDN'T know this before I joined the army, but there were three general types of checkpoints, and mine was the dumbest. Some checkpoints were placed in the middle of a Palestinian village or on a main road, like Route 433, that linked one Palestinian town to another; those soldiers checked them while they were inside their land. This may sound crazy, but these were the places most bombs and guns were found. Others checked people for medical permits, people who could only get the treatment they needed in our hospitals. Even if an ambulance came howling and the sick person was howling too, they checked, because of that one pregnant woman from when I was in fourth grade. The one who had a nine-month-old fetus in her stomach and a bomb with a diameter of thirty centimeters under her gurney. Both these types of checkpoints showed that we would not let our lives be cheap, but my checkpoint only showed that we wanted our homes to be cheap, and that the Palestinians' anger could be bought, that very same anger that was so deep it sometimes killed us.

Most days there were workers in line who didn't make it through, and the Israeli contractors who waited for their workers at the other end of the checkpoint would curse at us soldiers. And the Palestinian workers would curse at us soldiers. I was usually called a Russian whore, except for one time when someone called me a German bitch. That made me smile, but only for a minute.

THE WEEK before the day I first saw Fadi, one of the Israeli contractors followed me behind the sand dunes where I had just finished peeing and asked me why there were only five soldiers checking people but ten soldiers checking cars. He said that every time one of us went to pee the line slowed and that this was no way for something professional to operate, that a businessman like him didn't need to be subjected to the mercy of the bladder of a teenager. He didn't catch me with my pants down, but the fluid that had soaked into the sand stood between us. I had no answer.

"I don't work for you," I told the contractor. I thought he would curse me, but instead he asked another question, which was worse.

"Who do you work for?"

When I lowered my eyes and stood without words, I saw that fruit flies swarmed over the wetness.

IT WAS getting close to when we would have to start passing the Palestinian men through into Israel. I heard Hebron's muezzin through the speakers singing the call of prayer and looked at the first rays of sun spreading like dots of ink. I was so tired I had to slap my face so that I would not fall asleep standing up.

I hated so much and mostly myself when I was this tired. There was sour sloshing in my stomach and up my throat, and I could smell the stench of my own breath mixing with the smell of the toothpaste on my yellow teeth. I hated how disheveled I looked, like a child drowning in a green uniform, playing make-believe. I hated that even though I was wearing a bulletproof vest, and even though I looked like a kid holding a gun, my breasts were so large that I knew they showed through all I was wearing. I hated so many things I said—a long time ago, some lies I told when I was drunk at a high school party, a party I should have stopped but didn't when I was a senior. But mainly I hated the dumb chatter I exchanged with the Ethiopian and Moroccan girls in my unit outside our caravans on all nights while we smoked our lives away into the smallness of the night. They were worse than the girls in high school.

Waking up every morning was a tragedy, like killing your own mother, or losing your virginity to a guy who will only sleep with you once, and realizing what you have done just as you are forced to open your eyes. The walls pounded my eyes and head and neck like I was waking up inside a white, shiny boom box. And I never liked music. I would give so much, everything, for sleep, or so I thought. The problem was that every evening I would forget just how much, and I became scared of that bed where tragedy took place every morning. I went to sleep only when I couldn't help falling asleep.

If I could I would burn the blue beret on my head. But it was on my head.

More men. More men. More men.

I wanted to say that day that there was only one of me and demand to go back to my shabby dreams, but my shift was starting. The gates opened, and the metal rotated, and the men went through the machine that lit up green or red, then they stood across from the cement barricade that protected me and the four other soldiers checking IDs and bags.

א

MY OLDER sister Sarit told me that if I insisted enough, the sorting officer would cave. That all I had to do was say, "I won't go, I won't go, I won't go." She even specifically warned me that the worst thing that could happen was that they would place me in a military police unit and make me wear a dreadful blue beret. No other soldier would ever want to talk to me, because they would all see my blue beret and fear that I had the authority to write them up and report them for having a red hair tie instead of a black or an olive green one, or for wearing their everyday uniform coat over their official uniform, or for listening to headphones while crossing the road, or whatever stupid shit military police soldiers were responsible for writing other soldiers up for.

I told her to stop talking. So my sister said anyone that got placed in military police was an idiot. She said there were other army positions to be careful of, and that of course the best was what she was, a paratroopers' instructor, and I told her to stop talking.

"They might tell you that they'll put you in jail. That no one will ever hire you after that. That Mom and Dad will disown you. That you will never find love. That you will become a homeless person. Whatever it is they tell you, just say, 'I won't go, I won't go, I won't go,' and eventually they'll assign you somewhere else, and—"

"Stop. Talking!" I said.

In the sorting officer's office the day I was drafted, the sorting officer spoke before I sat down.

"Military police," she told me. Of course that was what

she said. Naturally. "It is the only boot camp I have open this week."

"I won't go," I said.

"Everyone says that," the officer said, and crossed her arms. She was smiling.

"I won't go. I am smart. I got good grades. I can translate things."

"I don't have any intel spots. All I have is the spots they give me, and all I have left is military police. Besides, they are trying to diversify the unit, make it more socioeconomically diverse or something, and you have great grades."

"You mean that everyone there can't read. I won't go. I am not about to spend two years of my life handing out reports in some bus station to soldiers who are wearing yellow socks," I said. I was afraid, shy about how confident I was. This was my first day as a soldier. I was eighteen and spiteful. After graduation, when there were no more girls to be bitchy to, I read a lot and followed sophisticated American TV shows: *The West Wing*, *Sex and the City*. It was just my luck that I was randomly drafted last.

"Look, if you physically resist going, I'll have to throw you in jail for a few weeks that won't count toward your mandatory service time, and then when you come out I'll still place you in military police."

"I won't go. I won't go."

"There is more to military police than the proper-appearance write-ups. It is actually a really important role. Different soldiers do different things. You'll like it, I swear."

"But I won't go," I said. I believed it when I said it.

"Oh, but you will," the officer said.

"No."

"Your parents will never speak to you again."

"No."

"No one will hire you."

"No."

"You'll have regrets."

"But I won't go."

In the end I went, because the officer knew even before I did that I'd go. That I was always going to go.

א

THERE WAS actually nothing special about Fadi, the man I noticed that day, or so I thought until I looked, and stopped, and thought hard. It had been a few months since I had thought hard, so I wasn't used to doing it.

He was one of the first men to show me his ID that morning. He passed through the machine with a lowered head and put his ID on the cement barricade. It was a green ID. It said his name was Fadi. Inside the ID was the white permit. It was stained brown, but it was the right permit, the construction-work permit that was the only permit we were allowed to accept at that checkpoint, other than a medical permit. I pointed to his plastic bag.

"What's in there?" I asked.

"What is in there? What could be in there? Food. Pita," Fadi answered. His voice exploded at the vowels.

"Can I see it?" I asked. I signaled with my hand. I didn't always check all the bags. I was supposed to check them at random, so I usually checked every third or fifth one, but suddenly I didn't want this man to leave me. There was something about him. His outfit was standard—a cheap old button-down shirt that was meant to garnish him with dignity but only intensified his sadness, its collar mocking his drained, barely shaven face.

He had murky rims under his eyes and hairs in his nose. He smelled of sweat and aftershave. He was like the rest of them, but he stood with urgency. He did not want to be there. He was almost not there, but he was. He was clasping his plastic bag and he was almost not there but he was and I could feel my eyes jolt.

"Can I see it?" I asked again. I was crying, but it was a physical cry, one brought on by exhaustion and the wind hitting my face. I cried all the time, but only physically. The man, Fadi, still would not let go of his bag, and I knew, I decided, that I would sleep that night and think of him. There was something about him, and that something would help me sleep.

Fadi flipped the plastic bag and shook it, and pitas fell to the sand like leaves. This was not the first time one of the men in my line had done that, but there was something different about how he did it, how injured he was by my request. It was more than a gesture. Behind him I could see Yaniv sticking his head inside the car of one of the Palestinians and making small talk. Talking very small, I was sure.

"Here, here you go. I don't need food. You have it and be happy," Fadi said, and then took his ID from the cement barricade and walked away, flailing his arms.

א

AT NIGHT I could hear the Ethiopian and Moroccan girls talking and smoking in the wooden pergola outside our caravan. They were talking about what's better, to tell a friend if someone is gossiping about her or not to tell a friend. They were stupid. Their problems were all outside of their heads. Everyone in the transitions unit was stupid. It was a unit designed for stupid poor people. People the army thought could do little except check IDs. We were stationed in places just as dangerous as the exalted infantry units, but when an infantry soldier passed through our checkpoint with his green or red or brown beret, he pointed, and then he laughed. He was a hero and we were not heroes; we were just the police.

I buried myself under the wool blanket of my field bed and thought of Fadi. After boot camp, when I was first stationed, I used other things to make me sleep. At first I thought about my boyfriend, about when we slept together, one of the dads of the girls I hated in my class, all the best times and times that never happened as I imagined but now I could imagine. In my thoughts my boyfriend was much stronger than I ever let him be in real life, and he would always start by pushing me against a wall, and I would always be surprised. In life, my boyfriend said that I should stop crying every time after it was all finished, because he would break up with me if I didn't stop, because it freaked him out. Also because he worried that if I kept doing it, then one day he would not be able to tell the difference between when I was sad and when I wanted sex. In the end he broke up with me, and he was also right. I would always cry when I remembered the sex, and so

I stopped thinking about that at night in my field bed because I assumed I cried too much during the day already.

For a week I thought about *Dawson's Creek* and *Ally McBeal* when I tried to fall asleep. Shows that were popular before I had a boyfriend. I remembered every episode. I remembered the punch lines and the way the light fell on the water. But everything that seemed so wonderful to me then, the things I imagined myself doing if I were a part of the show, the characters I thought I could be or meet—none of it seemed interesting anymore. I knew I would never enjoy watching those shows again.

Then I thought about the games I used to play with Yael. The time we pretended we were reporters, the time we pretended an elevator was a spaceship, the times we let Avishag join and play Exquisite Corpse with us. All the stories we made up. But after a while I realized I was inventing most of those memories. I stared at the bulletproof vest on the floor and realized I did not truly remember what it felt like to play games. And I knew if I invented any more memories of games it would only remind me of the memories I had lost, so I stopped.

This is how small my life was: after the games, after my third idea, there was nothing more I could think of.

The evening I began thinking about Fadi, he became my new idea. I imagined him talking with his wife, Nur, as they smoked a hookah stuffed with apple-flavored tobacco on their sun porch. I imagined that must have been the evening Nur put her foot down. On the specific evening I was imagining, an evening from the past, Nur asked Fadi to get a job in construction in Israel. Fadi did not want to go. He did not want to take money from the Israelis. He did not want to be torn from his dreams only to stand in line for hours and wait for a girl half his age to bark orders at him. He did not want to go. He wouldn't.

"I won't go," Fadi said.

"But we have five children," Nur said. "We need money for Nadia's university. We need better formula for the baby."

"I won't go."

"But you haven't worked in months. You won't find a job in Hebron."

"I won't go."

"But I will leave you if you don't. I will leave you and no one in the family would blame me for it and you will die alone."

"I won't go."

"Oh, but you will," his wife said and looked out to the lights coming from a neighbor's home, and because she knew that he would surrender, he did surrender and he did go.

I felt sleep touching me then leaving, touching me then almost staying. It was hard to breathe under the blanket. Outside, I could hear the girls talking and smell their cigarettes and shampoos. They said "calories" many times, and also "That's what's really bad."

I tried to think of what Fadi could be doing right then, rather than in the past, and decided that he must be arguing with Nur. That he was yelling at her as she made him his pita sandwiches filled with okra and hummus for the next morning. That he was still saying he wouldn't go. That Nur, beautiful Nur, was not even looking at him, but that when he said she was the devil she threw his sandwiches in the trash and then walked behind the kitchen counter and passed him and that all Fadi wanted was for her to touch his shoulder for one second, but Nur walked right by him and into their bedroom and Fadi fell asleep on the floor in the kitchen, his head resting on Nur's coat that he pulled from the coat hanger by the door, by the door, the closed door, that door that is closed—

When I woke up the next morning, I was tired, but less.

The ride to the checkpoint was usually all the torture that is inherent in movement. Breaths and moans and the webs of sleepy eyes of all of us jumbled. I was yanked from slumber and immediately boarded the bulletproof green van, with its miniature barred windows and thick metal skin. My head bobbed and smashed and hurt as the van glided along the territories we occupied. When the movement halted, all I arrived at was men, a line of men, all these men, waiting for me, raging through stillness.

The ride the morning in which I was less tired, the morning after I first thought of Fadi, was almost just a regular nice ride, though. Almost, I swear.

א

I SAID no again when Yaniv asked me to do cars for a bit, and then he told me a dick is like a boomerang.

"A dick is like a boomerang," he said. He was chewing gum like a dumb cow, but he was a boy. "You understand?"

"No," I said. "I don't understand."

"You know what it means to throw a dick at someone?" Yaniv asked. "It means that you are showing you don't care about them."

I had never heard this expression before. There were so many expressions I never heard before I joined the transitions unit. Hyperbolic, Moroccan, so many inane forms of speech.

"Well, I actually don't care about you," I said.

It was true. I hated him, and on mornings like that one when I was not so tired, I hated him even more than I hated myself. I hated the way he chewed gum as he high-fived the people he knew in the cars. I hated the way he would kiss all the girls who would let him on both cheeks. I hated his co-logne and that he plucked his eyebrows. I hated that he wore a giant golden Star of David around his neck and that he sang Mizrahi music to himself and always talked jokingly about how much he hated our officers and his blue beret and of how he guessed that this must be his messed-up destiny. I hated that he smiled and that despite his whining I would some-times catch him enjoying it—he loved bending down and sticking his neck inside windows and chatting up the drivers, and he did not understand the difference between horror and honor or he did understand but didn't care. He lugged his neck as if it were light.

"Well, that's why the whole point is that a dick is like a boomerang. You throw it at someone, and it comes right back at you," Yaniv said.

When I saw him smiling and sticking his neck down a window later that day, I thought about telling. I knew every-one would hate me for it, but I actually thought about telling my officer, who was walking between the cement barricades and the cars and must have seen Yaniv sticking his neck in cars, chatting and kissing babies and taking figs and olive oil bottled in used Coca-Cola bottles. The officer saw everything, but if I told, he would have to do something; he would have to. If I were an officer, I would never let one of my soldiers violate regulations like that. The regulations we learned in boot camp said that we must always place our guns between our bodies and the open windows of the Palestinians passing through checkpoints. That the Palestinians had to put their IDs and papers on the hood of the car and then close the window as the soldier approached to look through them. No one followed that, but at least they didn't kiss babies, and they didn't lie about their bad backs and—

I truly might have told on him except Fadi was back. I saw him nearing the head of the line and I knew that he was hoping I wouldn't be the one who would call him to approach the barricade. I watched him lower his stare and scratch his nose and kick the sand and hope for someone other than me. But I was also watching the other soldiers and delayed the man I was checking by looking long and hard at his ID until I saw that it was about to be Fadi's turn and that all the other soldiers were still checking IDs, and then I called for him.

He looked me straight in the eyes like he did not know me at all or like he wanted me to die, but I knew I knew him and the sum of him.

This is how I knew: he did not have a plastic bag. I had been right in imagining what I had. His wife had not given him pitas the night before. He was wearing the same button-down shirt, and his face was marked with edgy sleep. He reeked of sweat.

It was not that I believed that all the things I imagined happened in real life; it was that I thought that maybe it would be better if I did believe them, and I was not crying, and I wanted to keep being less tired.

I watched Fadi walk away after I gave him back his ID

and papers. A contractor with a cigarette in his mouth put a hand on Fadi as soon as he neared, and I could see Fadi's body flinching, how much wrong was in that very touch, how he wished he could punch the man, or scurry, or revolutionize his life, but he couldn't.

I knew that that night I would fall asleep thinking about Fadi coming home and punching his wife, Nur, just one punch to the jawline and then Nur's calm.

א

I SPENT the weeks prior to my draft trailing after Mother, who was holding the list of supplies the army had sent and comparing prices across stores, in outlet malls that were placed hours away from our village up north. Seven pairs of olive green socks. Sunscreen. Toothpaste. Enough sanitary napkins for two months. Mosquito repellent. Twenty sturdy rubber bands, to hold up the bottoms of the uniform pants.

My huge backpack, the one our high school gave to every graduate, was printed with the blessing "Go in peace, dear graduates. We are here for you and we will always love you." The backpack was packed and ready for the morning to come.

Mother and I took a bus to the Haifa drop-off spot, where another bus was waiting to take all the northern kids to Tel Aviv, to the central sorting base, where we would get the military equipment and our assignments for the next few years.

Girls with too much makeup held signs with painted hearts and kisses. These girls were crying and hugging and screaming to their friend as she climbed on the bus. "Read our letters only once the bus pulls away! We love you, babe!"

A boy kept trying to get his girlfriend to stop kissing him.

She was teary and her nose was dripping, but she would not stop kissing him even when he had to get on the bus. One boy who wore a yarmulke brought his whole family. Really, that must have been the entirety of his family. All grandparents. All aunts. All uncles. All and all. They were crying. But also clapping. All of them.

I had thought about telling my friend to come, Yael, but I didn't, because Yael was more my only friend who was not yet drafted than my actual, true friend. Because I was not a girl who had friends. I had a herd of retarded girls who followed me around for most of high school, but I never quite saw the need for friends, and I actually liked that it was only Mother and me that day. It was as if it proved my suspicion that friends are frivolous at the end of it all.

Mother kept on humming a song I had never heard before as we stood in the parking lot and waited to hear my name.

"Stop it!" I shouted, and then Mother started to cry. She was nervous because I was her last child; because I was her weakest.

Mother stopped crying right before I was called to get on the bus. "It's going to be Ok," she told me. "Everyone does this. These will be the best years of your life," Mother whispered. She held my face in both hands.

"I am fine. I am sure I will be home for vacation in no time," I said.

"Yes," Mother said. "Yes," she said, and she didn't let go.

"I need my face, Mother," I said. "I need my face."

AND THAT night, the night after Fadi came to the checkpoint with no pitas, Fadi came to visit my head without me even trying.

"I won't go," Fadi said. "Don't make me go to work again." He was on the floor of his kitchen, sobbing.

"You are not a teenage girl," Nur said. "You mustn't cry like that. Grown men don't cry like that."

Fadi stood up. He watched Nur chop onions for the weekend casserole. "I won't go," he said. He was choking on his words. "My life should be more than this. Avi the contractor said he bought his son a new bike this week. He has a bike, and he is a quarter my age. I never had a bike. This isn't fair."

"Who do you think you are? Do you think you are some spoiled Israeli boy? You are a Palestinian man and this is your life. This is what we have to do," Nur said. She wiped her neck with the dishcloth, and this disgusted Fadi. He had noticed wrinkles around her neck, hanging, useless skin that was not there when he agreed to marry her, and this disgusted him more.

"Who is 'we'?" he asked. "There is only me. And I know who I am. I won't go."

"Oh, but you will go," Nur said, so knowing and old and chopping onions.

And when she smirked he could feel his fist clenching and he threw it for the blow—he felt his knuckles grazing the blade of the knife and tearing as his fist was in the air. Nur held up the knife, but Fadi didn't stop, and he punched her, just once, one punch to the jawline.

ℵ

"I CAN'T throw a dick at you," I told Yaniv the next morning. The sun was not yet seen, and I had woken up less tired. I had woken up with enough energy to look at myself in the discolored mirror in the bathroom caravan. I hadn't looked at myself in months. I had grown accustomed to washing my hands with my eyes planted at my feet.

"What?" Yaniv asked. He had his arm around one of the Ethiopian girls who was also assigned to check cars. They were pouring packets of sugar down their throats and singing Mizrahi music into the defenseless sands ahead.

"I don't have a dick, so I can't throw one," I said. I was so not tired I decided to mess with him for pleasure. I knew this would drive him crazy. It amused me that he would actually believe there is anything in this world he could understand that I didn't.

"It's an expression," Yaniv said. "It's like, not for real. It means showing that you don't care, you understand?"

"No, what do you mean? Do you not know that I don't have a dick?"

"Gosh," Yaniv said. He breathed in. "It's . . . it's an *expression*. Don't you understand?" he stretched out his arms, imploring. He was clearly goaded because he didn't even notice that he shoved the Ethiopian girl a little.

"I don't understand," I said. "You are stupid to say something that makes no sense."

"But . . . it's an expression," Yaniv said. It was clear by his pouting and rapid chewing that he was searching for words that had never been his. Words like "literal" or "representative" or even "figure of speech." I let him search for what was not at all there until it was time for the gates to open.

Fadi didn't try not to get me as his checker this time. He didn't try anything. I didn't even notice him in line, and there he was, placing his ID and papers on the cement in front of me like he didn't even know me. I made him wait before I took them. I pretended to look at Yaniv, who was hunched down and deep in chatter with a Palestinian inside a car. Cars began to honk; he was holding up the entire line.

Then I looked and then I saw and then I was afraid, but only for a second.

I expected it, but it still truly scared me for a minute when I saw it. Scared like someone had just convinced me I was God, or already dead, or on fire.

Fadi's knuckles were wounded. Cut. Blood had crusted on them.

"Did you hurt yourself?" I asked.

"Yes," Fadi said. "I hurt myself."

א

THE SORTING officer who placed me in military police was right. It was a common misconception that every soldier who wore a blue beret spent her service days giving out reports to soldiers who wore their uniform the wrong way while using the public transportation. I was placed in the transitions unit of the military police, the one that had nothing to do with military attire and everything to do with IDs and checkpoints. Still, it was a very common error, that instant fear of blue berets. When I took the train home on my very rare weekend vacations, other soldiers hushed when they noticed my blue beret. Then they ran away. I felt like an ogre or an Iraqi dictator or like I was ugly, which I was—I was ugly, wearing that beret.

There were nice things about it, though. There was always at least one soldier on the train who ran away and thus effectively gave me his seat, even when the train was jammed. I always had the quiet I needed to read my *TV Guide* or American novels. On school trips I never had quiet on the bus. Everyone always wanted to know what I thought we should do about a girl who stole someone's boyfriend, or for me to make sure Yael let everyone copy her homework, because we used to be friends and I was the only one she still kinda obeyed. On the train, as a soldier, I never had to worry about anyone's problems or weigh in on gossip.

One really cool thing that happened because of the blue beret is that one time a soldier, a boy, wept when he saw me. He must have had a bad record and knew that he was wearing something wrong, missing something, and so he cried and ran, cried and ran faster.

There were some, few, nice things about the blue beret, but none of these things meant having friends. None of these things were things I could imagine in my head before I fell asleep.

ℵ

THAT NIGHT, after the morning Fadi told me he hurt himself, I imagined that Fadi was now sleeping on the straw doormat outside the front door of his house. I imagined that his Nur had changed the locks on him and that he had to pee in the street and that he stayed awake till two in the morning so he could pee because he was so ashamed the neighbors might see. He was so ashamed of how much it hurt, that humdrum, human urge, and of the relief he felt when he finally did pee. Of how empty he felt afterward. As if he had emptied out who he was and all he had to show for it was a puddle of urine and a doormat for a bed and a locked door. He woke up to a three-legged dog peeing on his face. He only got one hour of sleep, but it was time to start walking toward the checkpoint, and he did walk, and as he walked he thought that his whole life was his fault, but I knew that it was actually mine, that I was the one who was imagining these things for him, and I felt a tad guilty about bringing him so low, but I also fell asleep within minutes of imagining, and that was a blessing. I had never used the word "blessing" before, not even in my thoughts. People like Yaniv used it all the time, but now it was the first word that came to mind and the only one.

And besides, all of this—the doormat, the locked door, the urine in the street, the three-legged dog—it was only in my head and for my sleep, because the next day Fadi came to the checkpoint driving a car.

א

I WAITED and waited and waited for him. It was past nine, and I found myself elated by every nearly identical worker who showed me his ID but was not my Fadi. I knew it could not be true but was also convinced that after Fadi had woken up as the three-legged dog was peeing on his face, he had started walking toward the checkpoint but then thought better of it and turned around. That he had decided, for real, for once, that he wouldn't go. I was not sure where he had gone after he turned around, and I was sure that was only because I had fallen asleep before I could imagine it. I had fallen asleep so fast.

I was happy for my sleep. Happy for myself when Fadi didn't show up, that there must have been some kindness in my thoughts that I was just unaware of. I was so not tired I had time to hope that I was better than who I thought I was. I felt slightly like I had not joined the army. Like I had not joined the army yet. I looked at Yaniv and tried hard not to hate him. I could see only his body standing on the asphalt because his head was stuck deep inside the window of the car he was checking. I brought up his face, the face I could not see, into my head, and tried not to hate him. He had pointed, bushy eyebrows, like furry arrows.

Then I heard. The scream.

When I saw the red and Yaniv sauntering backward, I didn't understand that it was blood on his neck. I tried to think of what it was, but I didn't understand that it was blood. I would later remember that I could see by the way Yaniv flapped his arms as he took a step, and then another, backward, that he did know that it was blood. There was something right then in this world that he understood and I did not.

Yaniv thumped to the ground and ceased moving. There was chatter all around me, but I did not catch the words. The voices of the Palestinian construction workers. The voices of the Israeli contractors. The voices of soldiers. They sounded different from one another but also like they were screaming the same words, words that I did not grab. I looked to the ground and saw my blue beret falling, plummeting, hitting the sand, and I did not know why but my hand reached for it and then froze. I was stuck in that pose, like a child trying to break her fall from a swing forever.

A shot was fired. I did not see who fired it, or where it hit; I only heard it, growing bigger as it passed through the sand and the line and the cement barricade where I was still trying to almost break a fall I was not having.

ℵ

THE MAN who stabbed Yaniv was Fadi. The shot that was fired at Fadi missed him entirely, and even though he was paler than usual when the officers yanked him out of the car, I knew it was him because I knew him so well. He had seen me through three nights of better sleep.

He did not look at me, not with his chin or his eyes, when they took him. He didn't know I existed, that I existed in the world and saw things.

His eyes were those of a man nuisance had died in.

ℵ

I FORGOT about Fadi. I did. And Yaniv. I forgot for a while. I only remembered two days ago. I remembered the ride to the checkpoint, the morning after Yaniv's neck. My head. I remembered my head. The metal skin of the bulletproof van would not give up on it the whole ride to the checkpoint. Boom and boom and boom. I kept on slamming my head on metal with each spin of the wheels, not learning. I kept on not learning and letting my head approach rest on my right shoulder, only to be banged again.

I only remembered, because of the van, when I came to

Tel Aviv two days ago and started looking for an apartment. I had some money saved to start out from the nine months I served as an officer and got paid. I filled out the forms to go to officers' school the day after Yaniv died. I didn't want to be just a retarded checkpoint girl anymore. I couldn't.

At any rate, I finished being an officer a few months ago, and now I am starting life. I obviously looked at the younger Tel Aviv neighborhoods first, the ones that are serviced by those big cabs, you know? The cabs that are actually vans, because the cab driver can take up to ten people and drop them off wherever they want along his route. Anyway, when I was looking for a place I took one of those Tel Aviv service cabs, the number 5, and the ride—I guess it was smooth. Honestly, I didn't even bang an elbow.

But just an hour ago I leased an apartment near Rabin Square. I won't be offensive and talk money, but let's just say that with how much I will need to work to pay the rent, the metal vans can't be too far from memory. And Fadi. I am paying for this neighborhood because the cabs here are the same as they are everywhere in the world. They are yellow, and cars. There aren't any of those bizarre van cabs.

And also, I know I remember Fadi because even though my sleep has been a blessing since the day of Yaniv's neck, lately, somehow, I have had a night, maybe two, when I had to watch TV until I fell asleep. I needed the colors radiating from the box into my eyes for them to shut.

א

THAT NIGHT. That night, I could hear the chatter of the Ethiopian and Moroccan girls on the pergola outside the caravans.

I went into the bathroom and looked in the mirror. I took my gun and put it under the handle of the door so that no one could enter it, though I knew the girls were all smoking, that they would smoke for hours, and that I would be left alone.

I took off my boots and then peeled off my socks. They were white, and I remember being most horrified when I realized that I had been wearing white socks that whole day, because we were only allowed to wear dark socks when we were at the checkpoints. And even though I was a military police soldier in the transitions unit, I was still a military police soldier, representing the blue beret and all.

Those white socks. I remember that this was the thing that had horrified me that night.

My belt, green pants, green shirt, green undershirt, bra, the underwear I had flipped inside out because I had run out of clean ones. I took it all off and I looked at myself naked in that stained mirror. The breasts that were too big, the new lines that had formed at the edges of my mouth.

I saw that I was a soldier then, and I looked and looked and looked, and I was not afraid. It was a few weeks before I turned nineteen. It was the night before I filled out the forms volunteering to go to officers' school. I saw that I was a soldier then and knew that I would be an officer, and I was not afraid.

I never showered that night. I thought of Nur; I thought that she must have showered and that she was already working on getting Fadi out of the Israeli jail, and that she was a strong woman, and then I remembered that I had created her, had invented her, and that I was a soldier and she was not real.

That night. That night I could hear the chatter of the Ethiopian and Moroccan girls on the pergola outside the caravans.

When I was in bed, unwashed, I heard them say that Yaniv's neck was cut almost in two by the knife the Palestinian in the car used to kill him, and I would have thought of Yaniv's face, his pointed, furry eyebrows. And I would have wondered what the girls meant by "*almost* in two," but I fell asleep before I could. I fell asleep without thinking of any single thing. It was easy. Anything is possible when you insist.

People
That
Don't
Exist

Person A

The Sudanese's body is still skewered on the barbed-wire fence. Nadav says the Egyptian soldiers and we, the Israeli soldiers, are like two children on a dock, waiting for the other kid to plunge in and claim the body. One arm of the Sudanese man reaches in a stroke over his head, and his tongue dangles. He looks like a frozen swimmer. Nadav says I am a special girl. He says, "Avishag, the only person you think about is yourself." It was not my shift when the Egyptians shot the man. When it is my shift, I stare at the fence through the green monitor for twelve hours and think about people that don't exist. We know each other well, the made-up people and I. But Nadav says that is the opposite of thinking about another person. We drive in the Humvee along the fence because

Nadav is an officer and he has to check on the older girls, the ones at the guarding towers and checkpoints. The base's gate-keeper asks for my soldier pass and I show her I have signed off a vacation day. It was a little hard to do, because the base never has enough new girls, girls who have to be watch girls for four months after they finish boot camp and do nothing but stare at monitors. Before we reach the bus station, I ask if it is bad I only think about myself. Nadav has forgotten he told me that once. He says everyone is sold on the idea that if this person or that person is different than they are, then *they* are not who they are, and that I am the only person in the world who is not sold on that idea because I only think about myself. I don't know what that means. I don't know if that means bad or good. I want a burger. Two.

Person B

After it is all over, after I am safe, I open my eyes and every-one can see that I am alive. I am the only girl in a hospital room full of injured men who are also from my country. They are silent but I scream, because I can, because I want water. The doctor woman from the little country comes over and asks a question in the language of the little country and the translator translates. The doctor wants to know how I escaped Sudan. She wants to know what I was thinking. She gives me some water in a cup. She means, the translator explains, what was I thinking of when I threw my body on the fence that was made from little knives. I didn't think, I want to tell the doctor. It was not my decision. I felt *her*. She was there. Mom. Mom. Mom. A million times and again and another time and more. She was a giant and a young girl and a grape and the wind all at once. She was there and then she was not. The guide who took us out of Egypt said, in Israel, in the little country, they don't believe in magic. They believe in people. In the little country, believe what they believe, do as they do.

Person A

At the bus station, Nadav gets himself two burgers but says I should only get one. He says I never finish two burgers. I say that's not true, but it is. I say this time I'll finish. I joke. I ask, "What if I am eating for two?" He lifts his eyebrows and surprises me. He says, "Avishag, let's keep it. Let's raise it on a pepper farm in the Negev desert and be happy." He is finishing his service in a year anyway. It is going to be awesome. It is awesome. It is the solution, to anything and everything. Nadav gets to say a lot of things to me, and I let him, because he is my first boyfriend, or because he is an officer. But then I laugh and I say I was joking, as if I would ever tell him such a thing in line at McDonald's. I say I am eating only for myself but I still want two burgers. And fries. I am eating only for myself, but it is true that I am pregnant. I don't tell him because I can't really feel it. My body still feels like it's just me. Even my body betrays me nowadays, and I betray it. The point is that it is just me in the world. I get hungry, sick, hungrier, sicker. And I don't talk too much anyway. I haven't tried doing something that stupid since boot camp. I still have half a burger left, and Nadav says I should man up. He is not leaving until I finish. I tear what's left of the burger in two and I stuff one piece down my throat. The pickle gets jammed sliding down and the ketchupy acid flows up, then the meat. After I puke on the floor of the bus station's McDonald's, Nadav says that's the perfect example of how I think only about myself. I want to tell him he is right, but I have to catch the 72 bus.

Person B

You'd want to think I don't exist, but I do. This happened. This is what happened. He drove a three-wheeled bike with a carry-on like a cub, and that's how he made money in the camps. He was my mother's husband but not my father, and in months he had made enough money for the three of us to pay for the guide to take us first to Egypt, and from there to the little country. We were not allowed to say "Israel," but people called it the little country. Everyone everywhere in Sudan whispered about it, about how to get to the little country, how that was the solution. When they came and started killing people at the camp, my mother's husband hid me under a blanket in his bike's carry-on and no one touched me and no one hurt me and I was safe, but only in a way and only for a while. The three of us were safe, and we all survived the first day. That was a problem. The guide said he was leaving the next morning and he wanted more money per head, so much money, if he was going to take anyone at all. That's when I knew I would have to kill him. My mother's husband. And from that it was very easy to know that I would have to kill her too. Everyone at the camp was saving to go to the little country, and now everyone needed more money and in every tent sons were killing their parents for money and fathers were killing their children and wives— depending on who was stronger. But they, my mother and her husband, went to sleep. They loved each other. They loved me. They went to sleep but really they were waiting to die, because once the people hit a camp, they don't leave, they come back the next morning and the next, and morning always comes, that is just a fact, until soon the last person in the camp is no more and so it ends in days. The story ends in days. I wanted the money we already had, but they said no, that they are going to hope and hope, and the money was barely enough for one person and if we go, we all go. There is hope; they thought there is always hope. They believed in magic. They didn't fear me because I was not a son. I was a daughter, and short, very short. That's why I had to use fire and not a rock; that's why I had to be fast, and I was. I got the money; it worked. Soon I started believing in magic, too.

Person A

The 72 bus driver stops next to an ice cream store just because he can, and he buys his daughter ice cream—peach sorbet, actually—and all the passengers have to wait. A high school boy who sits behind him yells that that is no way to behave, and the bus driver says he can suck his cock, even though his daughter is right there and she is little and that is so wrong to do. I want to say something too because I am worried about being late for my doctor's appointment, but I don't say anything because if I were a bus driver I would totally stop for ice cream whenever I wanted, except I would buy apple sorbet and I wouldn't stop because my kid wanted ice cream, I would stop because I wanted ice cream, sorbet, actually. So I understand the bus driver's heart. Maybe that counts as thinking about another person, and I want to tell Nadav about this but I can't, of course, because he is already back at the base, because I am alone. At the clinic the doctor says I have two options, and I am excited because my favorite thing in life is when I get to make a choice, and I didn't think I had any choice in the matter; I thought it was just this thing I had to do, like all of regular life, like the army. The doctor says they can suck it out and scrape what's left, or I can take two pills, and then the fetus would just fall away on its own. I am conflicted. If they suck it out, they'll do it right away, and I am kind of bored and anxious to know what that would feel like, if I would feel any different or even sad, which is something I haven't felt in a very long time. But if I take the pill I could just leave right away and go back to the base and then maybe my officer would let me sign only half a vacation day off and then I'd get to save that half day, because the watch girls' officer is very nice; he is friends with Nadav. Also, it could be interesting to just do my shift and smoke a cigarette in the watch room while a tiny tiny baby is falling out and no one knows it but me. I didn't even know that pill thing existed! The wonders of science. I like it that both options are interesting. It makes the whole decision thing that much more special. But in the end I decide on the pills just because I miss them. I miss the made-up people on the green monitor.

Person B

The magic that happened after I left the camp was a very unusual magic; it was brought upon me by my mother, and it was not the magic you'd expect. You may think by what I will tell you that I was very lucky, but I was not. Some people had to walk out of Darfur into Khartoum, but my group only walked for a few hours, and then our guide transferred us to the truck of a Bedouin. One of the other women had to sit in the front of the truck and pretend to be the Bedouin's wife, and the rest of us sat at the back between wooden boxes of potatoes and flour. As I watched the Bedouin take the woman's hand and help her climb to the front of the truck, that's when I heard it first, inside the holes of my ears, the two disapproving clicks of someone's tongue, and it sounded like my mother, I think. *No good, this is no good,* I heard a whisper thumping at the front of my forehead. The woman who climbed to the front looked about eighteen, my age. Her skin was unusually fair, almost like that of the Indian work immigrants. I then realized that no matter what happens, if I live or die, even if I become a queen, my skin will never be as fair as that woman's. I will never be that beautiful. This broke my heart; it broke it very much. Everything was in vain. I had never thought about anything even remotely resembling that type of concern before, but now it was all that I could think of, my skin. For all the hours and days as the wheels rolled through the sands, I cried so much the others offered me their rations of bread and dry beef. They could not imagine what I had seen that could possibly make me sadder than they were, because they had seen the worst, and this softened the hearts of even the sons who had broken their fathers' skulls with rocks. Still, I cried because the movement of the wheels offended me. I kept on thinking that it did not matter if or where we'd arrive. My mom and her husband would still be dead, and it would be me who had killed them. Worse than that, I would still be me, and I had nothing anywhere, and I would be nothing anywhere. When we arrived in Egypt, our guide was terrified because they had just busted two trucks bringing in illegals and they didn't just kill the illegals; they killed the Bedouin guides too. But we were let in without an incident. That's when it all turned darker, then even more dark.

Person A

Four hours after I take the second pill, I think I am going to die, but I know I won't. My stomach hurts from the outside, like a drummer is hitting it with bare hands. I crumple forward but I crank up my neck, because I know they'll yell if I take my eyes off the monitor. In the eighteen years I have been alive, there were times I thought I'd die but then I lived and I lived and I lived. When I was first stationed here two months ago and had my first shift in front of the green screen, I made it till the fourth hour, but then I thought I'd for sure die. All around me there were girls staring at their strip of the fence and I could not understand how they did it for twelve hours, and then again, and then another time, and more. I kept on thinking this was my life for the next four months, until I was allowed to do checkpoints and guard towers, until I was "broken into the unit" as Nadav called it, and I couldn't even figure out how to make it till the next hour. The green pixels swam inside each other. I'd gone cross-eyed. I counted till a thousand in my head, and again and again. Then I decided to die, or at least shoot my foot after the shift so that they'd have to release me from the army. I thought about which foot I should shoot, the right or the left, and that was sort of fun and helped me pass time, and just as I smiled, that's when I saw them. Between the pixels, static white streaks formed the shapes of people, hundreds of miniature people, my people, the people that don't exist. This was not the first time I had seen those people, but I hadn't seen them since six years before, when I was twelve, the last time I had lice. The first time I had lice I was eight, and I thought I would die but I didn't. I scratched my head with a pencil really hard into my scalp, and when I took the pencil out there was lice with blood on it. I didn't think that would kill me. Still, I told my mom, and then with a brush she smeared gasoline all over my hair and made me watch TV with a handkerchief on my head. The lice were escaping my head like from a gas chamber. I could feel them flicking away and see them crawling all over my neck, a stream of tiny legs and round bodies. I didn't think that would kill me either. It was super cool. But then my mom said we had to get the eggs out too. I had to stand in the shower for hours while she passed a lice comb through my hair. She would also talk to me, and I hated that the most because at the time she was very busy with having three children, teaching high schoolers history, and having no husband, so she figured she would use the time effectively to lecture me about how I never put the dishes in the sink, how I always left my backpack by the front door, how I brought mud into the house, and how all of those things were killing her and that her only hope was that I would grow up to have a daughter who was just like myself, so that I'd finally understand what a shit I was. I wouldn't have thought any of that would kill me except I hate swear words, I hate them now and I hated them then when I was little, and they made me feel lumps in my throat whenever she would use them, and she used them a lot when she took out the lice eggs. It took her four years to get rid of the lice once and for all, and at the beginning every single time, I had to stand in the bathroom and I thought I was going to die every time she cursed—until I invented them, the people that don't exist. They were made of the brown dots on the white tiles of the bathroom floor.

Person B

I grew up hearing stories about people who were abandoned or raped by their guides and left to die midway, but in Egypt the twenty people in my group were invited to stay for a few days with the Bedouin's real wife on a vineyard. The wife was very wrinkled but could read and did read from her Quran every night, and I couldn't read, and then came the thought that I'd never learn how to read, and I thought that even if I did learn how to read I would never be very good at it and I had already missed out on eighteen years, so what was the point? Again I could hear my mother's disappointed tongue clicks, the *no good, it is no good* whispers. I had never thought thoughts even similar to that in my whole life; these thoughts were in my head but they were not my own. I realized they were magic, and that magic can exist, and that it is evil. The magic just got stronger and stronger. The Bedouin and his wife were very kind to us and most of all to me; they smiled like children in the morning, and the wife even took me on a walk in the vineyard, and then came the thought that I would never be this kind, not to strangers and not to anyone in the world, that my heart was dark like coal, like a witch's, and wasn't that a shame and wasn't there nothing in the world that could make that better? We walked along the vineyard, and for a second, for the first time since I left the camp, everything was a little good, everything was real and without magic. I'd never seen grapes before. I leaned in between the green leaves and stared at one, just one grape. It was perfectly round and green and so peaceful I grew jealous of it. Its skin was smooth and it glowed in the sun so that you could see lines lengthen within, lines of mystery and flesh and dignity. I touched it, gently. And then came the tongue clicks again. The *no good* whisper.

That's when I knew I was done for, when that thought came; that no matter what happens, no matter what I'd do, it would all be in vain—I could never, ever, even in a million years, become a grape.

Person A

I made up the game I play with the people that don't exist when I was eight and had lice; I used to pretend the people were the dots on the tiles of the bathroom floor. Now I play it with the people I pretend to see between the pixels of the monitor during my entire shift. I don't even notice the twelve hours pass. When my shift is over, I even miss these people. The game goes like this: I pretend some group of pixels on the monitor is actually a group of people. Sometimes they are in a country. Sometimes they are in space. Other times they are just in a gigantic room. It doesn't matter. Then I pretend that I am their ruler, and I make a special announcement, that one of them has been found to be very special, the most special person of all. Sometimes that one person is very good at sing- ing, another time that person is the smartest person ever to be born, and one time she is the kindest person in the world. But that person, always a girl, doesn't know that she is so special. She thinks that she is a nobody. Usually she is just the tiniest pixel, the one at the edge of the screen, and when I tell her what she actually is, let me tell you, she gets so excited she can taste her heart in her mouth. She could never imagine. Then the game starts again with another group of pixels, maybe the pixels below the broken willow tree or the ones at the very bottom. I never get bored of it because I think my memory is so shot by now that soon after one round of the game is over I forget all about the people. I forget real things too, like all the games I played at school with Yael and my favorite shows and the sound of Dan's voice and my mother's birthday and who I am. Nadav says that happens to a lot of watch soldiers, that it's the job. Nadav thinks that I have gone crazy, that I am too calm, complacent. He asked me what I thought about all the Sudanese that jump across the Egyptian-Israeli border, and I said they only distract me from my games with the made-up people, because if they jump through my part of the fence, I have to report it on the radio, and when they get shot, even if they don't die, that can be very distracting. Nadav was mad at that response, so I thought maybe I sounded anti-Zionist, so I added, "But of course I also think the Egyptians are animals." Then Nadav said I was naive. He said that we can't shoot the Sudanese because that would look bad, but we also don't want them here because then we would have to give them jobs, and they bring diseases, and they lower the Jewish rates. So we let the Egyptians shoot them instead because the Egyptians don't care if they look bad because the world already thinks they are bad but forgives them because they are Arabs. I couldn't quite follow his whole explanation, so I looked into the white of his eyes and imagined a room full of made-up people. That's when he told me I only think about myself. I couldn't win. But I didn't care so much then. Now I wish I did. My stomach is cramping as if it is trying to push itself between my legs, and my eyes twitch so much that all the made-up people are gone and all I can see is a fence through a green monitor and that one broken tree, and I still have eight hours left on my shift. The Sudanese man's body is still skewered there, right at the edge, smudged on the bends of the monitor.

Person B

We walked toward the fence of the Israeli-Egyptian border in a single line and in utter darkness, one hand on another's shoulder. The guide had left us an hour before and told us to just keep walking straight and pray to God. I didn't know why I was walking, but I didn't know what to do if I didn't walk, so I did. Ahead there was a willow tree; it was broken, but its top half was still green, lying on the ground. The magic thoughts, the *no good* whispers, got worse with every step. I tried to convince my legs to just reach the tree, and then we'll see. I could never fly like a bird, so what was the point? Step. Tongue clicks. *No good.* I could never be a man, so what was the point? Step. Tongue clicks. *No good at all.* I could never be a child again, so what was the point? Step. Tongue clicks. *No good, no point.* When I reached the broken tree, I told my legs that now they just needed to reach the fence ahead, to just take a few more steps. But it was too late. The *no good* whispers reached all the way to my sandals, and they were stuck in the sand. I stopped. The woman behind me and the man in front of me turned to look at me, but all they could see were my eyes, and we had been told to make no noise because of the watch-towers, so they quickly walked away from me. I could never stop the magic, the thoughts, so *what was the point*, I thought, and that's when the lights came on from the Egyptian towers, towers we had not seen at all but that were so close I could see the paint peeling through the flashes, the paint peeling and the gunshots and the screams and the fence ahead; we were so close and they were all running, but I stood still until something pushed me from the back, a gunshot, and my head fell and got buried deep in the branches of the broken tree and then the thoughts and the world grew quiet and cold, but only for one small minute.

Person A

We get a ten-minute bathroom break every six hours, and that's a good thing because I have to change my pad, and it is also good because, right then and there, I also decide to change who I am. And it is not because of what Nadav says. I don't care what Nadav says, I never have, because no matter what he says he still tells me to show up every night at his tent. It is because now that the pain has made it so that all the people that don't exist have disappeared from the monitor, I realize that I won't be able to rely on them forever. That it is time to start caring about someone who is not myself. I only have a few minutes of break left to start caring about someone other than myself, so I concentrate very hard. I close my eyes and I start with the baby. I never considered having it, and the doctor didn't even ask me. She assumed. They always assume about soldiers. I try to imagine that we do the kinds of things I did when I was a kid, but after five months of green-monitor shifts my memory is so shot I can't remember anything about being a kid that well, well enough to pretend about, well enough to remember the smell. All I smell now is blood and sweat. All I remember well is the lice. So I try to imagine myself combing my little girl's hair with a lice comb, but that doesn't work because when she turns she has no face, just a blank circle in the color of skin. And I think that that's the opposite of thinking about another person, to give my child a head with no face, so I stop imagining her as she would be and start imagining her as she really is, and I try so so hard to feel bad. I even rub my eyes and try to cry. I imagine the baby like you see in pictures of fetuses on the abortion pamphlets, as small as a fingernail and cute like a curled-up alien; I imagine it swimming all happy inside blood and tissue, until suddenly it is pushed out toward a huge, scary light and it knows it is going to die. But that's more of an interesting thought experiment than sadness because I know the baby doesn't really know it is going to die. I switch to thinking about all those Sudanese that get shot by the fence every night, how they come from hell and walk and walk with blisters on their feet only to die, but I only have two minutes of break left and besides, you have to understand, it is hard to feel bad for them because in all truth they look African and different from anyone I ever talked to and there are so, so many of them and they always die, and also my stomach starts feeling a little better and I decide that maybe changing who I am is going to be very hard.

Person B

Tongue click, *no good* whisper, what is the point of anything if I am never . . . if I am never all these millions of things? The magic had won. The thoughts were everything; soon there would be no me. My shoulder was warm and wet from the gunshot, I could hear fewer screams of others, and I could see the fence. There was sand in my mouth and I waited for it to be over. I didn't feel sad; I felt relieved, saved. I bent to the side not because I wanted to breathe but because my body made me. I curled up my legs and hugged the broken branches of the tree with my arms. I put my chin between my hands. A curled-up creature. My shoulder got warmer. Then my other shoulder got warm too, but a different type of warm, warm from the touch of someone who wasn't me. Warm like forgiveness, warm like a mother.

Person A

The people that don't exist, I still can't find them on the green monitor when I come back from the bathroom. The other watch girls are all excited. Gali, who did boot camp with me, tells me the excitement is because once again some Sudanese people tried to jump the fence, but the Egyptians shot almost all of them before the Sudanese even realized they were close. A lot can happen in ten minutes. I close my eyes to wipe the tears with my eyelids before they roll down. I am crying, but only because in this very second a jab cuts through my stomach, a different pain than before, a pain like no other, and I think now the baby is for sure gone. I only close my eyes for a second, and when I open them there still aren't any people that don't exist on the screen, there is only that broken tree, but also, next to it, a person on the ground. The person is much larger than the made-up people usually appear to be on the screen; it is as large as the Sudanese people usually appear on the screen. It is the size of a fingernail and cute, curled up like an alien. I can see it breathing on the bed of sand. We get in trouble if we touch the screen because it gets scratched, but I don't care. I am thinking about someone who isn't me. I reach and touch the green monitor—it is cold and far and real. I pretend to touch the child I'll never meet. I pretend I don't exist. For that while only, it gets to be only her.

Person B

Lying there on the sand by the broken tree, I could see the fence, and I could feel someone touching me. I felt someone's hand on my shoulder for a very long time. It wasn't a broken branch. It was a touch. A glassy, forever touch. *Mom,* I thought. A million times and more times and more. *Mom,*

Mom, Mom. Once, after my father left, she taught me how to make rice. She held my hand; we stirred together. This was all a very long time ago. She held my hand, but I was small, and the rice came out hard. She said it was the water's fault. She said the water was no good. But that was the night she stopped braiding my hair. She didn't braid it that night, and not for any night after, or maybe it was that that was the night I stopped asking. We still ate the rice, and then we went to sleep, and then we woke up. That night, when she held my hand and we stirred—that night could have lasted forever but it didn't. That other night, by the fence, by the broken tree, that night didn't last forever either. Lying on the sand, I could swear, someone was touching me. But as hard as I tried to hear it, my mother's voice was fading. The *no good* whispers grew quiet, then died. That old evil magic, it was now gone. And still. Someone's hand, I couldn't see it, but I could still feel it on my shoulder. That touch, it was not my mom. I knew, on the hospital bed in the little country, in all truth I knew it could never have been her who was touching me by that fence. Being touched like that, from such a distance, it was like being the grape I could never be—I could see it, but it couldn't see me. When I touched the grape, my finger patted the green surface and it was cold and far and real. What happened was that someone was there but then was not, and then I, I got up and I ran to the fence made of little knives and I jumped it. Only me.

A Machine
Automatic
Gun That
Shoots
Grenades

One day, thirteen days before the war, I turned beautiful. It was the best. Don't let anyone tell you there is anything better that can happen to a woman.

The day started in the farthest shooting range, the one with safety sleeves long enough to play with the ALGL weapon. It was a great morning, a morning that felt like a beach morning; it smelled of sunscreen.

"Yael," Hagar told me that morning, "today will be an Ok day."

She had said that to me every morning, though, since we became friends. This was a few months after Dana accused me of stealing her stuff and said the only way she wouldn't tell would be if I moved into another caravan. Hagar's caravan was the only one with a spare bed. The girls weren't happy about me moving in. They ignored me at first, but on that day I had already gotten them to like me. On that day I had friends.

That day with the ALGL, then, was something more than Ok, because by then I had made friends with the girls in my new caravan, my first real army friends. An automatic light grenade launcher by name, the ALGL weighed as much as a second grader, and we lazily dug a hole in the sand up to our knees to stick in its pedestal. The ALGL hadn't been used by the Israeli army in over ten years, and aside from weaponry instructors like us, only one soldier in each platoon was trained on how to set it up and aim with it. Setting up was complicated; it involved twisting knobs just enough times and lining up parts in certain angles. But once the froglike machine was planted in the sand and the string of grenades was loaded, aiming was easy. You pulled your hardest to the right. You pressed the trigger with both thumbs.

Hagar evaporated an abandoned Subaru in the range with her fifth grenade. In seconds, she shot ten more.

"A machine automatic gun that shoots grenades," Hagar said, and removed her safety goggles and helmet. "Now, you know that has to be something only a dude could come up with."

I looked at the Subaru's remains through the binoculars, a kilometer and a half away. The dust swirled above it, the wheels black splotches. Each grenade had a five-hundred-meter killing radius.

"I think you are supposed to say 'automatic machine gun,' " I said. "It's the other way around."

Hagar ignored me. She got up from the sand and took the binoculars. "I can almost hear it, the conversation when they thought it up: 'Hey, dude, you know what would be way cool? If we had a machine automatic gun—listen to this—that shot grenades!'" Hagar lowered her voice and grabbed her crotch. Neta and Amit laughed, but I only smiled.

She wasn't that good at impressions, and her long blonde hair was blinding when it met the June sun radiating from the dune. She was unmistakably a girl, and besides, it had been her idea to kill time with the ALGL that morning, and she was no dude.

It was me who told the girls I'd pass on a turn with the dumb ALGL. I remembered from basic training what the recoil felt like, how it electrified my chest cavity, and I was happy, so happy, just being with the three girls. The morning was good, and when Hagar smiled back at me, there was a stain of peach lipstick on her teeth, and there was nothing anyone could do but love her.

"Stop thinking dirty thoughts," she told me.

"I can't help it," I said. "I can't believe I have a whole week coming up with the American."

Hagar knew Ari the American better than all of us because she had been assigned to train his foot-tracker rookies during their M-16 week three months earlier. On the side, as one of its less important missions, our base held the boot camp of the Bedouin foot trackers. Ari and another guy, Gil, had been pulled from their infantry unit to our base to serve as the foot trackers' commanders, because the Bedouin foot trackers were retards and they couldn't command their own boot camps. The next day, I was starting the M-16 week with Ari and his new soldiers. I was looking forward to having something to do. I was looking forward to it because even though I had a boyfriend, ever since I had cheated on him with Boris, there hadn't been an hour when I didn't think about doing it with someone else. More specifically, Ari.

א

DURING THE war, I tried to remember what we used to do all day, but I couldn't. Each day was its own day. The months before the war were slow. The youth in Hebron had calmed, and two of the boys from Hidna village got such a beating when they were caught after they stole the fence, none of the other boys came back to the base again. Our small base conducted five-day trainings every month for the platoon that took up the rotation around Hebron and along Route 433. We refreshed their sharpshooters, and the rest of the month we didn't have to guard, because the platoons had enough people they could spare a few to guard the base. It was a great place for a teenager to be stationed back then. Most days were any girl's call; for Neta, Amit, and me they were usually Hagar's call. Some days, she would feel like shooting some weapon we had learned about in training ("I have this feeling," she'd say, "I think it's nostalgia"), and the weapons warehouse officer would let us take the weapon because technically it was the weaponry instructors' responsibility to make sure all of the wartime machines worked. We never played with the same weapon twice, because afterward we were always too lazy to take the weapon apart and rub the tar inside with a cloth soaked in gasoline, so that the weapon wouldn't rust and would work a second time.

א

AROUND TEN that morning, we called the van driver on the radio to take us back from the range. The four of us occupied the backseat. Neta and I had strawberry lollipops in our mouths, and my fingers were sticky. Neta's ponytail was bobbing; Amit had her head in Neta's lap, and she put her sandy boots over my legs. On my right, Hagar was doing something to my hair. Her long fingernails felt good when they scratched my scalp; their smell of nicotine mixed with her cucumber perfume relaxed me.

"So then I asked him what he liked about me, why he wanted to be my boyfriend, and you know what he said?" Dana asked Tamara. They were talking about Dana's twenty-seven-year-old boyfriend. The two of them were yapping away in the two-seater in front of us. The van had picked them up at the gasoline fountain next to the weapons warehouse, where they had just finished cleaning their own personal M-4 guns. They cleaned them there every week. Like they anticipated being shipped to Iran or some shit. Any day now.

We picked Ari and Gil up near a large metal container the size of a classroom. It was an emergency storage container. The word "greens" was graffitied on its front. The rumor was that it was only half full of green bullets, that there was some room inside of it, and that Gil once snuck his girlfriend to the base and got with her inside that container.

I couldn't see Hagar's face, because she was still working on my hair, but I knew she was rolling her eyes at Dana. There were only sixteen females in our training base, all of us infantry weaponry instructors. The caravan in the female residency lot had four rooms, so each four-person clique got its own. But Hagar hated it that we still had to listen to the others on the van rides.

"He said he liked me because I was normal! What does that even mean?" Dana asked.

Dana and Tamara lived in my old room, room 2, the room Hagar called the "family: the future" room, because all the girls in it could talk about was their boyfriends and their future families. Room 4 was called the "family: the past" room, because the girls who lived in it chatted only about their parents and siblings. Room 1 was "the dead" room, because they talked about the dead, even though there had been no action since we were drafted. These were dead they knew from, like, high school, but they still talked about them.

This was the way the army worked. We were all killing time, and at the end of the day every person liked to talk about just one thing. For my new room, it was sex.

"He explained that before he met me, all the girls he knew from Haifa were weird, so I guess that's a compliment, but still! I mean you tell me, Tamara—isn't it shocking that 'normal' would be the adjective he would choose? I mean, is this why he loves me?" Dana went on.

In life, Hagar said, only three things made her happy: the smell of gas stations, Marlboro Lights, and sex, and her only regret was that she could never delight in all three at the same time because gasoline was flammable.

She finished with my hair, and she tied it quick and tight. Then she pulled on Dana's ponytail, and when Dana turned, Hagar asked with a voice loud enough so that Ari and Gil in the front of the van could hear, "Hey, Dana, how good are your blowjobs?"

Dana's face turned red. Neta was moving the lollipop in

her mouth in and out. She wasn't the brightest lightbulb, but she was my friend, and I joined her, and it was so summer, and we made Amit laugh.

"Hey, I'm just trying to help," Hagar said. "I just wanted to save you time and let you know that that's why he loves you—you must give pretty good head."

That was when he turned. Ari. "Hey, play nice," he said.

His eyes were green, just like those of Dan, a boy I loved when I was a mousy middle schooler. But now Ari looked at me like I was anything but mousy.

I swear he did!

I looked down.

This is what he said next: "Hey, you are beautiful."

And I didn't see, but Hagar, Amit, and Neta swore he was still looking at me.

ℵ

BACK IN our caravan, my face was burning. It was noon. I was sure one of the girls had put him up to it.

Hagar, Amit, and Neta didn't speak to me at all the first two weeks after I was placed in their room. I used to think that Lea knew how to control a flock of girls like no other, but that was before I met Hagar. During those first two weeks, the number of guys they each mentioned sleeping with was double-digit, while I had had a boyfriend for seven years and only cheated on him once, with a short Russian soldier. They hated the idea of me, or anyone, having a boyfriend. But I hated Moshe, the real boyfriend I had.

When I started hating him, it was not his fault. It was my first Passover at his house. I was sixteen. I was passionate. Ok,

I was passionate. I was passionate about work immigrants, Ok, about immigration rights and all. I was young. I was talking very fast. It was past midnight. We had finished eating, said our last prayers. The white tablecloth was stained red, yellow. Empty wine bottles, dirty napkins, toothpicks, chicken bones. His cousin was twelve. She had a lisp. She was listening to me. "I can't believe this is how we treat the people who build our homes!" she said. She really didn't know how our country treated work immigrants, and she wanted to know more. I talked faster. I talked more. I was sixteen. I don't even know if it was how much I spoke or the simple way I looked. I wasn't a pretty girl, and I knew it.

I remember the weight of his father's fingers on my shoulders. The parch of the wine as he opened his mouth. He caught me midsentence. "Let me tell you, son, I just hope for you that she's at least a good lay."

They pretended not to hear. He was drunk; it is what you do. I didn't blame my boyfriend. I hated him. I wasn't trying to prove his father wrong. It was how it happened. When we slept together, I did quadratic equations in my head.

During our last time in bed before the war, I asked him, "How come your mom always puts tahini in her eggplant salad?" He kept at it. There was a sticker I had peeled off an orange on his ceiling's fan. I had put it there on my break the month before so I would have something to look for when I came back.

"I hate tahini," I said. "Eggplants are so much better with mayo."

"What?" he said. He was breathing fast. It was a Friday night. We had just finished the Sabbath dinner. Eggplants were my favorite vegetable. His mom knew that. I hated tahini. She knew that too. He was too heavy on top of me, the room too hot; I grew angry fast.

"She is cheap, that's why," I said. "She knows tahini will last longer than mayo."

"Shh," he said. "Someone could hear us."

Hear us talking about eggplants? I went back to tracking the orange's sticker, around and around and—

And when Hagar finally addressed me, late, in the dark, when the four of us were on our field beds, answering her question was too easy.

"Of course I think about sleeping with guys who aren't my boyfriend. I even did it once with a soldier I trained. And I think about Ari the American. All the time. I am thinking about him right now."

Answering the rest of the girls' questions wasn't any harder.

"Of course Ari and I would do it outside!"

"I think, just from his height, it has to be at least that big."

Soon the three girls were the nightly audience for my fantasies. I had friends. Finally. Hours and hours went by, and I never ran out of things to say. Hagar always asked for more about Ari. Dirtier, larger, in colors. Like the movies. Like America. I didn't know where Ari was from, but he had that accent people referred to as Anglo-Saxon.

נ

THE GIRLS swore they didn't tell Ari to say I was beautiful in the van. So I said the only other option was that he was trying to kiss up to me, so I wouldn't work him hard the next day during his Bedouin soldiers' M-16 week. "Have you thought about the other other option?" Hagar asked, and she handed me her hand mirror. "You look hot," she said.

On the van, Hagar had braided my hair in two braids and wrapped them around my head so that the skin around my eyes was tighter. My nose looked long but noble, my cheeks were sunken inside, my eyes glistened. It must have been more than the hair—I had lost weight since I joined room 3, the sex room, because all the girls did was smoke and drink Diet Coke. My yearslong acne had cleared up, but it was only that day, through Hagar's mirror, that I noticed it. In the mornings, Hagar would sometimes get bored and wake me by plucking my black eyebrows, and it was only then that I noticed how gentle my gaze had turned because of it. I had spent years trying, but that day I turned beautiful, accidentally, and it shocked me.

I think I loved Hagar the most in that second, when I turned to look from the mirror to her and realized that she and the world must see what I saw in the mirror just then— me, beautiful.

נ

"WE NEED to cool ourselves down," Hagar said. "Let's put ice water in our veins already." Back then, that month, putting ice water in our veins was her favorite pastime after guns. It was one of her stranger ideas. She said putting ice water in our veins would probably feel like winter inside of summer, and that we should probably try it.

Getting the frozen IV bags we put in our veins was this whole production. The kitchen sergeant let the four of us use the industrial freezer for our frozen IV bags because he was in love with Neta. One of the medics from the clinic gave us new IV bags and all the rest from the emergency supply room because he thought he was in love with Neta, until he began sleeping with Hagar and then thought he was in love with her more.

We were invincible.

Hagar pinched the vein on the flip side of my elbow hard. "Ouch," I said, but I was smiling.

"Can it be my turn to stick the needle in you this time?" Hagar asked.

"I love what you did with my hair," I said. "You can stick whatever you want in me, hon."

"Aw, baby," Hagar said.

The four of us went outside the caravan in our bras and underwear, ignoring the stares of the girls who were smoking.

Using her teeth, Hagar tied green elastic above my elbow, and I started opening and closing my fist. Then she stuck the needle, swift. She got up and clipped the IV bag to a cedar branch above us.

After she finished with the veins of Neta and Amit, Hagar did herself and lay down on the cement, smiling. "Refresh me, God!" she shouted.

We were lying on the cement in our underwear. Amit let me borrow a pair of her fake Prada sunglasses. It was noon and I could taste the heat.

I thought of Ari. The cold was swimming close to my head. The ice water in my veins was a ghost licking me from the inside. I changed the speed of the drip to faster, and it made my eyes buzz. It was one of Hagar's stranger ideas, but not her strangest. She had so many ideas. She wondered what would happen if we put Diet Coke in our IV bags, and I had to tell her that would mean putting oxygen in our circulatory systems. That it would kill us. I don't know why I knew that. Neta and Amit said they hadn't thought of that. Hagar said she hadn't either. Then she said, "But think about it, what a way to go!"

On the cement, Hagar said, "So. You. Ari. Bedouins' basic training. Exciting. Exciting."

I didn't say anything. I let the girls wait.

"So I heard an interesting rumor," Amit said. "I heard they might start giving the Bedouins M-4s now, instead of M-16s." I knew she was trying to throw us off the topic of Ari, because they all liked to pretend they were not interested in my fantasy talk, particularly at moments when they were most eager.

"Like they would ever waste green bullets on those retards," Hagar said slowly.

An M-16 has a range of 100 meters, and regular bullets. An M-4 has an aim that magnifies by ten, a range of 250 meters, and green bullets. The green bullets have a mass in them that weighs 0.008 kilos. They go further, more accurately, because they are heavier, so the metal coils inside the M-4 barrel are wrapped tighter to give the bullets more spin, more momentum. The M-4 is the gun that can actually help you if you need to shoot someone and hit them fast. But if you used a regular bullet with it, it wouldn't make it past 75 meters. It would never hit where you aimed.

We were silent for a while, but finally I couldn't wait and I could not let them wait any longer for my words, the words I thought were dirty. "Hagar," I said, "I am actually going to get with Ari."

"You have been saying that for months," Amit said. She had her head on Neta's bare stomach. Neta and Amit had been best friends before the army, and they were lucky enough to be stationed together. And if they were best friends before, they were now each other's sister, parent, everything. When we smoked hookah and played truth or dare with Ari and Gil, they didn't complain when they had to kiss each other. "It's like I am kissing myself," Amit said. "It's kind of a trip!"

"You just wait and see. This time I mean it," I told them. I opened my mouth to taste the sun. I was frozen from within; I was pretty; the sun didn't scare me. "He is going to take me in the ranges. In the clinic. On a coffee table."

"A coffee table?" Neta asked.

"It is this thing they have in America," I said. "Go with me here."

"But I heard he was Canadian," Neta said.

"He is Australian," Amit said. It was one of the only things I ever heard them disagree on.

"Yep, New Zealand, Australia," Hagar confirmed.

"Whatever he is, he is mine," I said.

We had had that exact conversation plenty of times before.

"Listen, girls," Hagar said.

"Yael." Hagar said my name. She said it the way I said Avishag's name on one of those rare moments when I needed her more than she needed me, for just a second.

"Do you think they torture him?" Hagar asked.

For the past five days, since it happened, Hagar had been making us talk about the soldier they took in Gaza. Hagar lived in his school district, and we all knew she knew him, even though she said she didn't, she was just interested in the topic of torture.

"I don't know, Hagar," I said. It was the truth.

"No, they are not torturing him; they give him chocolate

and take him to the park," Dana said. I smelled the vanilla and sweat on her skin. She was the one who had made me move rooms, but now she resented that the girls in the new caravan accepted me. She loomed above us on the cement. "You girls," Dana said. "No brains, no worries, huh? He is probably getting the life beat out of him right now."

We were silent for a second. Then, careful of the needle in her vein, Amit took off her bra. Neta did too. It was what the two did to scare Dana off. Nudity made her uncomfortable. Hagar still didn't move.

"So first, Ari is going to turn me over," I began, ignoring Dana. A minute later, she ran off, screaming that we were all disgusting. Somewhere in the midst of my fantasy, we all fell asleep, our IV bags empty. In my sun-hunted dreams, icy from within, I visited Vegas, then Bel Air, then the bridge the *Full House* girls drove on. When I opened my eyes, I was the only one left lying on the cement, and Ari was standing at the gate of the female residency.

He was! I swear.

"I need help," he said.

Ari had a fear. He was afraid of doing the set of moving targets with his soldiers.

Since I was a weaponry instructor, I was naturally a fan of the moving-targets drill. It sounded bad, but it really wasn't. The soldiers on the other side of the shooting line would walk around inside a ditch. Their target would be tied to two sticks, so it'd be tall enough for them to hold up without exposing their arms. They'd have goggles and helmets and bulletproof vests. Ari and I would talk on the radio and have a safe word for when he and the soldiers in the ditch could climb out and switch places with the shooting soldiers. The ditch had been clogged that past year, so this was his first time trying it, but I knew he'd do fine. I believed in that drill, as a weaponry instructor. If you were going to shoot someone, odds are he'd be moving; it was important to practice. But Ari had a point. It was a little crazy, or at least it could have sounded crazy to me if my basic training had not been as a weaponry instructor and I had not been told that as a weaponry instructor I must be a fan of it.

"I just mean, really? With all the money the army spends on Popsicles and lollipops, am I really going to train my soldiers on shooting at moving targets by giving half of them a stick with a cardboard target tied to it and sending them behind the shooting line?" Ari said that day.

So I told him we could practice shooting first, just the two of us.

Practicing just the two of us was a good idea, I thought. Most of the Bedouin foot trackers spoke little Hebrew and had a tendency to get into fights where they tried to bite each other's ankles off, so it was always good to practice for them.

Ari and I walked on the pebble road leading to the shooting range where the ditch was. During the walk, Ari told me that he had been pulled from his regular unit to make the Bedouin foot trackers into soldiers, and that he believed that was worth immigrating to Israel for. He said that foot trackers walk in front of the force, looking for tracks, and that during wars they go fast, the fastest. He said that these were guys who needed to know how to fight and that if they didn't, then it was all on him.

"Do you think they can really know what happened in a sand dune just by looking?" I asked him.

That part wasn't his responsibility, he said. He said that

Bedouin know how to spot tracks from birth. They have elders who serve as professional trainers to sharpen that skill.

"But I believe they are good," he said. "They say if you stood on a hill tomorrow, two years from now a good foot-tracker would still know you had been there, and when."

Once we arrived at the range, before he walked behind the shooting line, Ari put his hand on my shoulder. Then he went down the ditch, helmet, goggles, radio, and all. He was holding a target attached to a long stick, and I could only see the target. I looked hard to make sure no part of his body was peeking outside the ditch. I was behind the shooting line.

I shot at his target. And again.

But Ari wasn't walking fast enough. I went out of position a few times to yell through the radio, "Faster, much faster," but it didn't help. The first eight bullets I hit so they made the shape of half a heart in the place where the soldier printed on the cardboard's heart would have been. Then I thought better of it. I wondered why our targets all had soldiers in green uniforms printed on them, why we were shooting at ourselves this whole time. The next bullet went to the head. The nose. Then one to the right eye. As I did after every bullet, I closed my eyes, emptied my lungs, aligned my aims. When I opened my right eye, the target was gone. Ari had climbed out of the ditch. He was lying on the ground behind it, motionless.

I walked over to him. The walk was heavy on my heart in fear.

He still had his safety goggles and helmet on. When I cast a shadow over his head, he opened his eyes. "You killed me," he said.

"I didn't," I said. "But I could have! Why didn't you say

something before climbing out?" My heart shouted inside of me.

"You killed me. I was so young. I should have had more sex. I should have gotten that second burger," he said.

I tried to stay furious at him, but I couldn't. "I killed you," I said.

"Come here," he said. He held his hands up, kept his back stiff.

I sat on his stomach, one leg at each side. His hands grabbed mine. I let my hair fall on his neck.

Hagar would have handled it differently. But I had been a less-than-pretty girl for the nineteen and a half years before that day, and I had been thinking of Ari for the last three months, and somehow I knew that when dreams come true, you have to drive them. Odd, but what I wanted was to talk his brains out. He knew so much, I thought. I wanted to talk about things Hagar said. Ask questions. Know—everything—right then.

"Do you think it had to have been a bunch of dudes who thought up the ALGL?"

"I think Americans thought up the ALGL."

"Are you American?"

"I am from New Zealand, but I say Australia."

"Do you think they torture him? The soldier they took in Gaza?"

"No."

"Are you lying to me because I am a girl?"

"No. He is just a boy from a tank. They know he doesn't have any intel."

"Are you lying to me because I am a girl sitting on you?"

"No. Common sense says he is only good for bargain, and in a bargain, the healthier, the better. People don't just torture people if they don't have to. This is the real world."

Ari moved his palms from mine to grab my arms, balance me. We were playing seesaw.

"What was the happiest moment in your life?" he asked. It was a line. I didn't mind. I leaned deep and kissed him. I wanted to say, "Right now," but that was easy. I wanted to say, "Right now," but it wasn't true.

From the range, Ari took me for a long walk. We ended up in that emergency storage container. The one that had the word "greens" graffitied on its front. It was as wide as my childhood classrooms and tall enough so that even if Ari jumped the highest his long legs could take him, he still wouldn't reach the ceiling. There were no green bullets inside. There were two tables that I recognized as belonging to the foot-tracker rookies' caravan classrooms, and on them there were purple sheets and a pillow. In front of them there was an old radio on cement blocks. It was almost a room where you lived, a living room, but it was a container.

We sat on the tables in front of the radio.

"How come there are no bullets here?"

"The supply officers got lazy. They always forget to order new ones for the training rounds, and it takes a few months to get greens, so they just tapped out the emergency supply."

"What if there is an emergency?"

"What emergency?"

"I don't know, a war?"

"There isn't going to be any war," he said. I believed him.

The daylight was fading outside, but inside the greens container, Ari lit four military flashlights covered with red filters.

Lying on the tables covered with his purple sheets, I put my hand on the back of his neck and felt it stiffen. Then we loved each other for a while.

"I bet you bring girls here all the time," I said after.

"Not really," he said. "You are the first girl that mattered," he said. I believed him. I still believe now. Sometimes I believe things I know are not true.

נ

THIS IS true, in every way: he was wrong about the war because then there was one. You can look it up. The second Lebanon war. July 12, 2006. It is true like history; a lot of things that could have not happened, but the truth is they did.

They say in two minutes the ALGL the soldiers took from our base to the border brought down an eleven-story building in that war. It worked just fine even though we didn't clean it after we used it. It took down a school. Seventy-three people. If you were to look it up, you might even find their names. Also the name of the soldier they took before the war, in Gaza. The one from Hagar's school.

When I finally had time to look in a mirror again, it was a Saturday two weeks into the war, and I wasn't beautiful anymore; I was me. I tried to pull my hair up; I pulled it tight until it hurt, but that girl, she was gone. I handed Hagar back the mirror she had given me. We had slept in the ranges, an hour here, an hour there, on the asphalt, for a week, and we were having our first shower in the caravan, our first break from training the reservists. We had run out of green bullets the night before.

Ari had been dead for five days already. He and Gil were

pulled from the base to fight in Lebanon the day the war broke. Our officer told us seven hours after Ari died.

Two weeks into the war, at seven in the morning, the batch of reservists that came that weekend, over a hundred of them, stormed the caravan of the weaponry training officer. We stood by his side as our officer tried to shout over the mob. The reservists came for three days to train in our ranges; there were reservists in ranges all over the country, before they went up to Lebanon. They wore green, they had guns on their backs, but they weren't soldiers. They had beards, long hair, jobs in factories, jobs elsewhere, mortgages, wives, children.

Reservists, they went fast in that war—not the fastest, but they went fast. They kept on coming to our base and then leaving. "We have been training with regular bullets our whole time here," one of them shouted. "We are going up tonight. This is insane."

"I assure you no one is going to send you up to fight without greens," our officer said. He had fear. "I have people working on opening our emergency greens container as we speak."

But. There were no green bullets in our base. Only an empty container in which Ari entertained girls. A place where you live, almost, a living room, but it was a container.

I looked at the men. All these men; I knew something terrible these men did not know. These men, a few of them are dead now, and that day, before they died, I knew something terrible they did not know.

The green bullets go further, more accurately, because they are heavier, so the metal coils inside the M-4 barrel are wrapped tighter than the M-16's, to give the bullets more spin, more momentum. The M-4 is the gun that can actually help you if you need to shoot someone and hit them fast. But if you didn't use a green bullet with it, it wouldn't make it past 75 meters. It would never hit where you aimed.

At first I thought I was the only one who knew there were no green bullets in the emergency container. But then I looked to my right, at Hagar.

Then I looked quickly at the sand, then again at her. I forced myself to look at her face. Her eyes were closed and she was breathing fast. I had never before seen her afraid. Perhaps she had never been afraid before. Her face looked not her own, more beautiful, gone from this earth.

She knew too. She knew what wasn't in that container. She had been there. She had been there with him. Maybe on those same purple sheets.

She knew the men would still have to go, as is, with their M-4s and no green bullets. These reservists, the husbands that we could have had if we had been born ten years before— some of them would have not died if the color of their bullets had been different. This is a historical fact. The government admitted it in the report later—the one about how we weren't prepared for that war.

At first, for a second, I wanted to yell at Hagar for lying, for not telling me she had already been with Ari, for the madness in her encouragement of my attraction to him. I could almost see it; her hand on the back of his neck, and his neck growing stiff. Ari.

But then for one second, I thought of Ari only, Ari climbing out of that ditch.

"You killed me," he joked. He thought that this was very funny.

And then I looked at Hagar's fear, her closed eyes. I looked at a girl who was afraid for the first time in her life, and maybe only a little, and maybe for the very last time.

I breathed in the gunpowder that was on all of our fingers and the cedar trees of the base. And I just understood that there are people who live for the fight; for the moments before you lose or win. People for whom this world is not enough; they want ice water in their veins, beauty at any cost, climbing out of ditches under gunfire, exploding necklaces of grenades. Fascinating people for whom torture is not even within the realm of imagination. And I looked at the many men on the sands. Each one of them had shoulders much wider than my own that I knew would probably do him no good in what was to come. And then I knew: those fascinating people—I was never one of them.

II

The
Diplomatic
Incident

The first thing we need to know is that when the diplomatic incident occurred, Yael was stationed at a training base near Hebron. Lea was in officers' training school. They had nothing to do with it. Avishag was on the Egyptian border when the incident unfolded, in guarding towers and at checkpoints. She got through the months of her watch-monitor shifts just fine. She was serving in the army's only female-dominated infantry unit, as a common soldier on the border, when it happened. But Avishag did not have the power to script what happened that day. We could blame Avishag, or Israel, or Egypt, or even America if we felt like it. But what good would that do us?

The second thing we need to know is that infantry officer Nadav has no complaints with us. None. He is not pointing

any fingers at his school friends, or at his dad, or at the Israeli government, or at any government, really, and he is not
about to blame it on "War." If Nadav has a problem with anyone, it is with God. When he was seven, six even, he would
often stop in the middle of his homework or in the middle
of watching the Ninja Turtles, put his miniature chin in his
chubby hands, and say, "If I have a problem with anyone, it
is with God."

He would actually say that. A six-year-old! He was very
mature for his age, our Nadav, and absolutely adorable, even
before his mother died in the bus suicide bombing of line 5
(the 1991 one, by Afula Central; not the first one, the one
that was in the spring). And it was the little things that Nadav
would like to complain about. Like when you have your birthday in kindergarten and they make you bring your parents
and cake to school. Nadav only had his dad and the cake was
store bought. They made Nadav sit on a chair surrounded
by balloons in front of the entire class and stare at the cake
that rested on the tiny table. When he blew out his candles,
the smell of dead fire mixed with that of the balloon rubber
and cheap chocolate icing. On his right, his dad was trying to
make himself small enough to fit on the child-sized wooden
chair. On his left sat no one.

He is just saying, if you make a plan that every child
should have two parents, and then you make a world where
everywhere you go there is a right side of a kid and a left side
of a kid, a wrong and a right, a white and a black, a chair and
another chair, a dad and a mom, a mom, well, it is just not fair
to all of a sudden say to just one specific person, "Sorry, you
are not going to fit in with the plan." Nadav is just saying, as

a God you shouldn't go around doing shit like that. It is sick, that's what it is.

That's all officer Nadav has to say. He does not wish to talk further.

ﬡ

WE MAY think that Tom had the easiest job in the Israeli Defense Forces, but he knew that in all truth he actually had the hardest job in the whole world. Yes, he did spend his entire service in Tel Aviv, only a five-minute walk from Azrieli, the biggest and brightest mall in the country—that is, after all, where the headquarters of the army are located, and the general chief of staff's office; and he did get to go home every night at eight o' clock and sleep at his parents' house, even; and all he had to do for the eleven hours he was on duty was to sit behind a wooden desk and stare at a red phone. But wait—do we really know how hard it is to stare at a red phone that never rings? Every day, from eight to eight, with only two thirty-minute breaks for eating and peeing? For three years? Put nothing but a phone on your desk and try staring at it. You won't make it past fifteen minutes.

There are thirty-four cubicles in Tom's office, and luckily for him his is located so that if he stretches out his neck he can see the two leaves of a ficus plant and the clock on the wall. He has made a deal with himself that he can't start thinking about Gali until he only has fifteen minutes left. Before that, he does everything else. He plucks his eyebrows with his fingers. He counts his teeth with his purple tongue piercing. He thinks of Katie Holmes, then Shakira. But of Gali Tom doesn't daydream until there are only fifteen minutes left in his shift. He can't; otherwise it hurts too much.

He is going to see Gali tonight for the first time in two months, so that could explain the third leg he immediately gets as he allows the smell of her Herbal Essences pomegranate shampoo to resurface in his mind, but we know he actually gets it every time he lets himself think of her. The worst is when he gets it right in the middle of a shift. There could be the tiniest speck of dust in the still office air, he could sneeze and remember the time she sneezed when he last saw her— her tight copper ponytail bouncing up and down—and that would be it: he would be done for for the remainder of his shift, and it would hurt.

~

Does anyone know how to say "Don't do it" in Ukrainian? We should have learned how to speak Ukrainian. Not the whole language—it would have been enough if we just knew how to say "Don't do it." Anything could have stopped Masha that day. She was not really all that bad of a girl.

Even though Berezhany, Ukraine, is a small town, Masha got to be alone all the time because of her job. She was responsible for numbering and filing the completed order forms of the shoes that were made in the factory on any given day, so she only really had to work after other people had already been working for quite a few hours making the shoes. She didn't have to be at the office until noon each day, and sometimes even if she came in at one Julian would let her get away with it. She got to have lunch with her old mother, who would kiss her on the forehead when she stood at the threshold heading out. When she walked through the market to work, she got to stop by the tomato man and watch him as he restacked his tomatoes into a perfect triangle and then started all over again, sighing. All the children were at school, all their parents were at work, and the only people around were the elderly and the unemployed, who all roamed the streets with patient, soft steps. Everything was ordinary, but lighter—like seeing a video recording of your bedroom when you were not there.

At first she liked staying in the office and recording the completed order forms after everyone was already at home, having dinner with their families. All the cubicles around her were dark, and she would close her eyes and imagine that if someone were to look at the office from an aerial view, all he would see were two dots of light sparkling in the dark of the office—her cubicle and Julian the boss's office.

But then she got bored. She had been dating Phillip for two years, and when she would look to the cubicle on her right, she would see a framed picture of a stranger's family by a Christmas tree, and she would see herself as the wife, holding the little one and pointing up to the Nativity star. And when she would look to the cubicle to her left, she would see another framed picture and it would be her as the wife again, a little fatter and redheaded this time, and surrounded by four boys with too many freckles.

The first thing she took from the desk of one of the cubicles was a pen. It was red and had teeth marks on it, and she placed it two cubicles to the right of where she had found it. From that cubicle she took a stapler and placed it four cubicles to the left. But no one noticed, even though she waited for a week, then two more days. Deep down she knew that sooner or later she would get to the pictures. She loved imagining what it would be like to look up from your cubicle one day and see that your wife wasn't your wife, and your kids were not your kids. Or better yet, what it would be like to have a picture of another family at your desk and never notice.

And no one did notice. And a week passed, then two days, then a month. Soon, none of the framed pictures on the desks belonged to their rightful owners. She was beginning to rotate them, spending a whole night arranging the pictures of the wives in a pattern of blonde, brunette, blonde, when—

"You are a bad girl, aren't you?" she heard Julian whispering from behind her. His wife's picture was the only one she couldn't touch—he always spent his nights closed in his office. But something else told her she shouldn't do it. That something told her she should never have started the job in the first place, and that no good was ever going to come out of a job that requires you to stay in the office until midnight with your married boss. Masha had always been a smart, observant girl.

Don't do it, Masha.

Julian gently grasped her by her boney wrist, but she clenched the picture frame she was holding strongly in her hand and looked him in the eyes. She breathed once. She breathed twice. She was breathing.

And that was that.

א

WHEN TOM and Gali first kissed in high school, he swore he would never let a girl like that go. And he never did let her go, except the army came; then he and Gali wanted different things; then they were different things; then they seemed to be in different places all the time. It was clear to Tom from the time he was ten that he was not going into anything resembling combat. The official doctor's note that got him out of combat service cited chronic migraines, and the truth was that the problem did have something to do with his head: he paid 120 shekels a month to get his auburn hair highlighted, and he would die before subjecting his hair to a helmet. His eyes were the shade of green that required just a touch of eyeliner every morning to make them stand out. He knew he wouldn't be able to keep up with that while fighting terrorists and all.

But it was also clear to Gali from the time she was ten that she wanted to fire off weapons and make things explode and run after suicide bombers on the hills. Gali knew her parents had made her limbs from scratch, and she always hoped that those limbs had a purpose. Luckily for her, by the year she was old enough to join the army, the first-ever predominately female infantry unit was already in existence, and the opportunity was too good for her to pass up. Despite what we might be inclined to think of her, Gali actually enjoyed the company of female friends quite a bit and was always popular among them at school despite her looks. But little did she know that they were going to put this experimental female-friendly unit on the Egyptian border, on a border that had been peaceful for the last thirty years. Now she was stuck guarding in towers where nothing ever happened and manning checkpoints where the most excitement was when someone caught smuggled DVDs or smuggled people or smuggled produce or smuggled pot. Her hands were tied most of the time; someone higher up would give an order to let whatever those things were into Israel. She only got to go home to see her boyfriend once every two months.

ב

AND NOW it is Friday. Tom has the weekend off, Gali has the weekend off too, and it is *the* weekend. She should be coming into Tel Aviv's central bus station right now, or maybe she is already in a service cab on the way to his house. Tom gets every other weekend off, but again, this doesn't mean he agrees with us that his job is easy. Staring at a phone he knows is not going to ring. When he first learned he would be stationed at these offices, only twenty minutes away from his house, he thanked his mom profusely for pulling all the strings she had with the wife of the general chief of staff's personal assistant. They treated him like a king, in a way, and his direct commander even said that he could choose which phone to sit by. Each phone was meant to be a forever open channel of communication between the Israeli army and the armies of other countries, and Tom was even given the opportunity to choose the phone given to the Lebanese army, which had rung many times during that recent nasty war.

He knew the phone connected to the Egyptian army would probably never ring. And he knew that even if it did, the phone call would have nothing to do with Gali. And he knew that even if the phone call did have something to do with Gali, it would almost a million percent not be her on the line. And still he chose Egypt, because if he was going to spend three years waiting for a phone to ring, he wanted to preserve the possibility that maybe, somehow, in a weird and unbelievable way, that phone call was going to be from her.

א

"ONE DAY is onion; another day is honey," Hamody's uncle mumbled, signaling his wife to fill his china white coffee cup by lifting it and tilting it side to side.

"But uncle," Hamody said. He wanted to say, "But uncle, I love her," but he didn't, because he didn't want to sound cliché.

"This too shall pass," his uncle continued. "Moa'alems don't marry Christian girls."

Most of the time Hamody loved that his uncle was the head imam of the entire western part of Egypt. Most of the time he loved his uncle more than anything in this world.

"She will never marry you either," his uncle said. The smoke in the room got into Hamody's eyes. He wasn't crying. "Better one bird in your hand than two birds on the tree," his uncle said, and laughed.

But Hamody wanted the girl precisely because of that. Not because she was a Christian girl, because she wasn't really; at least not in Hamody's eyes. She wasn't a Muslim girl in his eyes either—she wasn't a girl at all. She was a bird on a tree, that one, waiting for Hamody to climb up, too strong headed to use her wings and fly to him. During his junior year of high school he had watched her walk to the grocery store every Friday with her baby brother under one dark arm and a chorus of her other siblings humming around her. She would balance the wheeled grocery bag with her other dark arm. Whenever young men offered to help her with her groceries, and they did, what she would do was place the baby in their arms and continue wheeling away the groceries.

"Why, thank you for your help," Hamody heard her say once to one of the many unsuspecting suitors who were left cradling a fussy baby, running after the dark girl in silent disbelief. And Hamody laughed, and he laughed.

"Why put a healthy head into a sickbed?" Hamody's uncle said. Hamody could feel the river of creamy black coffee gushing through his veins, pooling in his brain. He had wondered before why he had ever told his uncle about his feelings, and he now remembered that it had not been him talking the other week; it had been the coffee.

"Oh, Hamody. God hands his treasures to every person on this earth equally; it is just that some people choose not to enjoy their treasures," his uncle said. "We can't want everything we see, only what we can have."

אַ

"DUDE, WHAT are you doing here so early?" Tom asked Oleg, the Russian guy who covered the night shift on the phone connecting the Egyptian army and the general chief of staff of the Israeli forces.

"You know, bus got in early, figured I'd spare you the last five minutes," Oleg replied.

Tom was really in awe at how bighearted those Russians could be sometimes. He wouldn't add a minute to his time there. He got up, careful to use his JanSport backpack to cover the front of his pants, and walked all the way through the office and by the barbed-wire fences of the base and right through the gates that led to the heart of the bustling, gaudy streets of Tel Aviv. The Azrieli mall tower loomed above him, shining like a mouthful of diamonds. Cars were chasing and catching one another's colors on the highway. It was then, standing by a street vendor of organic juices made from oranges and wheatgrass, that he could feel something vibrating inside the pants of his green uniform. He pushed the M-16 further down his back and reached toward his pocket to read Gali's text.

> plz dont be mad stuck in the base till 2 weekend
> from now plz reply plz don't be mad i miss u

Tom put the phone back in his pocket. He was already starting to feel it hurting. And we do know, we do, how impossible it is to do nothing but stare at a phone for eleven hours. Yes, a phone. And so we cannot really blame Tom for not texting Gali back, and we cannot truly blame him for where his legs took him next.

א

IT WAS already ten at night, and Tom still hadn't texted Gali back. She knew because even though she was not technically allowed to bring her cell phone with her to the border checkpoint, she still did it, putting it on vibrate and hiding it between her heart and the bulletproof cement vest she was wearing. From afar, she sort of looked like a man, or a frog, or a frog man, with her green outer vest full of bullets and smoke grenades and green helmet on top. When Jenna the

Russian was taken to the hospital for dehydration (that stupid overachieving cow), Gali volunteered to stay on base even though it was time for her weekend vacation at home.

"Hi, Gali. Would you take a look at this ID?" Avishag asked. She was the other corporal on truck-gate duty with Gali that night. Her straight hair was jabbing out of her helmet as if it were suffocating at the roots. Officer Nadav was sitting on a white plastic chair overseeing the two, cracking his fingers and leisurely observing Avishag's every move.

The ID Avishag showed Gali read, "Mustafa Al-Zain." He was an Israeli Arab, according to his ID, which seemed pretty valid. In his picture he was smiling so hard his red nose was curling inward, and although his ID said he was forty-two years old, he looked about twenty, and rather sweet.

"Hi, Mustafa," Gali said, leaning carefully toward the front-seat window, aiming at it with her M-16 as the procedures required. "Your ID says you live in one of the villages up north. What are you doing all the way down south?"

"Come on, dude, don't give me a hard time. I was just seeing the beauties of Egypt. Can't a man just see the beauties of Egypt?" Mustafa replied. Behind him were nothing but hills of sand, like giant tan spoons lying upside-down on a beige dinner table.

"But in a truck?" Avishag chimed in, faking a curious tone and raising her eyebrows.

"Yes, can't a man just see the beauties of Egypt in a truck?" Mustafa said, trying his luck. But it was already too late, and he knew it. He was pressing the button to open the back of the truck as he was talking.

The truck was empty for the most part, except for three small carton boxes. It was rather clean, too, and smelled of

Febreze. Gali knelt down from all her height and looked inside one of the boxes while Avishag lit her way with the massive, painfully bright flashlight. For a moment there, the two resembled searching pirates, or searching pirate princesses, at least in their inner eyes.

On top were oranges, and that was okay because it wasn't a large enough amount that he would have to pay customs. But at the bottom of the carton box were hundreds of bootlegged DVDs. *Shrek 2, Love Actually, Harold and Kumar*; also *Riding Miss Daisy* and *Gangbangs of New York*.

"Officer Nadav!"

"Nadav!" the girls shouted and climbed out of the truck.

Nadav got up and walked toward the girls with a slow step and stroked his cheek with his palm. He was only a bit taller than Gali and about thirty centimeters taller than Avishag. He gently placed his hand on her shoulder and squeezed. His voice sounded as if it were squeezed out of him also.

"What's the problem?" Nadav asked.

"Movies," Gali said.

"How many?" Nadav asked.

"Probably around a thousand," Gali said.

"Not a problem, then," Nadav said.

"But—" Avishag tried.

"No but. If we detain him, it will be days before we get anyone from legal to press charges and take away the movies. He'll be out in no time and just get smarter about hiding them," Nadav said. He wasn't looking at the girls as he was talking; he was looking at his hand on Avishag's shoulder.

"So again we do nothing?" Avishag asked, but Nadav just stroked her behind the ear with his index finger and smiled.

"Thanks for being bitches," Mustafa shouted as his truck

drove away, leaving behind it a cloud of dust that penetrated the nose, the ears, the mouth, the pores of Avishag and Gali's faces.

ℵ

OF THE twenty-four hours in any given day, Gali and Avishag spent six hours on a border checkpoint shift, eight hours on a guarding tower shift, and the remaining ten hours doing what they wanted. Of course we know that you have to shower every day (they check), eat in the cafeteria tent (they don't check), keep your weapon clean and your vest fully equipped (they say they'll do random checks, but they don't).

And sleep. You need to sleep.

But that still left the girls with some time. There was still time, all this time, hovering about them.

ℵ

"YOU SAY you love me, but you never listen to a word I say," Avishag said.

She liked being in this room. Aside from the wooden shower caravan, this officer's office was one of the only spaces in the whole base that wasn't a tent. And it wasn't wooden either; it was a room made out of white cardboard, dropped down by a tractor in the middle of this nothing. There was even a green plant, a desk, and a sofa in it. And it locked from the inside.

"I do listen," Nadav replied. He put down his M-4 underneath a chair and sat down, then bent down to remove his military boots.

"I don't even understand what the point of us being here is—we never do anything about anything," Avishag said. "And I thought being in combat meant something. I thought after I was done with the monitors I would actually get to do something other than just watch."

"I know it is hard, sweetie," Nadav said. He glanced at his black Swatch and began to unbutton his green military shirt.

"It is hard because you suck. You never let us arrest anyone. All you care about is how much downtime you get. What if the girls in the guarding tower are calling you on your radio right now? You don't even have your radio turned on. And what if we get caught? And you never come when I am guarding to check on me or, anything, and you, and you—" Avishag said. It felt as though it has been forever since she had spoken for this long.

She tried to continue, but Nadav went over to the sofa. He lay on top of her and grabbed her thin arms. "Shhh, listen," he said, and kissed her ear.

"It is not fair," Avishag said, but her voice was already failing her again.

"It is not fair for me either, having to baby all of you girl soldiers," Nadav said. He covered her mouth with his hand. "Do you think I like being the officer of this 'female infantry experiment'? That I chose this? Some days you are the only reason why I even have the strength to put on my uniform."

He kept her mouth covered, even though there was no need. Avishag was not going to talk. Lying on that sofa, Avishag questioned why our world even gives us words.

א

THE FIRST time Tom went to 52 Allenby Street was with Oleg and his two cousins. It was three months ago, on Tom's nineteenth birthday. Both he and Oleg had the weekend off, which almost never happened because they usually took turns with their phone shifts, and Gali was not going to get a break for at least another month. Tom was so down and in his own head that week that Oleg sometimes had to shout at him just to get him to notice his shift was over. He tried to cheer him up by giving him an entire bottle of cheap Russian vodka, but to no avail.

Tom even suspected Oleg of switching his shifts around just so he would get Tom to go out that weekend, but at first Tom was in no mood.

"I just don't feel like partying this weekend, dude," Tom said, but it was not in the nature of our Oleg to take no for an answer.

"In Russia we say, 'No bitch is worth crying like a bitch about.' You understand?" Oleg said.

Tom was not convinced. "Didn't you once yell at me that you were from Belarus, not Russia?" he asked. He then looked around the street outside the base, hoping to catch a service cab that would take him back home already.

"Whatever, man. I am telling you, where I am taking you, dude, it will be a night to remember," Oleg said. He gave Tom his sad Russian puppy smile and pressed his chubby palms together, begging.

The service cab dropped them off in the clothing district, right by Allenby 52. The building looked like a regular clothing shop from the outside, but when they knocked on the metal door, a young, skinny Russian in sweatpants opened.

"Do you want some oranges?" he asked with a thick accent. "We have a tree right behind the shop. What do I tell you, this country has good oranges. It is on the house."

The room had two sofas and a huge dining table, but only two white plastic chairs. On the white wall there was a yellow poster on which prices were written in thick black marker. They misspelled "All-incloded."

"Oleg, what is this? You can't be serious. A whorehouse?" Tom whispered. But the Russian with the oranges could hear him, and he was laughing.

"Watch your language, will you?" Oranges asked.

But the truth is Tom was surprised to learn that he wasn't appalled. He was excited. Will these girls be hot? Could he ask them to do anything? Since that day back in tenth-grade gym class he hadn't even kissed a girl that wasn't Gali.

Before Tom realized it, Oleg and his cousins had paid and a middle-aged woman was there to walk them upstairs.

"What are you getting?" Oranges asked.

"Whatever is cheapest," he said finally. "I am not really . . . You know, I don't really do this type of stuff."

"That would be just blow job. Two hundred shekels. We can charge it on credit card as massage."

Upstairs, the hallway looked just like Tom's brother's university dormitory. There were rooms everywhere, as far down the green-carpeted hallway as Tom could see, but the middle-aged woman told him to go into the second room on the right. When she leaned over to point him there, her breath smelled of garlic.

The room was small, and the only furniture in it was a queen-sized white bed, draped with a shawl printed with a Middle Eastern pattern. The walls were white and smelled freshly painted. There was nothing on them.

The girl sat on the bed with her legs crossed. Even though her hair was bleached an industrial shade of blonde and her brown roots were showing at the top, and even though her lips were bright pink and her eye shadow purple, she still looked not much older than seventeen. She was thin. She was drowning in her sweatpants and the strap of her tank top fell from her shoulder almost all the way to her pointy elbow. Her skin was so white that against the background of the wall it was as if chunks of her were not quite there.

When she looked up, all Tom could notice were her eyes. They were so huge, so bulging and blue, it looked as if they were floating in the air.

The girl looked down again and got up to turn off the light. In the dark, Tom could feel her cold hand grabbing his and leading him to the bed. Before she could touch his belt, he got up and walked back to the wall and turned on the light. The room hummed silence.

"How about I just look at you," he said. "I am not really—" and he stayed standing by the wall.

The girl did not reply. She just sat there on the bed and looked down. Every so often she would look up, and Tom would look and look and look at her. She was beautiful in a way, and all eyes.

That was then, on Tom's birthday.

ℵ

AVISHAG COVERS her face with her hands, but soon it is hard to breathe because her hands reek of rust from climbing up the metal ladder to the guarding tower. It is noon, and her helmet is drenched in sweat and it makes her hair itch, but she is too lazy to touch it. Besides, she is not allowed to take off her helmet while guarding.

Gali is leaning her torso out of the tower and looking at her cell phone. Avishag wants to tell her she's stupid, that they are not allowed to have their cell phones while guarding, that they could get caught. But she doesn't, because she knows that no one is going to catch them here. That no one cares, really, about them there.

Through the binoculars Avishag can see two Egyptian guards in the distance. Technically the girls are supposed to look through the binoculars every ten minutes, but in reality they sometimes never look at all and there is no way for anyone to know. The Egyptians are not looking through their binoculars right now, and it makes Avishag feel good, superior. She thinks that one of them has a mustache, but she can't quite tell, and the thought of it makes her laugh.

The Egyptians are guys, but they don't have to carry anything on them. Not a vest, no extra bullets, no helmet. Just their thin brown uniform and their M-16. They don't even have magnifying aims on their rifles like the girls do on their M-4s. Avishag is beginning to hate the enemy, and it surprises and amuses her. Not because of the three wars and the dead and the land mines and the lies and all, but because they don't even have to wear stupid helmets.

Gali's long fingers are moving rapidly, texting then erasing then almost sending then erasing. Sweat gets in her eyes, a fly lands on her nose, and she is nodding her head, then shaking it to negate whatever thought she had just welcomed in.

But Avishag doesn't notice any of this. She is looking through her binoculars, thinking of herself, thinking of the enemy, and of a mustache, and that she probably just lost her mind, but it is funny how she still feels altogether the same.

It is only Gali who knows what we know, because she can look at the time on her cell phone. The girls have exactly seven more hours to go.

א

SAMIR LOOKS at Hamody's strong, dark hands as he gathers the coffee cistern and the ashtray from the floor of the guarding tower and puts them back in his knapsack. He watches as Hamody flings the knapsack with ease on his wide back, and he watches him as they both climb down the ladder, and he watches him as he jumps lightly onto the sand, barely bending his knees.

"Our four guarding hours are up!" Hamody says, smiling generously. "Say, Samir, you don't talk much, do you?"

Samir is grateful that there are only six other soldiers in the showers that afternoon. Samir doesn't undress quite yet, but he watches Hamody as he takes off his uniform. He keeps his gaze down, and when Hamody takes off his socks he can notice white cotton particles that remain stuck between Hamody's long toes.

It is only after Hamody is under the water that Samir begins to undress, slowly. He takes off his brown shirt first, careful not to touch the wet circles that formed under his armpits as he folds it and puts it on the metal bench. After he takes off his pants, and then his underwear, he walks quickly to the shower at the far left side of the caravan, waving his arms in a strange and distracting manner.

He pulls down the lever and faces the wall, and then steps closer. Careful so that no one might see.

א

"HI, AVISHAG, would you help me take a second look at these IDs?" Gali said.

The truck was pitch black, which was odd, and larger than the girls usually saw at the border checkpoint. Officer Nadav was sitting on a white plastic chair overseeing the two, cracking his fingers.

The ID Gali showed Avishag read, "Momo Levin." He was from a suburb of Tel Aviv, according to his ID, which seemed pretty valid. In the passenger's seat next to him sat an Egyptian man. His passport read, "Nadim Al-Hamid," and it too seemed pretty valid to Avishag.

"Hi, Momo," Avishag said, leaning carefully toward the front-seat window, aiming at it with her M-16 as the procedures required. "Your ID says you live right around Tel Aviv. What are you doing all the way down south?"

"Come on, dude, don't give us a hard time," Momo replied. Avishag wondered if she really did look like a man from this angle, her gun aiming forward and her hair all covered inside the helmet. Or maybe it was just that somewhere along the line, someplace along the line, it had become understood that everyone was a dude of some sort, and she was the only one who had missed it.

"I am sorry," Avishag said. "You are going to have to open the back of your truck."

Avishag and Gali both at one point had to use a public chemical toilet that hadn't been cleaned in over two weeks. They both knew the smell of a shirt drenched in blood at the elbows, after crawling training, and they both knew what it smelled like when they had to wear it again the next day. Avishag also knew the smell of the chest of a man who hadn't showered in days, and the smell of his unwashed hair. She even knew the smell of her dead brother's body, and how it mixed with the scent of fresh mud.

But even before the back of the truck was fully open, it was clear to both of the girls that they had never smelled something this awful in their lives. The smell was so strong that Avishag drew a strand of hair from under her helmet with all the force she had left and pinned it below her nose. She didn't even realize she was doing it until her head began to throb because of how tightly her hair was pulled.

The truck was three paces wide, and on its floor sat on top of each other twelve young women. One of them was a round-faced little girl, and she had a Coca-Cola T-shirt on but no underwear or pants. The few bits of the visible floor of the truck were brown and red and damp.

Avishag closed her eyes.

Gali closed her eyes.

Gali opened her eyes. Avishag did too.

Twelve pairs of eyes were staring back at them, waiting, breathing, and silent.

"Nadav!" Gali shouted alone. "Nadav!"

Nadav the officer got up and walked toward the girls with a slow step. He tried to place his hand on Avishag's shoulder,

but as soon as his finger touched her she bent down on all
fours, breathing in, then out, then more quickly.

"What's the problem?" Nadav asked.

"Women," Gali said.

"How many?" Nadav asked.

"Women, a little girl. They, Nadav—" Gali said, and she
pointed to the back of the truck.

Momo and Nadim stepped out of the car. Momo had his
arm around Nadim's shoulder, and more than anything she
had seen that evening, this sight had made Avishag sick. She
finally hurled on the ground, and remained there on all fours,
breathing in her own sick.

"They all have passports," Momo said to Nadav.

"And they got their visas with the stamps on the other
side and everything like this," Nadim added in his broken
Hebrew. He handed Nadav a pile of red passports.

Nadav looked at the passports.

"No," Gali shouted. "Don't, don't even look at it. You
know, you know they want to leave, Nadav," Gali screamed.

Nadav looked at Gali with his quiet eyes. "And how do
you know that, Corporal Geva?" he asked her. "Do you speak
Ukrainian?"

But at that moment, Gali wasn't even sure she knew how
to speak Hebrew anymore.

"No more buts or I will put you up for a trial with the
commander of the base. I am the officer on duty, and I say if
they have passports and visas, they have passports and visas,"
Nadav said.

As he closed the back of the truck, one of the women
stretched her neck out so much, Gali thought she could hear
her bones extending.

"Bye, guys," Momo shouted as his truck drove away, leaving behind it a cloud of dust that penetrated the nose, the ears, the mouth, the pores of the skin on Gali's face, but only hovered above Avishag on the ground, tucking her in like a sullied blanket of summer.

א

IT WAS only when the checkpoint shift was over two hours later that we saw Avishag get up from all fours. When Nadav put his hand on top of her head, she sprung up, fast.

She pushed him once. She pushed him twice. He caught her the third time and held her in a hug for a whole minute.

"Let's go rest," he said. "Everything looks better in the morning."

א

IN THE whole town of Berezhany, and maybe even in the entire land of Ukraine, no one had hair as beautiful as Masha's. It wasn't its color—although it was speckled with gold. It wasn't its shape exactly—although it did fall on her slim shoulders in waves like from a fountain. It wasn't its length precisely either, although she had kept it long, all the way to the small of her back, from the time that she was twelve and was allowed to wear it down, because the regulations of the middle school were less harsh than those of the elementary school. The thing about Masha's hair was the way in which it structured and restructured itself around her face. It was as if it had a life of its own. It always knew exactly how to fall around her face so that it would give her round cheeks the most flattering light, no matter where Masha was. In school, and later when she walked to the shoe factory at noon, and even when she was walking around on the weekends hand in hand with Phillip, it was as if she had her own personal lighting crew following her around, making sure she always shined, was always at her best.

So when she cut it short, right up to her shoulders, rumors began to fly across the town. Jakub the hairdresser thought the reason was what the reason always is: money. He thought she had probably sold it in a wig store because she found herself is some sort of an economic bind. Kalyna, the old lady who owned the house right by the small recital hall, thought that the reason was what the reason always is: love. She thought that Masha had fallen in love with a new young man and wanted to test the nature of his devotion to her by cutting off her hair. Eight-year-old Mousia, whom Masha used to babysit on Saturday nights, thought that the only explanation could be that Masha had gone mad. When she first saw Masha with her own eyes, walking through the market with her short hair, Mousia let out a shriek and ran all the way home to sob in her room. She even skipped the vocabulary quiz the second grad-ers were having the next morning.

In the end, it was Jakub who was right, because it was money, but Kalyna was also a little right, because who knows, maybe Masha was in love. But it wasn't quite exactly what they thought. You see, Masha had been fired from her job in the shoe factory because of her boss's jealous wife. Since Masha slept with the boss. A lot. And he had a wife. There were no other places of employment in the town that would take someone with no experience or training, and Masha was going to go to school, except she first had to make enough money so that her mother could keep her house, and, well. It was like taking two steps forward and your whole dumb life backward everywhere she went.

But wait. She could go abroad, become a nanny to some rich kids, cut off her hair (because let's be honest, if you had a husband you wouldn't want him around Masha and her hair either), make enough money for her mom to even buy the stupid house from the landlord, make enough money for Masha to go to accounting school, you name it.

But the job wasn't quite exactly what Masha thought.

ℵ

IT STARTED out as a thought, something that existed entirely in Avishag's mind, but by the time the two girls finished the long walk to the guarding tower, it was already a feeling.

Gali and Avishag climbed up there, and they sat, and they didn't say a word. And then an hour passed, and then it was more than a feeling.

It was a burning feeling, like fire ants eating at Avishag's skin from the inside. It made no sense to her at first because she had showered last night after she left Nadav's, and it was a good shower, long and drowning and kind to Avishag with the smell of soap.

And it didn't make sense. And it didn't.

And she sat, and she thought, and she didn't understand.

But then she did.

It was the uniform. The stupid uniform underneath the

M-16 and the ammunition vest and bulletproof vest, underneath it was the green uniform all along.

Avishag was wearing the uniform now, but she had also worn it last night when she was leaving Nadav's office and heading toward the showers. And she could feel it now: last night her uniform touched where he had kissed her; here, there, then lower, then on the other side. And now the same uniform was touching her again, and all of a sudden, out of nowhere, she realized that she could stand this no longer. But realizing it was not enough—she could still feel it; it wasn't in her head. She could feel his dried spit on her skin, it was real and close and so *there*.

There was no escape.

Except there was.

She unbuckled her helmet and tossed it on the ground.

"Avishag?" Gali asked.

Avishag took off her M-16. Then the ammunition vest, the bulletproof vest, and her dog tag. She sat down on top of them, as if falling, untied her sandy boots, and then took off her socks.

"Avishag, what is going on?" Gali asked.

Avishag's quick fingers unbuttoned her military top and then unbuckled her big brown belt. She took off her green tank top, then her red Mickey Mouse sports bra, then her underwear.

Finally, when she was completely naked, she got down on the floor of the tower and closed her eyes. The sun was roasting Avishag's skin in blows, like a child blowing on a ragwort.

א

GALI THOUGHT about shouting, or slapping Avishag, or even calling for help on the radio. But then she thought about the oddest thing.

She thought about how, during her first time, she was actually fully clothed.

It was only after Gali had her second orgasm that she realized that this was her second, that she had had one before.

The first one was given to her by the Jordan River. Every Passover in her kibbutz the kids would go bridge jumping to celebrate the end of the long Seder in the kibbutz's dining hall. But despite how tall she was, Gali was actually afraid of heights. She never quite got the courage to jump.

During her last year in the kibbutz, when she already knew she would be moving to Tel Aviv, Gali stood again on the cement wall of the bridge in her yellow Passover dress and looked down. She waited and waited. Everyone else had gone home. The pine trees were shedding their orange needles on the water, and old ripples were budding closer toward the river band and its lilac bushes.

A pigeon flew above her. Gali covered her eyes with her hair. She smelled shampoo; she took a step forward and jumped.

For a second it was like walking in air, and it was so unnatural, it was clear to Gali that something had gone wrong that could not be made right again. Her skin was sucked upward toward the sun.

She hit the water with a splash. A warm signal of feathery fairies traveled all over her body in that instant. Her toes curled. Her shoulders bent. Her funny bone laughed. She leaped up out of the green water with her mouth open, gasping for air.

But Gali's second one was on the day she met Tom in tenth grade, at his house after geography class.

And she was completely naked then, and it was still sunny out.

And it was Tom she wanted to think of now.

"You are so strong," he told her when she found herself in his bedroom on that tenth-grade afternoon.

"Really?" she asked. She was worried she might get sick. She worried Tom would kiss her, she worried he might not, she worried she might have something in her teeth, she worried she was too tall, she worried about the dangers of the city, how loud the city still was, even right then inside Tom's room.

"You look so strong," Tom said, and stepped so close to her, the tips of their noses touched. "Look," he said and pointed to the mirror on his wall. "You look so strong."

In the mirror, all Gali could see was her old self. But then she saw Tom in the mirror, looking at her.

She wanted his eyes to wash every part of her.

א

AVISHAG WAS breathing so heavily, naked on the floor of the tower, it was as if she had fallen asleep. There was no way anyone was going to visit the tower to check on the girls. No one had ever checked on them.

ℵ

IF WE could look into the seventh tower from the right on the Israeli side of the Egyptian border on August 7 in the year 2007, what we would see would be two Israeli soldiers with their eyes closed. They'd be on the ground. Naked.

ℵ

SAMIR WAS still not really saying anything, and Hamody had already smoked seven cigarettes and boiled two pots of dark coffee, so out of sheer boredom, Hamody decided to maybe try to do what he was in the tower to do in the first place. He picked up his binoculars and looked into the Israeli side.

At first he thought he was imagining, that maybe the coffee mix his uncle had given him was a bit too strong for him, but he gazed and he gazed. He washed his eyes with that sight, and it was real and far away.

On the other side of the border, two Israeli soldiers were lying on the ground, naked.

The first Jewish girl was long, and her breasts were small and firm. Her light brown hair rested on her shoulders. A gazelle of sorts, the type of girl who could give you a run for your money if you ever had to chase her.

The second Jewish girl was soft, big breasted, and altogether perfect. With her eyes closed like that and with her auburn hair around her like wings, she almost looked like the Christian bird from Hamody's town, the one he knew he could never marry.

Hamody lowered the binoculars and looked at Samir, who was sitting on a white plastic chair with his back to Hamody, looking back at the base in silence. Hamody thought of saying something, of bursting out in joyous cheers, of laughing the whole thing off, but then he realized he couldn't, or didn't want to, at least not with Samir. Hamody realized that he wanted to save this all to himself. And he suddenly didn't care anymore. His uncle had always told him, since childhood, that God hands his treasures to every person on this earth equally; it is just that some people choose not to enjoy their treasures.

Samir was still looking away, and before he knew it Hamody had his pants low, then lower, and he was using only his left hand to hold the binoculars.

א

WHEN SAMIR looked back, he almost couldn't believe it. At first he thought he was imagining, that maybe the coffee mix Hamody's uncle had given him was a bit too strong for him, but he gazed and he gazed, he washed his eyes with that sight, and it was real and so close.

Right in front of him stood Hamody. Bright, handsome Hamody, and he was exposed, and touching himself.

It was as if Samir's hands had a mind of their own.

When Officer Tariq climbed up the tower like a silent cheetah, Samir tried to hold it in. He really did. He could hear Tariq shouting, and he could see him grabbing Hamody by the collar, and he saw when Hamody handed Tariq the binoculars, and he heard Hamody shouting that it was all the Jews' fault, that it was some sort of a deliberate trick, a new Israeli evil strategy.

Samir could hear all of that and see it, but he understood

nothing of it. He also saw the glance of shock that Hamody gave him, the way he looked at him down there, at Samir *still* touching himself, at Samir with his pants rolled down.

But even as all of this was happening, and even though he had thought his brain had signaled his hands to stop, and even though he knew Tariq and Hamody were looking at him then, and they would know, and they would see it, even so, Samir couldn't help it. It was going to happen, it almost already happened, and then—

It did.

אַ

IT TOOK Tariq two minutes to collect himself and straighten up his beret and get on the radio with the commander of the base. It took the commander of the base five minutes to understand Tariq and two minutes to contact Abou Kir, the commander of the northern military region's headquarters. It took Abou Kir seven minutes to understand and thirteen minutes until the secretary of the Egyptian army chief of staff believed him that his matter was urgent enough to justify an urgent call to the highest-ranking officer in the entire Egyptian army.

Forty-two minutes after Tariq saw the naked Jewish girls with his own eyes through the binoculars, somewhere in the heart of Tel Aviv, a particular red phone rang for the first time in six years, and it was Oleg the Russian who picked it up.

It would take two months for the Israeli press to get a hold of the story, two and a half months for the Egyptian press, seven years for the BBC. But when the press did get a hold of it, they would title the whole situation "A Diplomatic Incident."

Right after the commander of the base found Nadav in the junior officers' office, where Nadav was spending time with corporal Rona Mizrahi, Nadav finally made the fifteen-minute walk in the sands to check on the girls in tower seven, to scream at them, to let them know the extent of the damage that they had caused. Nadav's pace was quick through the sands, eager, but by the time he climbed up the ladder of the tower, all he could find there were the girls covering the shift after Gali and Avishag's. Ilana Rotem and little Shonit Miller were standing there in the tower, biting their nails, fully clothed, and armed.

א

IT WAS Tuesday, and it would take two weeks for legal to get down and sentence both Gali and Avishag to seven weeks in military prison, the harshest punishment a female in active combat service had ever received by the lenient military courts to date. When Avishag's friend Yael heard about it, she thought it was hysterical that of the two of them it was Avishag who had ended up in jail. Everyone was surprised, but the girls were delighted to get a short break from the base. They would spend the seven weeks sleeping in their cell and playing cards with former on-base pot dealers.

But until then, there were still twenty-four hours in each day, and during eight of them the girls were back in the tower, their left hands on the handles of their guns, their eyes rotating through the binoculars, waiting for the variety of junior officers who came up every hour to check on them under the new orders of the commander of the base.

ℵ

AND THAT night, Tom was already starting to feel it hurting. And we do know, or at least we think we do, how impossible it is to do nothing but stare at a phone for eleven hours, so we cannot really blame Tom for coming back to Allenby 52.

This time when the girl looked at him, she kept her eyes locked on him and didn't look down. It was he who turned off the light. They both knew he was going to get what he paid for, and if he was going to look into her eyes, that would only be after. He kept his eyes shut the whole time.

ℵ

FOR SIX hours of the day the girls were still manning the border checkpoint.

It was Tuesday, and night had come, late and warm. In the back of a red truck, four blonde women were staring at Gali and Avishag; waiting, breathing, looking, not crying.

"Come on, dude." The driver got out of the car and pleaded with Avishag, putting his hand on her shoulder. "This is all approved and authorized. I got places to be," the driver said.

Avishag looked into his blue eyes. They were so large they took up half his face. Gali looked into the eyes of the women, and she did not remove her gaze, even though she had to blink. The truck was so small, one of the women, one with short freshly cut blonde hair, was sitting on her knees in a pretzel-like manner so painful it seemed as though the bones would pierce through her skin if she sat like that for even one more minute.

"I am not a dude," Avishag said to the driver, and she took off her helmet, and her dark hair fell down all the way below her shoulders. "I am not," she said. As she said it, she thought of the baby she didn't have and realized that no one could deny that it was true.

Nadav got up from his chair with a slow pace and stood between the girls and the open back of the truck. "Avishag," he said, "how about you put your helmet back on before we all get in trouble?"

"I won't let you do this to me," Avishag said, and she grabbed Nadav by the arm. "You don't know who I am. I am nothing like this."

"You," Nadav said, and he laughed. "All you do is complain. You, you, you . . ." He said it again and again. He pushed Avishag aside by the shoulder. He laughed. He repeated the word until it lost all meaning, until his speech was a growl, a foreign tongue.

א

THE DOORS of the truck are open, and outside the man who took Masha's passport in France is standing and talking with three soldiers with guns. One of the soldiers is chanting a sound, and in Masha's ears the chant becomes a song like the ones the elementary-school children sing at the end of each year in the small recital hall of her town. And soon the song is without a human voice; it is a mere melody, and then it is a battle cry, a faint one, and it is enough for Masha, and she leaps out of the truck and she begins running south, as far as her feet can carry her.

When her feet pound on the sand they send a shock that passes through her stomach and echoes in her lungs. Masha's thin legs coil underneath her stained skirt, and when they un-curl she can hear her bones cracking, laughing. She feels as though her legs are running faster than her heart can pump life into them, fast enough so that the wind is a soft curtain she keeps piercing through.

א

NOW, THERE are a lot of things we know. Masha is running south toward the fence on the Egyptian side, and there are land mines sleeping deep below where she is heading. We know that although Samir is already in jail, Hamody's uncle got him off easy, and he is already back in the tower, and the figure running toward his gate in the dark is close enough so he can see it without the binoculars. He already has a bullet in the barrel, and twenty-eight more in his magazine, and from a distance like this, we know that he can do just fine even with-out a magnifying aim.

And we know that no red phone is going to ring in order to ask for details about this figure coming from the Israeli side. We know that Tom is going to stare at the silent red phone, as always. And we know that Gali is going to shout, "Nadav," but it will do no good, and that Avishag is not going to shout his name, because she knows better, and we know that Nadav is not going to look right below Avishag's eyebrows and do what she wants, because we know Nadav has no complaints to anyone but God.

Hamody closes his left eye and looks at the figure through gunpoint. She is four hundred meters from the land mines, now three hundred. She is running fast. Hamody releases his safety and takes a deep breath. His fingers are a bit jittery from the coffee, but he knows how to calm his nerves. There will be no surprises.

And yet as we watch Masha's hair panting up and down in the wind, illuminating her from above like a gentle lamp, we cannot help but say:

Run, girl, run.

Faster.

The
Opposite
of
Memory

I wait for the bus to come get me.

I take off my uniform shirt but stay in a tank top. I let my hair down, let all the bobby pins plummet to the sand, let my curls drop to my shoulders; and then I hide my eyes with them. Because of the sun—it is so hot, my neck can't hold my head up.

I wait on the side of the highway. The sun is boom boom boom on my head. There is no bench, only a bus sign and the asphalt. No people in cars buzzing by, no one to be seen but me.

They let me leave the training base for the weekend because I said my mother was very sick. It was easy to let them let me leave. Dana, Amit, Neta, and Hagar were already discharged, and I enjoyed a special status as the last weaponry trainer who was there during the war, who was there when things were truly crazy and stayed after. Maybe they were scared I'd go crazy if they didn't let me do what I wanted. I said I had to check my weapon in at the base, because I'd be sleeping at the hospital.

The truth is I need to take the bus to get to the mall to celebrate Noam's engagement. She's the first of the girls in our class to get engaged. Avishag called; she'd just been in jail, she begged me to come. She said even Emuna would be there, she convinced her and everyone, so who am I not to come also? And who am I? During our weekly phone call last weekend, I said to her, "Emuna, I want to see you." She said, "Yael, you want a lot of things." But she told me she'd come. I usually see her every month on my break, and I said we were coming up to almost one month and a week.

א

I LIED about my mom being sick, and I have no problem standing here without my uniform shirt, particularly since I am all alone. I stuff the shirt and the beret and the green commanding lace inside my JanSport backpack without folding anything.

I sit on the sand and lower my head; close my eyes and wait for the wait to be over. I feel a respite from the sun and the boom boom boom of the day, as if an invisible tree, or more likely a cloud, had relaxed itself right above me.

But when I raise my head, I see that it is not a cloud but a person—a military police officer—looming above me. He is wearing the military police blue beret and holding an open pocketbook. He is not resting. He is busy looking at me, without blinking, so that I know I am in trouble.

I lower my head, close my eyes, and wait for the wait to be over.

I remember moments that are the worst but also moments that happen all the time.

א

IN SEVENTH grade, my mother drove my sister and me to school, and our car was right behind Emuna's car. Behind us stood Avishag's mom's car. I looked back and saw Dan sitting up front. I remember waking up that morning and thinking that my dream had hurt me, but I wanted to go back to it and say something more. My eyes were drained and angry. I put on my Dr. Martens and bell-bottomed jeans. We all wore Dr. Martens and bell-bottoms that year. My shoes were blue; Emuna's were also.

I could see Emuna's mother's blonde hair in its bun and Emuna, chewing the sleeve of her red sweater. I could still taste the hot chocolate I had drunk minutes before. Outside, drops of rain fell on the banana fields and I could see the bananas and the dirt through my partially open window. The radio was scratchy; it played an old song, a song about a girl with hair that looks like black gold.

"It's raining," my mother said. "Close the window." Even though our village is in the middle of nowhere, there were always traffic jams on the road leading to the school at this time of day. This was before they started the pickup vans. I liked it then. I liked looking at the cars ahead, particularly if I knew the people in them, and thinking of myself as a part of this chain, a note in this rhythm.

"Close the window," my mother said. She turned her neck and looked at me in the backseat. "It's raining."

At school, Emuna and I walked through the broken gate together, right into the fluorescence and chatter and linoleum floors. The girls all swooped down on my chair as we sat down, and I took out my Bible homework from my JanSport bag. We all had JanSport bags that year. Mine was black; Emuna's was purple and yellow plaid. She was the one girl who agreed to sit next to me that year, when Avishag and I weren't talking because of the fight we had had about my crush on Dan.

We were studying Jonah for the second year in a row. There was a new teacher, and she didn't know that we had already studied Jonah the year before.

The homework was even more insulting the second time around. I had a dream that night that Jonah told me, "You thought you were moving somewhere? You stupid girl." He was saying that to me while he himself was trapped inside a whale, trying to escape God like some dumbass who didn't know the rules of the Bible and how all the stories end.

We had to complete sentences by drawing lines from a column of questions—*Jonah went to the city of . . . God told the whale to eat Jonah because . . . God killed Jonah's tree because . . .*—to a column of answers.

"She'll let everyone copy, but I am first, so don't push," Emuna told the girls.

"I thought about you all weekend long," I told her then. "I thought about you all the time. I missed you."

Later that day, as we were eating our sandwiches (mustard-tomato-mayo for me, butter and cucumbers for Emuna), the new Bible teacher did not talk about Jonah but said that during the weekend her boyfriend had asked her to marry him when they were on top of the Azrieli mall in Tel Aviv. Under them, cars were buzzing, chasing each other, and the whole world hammered on and ahead. But not for our teacher, who said the world stopped.

Then Noam said that when she grows up she will be proposed to on top of the Azrieli mall, and we all agreed that was a good idea, except for Lea, who rolled her eyes. Lea always rolled her eyes.

The problem was that we didn't realize it wouldn't be our choice where we would be proposed to, or if at all. Noam's boyfriend proposed to her on the bus. They had just gotten a call from their realtor, and then he asked her if she'd marry him.

But she wanted us all to meet in Azrieli to celebrate. To honor a time when we were children.

א

WHEN I twist my neck and see the military police officer, I laugh. Sometimes you have to laugh. Sitting on the sand, I have to. I have spent two years in the army, walking in and out of the busy shops of the Azrieli mall with my hair down during breaks, riding trains with blue eye shadow on my face. Once I even wore my nose piercing, the one Hagar convinced me to get, while in uniform when I was taking a bus from Tel Aviv Central, where it is always swarming with blue berets, eager to write you up.

And here, in this nowhere, two weeks before I am done with my service, this is where I get written up. Now is when they find me.

"Your ID number, soldier," the officer says without looking at me. He is looking deep into the lines of his pocketbook, clutching the pen. Where the hell did he come from?

I lower my head again. I close my eyes.

"Your ID number, soldier," the officer says.

I don't answer. I raise my head and look at him, calm. He moves a bit, so that the sun again explodes on me. I squint and stare. He can't make me talk. He can't put his hands on my mouth, make it move and make air and sound come out of my throat. No force in the world can do that.

"Your ID number, soldier," the officer says. "I am going to ask one more time, and then you'll be in trouble."

I know I won't be in that much trouble. It will take a few days for the complaint to trickle from the military police down to my base. By then I will have only a few days of service left. The most they could do is make me clean bathrooms, but they won't even do that. My commanders love me. I am the oldest trainer left in the base. Hagar and the other two are already doing Europe. The base has been quiet since the war a year ago. No one will go after me now. I even think my new officer, Shai, is in love with me. After all, I have been a good soldier. I taught a lot of boys how to shoot.

"I am not a soldier," I say.

"You are wearing uniform pants and military boots. You are a soldier, and you have the chutzpah to walk around with half a uniform on?" the officer says.

"I am not a soldier," I say. "I am not."

Imagine that you know someone is something, you know

it for certain, but that person keeps on saying that they are not that thing—they deny it and deny it to no end. Is there anything you could do? There is nothing you could do. If I am a civilian, he has no authority over me. There is no rule that says civilians even have to carry an ID.

The officer crosses his arms, and I smile. There is nothing more I need to say, but I speak.

"These are my sister's pants," I say. "I am just a middle-school girl. And you are a big armed man who is harassing me. I should actually cry."

"Is your sister a soldier? What is her name? She can get in big trouble for giving you this uniform."

"She is ten," I say. "She is a very tall ten-year-old. I don't know where she got these pants."

"And the boots?"

"I bought them at Zara."

"You did not."

"Zara London, I swear. I am a well-traveled middle-school girl."

"Come on," the military police officer says. He is thumping his boots on the ground a little like a woman, even though he is a hairy man. He looks like he might throw a tantrum.

"I am not a soldier," I say. "I am not a soldier."

I keep denying who I am for a few more minutes. Then the bus arrives.

Sometimes I think of things and wonder why I never thought of them before. Sometimes I remember things and beg for mercy.

ℵ

I CLIMB into the bus and pretend to be looking for money in my purse. It is only when the door closes that I take out my uniform shirt and put it on without buttoning it and show the driver my military ID, the one that lets me ride public transportation for free whenever I am wearing my uniform.

The driver doesn't care about the shirt or the buttons or even the road. He is on his cell and signals me with his hand to step inside. As we drive away, I try to wave to the officer, but he is nowhere to be seen.

I sit by the window, two seats behind the driver. The red linoleum of the bus is bursting at the seams with foam and the window is covered in dust. I lower my head and close my eyes and I wait for the bus to get to Azrieli. I wait for the wait to be over.

All the time I fight. Why? It would have made no difference for me to get a citation for inappropriate public attire, or whatever it's called. No difference at all. Everything—Emuna, me, life, the bus, Jonah—would have hammered on and forward just the same.

On the next stop, a suicide bomber comes and sits right next to me. I have no proof he is one, but I have convinced myself that it is true, so I try to make sure. The last thing I want is to build an elephant made of fear. He looks in his fifties, and his step shows he is tired of the worldliness of the bus and this new land.

As he sits down he is rocking back and forth. His rhythm is that of a man who has given up on this world yet for some reason is still nervous. His seconds are loaded enough so that even in his weariness he finds a reason to worry. He is waiting for something big to happen, something that will change everything forever.

He puts two large black plastic bags under his seat. I can see a plastic container with brown cookies in it bulging out of the bag next to me, but that could be a diversion. A man like that carrying homemade cookies?

If I didn't suspect that he was a suicide bomber, I would guess that he is Russian. Something about how close his eyes are to each other, and his strange gray hat, a hat that does not belong to this country. But I am almost certain he is Arab: the accent of his grunt to me as he sits down, the way his eyes are sunken inside his face, his yellowing skin. And he looks like a suicide bomber.

Even though it is summer, he is wearing a nice jacket and slacks, a puffy sweater underneath. His clothes were nice once, but now they're worn out.

I quickly stand up. I look around but there are no empty seats on the bus and none of the other passengers seem alarmed. They are all leaning their heads on dusty windows, texting, or staring ahead in unison.

As the bus rolls us into a tunnel, the man begins to chant. I know what will happen. I have heard the stories on the news many times before. The woman who knew but didn't say anything and then lost her ear. The boy who texted his mother he was scared and then was dead. The bus driver who knew all along but thought he could pull over and call the police before anything happened; the bus driver who was afraid that doing anything would only make matters worse.

The man continues to chant. At first all I hear is "la la la," but then I realize he must be chanting the call of prayer, the one I heard entering through my bedroom window at five in the morning, every morning, when I was a child. The call, though tired by its journey from the Lebanese border, entered loudly.

"La ilaha illallah," the man chants. There is no other God.

I worry more about not dying than dying. That I will be left burned, blind, and a burden. That I won't be able to walk or use the bathroom on my own. That I'll want to die even more. I am scared of the nearness of it all, that everything will change in seconds and how do I prepare? What is it that I want to remember from before?

My blood buzzes inside the veins of my neck and my fingers jitter as if I am typing on an invisible keyboard. But I do not scream. I must not make a scene. You must never make a scene.

I ask the suicide bomber a question. Perhaps he will answer me in perfect Hebrew; perhaps nothing will happen.

"You are going to Tel Aviv, huh?"

"Ah-ha," he grunts. Just air. No words. And he closes his eyes and keeps on rocking and chanting, "La. La. La," his lips fretting.

As the bus rolls us out of the tunnel and the light hits his face again, his cheeks seem sucked upward, like a demon or a man of grace.

I notice that he is not clean shaven. Is it that God asks them to shave before they do it, or not? I don't remember. I think, *Ok, Ok, you have to make a choice,* so I get up and step over him. He will suspect and explode. It will happen right now.

But it doesn't. He looks back at me walking farther into the bus. So does another passenger, an Ethiopian woman holding her baby like she is afraid of what I may do to it.

I am scared enough that I sit on the back stairs of the bus, rocking back and forth with the bumps along the road. I am scared enough that I sit by the trash can, full of ice cream and tissues and shells of sunflower seeds. I can even stomach the glances of the other passengers, who don't understand why I got up from my seat, who perhaps have never been scared to death that they may not die.

But I am not scared enough to tell anyone, to scream. I am only scared the amount required to perhaps save my own life. Heroism has never been one of my qualities.

I think about her all the time, Emuna. More than I ever think about Avishag, even though she and I talk on the phone every day. Still. I beg for mercy and drain my brain; lower my head and close my eyes. And even then I think about Emuna.

א

ON ONE of the last days of seventh grade, my mother drove my sister and me to school, and our car was right behind Emuna's mother's car. My eyes were drained and dry and angry.

I could see her mother's blonde hair in its bun and Emuna, chewing the sleeve of her red sweater. I could still taste the hot chocolate I had drunk minutes before. The banana fields were all brown.

I still liked the cars and the traffic jams then. I liked looking at the cars ahead, particularly if I knew the people in them, and thinking of myself as a part of this chain, a note in this rhythm. I looked at her car and liked it that Emuna couldn't see me.

That's when I saw him. The man with the gun was still very far away. It would probably take him five minutes to walk from the banana field to the road. I watched him walk closer and closer. I didn't say a thing.

Emuna's mother's car moved ahead, and our car followed. Emuna was still biting her red sweater. That's how well I could see her—I could see her teeth.

The man with the gun was wearing a kaffiyeh. I knew, even then, that he came from Lebanon. That he was the only man to infiltrate the border since the army pullout. I knew it, I can't deny it.

I knew it was a chase, and I was inside a stopped car.

Their car moved ahead. Our car moved ahead. The man with the gun kept walking. Now, I could have thought, *Don't hurt us.* But I thought more. I thought, *Not us, them. Go there. Go there.* And I stayed quiet.

Their car moved, our car moved, their car moved. Then he pinned his gun to the window and shot Emuna's mother. He ran; he left.

Emuna in all that red, I see her.

This memory, though, is not the worst. What happened after was much worse.

א

AFTER THE bus pulls up to the sidewalk across from the Azrieli mall, I walk a few steps and cannot believe I am still alive. I feel like a carbon copy of myself, but after all, nothing happened.

The people scatter; the bus driver helps the Ethiopian woman get her stroller off the bus. The suicide bomber that never was marches alone toward a café, where people who are still very young smoke with their legs up on the tables outside. People, all these people, walk as if guided by invisible strings, across, along, diagonally, fast. I can hear the knock of their steps. The cars murmur like giant fruit flies, the music of the city all about me, touching me. The buildings throw their gloom and I think that even if the bus did explode nothing would have changed. All of this would still be.

ℵ

I OFTEN think I don't remember the funeral or the days after, but I know that I was there. I cried a lot, mothers other than my own hugged me, and then my mother hugged me at home.

I knew I wouldn't have to see Emuna because she was always gone in summer. That summer could have been different, I thought that it might be, but in the end it wasn't; except I kept thinking it was out of the ordinary that the village and the country had not yet exploded, that I had not yet exploded. I waited for a blast that would never come and that I did not deserve.

I remember something Emuna's mother had said the day Omer broke up with her and she said she wanted to die. Her mother said she thought her life was starting when Emuna's father asked her to marry him, and then she thought her life was starting when she did marry him, and then when Emuna was born. Or maybe it was my mother who said that about me?

The worst moments came after.

On one of the first days of eighth grade, my mother drove my sister and me to school, and our car was right behind your father's car. My eyes were drained and dry and ready. I had on my Dr. Martens and bell-bottomed jeans.

I could see you chewing the sleeve of your sweater. I could still taste the hot chocolate I had drunk minutes before. Outside, drops of rain fell on the banana fields and I could see the bananas and the dirt through my partially open window.

"It's raining," my mother said. "Close the window." I looked at the cars ahead and tried thinking of myself as a part of this chain, a note in this rhythm.

"Close the window," my mother said. She turned her neck and looked at me in the backseat. "It's raining."

At school I walked alone, behind Emuna, through the broken gate, right into the fluorescence and chatter and linoleum floors. The girls all swooped down on my desk as I sat down, and I took out my Bible homework from my JanSport bag.

We were studying Jonah for the third year in a row. It was the same teacher, and she had forgotten we had already studied Jonah the year before. Or maybe she didn't care. She was married.

Jonah was a prophet, but he didn't want to be a prophet, so God made him one anyway, even though he hid from God. After that, Jonah went to this town of bad people and told them they were really bad and that God was going to kill them all. The bad people didn't get mad at Jonah; instead, they turned good and God spared them.

Then Jonah became really sad because he felt like an idiot for telling those people God would kill them only to have God change his mind, and he was also dehydrated in the desert. Then he found a tree that saved him from the heat and God killed the tree. Then Jonah was very sad. And then God said, "You see, Jonah? You are sad about the death of this tree even though you didn't work at all to raise it, so how do you expect me not to have second thoughts about killing all those people I made?"

But God had promised Jonah a disaster. He had had Jonah make a scene for nothing. Jonah had thought the whole world would end, but God was never going to let that happen. I bet you he knew from the beginning. Some people, and God, know from the beginning that the world won't end. They pace lightly on sidewalks all around me.

We again had to draw lines between questions and their answers. Same questions, same answers, but it was harder to do this time.

God killed Jonah's tree because . . .

"She'll let everyone copy, but I am first, so don't push," Avishag told the girls. She took the seat next to mine. She smiled at me, as if we had never stopped talking. It surprised me, and then I was elated. I could not tell her that I had been saving the seat for Emuna. Not because of anything that had to do with Avishag. Not because I was happy she had forgiven me for falling for Dan. Because I did not want Emuna to sit next to me.

Emuna was real, and the same. She stood amid the girls like decoration and looked at me. They all did.

"I thought about you all summer," I told Avishag then, loud. "I thought about you all the time. I missed you." That was the pulse of the worst moments. The pulse of the world rolling forward.

ℵ

I RIDE the escalator higher and higher toward the open bridge that leads to the entrance of the Azrieli mall. In the highway below me the cars are chasing each other's colors; fast and again and more.

In the years since we all finished middle school, we have met at the Azrieli mall many times. All girls do. The enchantment died off the second, maybe third time.

I know exactly what is going to happen, so it does not even need to. But it will. Things that don't need to happen happen all the time. We keep doing them.

We'll all hug, the seven or eight of us who'll show up. Avishag and I will kiss each other on both cheeks. We'll all try on shoes we are never going to buy and buy tank tops we may never actually wear. The talk will be of boyfriends and college entrance exams and waitressing jobs and how good it is to be done with the army. We'll make fun of Tali and Lea for deciding to become officers. They'll repeat the old mantra of how easy it is to make money by staying in the army for one more year, because as an officer you get paid more than you would on the outside, and you don't have any expenses. I'll say, "But you? Lea!" and she'll shrug her shoulders, or slap my back, her movements mechanical, reminiscent of the authority she once had but lacking strength. We'll order coffee at the Aroma café and Lea will pour a sugar packet down her throat. Then we'll all laugh. The bathroom will be flooded and a woman who has no home will spit on us when we wash our hands with the industrial soap. Then we'll take the elevator to the roof, and one girl will say that from this height, the people walking the streets of Tel Aviv look like ants. Maybe it will even be me. "It is so good to be together," someone will say. "I absolutely love Tel Aviv," another girl will add. We will all hope we don't grow up to raise our children in a small town.

ℵ

WHEN I see Noam, she runs and hugs me. Then she shows me her ring.

"Topaz and white gold," she says.

It takes me a couple of minutes to notice that Emuna is not around. I think too much, and only of myself.

When I realize Emuna is not around, it excites me.

And perhaps this can be the boom. Maybe Emuna took off to India. Maybe she is in her childhood room, broken, in conclusion and after all broken. And maybe she decided that she just didn't want to see us, that this won't be fun, that enough is enough.

This all happened before, and it will happen again just the same, so in all truth there is no need for it to ever happen, this whole meeting, the mall, us.

I say I think about Emuna all the time, but I don't even ask about her. Not right away. I wait.

"I can't believe we are finally almost grown-ups," I say and kiss Noam on both cheeks.

Standing behind her are six other girls I have known since I was born. We are in front of a shoe store on the third floor of the epic mall, people walking around us, engulfing us, humming language.

"You are so crazy," Noam says. "How come you're not

wearing your uniform shirt?" she asks after I apologize for my sweatiness and uniform pants and explain I came straight from the base. "You'll get in so much trouble," Noam adds.

"If anyone asks, I'll just say I am not a soldier," I say.

"You can't do that, crazy face," Lea says and punches me on the shoulder.

"Well, I already did, Ms. Officer. I already said it once and I can say it again."

We laugh.

Aside from Lea, who also came straight from a base, they are all wearing bell-bottomed jeans. We never grew out of that.

א

EMUNA. I want to tell you something. Some things.

Do you remember that one time, in sixth grade, when we saw the movie? That was the first time we ever saw a movie in a theater. We sat that day on the floor of Lea's kitchen. There must have been eight of us. Lea called for a car. The smell of that call, to me, still, is stolen perfume and bananas and feet.

"We would like to order a taxi. A big one. There are a lot of us. And we're going to the movies," Lea said.

Remember the van that came and got us? The ride? We tried to make our faces and words and joy look like those of the adults we thought we were becoming.

"Here is a tip," Lea told the driver when we arrived at Nahariya's attempt at a mall. "A tip, as is customary."

The movie wanted to scare us. It was *Scream 2*. We screamed. Right after Neve Campbell shot Mrs. Loomis in the head, right as she said, "Just in case," all the lights went on and the movie stopped and an usher screamed, "Don't be alarmed. A suspicious object was found in the mall, and we need everyone to walk to the parking lot."

"Just our luck. Just. Our. Luck," Lea said in the parking lot. Remembering it now, I know these were the most adult-sounding words any of us said that day, but I didn't notice it then. The act was over.

"Remember this one time when we pretended we were wolves and crawled all over Nina's street?" I asked Lea.

"And?" Lea asked.

"And nothing," I said. "Just something I remembered."

"You do that *all* the time," Lea said. "Remember this one time *this*, and remember this one time *that*." She was imitating my voice, talking like a slow person. That year I still hoped she'd change back to the girl I used to play with, and the more I hoped the more she mocked me.

"Yea, she does that all time," Noam said. "It's annoying."

Avishag looked away. Not once has she ever spoken for me, I now realize. Not since the beginning.

But you.

And you said, "Leave her. Leave her alone."

And you. Remember?

Why don't you ever leave me?

צ

ONLY AFTER all the words without weight are done falling from our mouths do I ask Noam, "Where is Emuna?" I face her. "She is not coming, is she?"

Emuna. It takes me a long time to ask where you are. A long time.

I wanted to tell you something. When I am with you, when we are breathing the same air, I also remember you; still and always and all at once.

Ok.

"Oh, Emuna? She just went to the bathroom," Noam says. "There she is, right behind you," Noam gestures with her chin.

I can smell you, standing behind me and real, before I turn. I smell the industrial soap of the Azrieli bathroom on your hands. I smell the urine that soaked into the frayed ends of your bell-bottomed jeans. You are right here.

The smell is the opposite of memory. A thing other than other.

Means of
Suppressing
Demonstrations

Shock

Lea, the officer, had stopped feeling her own body. She lay on her back on top of an antisniper barricade, holding a newspaper page, blocking the stars. She had to stretch her arms to hold the wide page above her head.

"Oh," she said.

"The army didn't do it," Tomer said. He flicked his cigarette butt down to the asphalt of Route 433. He was talking about Huda, the little Palestinian girl on the beach. The newspaper picture showed her screaming amid red sand, near the body parts of the six people that were her family.

"I know," she said. "This is a manipulation."

The world said the Israeli army had done it with an air

strike, but the Israeli army knew that the family had been killed by a dormant shell that Palestinian militants had left by the ocean. Lea looked at Tomer. The orange light of the road lamps lit him from behind, so that he could have been a demon. He was nineteen, two years younger than the officer.

"It's just that I can't feel my body all of a sudden," she said.

"Again?"

Lea often told him that she couldn't feel her body. That she could move it but not feel it. That those were two separate things. He never questioned her; he pushed her. This was what she wanted.

Tomer took his weapon off his back and pressed her shoulders into the cement. When their pants were pulled down, he pressed his hands on her neck, then her arms. He called her "Lea" during the day because this was her name, and because she said he could. At night, when he was pulling her hair so tight her scalp buzzed, he called her "officer," because this was what she said he should call her then, and this was what she was. She wanted him to call her that then, because it was when he was closest and roughest that she knew he most needed to be kept at bay. When she looked to the side, she could see the warm glow that came from inside the homes in villages of other people.

She knew her service days were nearing their finish line but could not feel it. She could not imagine or remember any of the things she had wanted before she became a soldier, and she struggled to find things she wanted for her civilian life ahead. She guessed she must want a family or to get into a good school, but she guessed it from the data around her. She did not feel the want herself. When she had first begun feeling this way, less than a year into her service, after the neck of one of the soldiers at her checkpoint was cut almost in two, she had decided the only reasonable thing she could truly want must exist inside the army, and so she decided to become an officer. She did not want to be a dumb checkpoint soldier anymore, the type whose neck could get cut almost in two. She wanted to be able to yell at soldiers who put their necks where they might get cut. She grew to accept that her service days would begin and end in the transitions unit but figured that if she had to be at a checkpoint she might as well be a checkpoint officer.

Tomer did almost everything she asked him to without asking a lot of questions. He was a reasonable nineteen-year-old boy. And Lea, she had this certain beauty, after all. A cold, humming, unfazed beauty, and great breasts. She was also the only girl who was sprinkled inside his days. And he was passing his own time—his own time as a soldier.

Lea woke up alone in her field bed the next morning. She was in her own tent because she was the only female at the post.

It was an odd posting. Route 433 bred oddness all along it. It cut through the West Bank but had been closed to Palestinians since 2002, when the motorcyclists were shot. The army somehow needed four soldiers and a commanding officer for an improvised checkpoint every hundred or so kilometers, so she found herself commanding four boys who manned daytime guarding shifts in an always deserted checkpoint. All so there would be someone to say, "Sorry, the road is blocked," in case someone did decide to show, even after all this time. This had little to do with her earlier service days in a gigantic checkpoint and had almost nothing to do with who she was.

This posting would have made her angry, except she knew her service was over in a few weeks anyhow.

She spent the day in bed reading a prep book for university entrance exams. She hoped to make high enough marks to study business. She was supposed to check in with the boy on duty twice a shift, but she didn't bother because nothing ever happened. Except that day something did. Tomer, who had the afternoon shift, called her military cell to say that there were three male demonstrators at the checkpoint.

"Have they thrown rocks or anything?" she asked.

"No, but they have a sign. And they keep on arguing with me that I, like, disperse them, even though I explained we don't have any means of suppressing demonstrations here."

"That's not true."

She was suddenly more excited than she had been since before she had been posted on Route 433. As an officer, she knew that every checkpoint had a supply box to be used for demonstrations. Finally, she thought, her training was good for something. And if the demonstrators insisted, she must aim to please.

She unlocked the metal supply closet in her tent and pulled out a wooden box. It was heavy, so it took her a while to carry it to the antisniper barricade and then to cross the road to the sun umbrella that marked the checkpoint.

"We had a lesson about demonstrations and stuff in boot camp, but I forget," Tomer said.

Two of the three Palestinian demonstrators were in their thirties, and one was just a boy, a boy with fingers in his mouth. They had one sign, a piece of A4 paper on which they had written with a marker in English: "Open 433." One of the men was wearing a Guns N' Roses T-shirt. He raised his hand, so she signaled him with her hand to step forward. She signaled him to halt when he was four steps away.

"Officer, we are here to demonstrate against the restriction of our mobility, which is a collective punishment and against international law," the demonstrator said in solid, accented Hebrew.

She put one hand on the handle of her weapon and one in her pocket. "How come there are only three of you? This is hardly a demonstration."

"I do apologize, officer. We have a wedding this week in the village, and, you see, other people, they are not serious," he said. He bowed a little as he spoke. "Is there any way you could disperse us just a little, enough for a press blast, or something?"

She had meant to be cruel, but the man was being rather sweet. He squinted his eyes at her as he spoke and looked more like a bank customer asking for an increase of his credit limit than a demonstrator. It made her feel, a little, like it was the real world.

"We'll see what we can do," she said.

She sat on the asphalt and opened the wooden box. There were printed instructions inside, tucked inside a sheer nylon sleeve. Tomer signaled the man to step back and wait. He sat by her and they both read.

The purpose of Means of Suppressing Demonstrations is to suppress demonstrations. It is intended to intimidate and at most injure, but the purpose is not to kill. One general guideline:

*   *Use from light to heavy: shock, tear gas, rubber. We must minimize damage when possible.*

Grenade 30, the shock grenade, was designed to stun and scare by creating a loud noise. The instructions said that if exploded within a two-meter radius of people, it could cause problems in the eardrums and light injuries from the plastic, so Lea told the demonstrators to step back a bit. They walked back while still facing the sun umbrella, and after a while, the boy took his fingers from his mouth and gave her a hesitant thumbs-up. She didn't quite know how to respond to that, so she gave him a thumbs-up as well—he was far enough. Then she quickly put her hand back on her weapon.

The shock grenade was orange and cone shaped. It had a red stripe encircling it. She held it in her hand and then bent to the ground to lift a rock. Her fingers were stiff around the rock's dry surface. She dropped it from the air into Tomer's hand.

"You are the soldier," she said. "And besides, it's been longer since I last learned about this stuff. Let's practice."

They pretended the rock was a grenade. She gave him the instructions as if she knew them by heart, though she had just read them moments earlier. She reminded him to keep the grenade in the palm of his hand and to secure the lever with his index finger. She explained to him how to thread the middle finger of his left hand inside the safety as if it were a ring and to pull the safety with a spin of his wrist, as he would if someone were to ask him what time it was. She raised her voice at him a bit, because he pulled his arm back for the practice throw without accompanying it with a constant look.

"The instructions say after you take the safety out you have to look at the grenade at all times, because you only have three and a half seconds until it explodes. What if you took your hand back and hit a wall?"

"But I know there is no wall behind me," he said.

"What if there were suddenly? What if a bird came? It is not nice to have something explode in your hand, even a shock grenade."

After a couple of dry runs, it was time for the real thing. The boy had his hand in his mouth again, and one of the men was wiping his brow with his forearm. The heat radiated from the asphalt between them.

"Ok?" she shouted at them. Then she and Tomer put their earplugs in their ears.

She thought that anything in this world that one could guard against with pieces of foam in the ears could not be so powerful, but every time a grenade exploded, she felt the noise in her hip bones like a jolt and in her mouth like a hint of metal.

She thought that the three of them would stay longer, but after four grenades the demonstration was dispersed. Everything went according to plan, just as she and anyone who was standing in her position would have anticipated.

During her school years, she had felt like every minute was part of a race. Get that grade. That boy. Buy that shirt. Be the most popular girl. Don't let any other girl disobey you. Throw the best parties. Go. Go. Go, before someone else gets there before you. But the army was a numbing respite from that eighteen-year-long, breathless race. The army—it began and it ended, and she knew that. All of it was owned by the predetermined dates of its start and finish, dates within which none of what she had done would matter. Whatever it was she did, the army would end when it would. She would arrive at the same spot, that same station near the base where soldiers returned their uniforms at long last. It was difficult to feel anything, knowing this. Most of her days were procedures and orders, going from one dot to the next in what appeared to be the one and only possible straight line.

She tried, a bit, still, sometimes, to jut out of the line, the way a drawn line jutted during her school years when her thumb on a ruler forced the pencil off course. She tried with sex, with hurt, and shocking newspaper articles, sometimes, but she did not try too hard.

Tear Gas

The newspaper page Tomer brought to the barricade that night was about a girl who had been killed by her mother. The girl was an Israeli Arab from a northern village, and she had become pregnant by one of her brothers, who had both raped her and were expected to receive a harsh sentence. The picture showed the girl on the day of her high school graduation, smiling and wearing jeans. She had a generous, good-girl smile, the smile of that schoolgirl you couldn't even gossip with about the actions of soap opera characters. The mother was expected to receive a light sentence, because the killing had been done in the name of honor, and with passion, and one has to respect another's culture. The mother had used knives and a cane and a plastic bag, and she swore that she had first urged the girl to take her own life. The article ended with a quote by a butcher from the girl's village, who explained how a woman shamed is always like rotting meat, and sometimes there is no choice. If you don't cut it off immediately, the shame will fester its way into the whole family.

The officer let the boys keep the newspaper that the delivery truck brought every morning, with the promise that Tomer would save her the most shocking parts to read at night. She didn't want to waste time reading the things that would make her feel less than what was most.

"I thought that little boy was going to cry," Tomer said. He was wearing his undershirt and uniform pants, even though she had told him she didn't like it when he stepped out of the residential section not in full uniform.

"No, he wasn't," she said. "It was just some noise. I didn't even think that would disperse them, but maybe they just wanted something symbolic." She could hear a radio from a house singing in a language not her own.

"It was like, boom!" Tomer said. Then they didn't talk anymore.

She hadn't told him she couldn't feel parts of her body that night, but on the cement they had acted as though she could not feel anything at all and everything was fair and necessary as long as the other soldiers could not hear their noises. The tents were only half a kilometer away from the antisniper barricade, and sometimes she screamed loud enough she thought she should worry.

Her hours, the sands. She passed through them like a ghost she had read about in a teenage book she had once bought at the supermarket. The ghost was in a house but could not open drawers or pick up a coffee cup. She could not move a thing and her existence did not matter, was not felt. Lea lived encircled by a fog made of cotton balls.

The demonstrators came back the next afternoon. She spent the first part of the day wondering if they would. She made mistakes on one of the practice tests she took, even on one math question that was little more than algebra and common sense.

The demonstrators came back, this time with earplugs.

She didn't need to carry the wooden box to the checkpoint this time because she had told the early-morning shift soldier to take it there just in case.

"What is it we can do for you now?" she asked the man as he carefully approached. He was wearing the same T-shirt as yesterday. The boy was the one holding the sign this time, but he still had his fingers in his mouth.

"The thing is, no one is going to write a story about a few noise crackers," the man said. "That's the thing, officer." He was cautious, like a customer who had bought a shirt and demanded a refund even though he had already worn the shirt more than once. But he stood strong, like he was determined to insist as much as he could.

"The boy could get hurt," she said. Tomer stood behind her, drumming on his collarbone with his fingernails.

"He is thirteen," the man said. "That's a man for you. That's bar mitzvah."

He looked younger. She remembered the instructions said that no matter what, means of suppressing demonstrations should not be used against children. She also remembered a long discussion in her officers' training school about children being anyone whom you could not possibly imagine already having had his bar mitzvah, wearing a suit and reading at the temple and all that. These demonstrators really knew their stuff—informed consumers or whatnot.

The Federal, the gun used for shooting gas grenades, looked more like a toy gun than any actual toy gun she had ever seen. It was essentially a brown tube with two silver handles, one in front and one in back. It looked like it had been spray-painted. The instructions for it were long, and besides, she didn't want the man to think he had the power to make her move faster, and so she shooed him away without a word of promise and sat on the plastic chair under the sun umbrella to read.

For some reason, the instructions were half history. By the end of a few minutes she knew that the Federal gun was invented by the Federal Police in New York, America, by a company called Federal, hence the name! In the army, sometimes, she had to wonder who wrote certain instructions for certain procedures and who supervised that writing. It seemed like each document was allowed to have its own life. Sometimes there were still surprises and a bit of life in the army. Small times.

The grenade used as the Federal's ammunition had a diameter of thirty-seven millimeters, and its gas was of the CS type. It was silver with a blue stripe and looked very pretty and technological. The Federal had aims, and this worried her because both she and Tomer were terrible marksmen, which is what had landed them on Route 433 in the first place. But the instructions said that the aims were not to be used, because the shooter doesn't aim directly at an individual target, since gas disperses, duh. She felt stupid when she read that, but probably not as stupid as the person who had designed the weapon. The instructions actually warned against shooting through aims, because gas could seep out into the eyes of the shooter. When she put her hand to her nose, she could smell a bit of the gas already, cutting into her lungs like grain.

The instructions said that the effective range was up to eighty meters, but it didn't say which range was close to being dangerous, and so she positioned the demonstrators at a distance that appeared to her to be about fifty meters, then thought better of it and told them to take a few steps farther back.

She licked her finger to check the direction of the wind but could not feel a thing. She loaded the gun with the grenade, pointing the barrel to the ground and then snapping it shut. She hoped for the best wind and aimed at a forty-five-degree angle from the ground.

All this time, she had not said a word to Tomer and he had not said a word to her. But then she signaled him to take her place holding the gun and said, "Literally, all you have to do now is press the trigger, but press it hard because the gun has no safety, so the designers compensated by giving it a stubborn trigger."

Then she waved to the demonstrators, and even though Tomer had not counted, had not warned, there was the slightest sound of a thing coming undone, and then the demonstrators' faces were red and wet and screaming and then they ran and were gone.

Rubber

There were not enough stars that night, and on the barricade Lea looked like she was crying. The lights of the homes around her went out one after the other. The picture in the newspaper page Tomer brought was that of a bird that in two years was said to be going extinct. The bird was an eagle with a gray tail, but the newspaper said it was called the white-tailed eagle, which had made her think the picture and story could have been lies. But the bird looked angry through its eyes in a way she had not known birds could be, even ones who knew they were going extinct.

"This is the worst you could find today?" she asked.

"There was no mention of the demonstrators," Tomer said. They had reported the incidents to the Route 433 headquarters over the phone by the end of the first day, but no one seemed to care too much about them.

Tomer was on his back too that night, looking at the paper and then over at her. He crushed her shoulder with his. "You are crying, though," he said. He had not seen her cry before. "Or is it the tear gas? You're the one who told *me* to wash my hands twice before touching my face," he said.

"I am not that stupid," she said. "I am going to go to TAU for accounting, you know." She had never talked to him about when she would leave before, and she did not know if he knew it would be soon.

"Then what?"

"My shoulder. You are hurting it."

She had known they would come the next morning, and so she could study without being distracted. She only made four mistakes on the practice exam, all of them in the English section. All of them she had known were wrong before she checked, but she could not have guessed what the answers would have been on her own.

She had known they would come back, and so she went with Tomer to the checkpoint at the start of his shift. What she did not know was that the demonstrators would come with lab goggles and surgical masks. They looked like mad scientists, and she wondered where they had gotten those costumes, in their pathetic town in the West Bank and all. The boy wore cheap plastic sunglasses over his goggles, and she smiled when she saw them, and so he smiled back.

But when the man with the Guns N' Roses T-shirt shouted,

"It's rubber day!" her face hardened. She used only her chin to signal him. She let him come closer than she had the days before.

"No," she said. "A rubber bullet could kill you guys. This has gone on long enough."

"But, but—" the man said. He thought better of the tone of his voice. He realized that he was not a customer, that he had every reason to be afraid of upsetting her. "That's the point, though. They are going to report rubber for sure. They always report rubber."

Lea shook her head.

"We won't ask for anything ever again, we swear."

She didn't move.

"We just want this one thing, and you can give it to us. I mean—" he said. "Think about that."

She thought about that and she knew then that she was done for, and that her face showed it. The man stepped away on his own, raising his arms slightly to signify that he was giving her all the time there was in the world.

"The boy has to move away because you have to be eighteen for rubber," she said. She wasn't sure if that was a rule but thought it might be.

The boy sat by the side of the road for half an hour and waited with his fingers in his mouth, and they wrinkled. That's how long it took her to read the instructions. Longer. Tomer was standing above her as she read.

The instructions warned that the rubber bullets could kill. Aside from that, everything about them seemed designed to entertain and complicate a soldier's life. It occurred to her to wonder how many soldiers had read those instructions recently.

The Romay was a metal barrel that you screwed onto the barrel of an unloaded rifle. Then you stuffed four steel bullets covered in rubber inside it from the top and blasted them out with a single demibullet you loaded in your magazine. If you blasted out fewer than four rubber bullets at a time, the demibullet would expel too forcefully, and the effect would be like that of real live fire. The bullets spread in a ten-degree angle from top to bottom, and you had to make sure you hit only the target's legs, because if you hit other parts of the body, the effect would be like that of real live fire. If the target was farther than fifty meters, then it was out of the range of the rubber bullets. If it was closer than thirty meters away, then it was too close, because the rubber bullets would have the effect of real live fire.

The instructions were written so that if the rubber bullets killed a man, it was the finger that pressed the trigger that was to blame. It must have been the finger that was to blame because the instructions had cautioned against every other thing. She wondered how this would work in most cases, when the demonstrators were not three cooperative individuals with an A4 sign but an actual angry mob. But she did not wonder too much because her demonstrators were three cooperative individuals, and so what she did next was measure.

She told them to go very far and then walked toward them, counting her steps, like she had learned in boot camp's measurement lesson. According to her calculations, they were a little less than fifty meters away from the sun umbrella. She signaled for them to take a few steps forward and then walked all the way back to Tomer.

The two men stood quiet, positioned in the exact measured spot where she told them to wait to be shot. They stood patiently, like tame children waiting for permission to go play in the park.

The kit had only a few demibullets, and so she put two inside Tomer's magazine. The bullets were the same as regular bullets except they had no copper arrowheads.

"Below the knees," she told Tomer. "Get on the ground and aim below the knees."

It was the other man, the one she had never conversed with, who took the hit. He held his leg on the ground like a soccer player who had sustained an injury on the field. But before it was dark he limped away. His limping looked worse because he was supported by the other man on his left, and by the boy on his right, and the boy was shorter; he was small.

Live Fire

The one thing that is not a means of suppressing demonstrations is live fire, and Lea knew that the cooperative demonstrators knew this—they knew all the rules—and so she knew they would not come back. That night Tomer brought the entire newspaper to her out of laziness, and he was so rough that she spent moments on the cement imagining her spine as a string, and then that it had knotted, and then that it had snapped.

But they came back. The two men came back with bits of mattresses tied around their legs with pieces of cloth. They looked like they were half sumo wrestlers. And the boy with wet fingers just came back as a boy.

"We won't shoot you with live fire," she said. That was the only option left.

"Please," the man said. He stepped closer. He stepped

closer without invitation, and so did the boy and the other man. "Shoot and miss, just shoot and miss."

"You have to have means and intent to kill for us to shoot," she said. "That's IDF Guidebook 101."

"Please," the man said. "We need to be in the newspaper. Page five, even."

But she said means. Then she said intent. Then she said means.

"Means?" the boy asked.

"A gun," Tomer said.

"Or a knife," she said.

"Or a rock," Tomer said.

He didn't know what he was saying, because with that, the boy slowly bent to pick up a rock from the asphalt. It could not have been there, but it was, because it was the rock Tomer had used to practice throwing a shock grenade.

She raised her gun to her shoulder and charged the weapon and aimed at the boy. Tomer raised his gun to his shoulder and charged the weapon and aimed at the boy.

It was before the boy heard the man whisper in Arabic that he dropped the rock to the ground, as if he had been caught shoplifting it.

Then the boy put his fingers in his mouth and the guns were lowered and she thought the day and summer and place were almost over, but Tomer spoke up behind her.

"We could technically arrest him for that," Tomer said. "We could, technically," he repeated, and shrugged his shoulders.

"Please?" the boy said. He wasn't asking her. He was asking the man. An arrest of a child was always at least page five, she knew. He'd be out in days; probably he'd be out in days.

The man shook his head, but then the boy said that the

thing is, they just wanted this one thing, and now they could give it to themselves, and then he told the man to think about that and the man knew that he was done for.

"Whore," the man said to Lea as Tomer took the boy by the arm. It was what he needed to say to her. After all, she was a female checkpoint officer, and he played the role of the poor Palestinian, but the word felt forced and she was embarrassed for him.

After the men left, she and Tomer walked behind the boy toward the base to make the calls about the arrest. It took the men some time to leave, so night was falling by the time they walked back toward the barricade, but the orange road lamps were not yet on.

She quickened her step, because she wanted to walk in line with the boy. She quickened her step suddenly and then grew afraid that she had startled him. Her hand jumped and grazed his.

It was the boy who could have been afraid, but instead it was she who was afraid, and more, because she could feel it then and too much—the drying wetness of his hand now on her hand, and bits of dust from the rock he had held, and the wind. She could feel it all at once. She thought of how Tomer would later that night slam the entirety of his weight onto her bones, pressing them into the cement barricade. For a passing moment, she wondered if during that time he would call out her real name, rather than "officer." She wondered if she should ask him, then remembered it was not an important detail to ponder. Those dates, the dates on both ends of her service. Whatever happened inside of them was decoration and air and would not change the place where she would end up.

She decided she would go ask to see the army psychiatrist

the next day and ask to get released early, even though she had so little time left to serve.

א

A FEW years later they opened Route 433 again, but it only lasted a few months. There are still soldiers who spend three years doing little but saying, "Sorry, road is blocked," to anyone stupid enough to try. When she heard the route was open, and then when she heard it was closed again, she could feel it: her own hand, the boy's spit, almost as much as she felt it then and there.

Sometimes, at dark parties in Tel Aviv and on street walks and in rooms, she felt the spit on her hand, even when she was not forced to hear about Route 433. She felt it at dark parties and on walks and in rooms where she was never alone, where she was always with a person other than herself, and it was when those persons called her name that she felt it. *What do you say, Lea. Thanks a lot, Lea. I agree with you, Lea.* Every time she heard her name in the dark, she felt the boy's spit on her hand that night on the walk.

That night, Tomer had trailed only one step behind her and the boy. They had walked, kicking stones, humming, staring at the stars before the lamps took some of them. She thought about all that had yet to happen but that she knew for certain would happen soon. The cement. The paper. The plea for shock.

"Lea," Tomer said right before they reached the base. "Let's remember to take bets on which page in the news this arrest will be. What do you say, Lea?"

And there was that silly question again, the one she had

just chased. It came back. She wondered what he might call her that night, though she knew whatever word of the words of this world he chose would not matter. It would not shift the pace of the steps of the days, or even the pace of the steps of that night.

As they walked, the boy put his hand in his mouth again, the hand hers had just grazed.

That night, Lea was twenty-one, Tomer nineteen, the boy thirteen. They passed by the cement barricade in silence and with synchronized steps. Through the eyes of a villager looking out from within the light of a very distant home, they could have been a family.

Once
We Could
Pretend
We Were
Something
Very Else

hree days before I left the village, something almost good happened: Lea once again started caring about something that wasn't exactly true.

"Listen, Yael. Miller killed an olive tree," Lea said.

"Yes," I said.

"It is the hardest thing in the world, to die. If you're an olive tree."

"Yes."

"This was intentional. Premeditated."

Lea turned her head away from the olive grove by her house and really looked at me, for the first time in weeks. She rested her cigarette in the ashtray. Night was falling around her backyard, purple, orange, huge. The shadow of the amputee lawn dwarf was lengthening, and the wind chimes rattled.

Lea squinted, suggesting. She wanted me to say her new wild thought out loud, the one that was still growing, the first one she'd had in a long time.

And of course, I did.

"I believe we have a murderer in our village," I said.

We were twenty-one years old. We had finished our military service, and I was about to leave the village for a job at the airport. I had been stuck in my parents' home doing nothing for almost a year, but Lea's extra time as an officer had only ended a few months ago. I'd lost touch with pretty much everyone except Lea and Avishag. It happened that way, that after all these years I ended up with the same best friends I made when I was in elementary school. I never spoke with Hagar or any of the girls I served with. Avishag was living with her mother at her grandmother's in Jerusalem. She worked in an office, filing papers. Sometimes I still called Emuna, but she was in college already, in America. Lea planned to go to school, even took some entrance exams, but then realized that she didn't know what she wanted from the future, and she didn't know how to study for the future either. I didn't know how to study for the future either, but I wanted it to come. I was thinking about a job.

It's been years since Lea and I pretended together. But it's also been weeks since we talked, since she told me anything that was true, even something true that wasn't.

The olive tree was very dead. It was just a stem, a short stem. Its branches had turned dark one by one and then fallen to the ground. We weren't there to see it all happen. We were in the army. When we came back, there was nothing left for us to do.

Miller's wife began screaming, as she did every night after dinner. We could hear every word, traveling across the olive grove to Lea's backyard. A drawer was slammed shut. Chinaware broke.

"Keep it down, you hooligans," I shouted. After Lea grew silent, it was up to me to shout at her neighbors whenever they got loud.

"Meshuganas," Miller's scream came back to us.

"Hooligan," Lea shouted. I pretended I wasn't excited to hear her voice loud again, although my mouth dropped open without my noticing.

"Monkey girls," Miller shouted. He called us monkey girls because our grandparents weren't from Europe. We liked it, though. At least I still did. We once really liked thinking we were animals.

ℵ

ONCE WE pretended we were wolves. We were twelve, and we were angry because after our bat mitzvahs our mothers told us we were now women. So we bit each other's ankles. The people of the village spotted us walking on all fours through the streets and around the banana fields. Our mothers told us to stop, but we put their pants between our teeth and wouldn't let go. On the street, we licked the toes of the girl in the wheelchair, and she laughed. When we got into Miller's backyard, he screamed, "Meshuganas," and chased us away with a shovel when we showed him our teeth. We howled stories to each other and we understood them until our bones were very tired.

We always pretended we had different ages, different names. We never ever told our real names when asked. Telemarketers, new teachers, new kids, vendors selling candy at the Arab market—they all wanted a piece of us. They didn't really want to know our names; it was just a strategy to make us think they liked us. To get us to talk to them. To buy what they were selling. We wanted them to care about us, even if it wasn't real. Once we cared so much, about everything. We wanted to talk to anyone we could. We lived so far away from the world. But we wouldn't give our names up. We were Esther and Meek and Olga. Never us. Our world was small then, but larger than life because it happened only in our heads.

ℵ

IF YOU are a boy and you go into the army, one thing that can happen is that you can die. The other thing that can happen is that you can live. If you are a girl and you go into the army you probably won't die. You might send reservists to die in a war. You might suppress demonstrations at checkpoints. But you probably won't die. A lot of things can happen to you after. You could get a job. Go on a trip. Go to university. Get married. Move back in with your parents. Lea and I both moved back in with our parents, back to the tiny village by the Lebanese border. By now I had a job waiting for me in Tel Aviv, as an airport security guard. My uncle got it for me. I could not have gotten it myself. Not then. It was good money. All you had to do was sit. It was good; even I could see that. Lea saw nothing. She didn't even see it when the ashtray on the wooden table in her backyard was overflowing. She didn't even notice when it was light out, because she usually woke up after sundown. Every time I came to visit, her mom would greet me by saying, "You have a job. You have a job, right? You hear that, Lea? Well, isn't *that* nice." And her mom would clasp her hands and go back to the kitchen, and then the two of us would sit outside, look at the olive grove, and smoke so much, we couldn't talk. There were only eighty-two houses in our village. One house right after the other, until they ended. Except for Lea's house. There was an empty lot that separated her house from the Miller house. It was an olive grove. Because no matter how much sense it made to put another house there, they couldn't do it because of the olive trees. It is highly against the law to kill an olive tree. You are not even allowed to uproot one.

We were girls. I know we were just girls. We did what we did in the army, and then it was over. If Lea was having a hard time talking or leaving her parents' backyard when we were twenty-one, it was not because of the past; I know that. I admit it; the problem was the future of the past. It existed outside our heads, too large.

‌ ‌

THE EVENING after Lea told me Miller was a murderer, I went back to her backyard, and everything was almost the same as it had been for the past few weeks. She was wearing her red pajamas. She was sitting on the plastic chair, staring at the olive grove, smoking. The one thing that was different was that she was holding a stack of paper in her hands. I wondered if she was going to spend her whole life sitting in that backyard, staring at that dead tree and smoking. That night, it didn't seem impossible. She dragged the smoke into her lungs like her life depended on it, until her face rutted. I didn't know what to say. When we were little, and friends, it was always she who spoke, who told me what we should care about next, who we should be. I sat by her for days and weeks, waiting for her to care about something, anything, even just a little.

And now she did.

"We have to let everyone know he is a murderer," Lea said. "He needs to know he is a murderer. You can't just kill an olive tree. You have to want to kill it, you have to murder it."

Olive trees live for thousands of years. It was always hard for me to believe that, looking at those trees by Lea's backyard. Their stems swirled into themselves as if caught midsentence, as if someone had just breathed life into them.

"I agree," I told Lea. I always agreed with her. I will always agree with her, no matter what, I swear.

"It is not a matter of agreeing; it is a fact," she said.

"I agree, but, Lea, how did you figure it out?"

Lea said that she'd been doing some research. Apparently, there is almost nothing in this world that can cause an olive tree to die. Specific types of fungus and bacteria can make it sick, give it tumors, but they won't kill it. There is a bug that eats its bark and a caterpillar that attacks its leaves. Flies can reduce the quality of its fruits. Frost and rabbits could kill it, but this was northern Israel, and there was no frost, and there were no rabbits. And rabbits could only kill it if one of them crawled inside, got stuck, and died, and the body poisoned the tree from within. It happened in Spain once, according to Lea.

"And then there is gasoline," Lea said. "If you pour enough gasoline by the roots of an olive tree, it dies."

I looked at the remains of the tree ahead. A dark end. A clear beginning of something that had no middle. Its stem broke off in such an abrupt place, I bet that even if someone never knew there used to be more of it, if someone had never seen an olive tree or even any kind of tree before in his life, he could still tell something was missing.

"The bar mitzvah!" I said. "That's when the murder happened!"

Lea nodded.

I remembered Lea's mother telling us when we first got back from the army that while we were gone the terrible Miller neighbors became even worse. They moved on from merely throwing their raked leaves in the olive grove. They threw a bar mitzvah for their son in the olive grove, even though it was not their property and they had no right. They brought in all of their relatives from England and made pita from scratch on an authentic taboon, while marveling over the pastoral and holistic nature of their lives on the Holy Land's border. In loud voices. "You have to understand," Lea's mother said, "these people are not originally from here, so they don't understand."

"The bar mitzvah!" I said again, and when I looked at Lea, she was smiling. An evil, honest smile.

"Miller used gasoline for the taboon," Lea said. "My mom saw him. The idiot can't even light a fire."

"But why would he pour gasoline by the olive tree?" I asked.

"Because he had some left over. Because the tree was close to the taboon. Who can understand the mind of a murderer?"

We paused.

"A murderer, mind you, not merely a killer," Lea said.

And then she showed me the posters she had made. Forty posters, on A4 paper. She had made them with crayons. Her baby brother's. At the bottom they read: "Murderer of an Olive Tree: Wanted Dead or Alive."

She had drawn Miller's face herself. She made out his receding hairline in black and red crayon scratches. It got murkier with each poster.

"Okay," I said. "Okay." I understood. I always understood her logic.

We left the backyard. We did.

We stuck the posters on the olive trees and on the benches in the street and on Miller's car and even on his wandering cat. Lea stretched the tape, and I leaned forward and cut piece after piece with my teeth. Then we both banged hard to make sure the poster was stuck just right.

By the time we were back sitting and smoking in Lea's backyard, Miller's wife had begun screaming and slamming things as usual. But we didn't scream at her to keep quiet. We counted till three and shouted, "Murderer! Murderer!" We got no response.

Even so, by the time Miller woke up, we believed he would know we knew what he was.

ב

ONCE I pretended I could get a man killed. Once I said that draft dodgers deserve the death penalty. My mom always says that she bets the Miller kids will leave for England without being drafted, and I agree with her.

I pretended I could kill a man when I was in the army.

This was a year after the war, right before I was done with my service. It was a game. I told my officer, Shai, that a man had winked at me. He was just an Arab construction worker, and I was just tired and far from home and bored. He had all the permits. He was brought to the base from his village to build a new part of the shooting ranges. "This is a mistake; I did nothing wrong," he said with his accent. "I have all the permits," he said. "I am building things in your base."

"Don't worry," Shai said. "Don't worry."

He covered the man's eyes with a weapon's cleaning towel. The man put his hands behind his back on his own, and Shai cuffed them with real metal cuffs, not the fake black plastic ones the corporals had. "Don't worry," he said, and he sat the man in the back of the Humvee. I climbed into the back and sat across from the man. This was my wild idea, almost entirely my idea, but it was Shai who executed it.

We parked in front of the behind part of the sand dunes. Shai the officer silenced the Humvee. The vibrations stopped. He opened the back door of the vehicle. "Walk," he said. "Don't worry," he said. But the man could not see, and he was breathing in and out, in and out.

"Walk," Shai the officer said. "You can do it," he said. He put his hand on the man's shoulder.

The man walked in front of us like the spaghetti man from dreams. It was hard on his heart in fear.

"Stop," Shai the officer said. "Face us."

The man turned as if on a hinge and faced us.

"Don't worry," the officer said. "But," he said, "you can't wink at girls. There are certain things you just cannot be doing in this world."

I opened my mouth to breathe. I watched.

"So what I have to do is, I have to give you a chance," Shai the officer said. "What is gonna happen is that I am going to shoot, and maybe I'll hit you and maybe I won't, but if I don't hit you, and you move when I shoot, then I will hit you for sure."

"Is that Ok?" Shai the officer asked. "Nod if you understand," he said. "You have to nod," he said. "I am sorry about that."

The man nodded.

I could see it but the blindfolded man could not: Shai was not aiming toward the man. His M-4 was pointing sixty degrees from the ground.

He shot. The man fell to the sand. He hit it with his face first. He shouted for a long time, but only after we couldn't hear the bullet anymore. One long shout, a shout for a minute, and then a small shout, and then he breathed.

It was a bad thing to pretend about. It was a mistake. I was never good at pretending without Lea. That evening was when I said draft dodgers deserve the death penalty. I said it to Lea. Over the phone.

א

THE WEEK after she got back from the army, Lea and I had one conversation. We had it in her backyard.

When we had it, missiles were falling, as they tended to do where we lived, since always. We listened to the exit booms and waited for the explosions. We had heard them so many times before, we were pretty good at guessing where they would fall. We saw the thick gray in the sky and it was like seeing the same sky we used to see when we were little, like we were still little.

"I missed home. We missed home, right?" I asked Lea.

"I missed home so much. That's all I did. I missed and I missed," she said.

"So much," I said.

"But these missiles, they remind me of the army."

"Well, they are missiles."

"Exactly."

"They are the same missiles from before we left, though," I said.

"Exactly. But not to me, you understand?"

What she meant was, we missed home, and we waited for the moment when we finally wouldn't have to miss it anymore. But now that we were home, we still missed it just as much. It didn't go away.

This is what I thought she meant, but then again, she had no interest in leaving home again, and I did, so maybe I didn't understand at all.

ℵ

ONCE LEA and I pretended we were fish and cripples and stones. And when the school put in an elevator for the one human damage ever to be caused by the daily missiles—the crippled girl—we printed rules for it. We called the elevator a spaceship and posted rules for proper conduct in it, "The Page for Spaceship Rules." No eating in the spaceship. No licking in the spaceship. No peeing in the spaceship. No speaking Romanian in the spaceship. No jumping up and down more than four times. The janitor took the page we made down right after he saw us hanging it and asked for our names. We were so happy we forgot all about the spaceship. Made-up names were our favorite thing.

"What *are* your names?" the janitor asked, looming above us.

We said we were Arnilan and Di.

נ

THE EVENING after we hung the murderer posters, when I came to Lea's backyard, everything was the same, except she was wearing sneakers instead of just socks, and there were two containers of liquids that had never been there before. The first was a big yellow gasoline container. The second was a bottle of peach schnapps that I recognized from her parents' liquor cabinet. Last time we had taken sips from it we were twelve. Last time I had drunk had been two and a half years ago.

"This is what we are doing now? We are drinking?" I asked.

"Who's we? There is only me. You are leaving tomorrow morning."

This was the closest that Lea had gotten to showing anger because I was leaving, and I couldn't help but think the alcohol must have had something to do with it. I wanted to be angry too.

I sat on the chair beside hers and took the bottle from her and had a sip. The pollen from the cedar trees had gotten everywhere, my eyes, my throat, even when my mouth was closed; the schnapps washed it away.

I tapped the gasoline container lightly and looked at Lea.

"What are we going to do to Miller?" I asked.

"He hasn't responded to the signs at all, you know. No call to my mother, no shouting through the olive trees."

I looked ahead and saw that Miller's windows were dark. Even though it was time, I couldn't hear him and his wife screaming or slamming drawers. I couldn't even hear the chatter of the children talking about their cartoons and the toys their English relatives sent them.

"But what are we actually going to do to Miller?" I asked. "And where did you get gasoline?"

"I found it. It is easy to find. And I am going to do to Miller *exactly* what he did to that olive tree."

"We," I said. And I added, "Exactly?"

"Exactly."

I understood Lea's logic. How she thought of things. Things that were real and things that were not. I knew exactly what she meant by "exactly."

Not too far from us missiles set fire to a banana field, and slowly the green fruit burned and the scent filled the night.

ℵ

You will think I am saying something that is not true or that I think what I am saying is true but it isn't, but I know it is true. When I was twenty-one there were times when what I wanted was to die. I don't know why, but it is true. But most of the time what I wanted was to go work in the airport because it was good money. This is even truer.

I had only been to the airport once. It was to visit my uncle, who works in security there. It was a little before the army, in the few weeks I had after school ended and before boot camp started. I remember watching a mother running to greet her son. She kept on rubbing her hands through his greasy hair when she reached him. He seemed blinded by the fluorescent light. He was wearing dirty clothes, a striped shirt and red Thai fisherman pants. I remember a young couple in line to enter the boarding gates. They spoke English and kept looking at their airplane tickets. The guy rolled a pink suitcase and rubbed the girl's shoulder with his other hand. A young security guard, wearing a blue uniform and a leopard-spotted handkerchief around her neck, kept on passing through the lines, asking the same questions. "Did you pack it yourself? Did anyone give you anything to take on the plane? I am only asking because in the past people were given packages that looked innocent and turned out to be bombs." She sounded sincere every time she spoke to someone new, but no one confessed.

I won't even have to ask questions. My uncle said the job he got me involves only sitting at a desk in between the airlines' check-in and the duty-free counters and making sure no one passes through who looks suspicious. I will spend hours and months and days watching people leaving. And they will all look suspicious. It is always suspicious when someone leaves. I'll never leave myself. After my shift is over, I'll take the train to Tel Aviv and sleep alone. Then I'll come back the next day. So that I can do the opposite of leaving again. People who see me on the train and don't recognize my uniform, newcomers, visitors, may think I am going to the airport to fly away. I won't even have to pretend. They'll think it all on their own.

‫א‬

WE WALKED through the olive grove to get to Miller's house. It was dark and the only light was the orange fire, far away and in the fields. I was the one who held the gasoline container. The olive trees were alive around us. We were drunk but felt drunker than we were. Not elated, exactly, but we felt for a few minutes like we were no longer waiting. The silver leaves were everywhere; the convoluted branches swarmed around our bodies. The trunks were stuck solid in the ground by their roots, but with every step we took the trees felt closer, animated, eager. The explosions from the missiles stopped.

Lea began running forward and then stumbled, held up her arms for balance, and stopped by a tree. Not the dead one. A live and short one.

"Think about this tree," she said.

So I did. I stood in front of Lea and looked at her face and I thought about that olive tree.

Lea explained a lot of things, her speech rapid, improbable. She said that the tree lives, and it lives and it lives and it lives. For thousands of years. Flies attack its fruits and they nibble through its branches and it thinks it should just die, but it doesn't. It lives, and then bacteria makes tumors grow in it, grow from the inside, dangerously and slowly, and no one knows and so then it thinks again that it will die but it doesn't; it lives and it lives. It stays; it stays forever.

"It hurts," Lea said, but she was smiling. I could see her gapped teeth in the dark. "It hurts to be in the midst of these trees. Can't you feel them buzzing with too much life?"

I stretched my arms out into the air and tried to feel her words.

א

ONCE WE pretended we were reporters. Ten years before, when Lea still wasn't too cool to hang out with Avishag and me, after the ocean one day, we pretended we were reporters and asked what happens in the morning. We asked it all day. We didn't just ask one person. We asked a lot of people. I was sucking the salt off the edge of my braid when Lea asked the first person.

"Excuse me, swimsuit lady," Lea called. We were running after a lady on a Nahariya beach. Avishag stayed on her towel. Our public pretend games always embarrassed her.

"Lady with the swimsuit! Excuse me!" Lea shouted.

The lady turned.

We were little girls and the lady was sorry for us.

"I am sorry. I am sorry," Lea said. She was always sorry first, never after. "But excuse me. We are reporters, and we need to know, what happens in the morning?"

Back then Lea could draw her hand from mine, fast and far away, and I would only notice minutes later.

"What do you mean, 'What happens in the morning?' Is tomorrow a holiday?" The lady said. The lady didn't know what Lea meant.

Neither did Lea. But she asked a man who smoked a cigarette the same question. He said that in the morning we wake up. We brush our teeth. We go to work or to school.

I didn't know what Lea meant. But I asked a woman eating watermelon and she said that maybe I thought she was someone she was not, because she didn't know what I was talking about and she didn't know what I thought she was supposed to do tomorrow morning. I told her I didn't think she was someone she was not, and she cursed me because she wasn't a woman, she was actually a young woman.

What happens in the morning? We asked and we asked and we asked. More than thirty people. To some of them we explained that it was for our school's newspaper. To others we said we were reporting for a kids' show. We didn't laugh once. I remember that day; it was good like spaghetti after swimming.

We hitchhiked back to the village late at night. We waited at the corner for hours with smiles and no words. Nothing scared us yet. There was no explaining why we asked so many strangers that question, no right answer we expected. God did not plan that day for us. It was so random, only Lea could have planned it herself. In the backseat of the car that took us, Avishag fell asleep as soon as we got in, but Lea and I were so lit we couldn't stop swaying our feet. She sank her teeth into my hand for a long time so she wouldn't roar by accident. That's how alive she was to me that day. She left marks.

ℵ

THE DOOR to Miller's house was unlocked. We crept in. I tried not to make a noise, but Lea just marched through the rooms of the house as if it were her own, her steps quick. We passed through the entrance hall into the living room. Some of the kids' toys were scattered on the carpet; expensive, shiny.

Miller was sitting in the dark by the kitchen table. He was

tossing a banana from one hand to the other, catching it, and again. He didn't look up from the table, even though we were standing so close he must have known we were there. Intruders. There were plates around the table, with peas and schnitzel and salad on them, and there were forks by the plates, yet the meals were only partially eaten, abandoned midway.

"Miller," Lea said. "We are here to pour gasoline on you. Just like you did to the olive tree." Her voice was steady, her feet planted solidly on the floor. She didn't look at me. She looked straight at the down-facing head of Miller. At his bald spot.

Miller kept on tossing the banana. He followed it with his eyes. He didn't look up.

When he spoke, his voice scared me. It was prickly, like it came from far away, from a place I'd never been.

"Ahh, meshugana girls," he said. "You are crazier than I thought. Have you finally, after all these years, come to set me on fire?" he asked.

"You killed the olive tree," Lea said. "It was thousands of years old, and you poured gasoline on it after the bar mitzvah."

"I did what? Why would I pour gasoline? We barely had enough that day to keep the fire going," Miller said.

"It is the only thing that can kill an olive tree. It is the only thing."

"Well, monkey girl, no matter. Set me on fire. She is gone. Took the kids." He began tossing the banana more quickly. "This is perfect, actually, just what would happen to someone who stays in this country," he said. "You can't scare me."

"Did she leave because of the signs we put up?" I asked, before I could stop myself. Lea gave me a puzzled look. She stepped closer to me. This was not part of her plan, talking to him about his wife, but I was curious, curious as a child.

Miller began laughing. His laughter sounded more like a baby choking. "The signs? The signs? It is the missiles. The war. It was always the war. She couldn't take it anymore, wanted to go back to England," he said. " 'We can't have something happen to the little ones,' " he added in English, imitating the voice of his wife. " 'This was all your crazy idea to move here.' "

He stopped tossing the banana and just held it in his hand. Then he did something fairly unbelievable, but it was true: he covered his face with his hands, still holding the banana, and began sobbing. It was hard to make out his words, but I think he said: "I should have gone with her. What's in a country without a woman?"

I was still drunk, but not enough so that this didn't embarrass me. I lowered my eyes and only then noticed that I was no longer holding the gasoline container. That it was now in Lea's hand.

She looked displaced for a second. She looked at me like a disgusted kitten. "Why are we talking about this?" she asked, and then she opened the gasoline container and stepped right by Miller's chair. "Miller, I will now pour gasoline on you," she said, and this was what she did.

She lifted the container high but then lowered it under the table and, making *whoosh* sounds, she poured the gasoline on Miller's pants and shoes. On his roots. The smell burst out; it made it easier for me to breathe somehow. Miller's face was still covered.

Lea put the container on the ground, closed it, and then began to head away from Miller.

He looked up.

"Where are you going?" he asked. "I thought you came to set me on fire."

"I came to do *exactly* what you did to the olive tree, and I did," Lea said.

"What the hell?" Miller asked.

"If you were an olive tree, you would start dying right about now, but you are not an olive tree, and that is the point," Lea said. "What you did is, you poured gasoline."

Miller began sobbing again, this time without covering his face. It twitched in red and veins and tears. "No," he said. "You ape! You said you were going to burn me, and this is what you'll do!"

"No," Lea said. "I can't; that's not what 'exactly' means." She stepped closer to him again, her chin high, strong. Setting him on fire would go against her logic. Since forever, she had done exactly and only what made sense in her world. This was my Lea. Glorious, rigid, a creator of worlds.

"Burn me! Just do it. I don't care," Miller said.

"No," Lea said. "This is what you get. You stay here. You sit here. This is what you get—" and she would have gone on, but Miller got up from the chair and grabbed her, twisting her arm so that her back pressed against him. Then he shoved the unpeeled banana to her mouth, and began cursing, calling her a monkey first, then rapid curses, curses I had never heard before. Lea kept her mouth shut tight, and the banana smooshed out of the peel, its soggy white smearing her face.

I ran toward Miller and kicked him with all I had. I kicked again and again and again and then Lea's hand was in mine and we ran and we ran, through the door and into the olive grove.

WHEN LEA was in boot camp, her unit was called up to help with the Gaza pull-out plan. They needed boot-camp soldiers to pack up the belongings left behind by the settlers who refused to leave without being dragged, and they chose the boot-camp girls of the military police. I had not been drafted yet. Lea would call me with stories of a little girl who began eating the sand when she told the girl she couldn't go back into her house, and of how bulldozers had made an entire college campus into nothing but red dust in less than twelve hours. She had stories, and she needed me as a friend again. One Russian woman set herself on fire right by the road where Lea was guarding.

"The thing that's weird is the Popsicles," she said. "I think they are afraid the soldiers would get too upset by all of this, so the army keeps on giving us Popsicles. It's like it is summer."

"It *is* summer," I said through the phone.

"I know," she said. "That's what's weird."

LEA AND I marched through the olive grove back from Miller's house. It was only five hours before I had to hitch-hike to Nahariya and catch the train to Tel Aviv. I kept on walking, my mind unquiet. One step, two step. I began to skip, and then I raised my arms in the air, and then I froze midmoment.

"Lea," I said. "Let's pretend we are olive trees. Let's pretend we lived and we lived for thousands of years and now we are alive."

Lea stopped walking ahead of me, but she didn't turn to look at me. "No," she said. "I can't."

"Of course we can," I said. "We can pretend. We could be trees if we wanted to."

"No," Lea said. "I really can't. I can't be a tree." She looked at the dry yellow ground.

And she kept on walking, her body growing smaller, until she reached her backyard. I didn't go after her. I stayed. And when I closed my eyes and opened them again, frozen still, she was not anywhere anymore, and it was just me, at a halt.

I tried and I tried to pretend that I was an olive tree. I told myself that I lived, and I lived, and even when there were tumors exploding under my bones and predators eating out my eyes, I thought I'd die but I didn't. I stood frozen, eyes open, my arms misshapen in the air; I tried forever to be an olive tree, I swear. But without her I couldn't pretend. I tried for hours. Until it was time for me to leave.

א

WHAT REALLY killed the tree was a rabbit. We have never seen a live one in the village, but my mother told me that when she went over to look at the tree a few weeks after I left, she saw the decaying body of a rabbit inside the dead trunk. She went over because Lea's mother had told her she could smell something very wrong, but she was too scared and worn out to search herself. The rabbit was curled up inside itself, and its fur was almost gone. Its flesh blended with the bark and worms. Had Lea and I gone over to the tree and looked, we would have seen the rabbit ourselves, but we didn't. In the end, we never came close enough to see it that night, or maybe we just didn't look. We never could have imagined a dead rabbit, because we had never seen a live one.

Lea left for Tel Aviv too, a few weeks after I did. She didn't tell me. I found out about a year later. My mom told me over the phone. By then I was not in Tel Aviv anymore. I found out about that a week after I left the country for the first time, before I took the first of many trips around the world.

Here is what happened in the morning, the morning I left. I took my backpack, the big one, the one I used in the army. I had filled it the afternoon before, before I went to Lea's, with all the clothes that still fit me, clothes I hadn't worn in over two years. Aside from clothes, the only thing I took was the Rules. "The Page for Spaceship Rules," the one I kept from school, after the janitor told us to take it down.

I stood at the hitchhiking spot, and I pointed my finger, and I waited. I waited beyond the shade, the asphalt stretching ahead of me, my back turned to the outskirts of the village, only burned banana fields at my side.

A green Fiat stopped, and it took me south and away from the border to Nahariya, the most northern train stop in the country. I waited with four soldiers and a mom at the train station. Then I took the train; I took the train asleep.

When I took the train to Tel Aviv, I didn't yet know about the rabbit. And I didn't even think or dream about the tree. I just slept. I woke up minutes before we arrived. The train station was swarming with people, all these people, walking here and there. A woman rubbed against my backpack and I was pushed forward. When I looked up, my eyes met a man. He was promoting a cell phone service. I could tell because his shirt read: "Connecting People." He smiled at me and stepped forward, a neon orange pamphlet in his hand. I stood there, frozen. The heavy backpack chafed my skin.

"Excuse me," the man said. "What's your name?"

"No thanks," I said. "No thank you."

And Then
the People
of Forever
Are Not
Afraid

Having been born into the Zubari family, the largest Iraqi family in all of Israel, even Avishag's hysteria was not her own. It belonged to the many women who lived in her time and to generations of Zubari women who lived before her in Baghdad. At first she called her hysteria sadness and nurtured it as if it were her child. One February morning, she woke up and forgot what it felt like to want anything. She was twenty-one, eight months out of the army, and she should have gone downstairs to grab her morning tea and the olive sandwich her mom had made for her lunch in the offices, but she could not, because she didn't see the point. Instead, she stayed in bed all day until hunger was acid pooling at the bottom of her stomach and she had to run downstairs and stuff her throat with frozen pita and gulps of water she drank by pressing her lips to the kitchen faucet. As she was running down the stairs, there was something she wanted, at least for that minute, but after she ate, she would climb back to bed because there was nothing else she wanted.

When the nightmares started, her grandmother said to her mother, "She has hysteria" and also "We don't want a repeat of what happened to her brother Dan." Avishag and Mira, her mother, were living in Jerusalem at the time. The house where Avishag lost the will to move was her grandmother's. Her mother had moved there before Avishag was drafted. In American television, being hysterical meant shouting and crying and turning red and breaking chinaware and laughing cruelly. But for the Zubari women, these were behaviors they engaged in regularly. When they did have hysteria, Zubari women were quiet and motionless, chinaware *you* wanted to break. Hysteria was not forever; it came and went. But it was a thing to hide—from future Zubari husbands, from the rest of Israel that wasn't Zubari and female.

When his ex-wife started allowing Avi to visit his daughter again, when she told him that Avishag hadn't left her bed in months, Avi didn't know what to do, but he knew this time he had to do something. He had already lost a son he barely knew. Then he remembered that when he first got out of the army the only thing that soothed the lizards in his brain was driving around the stone walls of Jerusalem for hours and nights. So he bought his daughter, who had never gotten her license, a used car. A car that was once used by a person who was now desperate. Six million Jews died in the Holocaust, and the car Avi got his daughter Avishag went for two thousand shekels below market price.

"Six million Jews, that's not nothing," Avi said to Avishag the day he gave her the car.

His daughter wasn't sure what nothing was not. She stared at him and then shielded her eyes from the Jerusalem summer with her hand.

"Two thousand shekels, that's not nothing," Avi said.

He had gotten the car from a survivor. He said, "She is a beauty." He said, "She is American." The car. The survivor was Polish. She survived the Nazis, but the whore couldn't play him in price.

Avi had come to Israel from Libya. He was sick of hearing about the Holocaust because he had never even been to Europe, not even to Turkey on one of those "all-included" trips. And Europeans, the ones who had survived and made it to this country, they were the ones who ruined his life.

He told Avishag that driving around in the car was the only thing that made his days breathable after he got out of the army. He wanted her to learn.

Six million Jews were killed in the Holocaust, and Avi had squeezed the woman who sold him the car two thousand shekels below market price. Not once had Avishag agreed to sit in the driver's seat. He would come often and take her for rides after he got the new car. Weeks passed. Then he couldn't come so much because he was busy being a contractor, or with his new wife, his new boys. Someone was always sick; one of the Palestinian construction workers was always missing his shift.

Then he'd wake up in the middle of the night. Thinking he had given up made his nightly sweats tepid.

א

"Smile," he told Avishag at the start of the day of their twentieth "driving lesson." It had been months since he had bought her the car. Avishag stood in her boy shorts in the parking lot outside her mother's building and squinted at him. "This is the part where you smile," Avi said. He took his Time cigarettes out of his jeans pocket.

Avishag pressed a chin to a collarbone and breathed out. When she glided her tongue behind her teeth, she tasted morning. It was past two in the afternoon, but her mother had managed to get her out of bed only ten minutes earlier. This was the earliest she had gotten out of bed all month. Those green boy shorts, she must have been wearing them for more than a week. Even her mother had given up on her. "Let your father take care of you for a bit," she said. "Let *him* deal with it."

"Blood-sucking dead fish, this whole family," Avi said and tapped the hood of the car, like a man would to another man's shoulder. "Your mother, and her sisters, and your mother's mother, and your sister, and you." He pointed at Avishag.

Avishag didn't want to be a blood-sucking dead fish like her father called her. She didn't want to be a blood-sucking dead woman. She didn't want to be a dead woman. But what she did want, she didn't know.

It was not her fault, Avi reminded himself. She had hysteria. This was hereditary, an Iraqi thing. At first he had still tried to ask her what was wrong. He had wanted there to be a certain thing that was wrong. He had hoped even for that thing to be a boyfriend, maybe an officer, someone who had hurt her, so that he could hurt him back. But when he asked her what it was, if there was a boy or even a man in her life, she said no. Lately, he didn't ask about much anymore. He just asked for her to get better.

"Please," Avi said, clasping his hands together, balancing his cigarette in his fleshy lips.

"Thank you for coming, Daddy," Avishag said finally.

"Oh hon," Avi said, removing his nicotine-stained grin and sunglasses. He tapped Avishag on her back. "All I want is for you to have whatever you want," he said.

Avishag wanted to climb back to sleep. She had been forced to get out of the house for a bit. Her mother had gotten her out of bed by splashing water on her head. Her eyes were open, and they still stung a bit, still remembered the shock.

Avi put his cheap sunglasses back on and blew a kiss in Avishag's direction by gesturing an explosion with his hand from his lips, a gesture more appropriate for an Italian chef praising pasta than for a Libyan father cheering up his gloomy daughter.

"Come on, kid, let's drive!"

This was their twentieth "lesson." Enough was enough, he thought. There are times you have to decide that it is enough.

He twirled the keys in his fingers. His key chain was the symbol of Jerusalem's soccer team. Avishag couldn't stop staring at it swirling around his hairy knuckles; it was yellow, black, and foamy. When Avi was Avishag's age, he was already married to her mother.

א

WHEN AVISHAG was five, her mother had hysteria. She had it for a year. Then another year, after she had their third child.

Avi could count on one hand the times he had seen her out of bed that month. With one of his hands, he broke an almost empty bottle of Araq on the granite kitchen counter. He could smell the anise; it reminded him of chewing the dark licorice his grandfather had bought him in a candy store in Tripoli. Avi went into the bedroom. His wife was lying there in the dark, her eyes closed, her lips pressed together. Avi was very, very drunk. He put the entirety of his weight over her thin body but she didn't wake up. He started crying. "Wake up. Wake up."

He started cutting. The glass of the bottle was much sharper than he could ever have dreamed.

Oh, and he did dream. He did. For years after that. A decade. More.

In his dream he was holding just a dot of shiny glass, and when he pressed it into the sharp collarbone of his wife, a red line, a geometric line, flew into the ceiling. When the line hit the ceiling, it became a hovering puddle in the air of the room and then suddenly came pouring down on the bed in a splash of red. In his dream, he was drowning in his wife's warm blood.

In life, he had merely injured her. The scar on her neck was no longer visible by the time they were divorced. In life, it was the social worker, the German social worker, who made her divorce him.

א

"THERE IS an empty parking lot by Motza," Avi said on the day of the twentieth driving lesson, and turned the wheel to

the right. He put in a tape, a song he knew even back in Tripoli, where all the women were dark and young, and daughters
like his didn't happen. "It is a great place to start learning to
drive," he said.

Avishag opened her mouth, but it was only to put a chunk
of her hair inside of it.

"Say something," Avi asked.

She knew better.

א

BEFORE AVISHAG met with the army doctor, the one who
signed the papers authorizing an early release from the military, Yael had told her that if things were really that bad on
the Egyptian border, all she had to do was say something. Anything, really. She could say she believed she was a butterfly,
claim she wet the bed, explain that it was her teddy bear who
bought her cigarettes. She could say she had already gotten in
trouble once and that if they kept her she'd just do something
to end up in military jail again, like she ended up after she got
naked in some tower. She liked jail so much it was harder to
get back to routine. Something, anything to give the doctor an
excuse to claim that she was crazy. It took two weeks to get a
referral to an army psychiatrist, but Yael claimed that getting
out of being a soldier was not so hard. They don't want the
liability. There are enough soldiers in this country.

But when the doctor leaned over his desk and asked,
"What is it you wanted to talk about?" she drew a blank.

She looked around his office. His ashtray was clean; the
marble sparkled. On his wall he had the map of the country,

like any other officer. On top of the drawers at the side of his desk, a dirty aquarium rested. The fish all swam in circles, gold and sapphire and gilled. Avishag had never seen a doctor before. The Zubaris, being Iraqi, did not believe in them. Choosing a crazy sentence from the millions of options she had was impossible. Her voice would not let her do it.

The doctor coughed and said, "Well?"

In the end she chose to say something that was almost true.

"This aquarium makes me think it is the Holocaust of fish."

She did not remember where she got that idea; it was scavenged from a bottomless body of water, but it was also not a complete fabrication. She was dismissed two days later. She did not talk to Yael much after that because she could not bear to tell her she had been dismissed for a crazy sentence she almost believed.

א

ON THE hills around Jerusalem, a pickup truck stood before Avi's car covered in neon bumper stickers.

"The People of Forever Are Not Afraid," one of them read. "We Have No One to Lean On But Our Father in the Sky."

"Don't do that, hon," Avi said.

Avishag had the tip of her black ponytail in her mouth. She opened her mouth wide, like an elderly woman, and it fell out, dangling on her chest.

"That's how I love you," Avi said.

AFTER THE rabbis finally approved the divorce, Avishag and her father were allowed to meet only with the German social worker present. Her hair was dyed blonde and mounted on her head like a sand castle, and her nose was small and pink—a snout. She sat on a leather office chair, but Avi and Avishag sat on colorful wooden chairs, the chairs of children. Avi's butt was too big for the chair; he squirmed like a fried worm. Avi had had to drive all the way up north, because that's where Mira had moved to. On the tiny desk there were puzzles of smiling ducks and Barbie dolls and books. Avishag put a lump of hair in her mouth and stared right at him. His son, Dan, refused to see him. The German social worker said he was big enough to decide that. He was twelve. Mira had said she'd bring the youngest girl if things "go well" with Avishag.

"You could read to her," the pig-faced social worker suggested. She wiped her nose with her wrinkly hand.

This was, by far, the stupidest suggestion Avi had ever heard. If things had turned out differently, this woman would be stuffing her mouth with a pork sausage in a café in Berlin just now, and he would be riding on a horse with his daughter across the markets in Tripoli, buying her dark eyeliner and purple scarves. In Tripoli, girls started wearing makeup when they were as young as eight, and they always kept a scarf across their faces. This woman, she was not even wearing lipstick, and he could swear that her exposed hairline was receding. This woman, she did not know what being a woman was.

"I don't read," Avi said. What he meant was, he couldn't read, not well enough for a book.

"Oh, I see," the German woman said. She must have thought he meant he couldn't read Hebrew, but really he couldn't read much at all. His family had fled from Tripoli to the refugee camps when he was ten, and he had forgotten the little he had learned. He had lived there, in the tents, which later became a caravan town, right by the ocean, until he was old enough to join the army. He had forever been behind the other kids. He wasn't smart enough to make out words.

Oh, but he could make his daughter, and he did make his daughter, and his daughter, she knew already what being a woman was. She was only eight, darker than even he was, and she took his face in her tiny palms like a lady, like a mother, and she said, "Father, I do not want these stories. I want your stories. Tell me your stories."

He had never told a story before. The German woman smirked.

He put his daughter on his lap.

"She has to stay in the chair," the German said.

"Oh, Ok," he said. Avishag went back to her chair. She took his hand.

"One time, in this one country, there was this one mom and this one dad," he started.

"I think your wife would appreciate it if you didn't get into personal issues with the child," the German said.

Personal issues! "The child" had been made by him. What could he tell her that wasn't personal? *Those Europeans*, Avi thought. *All this spiteful formality. They have no hearts. Hitler burned theirs.*

"One time, in this one country," Avi started again. He paused, then spoke again. And that was the beginning of the only story he ever told.

ᴎ

"Just do something," Avi said once they had reached the parking lot. He and Avishag were leaning on the front of the car. It had taken him five minutes to convince her to step out of the passenger seat, and even that was progress from the previous times. That was something, at least. He wouldn't give up hope yet.

He offered her one of his Time cigarettes, and they stood there smoking. In the abandoned parking lot, there was nothing but asphalt, yellow weeds, and a semi trailer with no wheels.

"Just sit in front of the wheel for one minute," Avi said. "For me." He clasped his hands and even considered getting down to his knees.

"I am too hot," Avishag said. "I am going back in." The cool air of the car, it was a small thing she wanted, and this for her was something, at least.

Avi thought about giving up.

Then he thought about that bumper sticker, the one glued to the back of the pickup truck. That sticker, cheap, pink, idiotic, real. "The People of Forever Are Not Afraid."

It was for his daughter that Avi had learned how to read. He had spent hours laboring over a single article in the sports section of the paper. And then suddenly, years later, he had noticed that he had read the whole section in one sitting, with ease, during a visit to the toilet.

He thought about his middle daughter every time since, whenever life was, for a moment, as easy as living. Playing soccer with his little boys, buying his new wife a gorgeous chunk of lamb, buying a used car.

His daughter opened the door to the passenger seat up front slowly, careful not to hit the curb. The door squeaked.

"Sorry," she said.

So she opened the door faster and indeed scratched the curb. "So sorry," she said.

Finally inside the car, she closed the door behind her gently, too gently; it didn't close. So she slammed it harder. *Thump.*

"Sorry," she said.

Too hard, she slammed it too hard. "Sorry, sorry," she said.

Inside the car, Avishag brought her palms up, as if defending herself from a bear.

Avi got into the driver's seat and stared at her with his palms under his armpits, his elbows resting on his belly.

"Sorry" a million times a day. "Sorry," her only word almost.

"Sorry."

This was her way of saying, *Do something.*

"Sorry about what?" Avi asked. "The only thing you should be sorry about is that you won't even put one hand on the wheel."

She had this way about her, his middle daughter. He hadn't spoken to the younger girl since he had left. He had never seen Dan grow older than ten and had been asked not to come to his funeral by his ex-wife's mother. The younger girl was now going by the dumb nickname "Tzipi" and was happy, Mira, his ex, told him one time after he dropped Avishag off from one of their "driving lessons." What she meant was, *happy not to talk to you.* But Avishag, she had this way of making him put words into her mouth. Stories, even. Sometimes he would drive with her for over six hours. They wouldn't exchange a sentence, and by the time he dropped her off, he would feel as though he had learned something, although he wasn't quite sure what it was. Like there was something more he could have done but hadn't.

"Just one hand," Avi said.

She was quiet for a long time. She was always quiet. But then. "You know," she said. "One time in the army I saw a Ukrainian woman get shot in the head."

"A Ukrainian woman?"

"Maybe she was still a girl."

Avishag brought the tip of her hair to her mouth and then let it fall.

Ok, Avi thought. *Ok,* and also, *at least now I know.* And he breathed.

"So, is this the thing?"

Avishag rammed her eyebrows at each other. She almost even turned to look at her father. Her face had more expression in it than it had had in a while. She was confused. "What do you mean? What *thing*?" she asked.

"You know," he said. "The thing why you won't drive and—"

"What thing? There is no thing. I am just scared of driving, that's all."

"You are just scared?"

"I just am."

And with that, Avi knew again what he had thought he knew before, but this time he knew it better, and for real. There was just her. There was no thing. There was just his daughter.

Avi reached over and opened the glove compartment. He could smell the sweat on his daughter's feet. He wondered when she'd last showered. He pulled out a purple scarf he always carried with him. His mother's. The only thing he had left of her.

"Close your eyes," Avi said, and Avishag did. He tied the scarf firmly around her eyes. She didn't move. He sprung his fist in her face. She did not flinch. He made sure she could not see.

א

THE STORY:

"One time, in this one country, there were people. Then a king came, and he wanted the country to himself, so he sent the people of that country all across the world. He put one sister in one part of the world and another sister in another part of the world. Some of them he sent to Russia. Others he sent to Africa. A few he even sent to live where polar bears live."

"Polar bears, Daddy?"

"Yes, baby."

"What happened then?"

"Then the people of that country lived all around the world. Many years passed. Millions of years. But they couldn't forget that they were really not from Russia or Africa, that they were from that one country, and they always hoped that one day they could come back."

"And did they?"

"Not at first, hon. They wanted to, but they didn't know

how. They didn't have phones then, so the people in Africa didn't even know if the people in Russia remembered them."

"So did they ever come back?"

"Well, then one year, the people in Russia and the people in Africa and the polar bears even, all the people and animals who never lived in that one country started killing all of the people who did once live in that one country."

"Did they drown them?"

"Drown them?"

"Like my fish?"

Avi thought of his mother's red and purple and swollen body the day they left Tripoli. Of how they had killed her. About the smell coming from the irrigation ditches all around the walls. When he was a child, he knew what death looked like. All Avishag knew at eight was about her fish. It had died when she was four. Her mother hadn't even made her see it. She had told her it drowned. That was a good thing. But it wasn't in any way true.

"Yes, hon, they drowned them."

"Oh no!"

"But some of them climbed out of the water."

"Good! And then what?"

"And then the ones that made it out of the water decided to go back to that country they left a million years before. They came back to the country from Africa and Russia and all over the world."

"And then what?"

"What do you mean, 'Then what'?"

"What did they do there?"

"They lived."

"But what did they do?"

"They lived. They lived like we live. They built houses and paved roads and planted trees. You know, they worked."

"And then what?"

The German social worker pointed at her Swiss wristwatch. Their time was up.

Avishag must have repeated the story to her mother, or maybe the social worker told. And Mira didn't care for it. The killing part. That was that. She won full custody. She took the kids and went to go teach in some northern village.

The next time he was allowed to see Avishag she was already nineteen. A soldier. Her shoulders bulked under the uniform. They met at a McDonald's in a gas station outside her base. It was the only thing open all night, and her only free time was at five thirty in the morning. She was an infantry soldier in Egypt, serving in the only female infantry combat unit, and one of the other girls must have wanted her to take her shift for her, because she walked in screaming on her thick military cell phone.

"What do you mean, you missed the bus coming back from your doctor's appointment?" she spat coldly and raised her hand to gesture for Avi with her fingers, *Just a second.* Her other small hand held tightly to the black handle of her M-16.

"Fuck you, faggot, you hear me?" his daughter said to the other watch girl on the phone. "I am not your mother that you can fuck me and bury me in the sand."

She hung up and sat in front of Avi. Her face was still dark, but her hair was raised up in a rigid bun, and her eyebrows were plucked in an odd manner that removed all the similarities to him from her face. There was no sign of the quiet, shy girl he knew. The one-shekel ice cream cone he had bought her was dripping on the red plastic table. The only women he had met in his service days were secretaries who wore green skirts and made the highest officers coffee.

"And what, exactly, do *you* want?" Avishag asked.

The next time he saw her was after his ex-wife called to report that his oldest daughter hadn't gotten out of bed in over two months, in case he was interested. The army had discharged her a few weeks after she had gotten out of military jail for some innocent prank, something involving nudity while guarding. But she wasn't the same when she came back. She was acting a little off.

"I'll come right over," Avi said. "I'll buy her a car."

"She can't drive," his ex-wife said. Her voice was tired, but it was still her voice, the one he hadn't heard in years.

In Tripoli, husbands disciplined their wives all the time. His father sure did. For years he had regretted that he hadn't met his first wife in another time, another country, where things would not have gotten so out of hand, where there were no German social workers. But he had met his wife when he did, where he did, in the immigration caravans. She had come from Baghdad, where her father was a jeweler. She spoke four languages. When they met, they were standing naked on the asphalt outside the caravans with dozens of new refugees, covered in the DDT, the pesticide that rained on them from airplanes above. The Europeans in the immigration office thought they could be carrying diseases. His future wife was naked and humiliated and white on the outside with chemicals, but dark in her eyes and through her heart, full of longing for the plane that had brought her. She was fourteen, four years older than he was. He promised her everything was going to be all right, even though he did not yet know her name.

"Everything is going to be all right," he told his ex-wife, Mira, on the phone when she called after all these years. "I'll teach her. I'll buy her a Subaru."

"A Subaru?" Mira asked.

"I am her father."

א

THEY DROVE for a long time. Over two hours. Avi could see them pass the military cemetery at Mount Herzl and the hospital on Mount Scouts where Avishag had been born. Mira's family had moved from where they had met to Jerusalem, but he had never lost touch with her. She had wanted to have Avishag in Jerusalem, even though they could only afford to live in Bat Yam back then.

Avishag's eyes were covered the whole way, but she could smell the air descending down the hill from pine and rock into a humid smell, a fried smell, beer, sunscreen, tar, the beach, just the ocean, eventually.

Jerusalem is landlocked. She knew they were in Tel Aviv even before she could see.

The car was not suitable for driving on sand, nor was it suitable for riding on this shaky fishing dock, but Avi didn't care. The wheels of the car rolled on the old wood. The whole way, he wasn't sure where he was going. He let the car drive him.

Avishag's father put his hand on his daughter's forehead, then removed her scarf. The sun hit her eyes in orange. She kept them open. The sun hit the water in orange, then the water hit her eyes in orange. And still. She kept her eyes open. There was no wind, and the Mediterranean was flat. No one around, not even a seagull, just her and her father in the car. He had driven the car right up to the edge of a dock.

"Do you want to change seats?" her father asked. "Be sure about this," her father said. "The sun is setting. Just sit in the driver's seat," her father said. "All you have to do is sit. This car isn't going anywhere."

He wanted to shake her, but he didn't.

After five minutes she decided she wanted to change seats.

That's how right some parts of this country can be sometimes, her father thought.

They changed seats. He had never before managed to get her to sit in the driver's seat.

He watched her hands, her small hands, as they clutched the wheel. Her hands were small, even for her small body, disproportionate. He had noticed it the day he saw her with her uniform, how unexpected it was to see a hand as small as hers clasp the handle of an M-16.

He remembered the soft touch of her palms grabbing his face when she was eight, the day he told her the first and last story he ever told in his life. Her hands were clammy, but her child sweat smelled sugary. He remembered her high-pitched, excited voice when she asked, again and again, "And then what? And then what?" And then he remembered when it was that their time was gone.

His daughter tightened her grip on the wheel. The sun was setting; he could see its orange strokes lengthening on the water. This moment too would soon pass. He and his daughter would switch seats; he would drive her away from the ocean and up the hills of Jerusalem all the way back to her mother's home. Even in that moment, silently watching and adoring his daughter's small hands, he couldn't help but worry, wonder. *And then what?*

He wanted more. He knew that it might be months before he would be able to get her in the driver's seat again.

Right before the orange sun thumped the water, he heard himself mumble. His lips said that if she wanted to, she could drive the car into the water. If they didn't drown, he'd buy her a new one.

He was joking but then he wasn't.

נ

SHE TURNED the key in the ignition. She didn't know what to do next. The car grumbled; her thighs shook with it under her boy shorts. She looked at her father. She touched the stick shift, it was difficult to move it, she didn't believe she could move it, it was like a sword stuck in a stone, but then it moved; it got stuck in one spot, then another; then her hand had no more strength, none at all; if someone had held a gun to her hand she could not even have made a fist.

She thought she was paralyzed, and so she tried to wiggle her toes, and it was a surprise: they moved, her long toenails curling inward inside her sandals. She could also turn her neck. She looked at her father. She didn't know what to do. He didn't know what to do. He thought he should do something, but he didn't know what. He thought, *There is never a bad time to start.*

He moved the stick shift for her. He could feel it, before she pressed the gas. Her foot. Her body. It was a part of him, and the machine and country.

א

UNDERWATER, AFTER she had opened the door and swum out, her eyes could see nothing but musky green. She remembered her foot, how it had moved, how it had moved the whole car, all that power. She kicked with her foot and she could feel the bottom of the ocean, soft and cold between her toes. Her hair scratched the surface of the water, and then her whole face was out, out in the warm air and sun. She opened her mouth, gasping for air. Then she didn't know what to do. She was sucked back down. She kicked with her foot again and could feel her body floating up, but not far enough. She thought of her father, but she could not see him, and she didn't know what to do but then she did. She punched the water with her fist. Then she kicked it with her leg. Then she punched it with her other hand. She kicked with the other leg. Hand, leg, hand, leg, hand, hand, hand, and again, and soon, though she was a Jerusalem girl, though she had never done it before, she was moving forward, floating, swimming. It was the oddest thing; she could barely breathe, ashen dots flitted across her eyes, but with each violent act of her body she could hear them, hear that she was hitting them, those who had drowned, in the Holocaust and in Tripoli and in Baghdad and the North Pole even, and they answered back not in pain but with questions, two questions. *Where to, hon? What's next, kid?*

After her father pushed his way out of the car, he swam out to shore alone and then watched her swim for minutes that seemed like days that were all years, years he had not seen her grow. And there was his daughter, swimming, and he knew that she would eventually reach the shore, and him. She reached the shore, her clothes dripping water, and sat on the sand very close to him, in silence. He put his wet arm around her and his heart pulsated into her forehead, her unsteady breath slowing, becoming one with his. She smelled his sweat and knew one new thing, one thing no one but her knew and that she had not known until that second but was now so sure of, her lungs might burst. She knew that she did not have that passing Zubari hysteria. That she was going to be sad her whole life, her life ahead.

1.5 Bedrooms
in
Tel Aviv

Ron looked at Lea. She looked like the world's mother when she worked. She cut open the wheat bread with delicate twists of her wrist, as if she felt each jag of the knife as it cut through the dough. She rested the romaine lettuce on top of the strawberry wedges as if she were tucking in children for sleep. She wiped her hands on her black apron and her large breasts swung under her loose shirt. She looked up. Her gray eyes met Ron's.

"What?" Lea asked. Ron realized he must have been staring at her, at his new employee. There were no customers in line. He was sitting on a plastic chair under the striped roof of the kiosk.

"Just thinking. What are you doing with your money?" His ears burned from having to come up with something on the spot. The sun hit the yellow leaves scattered on the boulevard so that he could see the heat in waves.

"I pay rent," she said.

"Yeah, but aside from that," Ron said. He recognized a tired quality in her eyes, one that did not exist in the eyes of all the other wannabes who came to the city. Still, it was clear she was from out of town. Her colorful T-shirts' necklines were all cut by scissors, and she had a backpack instead of a purse. Ron wondered what she had come to Tel Aviv to become. An actress? An architect? Nothing he thought of seemed quite right. He had been looking for an older employee, someone out of high school, past the army, and he had lucked out with her.

"I just pay rent. I have a one-and-a-half-bedroom apartment on a pricey street."

Ron wondered why she called her street pricey, instead of just saying the name of the street. He wondered why someone would live in Tel Aviv and work twelve hours a day just so they could afford the rent. He wondered what it meant, he always had, to say that an apartment has one and a half bedrooms. So he asked her.

"One and a half bedrooms? I never got that."

"What's not to get? There is a bedroom and then half a bedroom," Lea said.

She smiled. But she was not smiling at Ron. Two middle-school boys with a poodle ordered a sandwich with salami, banana pickles, basil, and popcorn, and her gaze had turned to them.

ٮ

IN THE midst of the city, where the Japanica sushi stand used to be, where Rothschild Avenue meets Allenby Street, Ron had opened the We Don't Judge sandwich kiosk. His buddies and parents were skeptical. The Japanica had been popular among the drunks who filled the clubs on both sides of the stand, but the city demanded a disgusting amount of rent for the space because of its location. Even though the Japanese cook and Israeli cashier had had to turn away about eighty customers each night, the business had still bled money and the Japanica chain owners had decided to cut their losses and close up after five years.

Ron had always been drawn to a challenge. He had gotten the idea for the sandwich shop at 7:00 a.m. on a bus home to Ra'anana after a night of drinking in Tel Aviv during a week-end break from the army. He hadn't eaten all night, but he was always picky about food and couldn't find quite what he wanted. Indian, vegan, fusion, Yemenite, pizza—nothing could be quite as good as the breakfast he would make out of his parents' fridge at home. So he decided to wait, and in his famished drunken state he got the idea for the sandwich shop. He thought the idea was great when he was drunk; he liked it even more after rolling it around his head while sober, back at his desk on the base. He served as an Arabic translator in one of the intel bases, transcribing and translating radio broadcasts from Jordan all day. The job was boring but cushy, and it gave him three years to think.

ONE OF the lunch regulars, an old man who spat when he shouted instructions, was giving Lea a hard time.

"Now, baby cakes, I want my yellow peppers roasted for two minutes and my red peppers roasted for ten minutes, and I want the edges cut off from the turkey slice," the man said for the second time.

"Of course," Lea said and placed her hand over the counter to touch his sun-spotted arm. "The usual," she winked.

"Ump," the man grunted. "Last time I could swear you roasted both types of peppers for the same amount of time."

She hadn't. She had followed his exact instructions.

"I am *so* sorry that happened to you," Lea said with a deliberate, grave face, as if the man had just reported that his granddaughter had been murdered while under Lea's care. "I am going to do everything I can to help."

It made Ron feel good, warm, that Lea took her job as seriously as she did. He put his heart into this kiosk. He wanted it to succeed, whatever it took. He had dropped quite a bit of money on a pepper-peeling machine (copper; made in Sweden). He had dropped even more money on a butane torch for crème brûlée (aluminum; France). It had taken him hours to figure out how the massive thing worked, but when Lea used it, it was a matter of seconds before the flame burst yellow and orange. Her eyes danced with it.

"You are such a good retailer," Ron said after the peppers man left the kiosk. He had intended for days to say something nice to her and then, maybe, ask her out to dinner. He wanted to wait for a good opportunity. "You are Russian, right?" he asked.

"Half German," she said. "And half Moroccan, but it doesn't show."

She looked sad that day, even sadder than usual. A few times she froze, stared, took small breaths like a child sipping soup.

"You are doing such a good job. Is this really your first job after the army?" Ron asked. Lea had ignored his compliment and turned her back to wash the guts of the peppers from the cutting board.

"Yes," she answered. "I told you at the interview I just finished my service."

"Did you work on the side during your service?" Ron asked. His shoulders were slouching; he had wanted to give her a compliment, but here he was annoying her with interrogations. This was not how he wanted the conversation to go.

"Not all of us were lucky enough to have Mommy and Daddy set us up with an office job. I barely got breaks," Lea said. She dumped a handful of caramelized onions into the blender but waited before she pressed the "on" button.

Ron was expected to respond. He had the urge to tell her that his parents did nothing for his army posting, that he had just worked really hard during high school on his Arabic classes because he knew combat was not for him, but he resisted the urge. His instincts had not gotten him very far. He was a pragmatic guy in business, and he wanted to be one in love. He suddenly remembered the slogan of the ministry of transportation safety campaign: "On the road don't be right; be smart."

"Where did you serve?" Ron asked.

"Military police. I was an officer."

"Like snitching on soldiers who do drugs and all?"

"No. Transitions unit. Checkpoints. West Bank."

"Wow," Ron said. He reached for what to say next, like an arm reaching through a hole too small for the rest of the body. "Couldn't have been easy," he said finally.

"It wasn't that bad," Lea said.

"Did you know anyone at the checkpoint where they stabbed that soldier right in the neck?" Ron asked. He remembered reading about it a while before. The newspaper had said the neck was cut almost in two, and he had wondered then what they meant by "almost."

That's when Lea turned on the blender. The blades spun, scratching the plastic, an ungodly screech.

א

THE TRUTH was, Ron's parents were not well off at all. After his time in the army, he worked like a dog at a gas station for two years so he could collect the preferential job benefits for postservice citizens from the government. You'd be surprised, but that's some money. His work friends blew it on trips to Thailand and Peru or university entrance exam prep courses. But Ron played with the money. He played in real estate, and then he had more money to play with. He played in the market, then real estate again. He had always been good with money, a risk taker, even when he was just a twelve-year-old dog sitter. He had never thought it would be so easy. By the time he was twenty-seven he had so much money in the bank he was embarrassed to look at the exact number. The bank statement burned a hole in his jeans pocket. He had nightmares about his parents finding out just how much money he had. He still lived with them in their three-bedroom apartment in Ra'anana. He was looking for apartments to rent in Tel Aviv. In the end he still settled on a one-bedroom apartment, because the price in the city for anything more was so revolting, his good sense did not let him pay it, no matter how much money he had. But before he found a place, when he was still looking through newspaper ads while sitting around the kitchen table and eating his avocado, lemon pickle, and French fries pita, that's when he read that the Japanica was closing, that they were renting the kiosk out. His mother kissed his ear before she headed off to work in the textile factory. That's when he knew. It was time. Life was starting, and he was ready to jump in headfirst.

ℵ

ONE NIGHT shift, Ron wondered if he was becoming obsessed with Lea. It bugged him that he thought about her so much, even though there was so little he actually knew about her, even though he knew he should stay focused on the business. For all he knew, she could be shooting him down because she was some sort of prude, a former religious settler, maybe? After all, there were plenty of other girls, girls in plastic heels, swarming in circles all over the city. And it's not that he was even looking. Throughout his service, he had been sleeping with a blonde from Kfar Saba who transcribed Spanish intel. She was a sweet girl, generic. After the army she got on a plane to Thailand like everyone else. Then came the e-mail, the one about someone else, someone specific.

Ron told himself not to lose his focus. Two film students

from TAU were still yapping about the new Natalie Portman movie, even though they had long been served their green olive and steak sandwich and it was past midnight.

"I just think the movie could have been a lot more interesting if she actually fucked the brother when she thought her husband was dead, if her husband didn't just suspect it because he was war crazy. Now *that's* complexity," one of them said. His feet were too long for the bar stools of the kiosk's counter.

"I agree—it would have been so believable. I mean, she thinks her husband's dead and his brother's this fuckable guy from *Brokeback Mountain*," the second film-school guy said. He had sunglasses in his long hair, holding it back like a girl's hairband. "What do you think?" he asked Lea.

Lea was listening to the two guys with her chin in her hands, her elbows resting against the counter. A crowd pleaser. "I haven't seen the movie," she said.

"Oh," the sunglasses guy said. "I'd say I'd take you, but I'd rather take you to a movie that's actually worth something."

"I will say, even though I haven't seen the movie, when in doubt, have as many characters as possible fuck Natalie Portman," Lea said. She was no prude.

"What a smart girl. I wish there were more girls like you in this city," the sunglasses guy said. He reached over the counter and touched a strand of Lea's hair. "When in doubt," he said and laughed.

It was only because this kiosk was making him spend all this time with her, Ron thought. He should not lose his focus. He should not obsess. He got up from his plastic chair and walked to the counter. He stood by Lea. She smelled of skin, of flesh. He counted to three. Then he reached over the counter and punched the sunglasses guy in the forehead.

The sunglasses hit the gray pavement but did not shatter. Ron wanted to unclench his fist but couldn't. He looked at the two guys who stood quiet, fuming. He looked at Lea.

"Just go," Lea said to the two film students. "For me?"

The tall one bent to lift the sunglasses off the street. It took him a while; he was drunk.

"For you," he said, then tapped his friend on the shoulder and pulled him away. The sunglasses guy walked backward a few steps, staring right at Ron. Then he turned his back, dramatically, and kept on walking away.

"Lea . . . ," Ron said. She was staring right at him, her eyes catching the orange streetlights. He didn't know why he had done what he had just done. He didn't know what to say. He had never had her, and now he had lost her.

"Hey," Lea said. "It's Ok."

Ron covered his eyes with his hands. She was a crowd pleaser. And that's what he was: a crowd; worse than that, a boss.

But then.

"Would you like to go out with me once Vera comes in for her shift?" Lea asked. She put her palm on the back of his neck. "Hey," she said. He had just hit someone, and here she was touching him for the first time, letting him stand so close.

It was strange. Even after she slowly took away her hand to grab a butter knife, he could still feel her fingers on his neck.

נ

A LOT of people think that brilliance in business comes out of an ability to make cold, sensible observations, but Ron's business sense came right out of his warm, open heart. Tel Aviv was full of tired, lonely people, people who had all moved to the city when they knew what they wanted but who had been quickly sickened by the race, by having to always get everything all on their own, by waking up in their tiny apartments, morning after morning, naked, sweaty, and afraid. To Ron all these people were the same, and they were not hard to understand. What they wanted was someone who would give them exactly what they would give themselves if they weren't so tired, whatever it was. Someone who would never judge.

The principle was simple. Each customer could ask for whatever he wanted in his sandwich and have it prepared in whatever way, down to the last detail. No explanation or demand was too long or too difficult. A falafel sandwich with no falafel? Rye and turkey with three spoonfuls of sugar sprinkled on top? A pizza slice inside a pita with mayo? Orange juice that was heated in the microwave for twelve seconds? No problem! If the customer wanted an ingredient the kiosk didn't have in stock, he could pay for ten sandwiches in advance and thus purchase a pink and lime green punch card and a guarantee that the ingredient would be available the next day and every day for the next four months. The shop was more than a gimmick—it was a solution.

LEA WALKED ahead of Ron down the streets of the city. Every time he caught up to her she started walking faster, until he somehow understood that walking this way was what she wanted, that this was the way she liked it. He accepted, he was in the business of accepting, and he trailed a few steps behind her. The streets were full of people, discarded toys, clothes, leaflets. Nothing in the city ever quite seemed to match. Even then, at 2:00 a.m., they saw a little girl walking all by herself, but she didn't look poor—she wore a Gap sweatshirt—and she didn't look lost. She was humming. On a bench, a skinny young boy and a middle-aged man with an accordion huddled over the sports page. Stores were out of line, bulging a little too much toward the sidewalk every so often. A shop selling hiking equipment next to a Judaica store—none of it made sense. With Lea walking in front of him, everything was strange but no less familiar.

At the LimaLima club, after a few drinks, when Lea disappeared and went to get herself one more, he still thought of the streets of the city, and his thoughts became weirder. Something was off, or maybe he was just not used to drinking so much. He remembered that a friend of his dad's had once told him that the people who had built the city had been so idiotic they built it so the streets went parallel to the ocean, so that everywhere you go you get a view of someone's porch rather than of the Mediterranean. The club was packed, the music so deafening, it blasted his chest cavity. In the darkness all he could see were tongues. He smelled parched breath and sweat and hair spray; limbs rubbed against his stomach, his ass; he pondered the possibility that perhaps the city was someone's half-assed idea, like the sandwich shop was his idea, that nothing was as it was meant to be, that maybe the city was never quite meant to exist on this earth, some bizarre cosmic glitch—

Lea threw her arms around his neck, careful not to spill her vodka Red Bull.

"That's your fifth drink!" he screamed into her ear. He too was drunk, he reminded himself, although he had had only three drinks.

When she pushed her tongue into his mouth, he was still pushing away the pesky thought that something was not quite right; he pushed it and pushed it. Then he pushed Lea's body closer to his and told himself he thought too much, that perhaps there were some disadvantages to being so pragmatic all the time.

On the dance floor, Lea's fingers slid under his shirt. Her fingernails scratched him.

"I am not the good girl you think I am!" she shouted into his ear. "I have done some pretty bad things." Her shout was the perfect volume—just loud enough so that he heard every word.

"Whatever it is, I don't care," he shouted back. He pulled her into a hug, the kind of hug you give a child. She was the best thing, a brilliant concept, the only good idea anyone had ever come up with, the only thing that fit just right, his brain decided.

א

HE KNEW it, actually, before his brain did. That she was right. For the first three months the We Don't Judge sandwich kiosk

THE PEOPLE OF FOREVER ARE NOT AFRAID   265

bled money like a slaughtered donkey. It did a little better than the Japanica had—their colossal mistake had been paying all this rent for a stand that only drew customers at night. No Israeli wants overpriced sushi for breakfast, and hardly any Israeli wants it for lunch, when the sun makes the fish stink. Overpriced sushi is a food you order in Israel when you are stumbling home or to another club after dark, when you can't bring yourself to care, when you want to give the girl you picked up whatever she wants and get everything over with: this one stupid night, your whole stupid life.

Ron's sandwich shop was open twenty-four hours, and he was there for fourteen of them for the first few months. He hired two of his teenage female cousins to take orders and an illegal worker from the Sudan to make them (and clean), but by August he knew he had to find new employees because his cousins had to start school. It was pathetic how many people in the city were desperate for a job, any job. His phone wouldn't stop ringing. Models, PhD students, theatre actresses. For every dozen phone interviews he had, he scheduled one girl for a trial shift at the shop. He knew the gimmick was not enough, that in order for the business to succeed he had to have the right human resources. A girl who wouldn't judge. A girl you'd want to buy a sandwich from. Lea.

In the interview, he asked each candidate to describe his or her dream sandwich. He asked them not to make something up just because it was original but to be honest, to tell the truth about themselves.

Lea said she would never dare to tell him the truth about her sandwich, about herself. That she was afraid he couldn't take it. It was the most pretentious answer he got for that question but also the one he most believed.

He didn't hire her because he wanted to fuck her. He hired her because she was good for business, simple as that. Falling for her the second he saw her was just a coincidence. Well, it was not a coincidence—what could a customer ask for other than being served exactly what he wanted by a girl no one could help but love?

א

SHE CUT in front of him after he turned the keys to the front door of his apartment. She walked through the door as he put the keys back in his pocket and bent over to take off his shoes. Her neck was stretched high, as if she didn't even register that he was there. She looked around the living room, picked up the remote, then threw it back on the sofa. She stuck her head in the kitchen area, switched on the light, then switched it off again immediately. She walked through the short hall, opened the broom closet door, shut it, then opened the door to his bedroom. He could hear her body landing on the bed. "Well?" he heard her say while he was standing in the living room. And he felt foolish, so foolish, that he wasn't already in there with her.

He realized he had never gotten around to fantasizing about sleeping with her. He had not expected her to sleep with him that night, but it felt as if it had all been planned, like the world had spun webs around his brain for years and eventually dropped him in those very moments, like the first time you see your favorite movie, and your mind already holds the memories of all the times you'll see it next.

ℵ

HE HAD been drunk, so all he could remember was falling asleep to the sound of his own moaning, but he woke to the sound of someone else's. It was still dark out.

He found her in his bathroom, her face red. She had been crying, but now she just held his towel to her face and stared, frozen, sitting on the tiles of the floor.

He turned on the light and the yellow blinded him.

"What's wrong?" he asked. "Do you regret . . . this?"

"I am sorry," she said. "I am such a mess."

"You don't ever have to be sorry with me," he said and sat by her on the cold floor. "Whatever it is."

"You don't want to be with me," she said and smiled. "I told you, I am not a good person. I have done disgusting things."

Even in his hungover, sleepy state, he was still a smart guy. He could guess what this was about.

"You mean to the people at the checkpoints?" he asked.

She nodded.

"That's everyone who has been there. It's not you. It's this fucked-up army; it fucks you up," he said.

"You don't know what I did," she said.

"Whatever it is," he said, "it won't change a thing. Tell me you had to kick a grandpa in the balls and I wouldn't care." Ron felt angry, sickened, at the city, at the country—at whatever circumstances had made Lea cry like that. It wasn't right. It had never been right, this whole seventy-year-long war. He had never realized that before now.

"What are we?" Lea said and laughed. "Are you saying we are like some sort of item now, as they say in this city?"

"Yes," Ron said. "We are an item. Come back to bed."

He would fix it, he decided then. Whatever it was that made her eyes so knowing the first time he saw her, he would fix. This was what he had to work with, and he would make it work. That's pragmatism right there.

א

HE TOOK it very far very quick—but he couldn't help it. The month he found out the sandwich shop was finally doing more than breaking even, that it was beginning to make a profit less than a year after he had opened it, he told Lea, "In a few years there will be enough money to start a family with." He was amazed at how well it was going. Were there any other food places in Tel Aviv that had managed to establish themselves this quickly? His brother had told him he would have to invest money for a good two years before it would start paying off.

"Watch it there, tiger," she said. She wiped the counter. She smiled. At him.

After the lunch rush, a middle-school girl with a brace on her face was giving Lea trouble.

"Your sign says that you will put whatever I ask for in the sandwich, and I want a baguette with pot brownies," the middle-school girl spat out.

"I wish I could do it, but we don't even have a liquor license," Lea tried to reason with her.

"I want what I want," the girl replied. She was avoiding the gentle way in which Lea tried to catch her eyes, the way Lea tried to humor her in whatever way she could.

"I know, sweetheart, I know—but my hands are tied."

Before they were together, "an item" as she called it, Ron

had wondered where Lea's supernatural patience for the customers came from, but now that they had been together for
a few months, he knew. Still, Lea had yet to let him come see
her apartment, hadn't even agreed to share a cab or tell him
where she lived.

"You know what it is like in this city," she said, resorting
to cliché when he asked her about it. "Your apartment is all
you are."

Still. He knew more than just the Lea who worked at the
shop; he knew another Lea too. He knew two Leas. Three,
actually. There was the Lea who wore dresses short enough
to be shirts to dance clubs, who dragged him through the
streets of the city from one club to another: the Cat & Dog
club, the Oman 17, all the big names. This was the Lea who
could dance for hours, whom everyone at the bar knew and
liked, and they would chant for her as she finished her fifth,
then sixth drink. The Lea who came to his bed almost every
night, giggling, laughing, acting as silly as a child and all at
once entirely a woman.

Then there was the other Lea, the one whose crying woke
him close to dawn, the one he caught in his arms as she tried
to run out of the bed, the one with hardly any words.

The third Lea, still his favorite, was the Lea from the sandwich shop, the star employee. She behaved exactly as she had
on her first day. But it was he who was different. How could
he not be?

"How about you get the fuck out of here?" Ron screamed
at the middle-school girl. "You are not being funny. Or cute.
Your face looks like a Rottweiler with that brace."

"You'll be sorry," the girl said. She flung her Manga backpack on her back and walked away.

"You didn't have to do that," Lea said. "I had it under control." She turned to peel roasted eggplants.

Ron was trying to calm down. Tel Aviv people pissed him off. This shit would never go down anywhere else, but in this city everything was fair game. A man could not even get away with a gimmick. When Domino's said they would provide thirty-minute delivery to anywhere in the city or the pizza would be on them, hundreds of people waited for when it was daylight saving time and then yelled at the delivery guy that he was an hour late and demanded their pizza for free. Ron had even started suspecting that the people of the city were stealing things when Lea and Vera looked away. Things had a tendency to disappear—utensils, cups—that day he couldn't even find the butane torch.

He watched Lea crack walnuts by rolling them on the wooden cutting board. Her ponytail swished. Something was different. He watched her as she bent below the sink to throw out the walnut shells. She moved slowly, methodically, bending her knees, keeping her back straight.

"Did you hurt your back or something?"

"Didn't I just say I had things under control?" Lea said. She stood upright again, grabbed a butter knife. She gave Ron an unnerving look.

"I am sorry, I am sorry. I just don't want you to hurt yourself," Ron said.

"*You* are gonna get hurt unless you shut your mouth," Lea said. She pointed at him with the butter knife. Then she stepped closer, dropped the knife on the counter, reached over. She grabbed Ron's hand. Her hand was soft, and when she smiled, Ron forgot his annoyance, forgot his question, forgot that questions could even be born into this world.

ᘓ

"I LIKE my job a lot." She suddenly spoke during one of those premorning hours when he held her in his arms. "I like being able to give people what they want. At the checkpoints you'd hear all these fantastical stories—everyone had a mother who had less than a day to live somewhere, the wedding of a child who had survived an attack by evil wolves—and all I could do was say that my hands were tied because they didn't have the right color permits, or because they were five minutes late."

Ron didn't know what he could say. He kissed her shoulder.

"Thanks for giving me the job," she said.

"Did you ever feel like looking the other way, letting someone through the checkpoint when you weren't supposed to?" he asked after a few silent minutes.

"I thought about it, a little, sometimes. Then that man stabbed one of us in the neck through a car window. We weren't supposed to come so close to the cars, but that soldier did—I guess the man in the car pretended to have a story too. And when I was an officer I couldn't just let people through, because then I was an officer."

Lea's body was much smaller than Ron's; it felt even smaller when he held it. When she drank too much, he sometimes carried her up the stairs. And still he knew she had done things that he couldn't; well, maybe he could have done them, but either way he hadn't. He had transcribed Arabic in an office. Knowing this made it easier and harder to hold this naked woman in his arms. Easier because he knew she was stronger; she didn't need him; she merely wanted him. Harder because he always wondered if his arms were clutching her strongly enough. "Couldn't have been easy," he said finally. His words still failed him, but he had to say something, and holding her so close, he hoped Lea would understand.

"It wasn't," she said. "Even though I never even liked Yaniv, the boy who was stabbed. He had these pointed bushy eyebrows, like furry arrows."

"That's why you didn't like him?" Ron asked.

"They looked like surprised worms."

"It is Ok not to like someone. You didn't know."

"Maybe."

א

THE EVENING after the girl asked for pot brownies, another jokester came. He was drunk, Russian, fat.

"I want baby meat in challah bread," he demanded.

"Baby lamb? Baby cow?" Lea asked.

"Baby *baby,* bitch," he said. "That's what I want."

Lea froze and looked at him.

"I can see it in your eyes you'd do it," the man said. The rims around his eyes glowed sickly yellow. "Your sign does say, 'whatever you want,' doesn't it?" he asked. "I can see it in your eyes you'd do it."

Lea looked at her sandals. Then she looked up. She looked to the left, to the right. Ron had never seen her so scared. It was as if the man had a gun to her head, as if the whole world were out there, waiting to chase her.

She ran out of the kiosk.

Ron heard her sandals slapping the pavement at a steady pace. "Wait!" he called.

He took a five-hundred-shekel bill out of the register and

handed it to the old man who always ordered the red-and-yellow-peppers sandwich.

"If you can just keep an eye on the place until Vera gets in for the night shift, I'll give you more," he mumbled.

He didn't wait for the old man to respond. He ran.

She was quick, but he was quick too. He caught a glimpse of her hopping in a cab and lucked into one of his own. Lea did not look back. He wanted to tell the driver, "Follow that cab!" but he felt silly. He didn't even know if saying something like that was legal in real life. Instead, he just told the driver he'd give him street-by-street directions. He told the driver he remembered the road to where he wanted to go; he just could not remember the place itself.

נ

IT *WAS* a pricey street. He watched her get off right by Rabin Square and walk down Zeitlin Street. He gave the driver a fifty without waiting for the change, got out, and walked slowly behind her. He followed her into the building and waited in the staircase until he heard her close a door on the third floor. He wondered how she'd respond, why he didn't just call her name. He realized he was curious about where she lived; and, as happy as he was knowing three or even four Leas, he would be most happy with just one, with just her.

He waited for five minutes. He played with the dust on the plastic plants in the hallway.

He knocked.

She opened the door barefoot, wearing nothing but a long white shirt.

"You shouldn't have followed me," she said.

"I had to see what a one and a half bedrooms looked like," he tried to joke.

She didn't smile. She looked tired, more tired than he had ever seen her.

"I am coming in," he said.

She moved to the side without a word, allowing him to enter.

He caught only a glimpse of the living room and kitchen before she pulled him by the arm. It looked like the apartment of someone's parents. The sofa's pillows were knitted and matched the paintings of fruit platters and bridges on the walls. He smelled incense; scented, burning wood.

In her bedroom everything moved faster than it did during the drunken nights at his place. She kept on grabbing his hands and putting them there, then quickly there, then another place. She pushed him, hard, onto the bed when he tried to touch her hair. He landed on his back and wondered how much an orthopedic mattress like hers cost and why he hadn't gotten one yet.

He asked her for the price, and she laughed, softened. He put his hand on the back of her neck. His Lea.

He surrendered. She did too, ultimately. They fell asleep.

ᴎ

HE WOKE up to the familiar sound of someone sobbing and for a second forgot where he was. Lea lay still by his side, and when he leaned over to look at her he saw that she was sound asleep rather than crying, breathing in a rhythm, more peaceful than he had ever seen her.

He heard it again. A sob. A moan. He walked out of the

bedroom and stood still in the short hallway in his boxers. He felt foolish, displaced, cold. The air conditioning was blasting, but he hadn't felt it under the thick covers.

He heard the sound again. It was coming from behind a door next to the bedroom.

The half bedroom, he thought.

He tried to open it, but it was locked. He knew Lea, knew her well enough to know where she'd hide a key. Whenever Vera was late for her shift and Lea absolutely had to go, she would lock down the blinds of the kiosk and hide the key under the trash can in the street. There was no trash can in the hallway, but there was an urn on the carpet, full of decorative fake bamboo sticks.

~

THE HALF bedroom looked exactly like a regular bedroom, except it was only half the size, and there was no bed, but there was a butane torch on the floor—aluminum, French; the one he had bought for the kiosk. The aluminum was covered in little red splotches.

And the man, of course. It was impossible not to notice the man. A middle-aged Arab man was in the room, on the floor, with his hands and legs cuffed. He was naked, and the skin on his back was burned. His face was a host of colors and bumps, yellow, red, blue. He looked up and opened his mouth. He was missing two bottom front teeth, so that one tooth stood alone, like a baby's.

Nothing made sense; nothing seemed to match. Ron opened his mouth but no words came out. He felt her hand on his shoulder.

"I don't expect you to understand," Lea said. "I saw him passed out drunk on a bench by the construction site under my building two days ago and I knew I recognized him. Fadi. So I took him. He killed a boy in my unit once. Cut his neck. Just reached in through his car and grabbed him by the collar and with the knife . . ."

"Didn't anyone say anything when they saw you carrying him?" Ron asked, his voice slow.

"This is Tel Aviv," she said.

"Help me," the man said to Ron in Arabic. His voice was hoarse, air with no vocal cords.

"It took me two hours to carry him up here. He was so drunk he didn't even resist, but I was worried I was going to totally throw out my back," Lea said. Her voice sounded sleepy. "He keeps on talking to me. On and on and on. You'd think he'd gather by this point I don't understand a word of Arabic. I thought he'd stop talking after I knocked his teeth out, but he won't."

"What did I do?" the man asked Ron. He looked at Ron as if he thought Ron had authority, as if he were a high-ranking Mossad agent who had finally come to do the right thing.

Ron's head was pounding, a hangover, although he hadn't drunk a thing last night. Lea kept talking.

"I can't stop either; I can't let him go."

Ron looked at the man and motioned him with his hand to stay quiet. He looked at his watch. In less than two hours it would be time for his shift in the sandwich shop. He picked up the butane torch.

He landed a blow on the back of the man's neck. The man crumpled; his face smacked the floor. It was an accurate, steady blow. Ron couldn't help but wonder if the blow had broken the torch, if it would ever work again.

He put his hand on the back of Lea's neck, and she stepped closer and wet his chest, then began to kiss it, small kisses, like a child sipping soup.

He thought.

Perhaps they could spend a few more hours in bed before they went to the kiosk. Put on some music, have a few drinks. Never mind that it was five in the morning; this job, this city, they were not the boss of them. Sure, he'd have to help Lea let the man go soon, and scare him enough to keep a secret. But there was plenty of time for that.

This morning was theirs.

This city is theirs.

And maybe everything is someone's imagination.

Please, don't judge.

III

The
After
War

And when the boy soldiers returned from the war they tortured the girl soldiers who waited for them. This took four days. In the end people died.

This was the after war, but everyone knew about it before it happened. Every reserve soldier was invited to participate, and very few people, perhaps just a few young girls, were surprised.

None of the women had to be there. Lea was married, three months pregnant—though she hadn't told anyone yet. Avishag was on antidepressants and seeing a shrink. Yael was in Goa, India, at the time, translating the lyrics of a traveling musical commune. They had all kept in slight touch over the years. They did not keep in regular touch with anyone else from the village, not even their parents.

Avishag had a driver's license. She drove the girls to the training base in her dead Subaru. They got stationed together because Shai the officer used to fuck Yael and he was waiting for her to come back from the world and fuck him more.

They came back, but they were no longer needed. They were women now. The younger girls hummed songs like milk and honey. "There is a love in me and it will rise and win you" and "Not always I come out with words." They were in front of their watch monitors in war rooms, fully geared at the gates; checking who everyone entering the base was. Calibrating weapons with the L-beat, a red laser that let you correct a weapon without firing.

"Hey, where do we rest?" Yael asked the girls huddled on the sands outside the war room. They were playing a new card game called Jungle Lies. The rules changed each month with every new deck of cards.

"You just got here," a young checkpoint girl said, throwing two cards down, taking three. "We don't even need you cunts."

"You threw out three cards and now you'll have to lose four cards the next round," Lea said. "And since I am an officer, I suggest you mind your words."

The girl took them to their housing in the Negev guns and ammunition storage caravan.

The women thanked her and she laughed like there was no tomorrow. "You shouldn't have come. We got this."

The Negev, named after the desert, was a modest machine automatic gun developed in Israel. The room reeked of gasoline; the weapons had recently been cleaned, and they were crammed against the wall. The floor was wooden, and weeds as high as the girls' knees sprouted through the cracks. There were four green mattresses in the far left corner.

"Well," Avishag said.

"LOL," Lea said.

Yael sang a song about a duck who wanted to ask questions, a song she remembered from when they were little.

Suddenly all the lights on the base went out.

"Why?" Avishag asked.

Then she slipped out of her red dress, her breasts hard in the daylight. Lea poured from a green bag the uniform and equipment that she'd picked up at the supply caravan.

The girls changed and gossiped.

The cardboard sign in the supply caravan read: IF YOU WILL IT, WE DON'T HAVE ANY OF IT. It was a joke, and Lea laughed.

They were on an abandoned base built in 2012 for the purpose of training firefighters, who arrived from different cities for one month every year, how to prepare for a fire like the one that had happened in the Carmel forest in 2011.

The base was yellow, oversized, American.

א

SHAI WAS talking on his cell phone, but when he saw Yael, he hung up. He walked on the sand toward her, and Lea and Avishag froze. Yael trod lightly.

Shai put both hands on her hip bones.

"I waited for you, and now I am leaving tomorrow with my soldiers," Shai said. He and Yael had met at a Jerusalem gay pride parade a few months after she got out of the army;

he was signed on for five more years, which suggested for-ever. They were waiting in line for colored ice, and their sweat mixed when a float with transgendered people dressed as fla-mingos pushed everyone closer together. They had known each other briefly before; he was her officer toward the end of her service.

Now Lea and Avishag watched Yael and crossed their arms. Even Avishag was interested. They waited to see what Yael would do; it seemed to Yael that other people were always waiting to see what she would do. As if she knew.

"Show me where and how you are taking them," Yael said. Then she kissed him. She never liked kissing. Sticking her tongue inside another person's mouth. It seemed like a poor survival tactic. She tasted the bread he had recently swallowed.

"What have you all been up to?" Shai asked after, instead.

Lea was married to the guy who had started the WDJ sand-wich chain stores. She was living in Tel Aviv and smoking her days away in cafés, writing porn books about Nazis fucking the life out of Jews in showers and seven-year-old girls losing their virginity via incest and double penetration. She used a pseudonym and was well received globally. Avishag had left her mother in Jerusalem and was living with her uncle in a small development town in the Negev desert, working as the youth organizer of the local Ethiopian scouts' troop and in-tegrating horse-riding lessons into their curriculum. On the side she drew fan-fiction comic books based on Emily the Strange called *Emily the Sad*. Emily the Sad was always losing her keys or missing her bus, but nobody helped her and then she would sit on a bucket in a poppy field and cry. Avishag scanned the images and e-mailed them only to Yael, but Yael never opened the attachments after the first one, the one where Emily forgets how to add and cannot figure out if she has enough money to buy a hairbrush. Yael was busy doing the world at the time, an idea she had promised to herself the day she quit her airport job with seven thousand shekels saved up, translating works she found in China, Romania, Zimbabwe, India, and putting them up online for free. And she wrote music. In all languages. Songs she put on the Internet and that people loved, though they never knew were hers.

"Geez, Yael," Shai said, after all the highly small talk. He himself had nothing to tell. "Is there anything you don't do?" he asked.

"Nope," Lea said, and she tapped Yael on the back. Yael felt her nails on her skin like moans. "Our little Yael is quite the renaissance-cunt-woman."

"All right," Yael said.

"Lea, please. We are in a war," Avishag said.

"I asked for the plan for tomorrow," Yael said. And she looked at Shai. Her stare was like a fisherman's string. She would not let him go.

א

SHAI EMPTIED the war room so the two of them could talk. The room was covered with maps on the wall, cereal on the floor, and rainbow hair ties and radios all over the desks.

Yael asked Shai not to go.

This was after he showed her the sketches of the school they were taking down, the location of each sniper, every window.

"You'll die. We cannot enter Syria by land," Yael said.

"I have to go," Shai said. "I am an officer."

"I'll do whatever," Yael said. She scratched his nose and got down, like a cat, on her knees. The floor was covered in dust and cereal; dead cells she could feel through her pant legs.

"Yael. You are paranoid."

"I'd walk around the base, the world, forever, on all fours, with your dick in my mouth."

"Marry me?" Shai asked. He looked down at her. He was joking, but they both knew that jokes are what's most precise when death feels intimate.

"I need to travel. But maybe one day."

"One day is not enough. Whatever is whatever." Yael knew better than to say no, so she said die and gave up. In truth she knew there was no real solution in her words. Not for Shai. On her way back to the caravan, grasshoppers were catching their reflections in the gasoline pools that had formed from all the weapon cleanings, and plunging into them.

ℵ

SHE ENTERED the caravan smiling. She figured she had to. The lights were off again.

"You are home!" Avishag said. She was braiding her thin hair after a shower, wearing a summer pajama set decorated with pies.

"Let's play story," Lea said. She pulled a soul candle from her bottomless pocket and lit it.

The girls got out their pens and paper and each of them wrote a sentence. It was a game they had not played since they were in seventh grade. Their enhanced version of Exquisite

Corpse. Lea got to see Yael's sentences but not Avishag's. She continued the sentence she saw. Yael's continued Avishag's; she never saw Lea's.

The stories they wrote were mainly about dead dogs making love in a place almost like Antarctica, modified song lyrics from *American Idol,* and stepmothers so fat they emptied the kibbutz pools they jumped into headfirst. The three pages went on in a circle, each girl folding the sentence she saw and leaving hers to be seen by the girl on her right, like a fan of the words that were in all of them, drowned in ink.

They did not set up a clock. They whispered across the beds the night before that they would wake up by themselves. "Natural awakening"—it was an army phrase no one used anymore, meant for those rare clockless dawns when you have nothing to wake up for in the morning.

א

THE BOYS were away, in a rolling bus or in another land, when the girls woke; only the younger girls were left. It was past noon already by the time the women felt that urge to step out and roam the base.

The hotter clique of younger girls were covering each other in ice and sunbathing naked by the flag. There was no one left to train in the base, no shooting range or open gate to watch on a monitor. One of the girls, a gorgeous one with a thin plume of blonde hair covering her neck, was jumping between the girls who were splayed on the floor. "Bim bam bap, I ate a rat," she sang as she jumped, and the girls had to roll over and increase the space between them, because she kept on succeeding to jump into the spaces no matter how far apart they got. "We are a rare breed, an odd bleed," the girl's chant rattled on as the three women walked away.

"So are we going to raid the guys' caravans or what?" Lea asked. "You know you always wanted to."

Lea stopped walking and approached Yael. She kissed Yael on the forehead. There was something softer about her. Her lips were shaky on Yael's skin. Perhaps it was the baby inside her, but Yael thought it was the mere unruffledness of aging.

They walked through the base and encountered the less popular younger girls in their red and leopard-print bathing suits. They were holding hands in a circle so firmly that their knuckles turned white. It pleased Avishag that the girls were playing a game she knew. A birthday game. The special girl of the day got to stand inside the circle and be the cat. Outside stood the girl who was the designated mouse. The goal was for the circle of girls to never let the cat break free of the circle. The girls were chanting an ancient army girls' song: "What a mess, what a mess. Whores get screwed for money; we do it for free."

"It's nostalgia day," a tall redhead, the mouse outside the circle, said to Avishag. She looked right through Avishag. "So you can join us, even though you are old. Later we can play teachers and schoolgirls, and you'd get to beat us with the L-beat laser-calibration sticks."

"That's thirty-four hundred shekels for each stick. You must be joking. Who here is a weaponry instructor?" Yael asked. Since she had first seen the young girls, she had been looking for her younger self. The shortest girl, the thin one. But she was nowhere to be found. The girls' bodies all reminded her of Amazons.

"There is no use for them no more," said a girl with dark circles around her eyes that were large enough to penetrate her cheeks. She was a weaponry instructor, and it showed. "The boys are entering Syria by foot. We are all kaput now. I wonder what will happen!"

"Ignore, ignore," Lea said, and brushed an imaginary spider off her shoulder. "I never liked children. Let's go to the boys' castle and have some grown-up fun."

The three could hear that the cat girl broke free as they approached the boys' caravan area. She broke the circle with the groan of a muffled robot. None of the women looked back to see her catch the mouse.

א

THE BOYS' caravan area was structurally identical to the one Avishag had slept in during her service days near Egypt. The rooms looked as if the boys had been asked to leave in the middle of dinner. The dark mud of a coffee cistern was spilled on a mattress. Yellow underwear stained brown was left on a threshold. Uniforms, razors, pretzels, even money, were scattered on the floors.

Yael heard a voice talking. It was the voice of a woman, but it sounded more like that metallic groan of the cat girl breaking free. The boys must have left a TV on, she thought. At the end of the long two rows of caravans, the "recreation room" stood open. She had always hated it, that because there were more boys in every training base, they were the only ones who got to have recreation at night. The girls could watch TV if they walked in accompanied during the day, but she was always guarding or training during the day. Unless you were fucking someone important, it was "No TV for you after supper, young lady!"

Lea was stuck inside one of the caravans. Avishag and Yael stood outside and watched her sniff mattresses and crusty socks.

"Is this the type of thing that gets you off nowadays?" Yael asked. "I thought you were a married lady."

"Oh dear," Avishag said. She rarely spoke for Lea, but obscenity made her eyes buzz.

"Kinda. It kinda gets me off," Lea shouted, still sniffing. "But really I am trying to detect Russian sweat.... Wait!" Lea looked under a field bed with a mattress covered in hot red sheets she had just breathed in. "Got it!"

She found three bottles that were part of a four-pack of peach schnapps, bound together by white plastic. Avishag hoped the Russian boy had not taken the fourth bottle with him to Syria. Russian boys tended to handle the automatic weapons.

"He must be a homo. What kind of guy drinks this shit? It's our favorite, Yael! This is too good to be true."

א

THE GIRLS stretched themselves out on the velvety broken sofas in the recreation room. Yael took a long swig and felt the ticking of her body slowing down. Lea was already a quarter of the way through her own bottle. Yael did not understand what the TV was showing. It was a video game, set up so that the player was the eyes. A woman with a machine's voice was reciting insults: "The results of the test from the previous level of the game conclude that you are a terrible human being. We weren't even testing for that," the voice said. The setting seemed like some kind of deranged physics lab. Cement and orange lava. Robots were shooting and speaking with the voices of children: "Where did you go? I don't hate you."

Yael passed Avishag the bottle. "I can't," Avishag said. "The medicine."

"Oh yeah, the super cool medicine," Lea said, and pinched Avishag on the cheek. "Tell me, little Avi, does Dr. Zhivago-bumble-bee up your dosage before or after he fucks you?"

Right as she said it Lea regretted it. Avishag looked down at one of her fingernails as if it were a war room monitor. Lea, oddly, was nicer drunk than sober, and she wondered if the cruelty bleeding into her words was the baby's way of telling her he did not very much care for peach schnapps.

"I have a woman doctor," Avishag said. Even though it was Yael who had left the country, it was Avishag and Lea who had met the least since their huge blowout after Avishag told Lea she'd been taking antidepressants. They had become friends again after the army, when Avishag needed Lea, with Lea eagerly telling Avishag exactly what to do to cure her sadness. Lea was disappointed in the end that Avishag found a solution that had nothing to do with her.

Yael thought she needed to say something but then realized that she always thought she needed to say something. So she didn't. She looked around the room, under empty pizza boxes and porn magazines, and found the computer game box. The game was called Human Engineering INC 2. She read the back:

*This game is a series of mathematic riddles that must be
solved or death and excruciating pain will occur. The player,
Many, is following the orders of a Cyber Intellectual named
GOD-DOS (Genome Organizing Detailer and Domain
Operating System) to complete tests in the Human
Engineering INC Enrichment Center, with the promise of
receiving frozen pizza if testing is finalized and the subject
is still alive and retains his taste buds and face.*

The automated woman's voice was speaking in loops, invisible. Yael closed her eyes and listened. "The Enrichment
Center regrets to inform you that the next challenge is impossible. Do not try to solve it" and "Honestly, this part of the
game was an error. If we were you, we would just kill ourselves already. Just what, as it says here in your subject 3288
file, your birth mother wanted to do when she gave you up
for adoption by putting you in the Dumpster, the night after
a sausage festival."

Yael pressed a button on the joystick, and then she pressed
all of them. Lea was drinking more quickly. Avishag was staring. Yael liked it that she had something to do in that awkward moment. Finally, the player on the screen jumped above
the lava. The woman's voice was heard louder: "Great Job!
You stayed hopeful and dedicated to your goals in an environment of oppression and negativity. You should really become
an activist and free some slaves."

The next phase of the game was conducted in an incinera-
tion chamber for badly wired battle androids. They slid across
a manufacturing line into the flames, mumbling like toddlers:
"I am badly wired. I only take up space. Thank you for end-

ing me and helping the Enrichment Center thrive!" Except for one android, who quietly repeated: "I'm Ok wired. I am *different*," until he burned. Yael wondered about the face of the American man who had written the script for the game. Then she wondered about those who played it. About all of those who had seen that chamber.

"Listen, girls," she said into the sun that penetrated the recreation room. "Listen girls"— that phrase again, just like all the times she had used it growing up.

"Oh, no," Lea said. "It's always a bad sign when she says that."

Avishag liked it that Lea was finally speaking again. She smiled, showing her teeth.

"They are going to kill us all. The boys. This is the game they play," Yael said. Then she pointed at the screen.

"Oh no, Avishag!" Lea yelled. "Yael thinks she is Jonah the prophet again!" She was talking about Yael as if she weren't in the room.

Avishag laughed. She took Yael's face in her hands. "Yael. You are not Jonah. We went over this in fourth grade. Then again in seventh."

Yael felt as though she could breathe in Avishag's voice. She had been missing the sound of that voice, the actual voice, with its dash of unmedicated cynicism. "I know I am not Jonah, duh," Yael said. In that second, everything started making itself a little good again.

"You are no Joan of Arc either," Lea said.

"Most certainly you are no Maid of Lorraine. I saw those e-mails you sent from Paris. What was it? Four guys in one weekend?" Avishag said, and then the three started laughing in such unison, had there been anyone near enough to hear them he would have thought a tractor must have caught the hiccups somewhere.

Lea was the first to stop laughing. "But really, if we forget about Yael reenvisioning a better production scheme for Bruce Willis's *Armageddon,* what I wanted to say is that Avishag, I am sorry. It is none of my business, your medicine."

Avishag took the bottle from Lea's hands. She poured the liquid into her mouth, paused, swallowed. Then she laughed. A laugh that dropped and rose like a yo-yo. This was the way she did it. This was how she started to cry.

"You are right, Lea. They wanted me to go to the army, so I go to the army. Then I am having all these thoughts and the thoughts are interrupting everybody, so they want me to take medicine. Then one of the scouts' moms finds out I take medicine, and now they want me fired. I'm going to have to move back in with my mother, who is still living with her mother. You can't win with these people."

No one in the world had heard Avishag talk for this long since the tear-gas commander. She spoke like she was opening a can with her teeth.

"Who are 'these people'?" Yael asked.

"Everyone who is not me," Avishag said.

Lea gently patted Avishag's knee. It occurred to Yael that she was the only one who hadn't changed, that the other two had but she felt like she was still she.

"It's not just you," Lea said. "I can't win with these people either. Ron's sandwich shops are doing amazing. But we still can't find a place big enough to raise kids in Tel Aviv. There is so much demand—there is simply nothing available."

They both looked at Yael. At first she thought they were

looking for guidance, but then she saw an embarrassed pinch at the side of Lea's mouth. They were looking at Yael as if she were an outsider.

"Don't look at me like that. It is not better out there in the world. Everywhere you go, it's just trains that never show up, noise complaints. Police cars sticking out of the sidewalk into major roads so that they force you to walk in the middle of traffic. It's like they want you to get run over."

The girls looked at her as if she were a wannabe in their clique. Desperation rang false on Yael.

"But. I haven't been everywhere yet, obvi," Yael said.

And then they all breathed.

א

FROM THEN on the days of war were nice to them. They watched Yes satellite TV all day. They all just had regular cable at their parents' homes and wherever else they lived, so the new channels were a blessing. They watched a *Gilmore Girls* marathon and a Discovery Channel show about honey badgers. They watched a documentary called *My Car Is My Lover*, and a *Night Court/Who's the Boss* marathon on the oldies channel. In the afternoons Lea and Avishag took the car to get food and alcohol in the nearby Arab town. Lea paid; they got fusion food: fried onions and Muenster cheese and basil on everything that could ever be carved out of bread.

Yael stayed behind when the other two went out to get food. She loved it. It was like babysitting for the richest couple in town after the children had gone to bed. She stretched her legs out and watched fuzzy shows on channel six, the children's channel. *Bully the Snowman* and *Wonder*

Shoes and *Chiquititas*. The songs bounded her, as if their notes were painted in water on the walls. The channel's theme song between the shows was her favorite. "The channel is my home. This summer the plane is boarding on the children's channel! Science! Art! Horror stories!" She breathed like she thought nothing of it in those hours. She was the ruler of a domain not her own. The song rang like trumpets when she closed her eyes. "The national channel is the true place! With it I am able, and it is always with me!" If Yael was crying, it was because only then did she start to understand why she thought it was, after all, pretty good to die for her country.

The women were happy in those days.

א

THE BOYS came back to the base after two weeks. Shai had died. A few others had too. The foot invasion had achieved nothing and the army was taking down Damascus and Aleppo with aerial strikes instead. The younger girls had left the day before, sent back to their original bases. They boarded the bus laughing and pointing their middle fingers at the three women. "Summer vacation is over, grandmas! We are going back to mommy and daddy." The blonde watch girl giggled at them, slamming her body against the window, looking just as ethereal with her breasts crushed on the glass. Yael thought of Hagar. The reserve officer called her on the phone to chat about the dead they both knew and said that, under the circumstances, the women could go home because the boys were only coming back to wrap up their equipment, and they would have no time to train with the girls or linger in the base. Then the boys would get a week at home.

Yael thought the right thing to do was to wait for the boys until the last bus got them, even though the women had a car. But when the boys arrived they looked through the three of them as if they had been airbrushed out of the base.

Ten guards from an artillery platoon were to guard the base until the firefighters arrived in a month.

It was only when everyone was all packed up and waiting at the gate for the late bus that the boys engaged. They teased Yael. There were twelve boys left, waiting for the last army bus in the sun. The boys said if Yael was going to do just one tiny thing to earn her reserve stipend, that thing would be the fattest guy in the group. That's Zionism right there.

"I am not going to pity-fuck Baruch," Yael said. "He is nasty as fuck," she said. She was sitting on top of the anti-sniper barricade by the gate of the base. She did not look at Baruch or Oren the officer, the one who had come up with the idea, when she spoke. Her words were mumbled because she had Lea's bobby pin jabbing out of her red mouth. Lea lay with her head in Yael's lap. Yael was twisting the sides of Lea's bangs into tiny braids, as if nothing mattered more than those auburn hairs. Lea's hair smelled of lavender shampoo. When Yael rubbed her nose, she smelled that the cleanliness of it had stuck to the tips of her fingers.

"Why would you say something like that?" Oren the officer asked. He stood with his arms crossed, turning his gaze from the gate and the road ahead to Yael. "His best friend just died on him, while you were here in the base jerking off."

"So his best friend died. My boyfriend died. Actually, a few of my boyfriends died. They tend to. Avishag's brother once died a long time ago. Big deal. He needs to find his balls and move on," Yael said. She was winking at Lea, rolling her eyes with the teenhood that the young girls infected her with. Avishag held her hands to her ears and closed her eyes.

"Find his balls and move on?" said Yoav. "Shai was not your boyfriend. He said he was not. If he was, you could have made him stay."

Yoav. The staff sergeant. He joined in the conversation.

א

AT FIRST Yael thought the boys must be kidding, that they must be just kids. They came with three gurneys and slammed the three girls onto them. They didn't tie them in for safety or give them helmets. As a weaponry instructor, any deviation from safety protocol disturbed Yael, and her concern grew when the boys jammed the barrels of their guns firmly into her back. She could not see the other two because of the dust clouds that rose from the run up the hill to the flag area, but it was clear to her that had the angle of the jam been different, her spinal cord might have been severed.

The boys let the girls drop like leaflets from the height of their shoulders right by the flag. Then they huddled in a circle, as if the world were their soccer game, and whispered.

"You are going to write, big, with stones, 'We Are Whores,' or we'll . . . we will torture you," Yoav said to the girls on the ground after a few minutes. "We will not let you go home."

Yael rose from the ground and sat on her bottom. She looked up at Yoav. His eyes were red. He'd been smoking weed. She could see that the snot in his nose was black, and she knew he had been too afraid to wash his face and be forced to look in the mirror since he got back. She could not believe he used the word "torture." It sounded cliché. Like he hadn't bought the vowels for it.

"We are not writing nothing," Yael said, low. "Nah, nah, nah. Come on." The old Rihanna song flew from her mouth. She remembered when Rihanna had overdosed the year before. How she had cried about it while looking at her delayed flight glowing in red in that tiny Romanian airport. "I like it, like it," she now sang on.

"Listen, girls," Avishag said. She removed her hands from her eyes. She had been crying for a while; the dry wetness blended with the new.

"You shut up with your baby talk," Yael said. She hadn't yelled at Avishag since they were in high school. Maybe that was a problem, Yael thought, and then waited for Lea to talk.

"I am a professional writer and I won't even write it in stones. Stones are so permanent. And I personally like 'S&M,' even on Facebook. I like it, like it," Lea said. She did not sing the lyrics.

And so the boys did not know what to do. They shrugged at each other, pointed their guns and made the girls go to their caravan, the Negev guns storage container that was already locked. They made the girls crawl on all fours.

א

"WHAT NOW?" Avishag asked. Night was dropping and all the lights on the base went out, then back on, and again.

"Now we are not scared. There is no fear in the world," Yael said. There was becoming much more of her with every word. "We have two bottles of sauvignon blanc and tons of pizza crust and pasta left and a whole bottle of Diet Coke, from that time you accidentally bought diet. I brought it here."

"You brought it here from the boys' area?" Lea asked.

"I brought it here. I thought it might be wise."

"So now we wait," Lea said. "You thought it might be wise . . ." she said, and shook her head, smirking. It was almost as if she were surprised by something for the first time; at who Yael was, at who she herself was. In her voice Yael heard that Lea got it but was not sure she wanted to.

The girls sat on their mattresses and looked at the door. They did not move. They wanted to remember everything that had happened in the seconds before.

א

AND SO it began.

The next morning Yoav entered alone and asked for a volunteer, and Yael volunteered by rising and walking and following him.

Avishag cried.

"OMG," Lea said.

Yael talked through the whole march up to the flag, saying she'd do whatever if he promised not to touch the other two, then giving up hope when she was already naked and saying that she'd do anything and gladly, if he only spared Avishag. She mentioned the dead brother, but in the end it did no good.

The twelve boys and three girls were all active participants. Volunteering proved unproductive.

Nothing that they did was very productive. But they tried.

Yael tried talking. She would not shut up. She said she'd been hitchhiking all over Africa; that she probably had exotic diseases and that this was really not a wise move. Lea only spoke on the walk back, saying that this was all rather interesting, that she might write about it or tell her husband about it—they had been meaning to spice up their bedroom routine. She lectured the boys as she was clicking her bra shut, her hands under her uniform shirt. Even Avishag could not be shocked. She kept her eyes closed and whispered apologies for the war, sympathetic chin nods about how difficult it is to be a young man in today's dating world.

The twelve boys found themselves inside a pickle.

א

THE GIRLS were fine that first night. Even Avishag was thinking ahead. She spoke as the other two were looking at each other, as if hanging each other and Avishag on the line between their eyes.

"We'll just have to do a lot of drugs. We'll travel somewhere and do a lot of drugs and then move on," Avishag said. She put her head on Yael's shoulder and Yael did not push her away like she usually did. "Yael, did you do a lot of drugs in India? Which drugs are the most optimal drugs for moving on?" Avishag asked.

"The way you talk sometimes, I swear . . ." Lea said. "I've missed it."

"Well, I wanted to do a lot of drugs, but it did not work out that way. I smoked pot once and felt like the window was pulling me toward it like a magnet. So I smoked pot in the woods instead, and then I felt like I must find a window so it can pull me toward it like a magnet. Later one time I accidentally did X at a rave in Goa, and it made me so paranoid I decided that drugs were really not my thing," Yael said.

"Paranoid! But X is the drug of love and trust!" Lea laughed.

"Maybe you should seek psychiatric counseling. There is something chemically wrong with you, perhaps," Avishag laughed.

"It was the realest thing. A Persian boy with long lashes was running toward me on the road. He screamed his name, it started with a J, and although I did not speak Farsi I knew that it meant 'the world.' He smelled of moss, and it was because he was holding a brook trout in his hand that I thought came from the rivers of Babylon but knew didn't come from there because brook trout don't swim there, and besides, he was from Persia," Yael said.

The heat and the thirst might have gotten to the girls, or at least to Yael. Yael would not let them drink the Coke for the first two days that they were trapped.

"You must have been tripping," Avishag said. "It must have been another drug. X doesn't trip you. I read about drugs in a pamphlet," Avishag said.

"But the thing was, I was not the only one who could see the boy. Two of the people I was hanging out with could see him too. And they pointed at the boy and hid behind me because they were scared that the fish was poisonous and it would kill us all if it touched us. I was scared too, but I knew I shouldn't be. The boy said he wanted his dad, but he wasn't angry—it was more like he was worried about us partying like that."

"That's a very strange story," Lea said.

"Stranger things happen," Yael said.

And then a boy other than Yoav opened the door. He was eighteen.

א

BY THE end of the second day, the boys had developed a routine. They knew each girl better than she knew herself. When Yael got back that afternoon, she got quieter, and this gave the other two the room to talk they had never had before.

Avishag told a story about a fifth grader in her Ethiopian scouts troop who painted nothing but severed toes. The severed toes would all have jobs, they would get married and go to the army, but they were all bloody toes. The school board was upset, and there was a meeting when all the parents decided that he must be sent away because he might cause harm to himself or others. Avishag spoke for him, but it did no good. Maybe that's why a mom followed her afterward and found out about the psychiatrist.

Lea asked Avishag for another story, to see if another story could make her realize that the first story was really not worth remembering, if she should regret not having the energy to write it down.

Avishag said that because chickens need a lot of calcium to make eggs, her uncle told her to crush all the empty eggshells into a powder with a stone and mix it inside the chickens' food. But one time she thought she'd try to see if the chickens could just eat the eggshells as crumbs. If they could peck at whole lettuce stems, she did not see why they needed the shells as powder. But what Avishag did not know is that when a chicken eats something that looks like an egg it becomes an egg eater. That was the reason for the powder.

"So an egg eater eats other chickens' eggs?" Lea asked.

"At first," Avishag said. "At first she only eats other chickens' eggs."

א

BY THE middle of the third day, they had run out of Coke. They still had some pizza crusts left. Lea had drunk most of the Coke—her body had forced her to—and she was so ashamed that Avishag kept going on and on about how it was she who had drunk most of it instead, and how sorry she was.

When the lights went off, Avishag stopped apologizing and cried. She was most afraid of the dark that was more than the dark she saw inside her eyes when she closed them.

Yael watched her own shadow; when she tilted her head, the shadow of her hair on the wall blended with the shadow of one of the guns so that it looked like the gun was trying to become her.

This was when Lea offered her solution. "You know. We do have ammunition. And automatic guns."

"We cannot shoot them. Don't even think it," Yael said.

"We can threaten to, you little whore. You don't control us," Lea said.

"We cannot. They hold our future in their bodies and heads," Yael said.

"You know, sometimes I really wish you'd stop talking like that," Lea said.

"Me too," Yael said.

"Me three," Avishag said.

The girls were speaking with thirst. The guns were still wet with gasoline. Mocking them, so near, sleeping with them as if on purpose. The boys were in charge. They didn't understand why, but they knew it through their bones. The door in front of the girls was not theirs to open.

א

ONE OF the girls' sweat had begun to smell different. It smelled like an alarm.

Avishag offered her solution. "We should just write it. It is just stones. Someone will move them. It's just words. We'll get back at the boys as soon as we're out. They'll be sorry later."

"Just words?" Lea asked. "Maybe."

"Just stones?" Yael asked. "Nothing is as written as much as a thing written in stones."

"Yael," Lea said.

And Avishag was preparing to talk more. Yael wondered if she had been encouraging her to talk too much, after all.

"No!" Yael shouted, and filled the other two with fear; of her, of the boys who might hear. "We are no Harry Potter. We don't get to have second chances. This is this. We are not Jesus. We don't get to come back. Either this is the Jewish state, or it is not."

"Yael," Lea said.

"Please stop talking," Avishag said.

"If we don't face this now, we'll hurt someone else later. The boys will never forgive themselves. Lea, you'll always watch TV instead of doing what you really want to be doing. Avishag, you'll always say 'sorry' when someone bumps into you. I will always hate me, me talking like this," Yael said.

"You sound very passionate about this issue," Lea said, and she smiled. And she didn't cry.

That night the boys came only for Lea, then again.

"Lea, princess," Yael said when she heard the boys approach the third time. "I don't know everything. I haven't been everywhere, *remember?*"

"Do or do not. There is no try," Lea said.

"May the force be with you," Avishag said.

Yael felt the weight of all the words and sounds she had ever shared with her friends like a waterfall exploding inside her mouth, in that moment. She needed to imagine a way out, and soon.

א

BY THE fourth morning the girls did not trade any words. Yael wanted to say something very powerful, to whisper an ancient truth, but the thirst did not let the back of her mouth form the consonants, and besides, she herself knew she was becoming silly.

Avishag was making dolls from the weeds that grew through the cracks on the wooden floor. Hearts and babies and cats. Simple shapes that were the cartoon versions of real objects. Weaving and tightening and ripping. Yael did not notice when she started doing this, but by morning there were six dolls and one becoming one in Avishag's peeling hands.

When Yael noticed this, she took the bamboo stick that

was holding up an anemones office plant that hadn't been there when the girls first came to the caravan. She made holes in it with her teeth, and then it was a flute.

For her to play.

"If you are playing for me, Yael, then don't. I told you a million times. I am like Shylock's daughter, Jessica. I cannot hear music," Lea said.

"We are not doing Shakespeare right now, are we?" Avishag said.

"I mean, that's a little gay, I admit it," Lea said.

"Right. Because we all know Hitler was gay," Yael said.

The girls looked at her. And they were afraid, and mostly, then, for themselves for listening to her.

"And by Hitler I mean Shakespeare," Yael said.

Then she asked for permission to sleep.

א

YAEL DOVE inside her body to find sleep. She imagined ocean waves beneath her, demanding calm. Then she thought of all the happy times when she sat on the floor and eagerly listened to the opening theme songs of her favorite TV shows and remembered all her tears that rolled with the song during the credits at the end of each episode. She remembered her childhood body, awakening flooded with delight that curled her toes and opened her nose in the middle of all those dreams in which she was taken by another human being for safe keeping. To a room with a bed that locked, where all that happened was that she was fed and pitied.

In her daydreams, the ones she used to have during history class, it was always a woman math teacher who took her and kept her. The woman always looked a little different: tall, blonde, dark. In reality all of her math teachers were men who did not see her. After she saw *Mean Girls* in high school, the image of the woman math teacher was fixed. It was always Tina Fey, or the math teacher she pretended to be in that movie. *What a stupid girl I used to be,* Yael thought. *What a stupid girl I still am.*

But then she thought more. And she opened her eyes.

"*Mean Girls,*" Yael said, while still lying down.

"Let's not talk unless it means something. My voice is tired," Avishag said.

"This means something. Remember how the girls in that movie always say the opposite of what they mean?" Yael asked. She sat up.

"All Americans always say the opposite of what they mean. Just look at their movies. All heroes. It's because they don't have real ones," Lea said. Ron had a strong anti-American bias that he'd picked up from doing some business with them, and Lea had adopted it.

"Right," Yael said. "We have to become a little American. We have to be the opposite of what we are. It will break the boys. Avishag, you stop being sorry. Don't ever say 'sorry' or 'thank you.' Just say again and again, 'I don't deserve this. I am a good person,' and Lea, you do the opposite. Apologize. Thank. Smile," Yael said.

"Do you think you may have Stockholm syndrome?" Lea asked. "I am just asking," she said. "I find this all to be very interesting."

"No," Yael said, calm. "I am trying to cause the opposite.

The boys must get the Lima syndrome. They must learn to love us, a little."

"But if we are acting the opposite of who we are, then they don't love *us* us," Avishag said.

"They are. They are loving what we can be. And we can be everything we want to be," Yael said.

"Now you are sounding like the national children's channel again," Lea said.

"And that's how you love me," Yael said, and she looked at Lea.

"And that's how she loves you," Avishag said.

א

IT WASN'T until the afternoon that the boys came. A little before that, Yael started to cry.

"You know, how come you guys didn't ask me how I am supposed to act now?" she asked. She was sobbing and pulling her hair.

Avishag and Lea did not speak.

"I have to not make a sound. Be the opposite of making sounds," Yael said.

"Okay," Lea said.

"So why are you crying so loud now?" Avishag asked.

"And pretty soon I may become a song," Yael said. And she moaned all her knowledge onto the other four ears.

The caravan was five steps wide and seven steps long and the ceiling was above the three girls on the mattresses.

ℵ

THE BOYS came and the boys took and the boys came and the women were what they were not. It was very hard to do.

ℵ

PEOPLE DIED in the after war: 6,422 civilians and combatants in Syria the following month.

ℵ

THE THING is, Yael's idea worked. The boys never came back, after.

In the middle of the fourth night Avishag opened her eyes. And she got up from the mattress. And she opened the door of the caravan. And she walked in the dark to the flag. And she walked in the dark to the war room. One step, one other step, and then more. And she found a flashlight. And it worked. And she walked to the boys' area. And around. At one point she thought she saw another light, and she grew afraid, because who would hear her, and who would help her? But in the end it was just the reflection of her own light in a neon sticker on a wall. She felt a pang in her stomach and remembered the decision of the tiny baby.

The artillery unit guards never showed for some reason.

Lea did not believe that it had worked. And at first she thought that even if it had worked it would not matter. It wouldn't change what was to come. The only ones who knew were the three of them.

That night in the caravan, Avishag came back. She saw it

with her own eyes that the boys had gone, but she did not know what it meant for the next minute either.

Yael had to convince them.

The first thing she decided was that they were not going to drive home that night. That they were going to save that night together. And then she was ready to answer questions.

They argued on the mattresses for hours. About whether or not what had happened to them was even interesting, about whether or not anything they did mattered. About their mattering, or not. When it was still dark out, right when they almost could not make voices anymore, the lights came back on, and then they talked more.

"No one but us will know about this anyway," Avishag said.

"Yes they will. Lea will write it. And in the end people will believe it. Because this actually already happened, and to us," Yael said.

ᴎ

Bᴜᴛ ɪɴ the end it was not Lea who told the story. No one knows who told it, and if, and how. What is true is that the women looked so present inside the lit caravan that night, the walls considered dying.

"I am very tired," Yael said.

"Avishag, do you want us to keep the lights on tonight?" Lea asked.

"No," Avishag said. "No, Lea. I don't want to be afraid anymore."

Suddenly all the lights went out.

Lea had the baby seven months later.

Operation
Evening
Light

When I was eighteen, Mom woke me up. She did it by
tapping on my cheek with two of her fingers. "Yael,
wake up," she said.

When Mom was eighteen, airplanes called her on the
radio. She spent three years waiting for airplanes to call her
on the radio. When they called, my mother would give the air
force planes her permission to land. They needed to land to
refuel. Her base was a fuel base. She was an air traffic controller. They waited for her voice. It had been recently hardened
by the encounter of first cigarettes and the struggle to conceal
youth. Without her permission, the airplanes could not land.
They needed her when they were in the sky and she was in
the control tower, drawing faces on her dark arm with pen

and thinking of ugly jokes she could tell the boys on the base when her shift ended.

Once, an Israeli plane that stopped for a layover in Athens was hijacked, and even though it was not Mom who rescued the hostages (Mom was a girl), it is true that if it weren't for Mom the rescued hostages would not have gotten sandwiches when the rescued plane stopped to refuel on its way home. She used to say that her job in the army was not important, but I thought it was. A plane can only circle in the sky without fuel for so long. She could have, in theory, one time, said no. She could have always said no, but she never did, she never said no in her life. A lot of people could have died because of her. She was eighteen when she arrived at that beach.

א

I woke up after Mom tapped me on the cheek with two of her fingers.

When I was eighteen I slept in her bed because I was afraid of the future. I didn't think much of going into the army, except for making sure I had the right underwear and a new watch, but then I saw a news story about a soldier at a checkpoint whose body had been exploded by a suicide bomber like a surprise, and then I became afraid.

It was not long after I saw the picture of the exploded soldier that I began snapping my fingers all the time under my jaw, to scare away scares. This was something I had done before, but not for years. Dad was angry because he was tired of sleeping in my youth bed. He said his legs were too long, and besides, this was not fair. Mom said it was fair because I was her oldest daughter, and she made me from scratch, and here

I was eighteen and going into the army soon. Then Dad surrendered because he loved her all the time. It was a problem.

"Hey, Yael," she said when we were both in her bed. "Say you want to be in the air force."

"I don't want to be in the air force," I whispered. "Mom, I don't want to be a soldier at all. I think I have scares again."

"Say you want to be an air traffic controller."

"But I already know I am going into infantry. That's what the draft slip decided. You can't be an air traffic controller in infantry. There is no air to control."

My mom was not listening. I never knew if she believed what she said. "Say you want to be an air traffic controller in Sharm el-Sheikh. Say Sinai."

"But. Mom. I can't be an air traffic controller. I'd get too antsy sitting all day and waiting."

"You should ask to be an air traffic controller in Sharm el-Sheikh. It is the best job in the army for a girl."

"But there are no Israeli soldiers left in Sharm el-Sheikh. There is no base there. We gave that whole part back to Egypt."

My mom passed her finger over the ridge of my nose, and again. "Yes. We gave it back before you were born," she said.

She said things that she knew were impossible like she thought they weren't.

א

ON THE day she was drafted my mom walked right into the sorting officer's office and asked to be placed as an air traffic controller. The sorting officer laughed. This was because her skin was dark and her last name was Yemenite and her nose was broken. It grew broken, like a disaster or a crayon painting of a toddler. She broke it when she was a child, falling from the back of the milkman's wagon one evening.

She was not aware on that day that what she asked to be was impossible. She asked her older sister what she should tell the sorting officer she wanted to do, and her older sister laughed. Her older sister knew that the sorting officer would not care what she had to say. Then her older sister wanted to laugh some more. She was not actually the type who laughs. She was a secretary in the army. She advised Mom to say she wanted to be an air traffic controller.

In those days air force bases were known for having built-in theaters and bowling alleys. Places Mom had never seen before in her life. Female air force soldiers were daughters of politicians and military men. Air traffic controllers were the daughters of combat pilots who later became politicians. My mom's father bought a lottery ticket every week and promised to make my grandmother a queen, but meanwhile worked for forty years as a dispatcher of Israel's only bus company. He was just an expected man who aspired in the most expected of ways. He died the year I was born, after he read in the paper that he had lost all the money he had ever saved in the market. He either did it himself or had a heart attack; either way it was something expected that killed him off.

The sorting officer's response to Mom's request was anything but expected. He laughed once. He laughed twice. She asked him why he was laughing and he laughed again.

"You want to be an air traffic controller?" he asked.

"Yes," Mom said. She was not the brightest lightbulb. "This is what I want."

I have heard too many versions of how the conversation

rolled on from there, and I don't want to tell you any of them. Sometimes when you tell a story you've heard too many times, you remember all the times you've heard it before, and you think that maybe it is not very real, and then you think that maybe you are not very real. Maybe you are another woman's daughter. What's important is that Mom became an air traffic controller. No one could believe it, but she did. The air force base she was placed on did not have a theater or a bowling alley or a swimming pool. It was located on a beach. She thought the beach was the most beautiful beach in the world. She said, not just Israel. The world. One time we saw a magazine picture of an abandoned beach in Zanzibar. She said the beach in Sinai where she served looked like that, but that it was also more. I asked what she meant by more, but she just said that it was more of everything.

When she took the bus from the sorting base to the Tel Aviv airport, the driver of the bus knew her. He knew her father. That was the price of having a father who worked for the bus company. You couldn't go anywhere without the help of those who knew the man who raised you. You could never pretend to be a tourist. The country and its roads owned you.

The bus driver asked her how her dad was doing and where she was serving. He asked her that but then immediately started cursing a passenger who told him to hurry the fuck up. The passenger was also a girl soldier, but she looked like she had been serving for much longer than Mom. Her uniform was tailored to her size.

Mom did not want to be rude. She sat behind the driver as he threatened the girl soldier that if she cursed at him one more time he would make her get off the bus. Mom felt good, so good, showing her new army ID and being allowed onto the bus because of it, and not because of her other ID, the one she had been using all of her life. The orange ID that said she was the daughter of a company employee. Mom only paid to ride the bus one time in her life, the day she took me to the army and didn't want to take the car because she was afraid of driving back home alone. By the time her dad retired, she was already married to a man who owned a company car, so she didn't need to take the bus any other time, because of that company car. Not a bus-company car. A car from a company that made parts that went into machines that made airplanes.

She thought the driver had forgotten about her, but as soon as he started the bus he was ha-ha angry with her. Up until that point, the only jokes Mom had ever heard from men and boys were ha-ha-angry jokes. The seller at the market was ha-ha angry with her that she bought his best fish for the Sabbath dinner. "You trickster, you! You took my best fish. What will my other customers say? Ha-ha, I am angry." The milkman whose wagon she fell off when she broke her nose. "You trickster, you! What were you doing climbing on my wagon anyway? Now every time someone asks you how you broke your nose you'll tell them you fell off my wagon, and they'll think I am a bad driver! Ha-ha, I am angry." She had four sisters, no brothers, and she went to a religious all-girls' school. Not because she was religious but because her sister had refused to go back to the public school after a boy told her a ha-ha-angry joke and then spat on her hair. So after that, all the sisters were sent to a religious school, because the oldest sister is always the strongest. Mom's dad didn't tell any jokes, not even ha-ha-I-am-angry jokes, because he truly was angry all of his life.

"So what? Now that you are a soldier you are too good to

answer a question from an uncle?" the bus driver asked. He was ha-ha angry. He was not her uncle, but he knew her father so he called himself her uncle. "How's Dad? Where are you serving?"

The collar of the green uniform chafed Mom under her jaw. What she wanted to do more than anything was make the chafing stop, but no matter how she straightened her collar it didn't help.

"Dad is happy. I am serving as an air traffic controller in Sharm el-Sheikh," she said. When she said it out loud it sounded so correct. This was who she was. This was where she was going. She needed to take the bus to get there. The bus company was there to serve her. So was the driver.

The driver was angry, angry actually, at her answer. At how confident she had become. This was, at least, what she thought, because it sounded like he was no longer joking, so all that was left was anger.

"Tell Dad that if he keeps on drinking and missing work, we won't cover for him for much longer, you hear me?" the driver told Mom.

She heard him. She thought that by now the skin under her jaw must be pink. But she didn't touch it.

"A house full of women, and you can't take care of one slow man," the driver said.

Mom leaned her head against the window. A lady with too many chins looked ahead with her neck stretched as if she were driving the bus herself. Mom looked at the lady as though if she only looked hard enough, she might never have to become her.

Mom had never flown before, and she was so eager to see the streets of Tel Aviv from above and to watch the crowded beaches and hotels becoming smaller beneath her that she thought she would stare out the window the whole flight, but instead she fell asleep. She dreamed of her father. He was chasing her like he did in real life, after she cut her oldest sister's shoulder with a razor so deep there was no choice but to take her to the doctor because she bled through all the fabrics they used to stop her blood. Mom and her sisters often cut each other when they were little. This was because they didn't have a pencil sharpener, so they used rusty razors to sharpen their pencils for school. They would stand around the trash can and sharpen, and then they would bicker over the same things all sisters do. Over the ways their faces and smells had turned excruciating to each other because they were so near, because they were so much like their own. The only difference was that they had razors in hand when they bickered.

In her dream her father had chased her just as he did in real life, and he was drunk, just as he was in real life. The difference was that in the dream he was slow. He kept trying to reach her, and although she did not want him to reach her, she also did not want to be one of five women who could not take care of one slow man, and so she ran slowly herself.

She woke up when the wheels thumped onto the asphalt and bobbed her head sideways. When she looked out the window, she saw sands that stretched as if untouched yet keen and an ocean so quiet she thought it had stopped stirring just for her.

א

MOM CALLED my most chronic problems *sulas*. Over the course of those three years at the beach, Mom once had to practice compassion so well so that it accidentally became a habit, so that she was able to live for the rest of her life without ever desiring half a thing for herself. I could tell her problems that didn't even have words, problems I could never tell my friends about, not even Emuna or Avishag, and she would give them words just so she could do something about them. She noticed my first *sula* herself. I didn't even have to explain it to her. It was she who explained my problem to me. She explained that a *sula* was a bad habit, like knocking on wood or biting your nails. That it was a type of habit that only you knew what you were hoping to gain by preserving but that you didn't have words to explain to others. Her explanation sounded perfect. She said it was the worst thing in the world.

What you have to realize is that every *sula* was a serious problem. A problem that you didn't remember what it was like not having and could not even imagine your life without. Almost like being pregnant when you don't want the baby or being infected with a deadly disease, but worse, because no one knew about it and because you suffered from it every second.

My first *sula* had to do with my neck. Or rather, that area under my jaw. One day when I was five I made a funny face that stretched it out. From then on, it felt as though I was doing it accidentally all the time, and when I looked in the mirror I started worrying that by making that funny face I would give myself a double chin. I was ten and worried about looking fatter in the face, because I had heard Mom say that once you gain weight it doesn't matter if you lose it; your face will stay fat until the day you die. It got worse. I somehow started believing that snapping my fingers three times when they were under my chin, so that I could feel the snap smacking the skin, would cancel out the influence of the funny face. I had no reason to believe that, but I believed it so much I couldn't stop. My fingers hurt so much I couldn't hold a pencil. I would swallow my mayo-mustard-tomato sandwiches so fast at school because I couldn't wait to have them out of my hands so I would be able to snap my fingers again. It was only when Mom tried to take a picture of me on the eve of the first snow that she noticed and screamed: "Sula!" Then she let me stay home from school the next day and watch my Argentinean soaps as she fed me pita and yogurt and clementines.

I would like to tell you that just knowing that there was someone out there who understood fixed the problem, but this was not true. After the problem with my neck there was that time Mom said that standing next to the microwave would make your eyes run away from each other. She said it to my sister, but I heard. This led to almost half a year of the eyes *sula*. I would roll them in their sockets till they screeched, then again. I couldn't watch TV. My head hurt so bad I would sometimes have to sit down as soon as I stood up. In the darkness of my bedroom I worried that I had rolled my eyes so much the darkness was my own blindness.

The teeth were the last of it, and also the worst. Teeth are worse than eyes. I had a whole summer vacation of freedom from *sulas* until I bit into a corncob and accidentally ground my front bottom tooth with my front upper tooth. I managed to get the bottom tooth above the upper tooth, and this hurt like nothing I had ever felt before, so much so that soon I kept on trying to create the same exact pain just because waiting for it to accidentally happen again was worse than feeling it. And I would do it again. And again. Chills would run down my moves and steps. I had to wear sweaters in the middle of that Israeli August. When September came, I would wait for class to end because I could not bear the grinding, then for lunch at home to end because I could not bear the grinding, then for the day to end, then for sleep. I was waiting, waiting, waiting for a relief that never came.

"I have to make it stop. I can't go on like this anymore," I told Mom.

I was paralyzed by a problem that wasn't even real. I couldn't even tell Avishag, let alone Lea.

Mom said: "Yael, I understand, I understand, I understand." She said it again, then again. She looked me in the eyes when she said it. Dad spent months sleeping with his legs folded in my bed. She understood me through the night. Had it not been for someone who understood a problem for which I had no words, I might have gone mad. Minutes chased hours that chased my sleep.

I don't remember when or how or why it went away. I remember that there came a point where I could only breathe when I fantasized about the moment in which I would no longer think about teeth and that there came a point where I was unable to even remember or imagine what a moment like that would be like.

But it went away. This much I know, because when the neck *sula* came back when I was eighteen, right after Dan died, all I could do was wait for the teeth to start.

א

THE BASE on the beach was small. This is the same beach where the president of Egypt would flee, years later, at the finish of a thirty-year rule, when the streets forced him to see they could not love him any longer. Today it costs over five hundred dollars to get a hotel room by that beach in Sinai, and it is so crowded that tourists who visit Egypt waste a lot of time finding a place to lay their towels, but back then twenty or so soldiers possessed that strip of land all by themselves, because it was declared to be a closed military area.

There were only two other girls on the base on the day that Mom arrived. She said that they were both blonde, with short hair. The blondes both grew to have many children, but only sons, and Mom said she could not have imagined it any other way, starting from the day she met them. She could never imagine them having daughters. Mom's black, sensitive hair reached down to her bony ass, and her nose was still broken. The girls were also air traffic controllers. They were the daughters of pilots. They were even dimmer bulbs than Mom was. The base was not a popular posting for air traffic controllers because it was far away and soldiers only got to go home once a month because the army could not spend much on internal flights for soldiers. Mom didn't mind. She had wanted to stay on that beach forever since the moment she got there.

The work in the air traffic control tower was simple. Back in those days planes landed there only once in a while, as part of the training of new pilots. All Mom had to do was look at the lane and make sure no other planes were on it, and she had to make sure she didn't give two planes permission to land at once. If the red phone rang she had to answer it, but it never did. Aside from that, all she had to do was wait. She showed up one hour early for her first shift and then one hour early for every eight-hour shift after that. She picked up smoking and spent all of her pocket money on cigarettes and always made sure she gave more cigarettes to the other two air traffic controllers than she smoked in a day.

Aside from the two blonde girls, there were about twenty other soldiers in the base. Most of them were fuel fillers and ground technicians for the air force. There was one cook, the oldest of all the soldiers, a twenty-seven-year-old man from a kibbutz in the desert who used to make ha-ha-angry jokes at Mom all the time and say her skin was dark as an old choco-late cake or shit, and that she should not be allowed in his dining room because it was a health risk either way, and who gave her kisses on her neck and hard-boiled eggs he had left over.

א

THE FIRST time Mom ever told me about that beach was after I explained to her about the problem I had with my neck, about how it all started when I began to worry that I might have a fat neck. She reached for what she could say because it was she who had told me that once you get fat you will for-ever be fat in your face.

"You know, you don't have a fat neck, but even if you did, and you never will, know that that's not going to kill you. You know, if you are nice, boys can't even see you are ugly. Being a good sport and a laugh is much more important than being pretty. Boys and girls don't like a sour girl. When I was in the army, there were two beautiful, sour girls at my base, and even though I was ugly all the boys loved me because I always smiled."

"You weren't ugly! Are you saying that I am ugly?" This was before I knew about Mom having broken her nose.

"No! You are the most beautiful girl in the world. But it is important to laugh a lot. We need to get you laughing more. How come Avishag and Lea never come by anymore? We need to think what we can do."

Later I started dating Moshe and believed one person didn't think I was ugly. Later, in the army one day, after Hagar did my hair, I even became convinced the whole world could find me beautiful.

At some point during her service, Mom got plastic surgery on her nose. It sounds terrible to say, but it is the truth. It was broken and then it was not. I am not sure where she got the money, how she got it done, but she did. The first picture I ever saw of her is her in a full-length yellow bathing suit. Two shirtless boys are lifting her by the arm from either side, and she is laughing so hard the back of her throat shows. Her nose is perfect and long. The beach where Mom swam in a full-length yellow bathing suit, the beach where boys loved Mom, is not the border anymore. On the new border, the closer border, there are today, ten years after my service, torture camps for Eritreans run by Egyptian Bedouins. They promise the Eritreans they will help them get to Israel through Egypt. For money. Then they chase them, keep them, and send an ear or a finger to their families and ask for some more money. But when the end of the beach was still the border, boys chased Mom on it until the skin under her feet grew firm.

My cousin called, whispering and giggling, one time to ask if it was true what she heard, if it was true that Mom's nose wasn't real. I was always jealous of Mom's nose because of how noble it was, and as I looked at her washing the dishes in a torn T-shirt and head scarf, a woman who spent hundreds of shekels on the right acne wash for her daughters but hadn't

changed her own toothbrush in years, I could not believe she
had ever been a woman who would get plastic surgery.

"Well, my mom did say it was because your mom's nose
was broken or something, but *still*, isn't it funny?" my cousin
whispered through the phone. When they were little, my
mother had cut her mother so deep, she bled through all the
fabrics in the house.

"No," I said. "It isn't funny." I never asked Mom about
her nose.

א

THE MONTH before an airplane was hijacked and Mom had
to accidentally make the case for compassion was the happiest month of her life. All the boys on the base loved her when
her nose was broken because it was so easy to love her—there
was no danger of falling in love with her for real because of
her nose, and she was such a good sport, and she tucked them
in at night after a game of backgammon and let them drown
her in the ocean and let them feel no shame about holding
an eighteen-year-old girl in a bathing suit in their arms. Mom
grew happier each day. She didn't fly home once after she
arrived on the base, back to that Jerusalem building with the
babies and lost lottery tickets and drunken chases and slaughtered chickens and bleeding sisters. The salt air made her hair
bigger. The waiting in the control tower made her thoughts
longer and the faces she drew more interesting. The boys who
made her their queen and relief made her less afraid to think
of memories she had spent her whole life convincing herself
she did not have, so that she did not have to always distract
herself, so that she was less of a less-than-bright lightbulb.

By the time her nose was fixed, the boys thought it was a miracle. Like when, on the Argentinean soaps, the couple finally finds out they are not brother and sister after all.

When she walked on the sand dunes, the boys clapped. The two blonde girls, who later grew to have only sons, then grew quieter. Then they helped her cut her hair right above her shoulders and followed her wherever she went. If it weren't for what happened next, Mom would have been on her way to becoming a dictator or, at the very least, an evil politician's wife, or maybe even an evil God.

It was on the day that Ari Milter bit Joseph Gon's cheek during a fight that was about guarding shifts but was really about Mom's midriff that Germans and Palestinians hijacked an Israeli plane that stopped for a layover in Athens. Two hundred and sixty civilians were on the plane. It was the hijacking that led to Operation Entebbe, or Operation Yonatan, as I know some call it, because of Yonatan, who was killed.

The hijackers landed in Libya to refuel. A passenger who was a nurse faked a miscarriage and was released during the layover. She had a British and an Israeli passport. Her mother had just died, and her father was ill. She had married only weeks before. She was not pregnant, but she managed to convince the female hijacker she might be losing a baby.

From Libya the hijackers ordered the pilot to fly to Uganda. They landed the plane in the Entebbe airport. Idi Amin, who had started out as an army cook just like the army cook who used to give Mom hard-boiled eggs and kisses on the neck, was then not a cook anymore but the ruler of all of Uganda. He cooperated with the hijackers, so it was easy for them to gather all of the passengers into one of the terminals.

The Germans started screaming orders, separating the Jewish and Israeli and Gentile passengers into different groups.

The captain of the plane, who was a Gentile, insisted on staying because he said he was the captain, after all. His eleven crew members stayed also. None of them died, but Air France suspended the captain for staying behind. In the end he got a plaque from Yitzhak Rabin, who was the prime minister of Israel then, for being a protector of Jews, and then Yitzhak Rabin was the prime minister again and was shot by an Israeli Jew who hated him.

What matters or not is that the captain stayed, although it is unclear what help he was to the rescue mission, if at all. The hijackers wanted all these European nations and Israel to release freedom fighters and anarchists who were in their jails. Everyone, including Mom, thought this was what was going to happen. The soldiers of that beach wondered if the plane with the freedom fighters was going to fuel at their base, and if so, whether or not the cook was going to try to stop the plane from flying off with the freedom fighters because a freedom fighter had once blown up a bus the cook's mother was on and made her become blind. She was urging the cook to kill her off already all the time. The hijackers said they would start killing people off on July 1, but in the end they agreed to wait until July 4 because it was a symbolic American date. A seventy-five-year-old woman called Dora started choking on her food, so the hijackers let her go into a hospital in Uganda, because it wasn't July 1 yet and they couldn't kill her then.

א

NO ONE believed there would be a rescue mission but the people who were sent to rescue the hostages. When Mom's red phone rang, it was five in the morning and she was alone in the control tower. She was drawing the face of a girl on her own ankle. She didn't know why, but the girl kept on looking either surprised or angry, and try as she did to fix the girl's eyes, Mom couldn't. She was left with a blotch of blue ink on her dark skin.

When the phone rang, she screamed. This was because she was at peace then and because she had never heard a phone ring before. They didn't own a phone at the Jerusalem apartment. There was a pay phone at the entrance to the market. When she picked up the red phone, she heard the voice of a man on the other line. It sounded nothing like the voices of the pilots coming through the radio. It sounded like the man was standing right there in the room with Mom, breathing the words into her ear.

The man asked for her name, personal ID number, and rank. She had to say her last name twice, because it was a Yemenite last name, and the man was surprised. Then the man told her that if she were to reveal his orders to anyone on the base or in the world she would be prosecuted in a military court and risk the lives of over a hundred Jews.

Everyone thought the hostages would die or be exchanged for other hostages. No one believed in the likelihood of rescue. Everyone but Mom seemed to have a friend of an aunt or a teacher of a brother who was one of the hostages. It only took one worried soldier to tell his worried mother and then the whole country would know the hostages were in the air, even the Arabs of the country. Even when the plane was in the sky, they were afraid someone would shoot it down. They also didn't know Dora was already dead and in a trunk. They thought that if they only kept the operation secret they could still save her from that hospital.

But they needed sandwiches. The hostages hadn't eaten in days. They were expecting to land them in a field hospital the army had built in Kenya and feed them there, but none of the hostages were injured, so there was no point risking the landing there.

The man on the phone asked Mom to tell the cook he must make as many sandwiches as he could.

"What type of sandwiches?" Mom asked, and the man became ha-ha angry with her. Ha-ha angry, but actually relieved because he thought he was sending men to die on top of the hundred Jews who were going to die anyway, and here was this sweet girl with a voice softened by the encounter of first cigarettes and the shock of youth asking him for culinary advice.

"You choose," the man on the phone said. "I am a lieutenant, and here you are a private asking me for sandwich advice. That is your job."

Mom had twenty minutes left until the end of her shift. She drew two more faces. She thought of her favorite sandwich. Pastrami with mayo and red peppers. They didn't have any of these ingredients in the base because all of these things were good only because they go bad quickly.

In the end, giving instructions for the preparation of the sandwiches for the rescued hostages was the most complicated thing Mom had ever done in her life. It was a thing she never thought she could do and would never have done, and it was because it was so hard that once she did it one time, she knew she could do it again and it turned into a habit.

Mom had to make the case for compassion.

"It's a prisoners' exchange, isn't it? They are going to land those Palestinian prisoners at our base to refuel before they take them to Uganda, and they want *me* to make them sandwiches," the cook told Mom. He didn't even try to kiss her neck.

"I can't tell you what it is. The man on the red phone said that I can't."

"Red phone? That's got to mean a prisoners' exchange. And they want *me* to make them sandwiches?"

"I can't tell you what it is. But you do need to make sandwiches. A lot of sandwiches. As many sandwiches as you can."

"I'll make them sandwiches all right. I'll spit in them. I'll pee in them. I'll use rat poison."

Mom did not know what to do. She remembered that she was the daughter of a slow man. She remembered how delighted she had felt when the blade of that razor pierced too deep into her sister's arm when she was a child. She fondled the ridge of her nose and remembered that it was now straight, and that she was beautiful.

"Please don't do anything bad to the sandwiches."

"Why not?"

"You can't; I won't let you," Mom said. Sometimes she liked to say things that were impossible as if they weren't. "You can't," she said.

Had she been born the daughter of a pilot, had she not lived for twelve years with a broken nose, she might have told the cook that he couldn't enough times that it might have worked. But because Mom was not born any of these things, she had to say more. She had to make the case for compassion, not because she wanted to but because she was bound by the circumstances.

"What if one of the prisoners is innocent?"

"My mother is blind," the cook said. "My dad has to take her to the bathroom and sit her on the toilet. And in all likelihood none of them are innocent. The army barely arrests all the people who are guilty."

"What if one of the prisoners just made one mistake? Something they didn't want to do and before they knew it they were doing it?"

"Then it is fair, whatever I do. Then they know they made a mistake."

"What if something happened to them?"

"Like what?"

"Something. They were doing something else and then something happened to them. Haven't you ever done something else and then something happened to you?"

"Like what?"

"Something that happened to you. You were in one place and then you were in another, like you took a bus but you didn't remember why you wanted to take it once you got there."

"I don't take buses," the cook said.

"Please don't do anything bad to the sandwiches."

"I don't take buses."

When he said he didn't take buses the second time, she knew that he understood her. She only understood herself word by word, but by the time she stopped talking, another person who was a cook who used to kiss her neck even when her nose was broken understood her also.

After she finished her three years, Mom took the three thousand shekels her father gave to each of his daughters after they finished their service. She flew to France and worked as a nanny and met a man she loved too much and who made her want to live a very expected life on the day he told her they could not be together. When she flew back to Israel, she had just enough money to register for summer classes in drawing, but nothing more. Her older sisters were already teachers or social workers or mothers. She would later grow most ashamed of taking those summer classes. That was her final landing from those three years of glory on the beach. I have never seen anything she drew, have never seen her draw. After I was born.

א

NO ONE believed there would be a rescue mission except for the people who actually rescued the hostages. Only one of the people who rescued the hostages died. The name of the dead was Yonatan Netanyahu. His younger brother became the prime minister, then again. The planes did not stop on the base on the beach to fuel on the way to Uganda. They stopped in Nairobi, Kenya. At that time, the government was still talking about the possibility of coming in through the ocean for the rescue. It was only in Ethiopia that the rescuers got permission to go ahead with their plan. They landed in the dark, a smooth landing. Cars were waiting for them there; one of them looked exactly like Idi Amin's Mercedes. One of the Ugandan security patrollers, who had never gotten his license but was always interested in cars and always hoped his first car would be a Mercedes, knew that Amin had changed his car the week before. He called his friend and they stopped the car. Then one Israeli soldier shot him dead with a silenced gun. Then the Israeli soldier shot the friend. The car began to drive away. A soldier named Roy looked out the window and saw that the friend was still moving. Roy was a sergeant and twenty, and all of those who died during the rescue lived on his shoulders now. He shot the friend dead with a Kalashnikov through the window, loud. This was how the hijackers knew they were done for three minutes before the Israelis busted into the terminal. They hid in the bathroom and one woman hijacker cried, but in the end they were all killed.

It was the Israeli soldiers who accidentally shot fifty-four-year-old Ida. She had immigrated to Israel from Russia, seeking safety. They also shot a nineteen-year-old boy who would have been a soldier just like the Israeli soldiers who accidentally shot him when they burst in, but he was born in France and studied in college. One Israeli soldier was shot in the neck by Ugandan snipers and could only move his eyelids until the day he died, thirty-two years later. Forty-seven Ugandan soldiers died. Hundreds of Kenyans died two days later, because Idi Amin was mad that they had let the Israelis fuel. They hadn't let the Israelis fuel; they were just people and Kenyans, but then they were dead. In 1979, after the Ugandan-Tanzanian war was over and Idi Amin was gone, they found the body of Dora, the woman who choked on her food. And was sent to the hospital. They found it buried on a sugar plantation twenty miles from the Kampala hospital. Ugandan soldiers had dragged her from her hospital bed a few hours after the rescue mission was over. Her Ugandan doctor and two of the nurses tried to stop them, so the soldiers shot them and left them to die in the hallway. They shot Dora after they put

her inside the trunk. They shot her right before Mom's red
phone rang.

ℵ

I USED to think my mother lived for me.

The Entebbe rescue mission was the most successful
hostage-rescue operation in history. Armies modeled their
rescue missions after it but kept on failing because of reasons
that were not their fault. The earliest imitation failure was
Operation Evening Light, in Iran, ten years before I was born.
The Americans never even had a chance. Airplanes kept on
not having enough fuel, then crashing into each other, then
catching fire, then forgetting spare parts of themselves in lands
that were too far. In the end, people died. Then there was a
prisoner exchange. I would like to tell you that before I went
into the army I thought about the daughter of the American
woman who was in a control tower and had to tell an American cook to make sandwiches for the prisoner exchanges and
did not care if he put poison in them or not, but in all truth
I was so afraid I only saw my fingertips and thought only of
myself.

ℵ

"MOM. I am scared. I am scared of going in."

"What do you have to be afraid of? You are eighteen, Yael.
Your sister did just fine. All of your friends have been drafted
already."

"Of the possibilities. Of all the things that may happen."

"Like what?"

"What made you convince the cook not to poison the sandwiches? Tell me. Tell me again like you never told me before."

"What are you talking about? I was just following orders," Mom said. Sometimes she said things as though she had never spoken other words before.

"I am scared that they will put me in a checkpoint, that I might explode."

"That only happened to that soldier because he wasn't following orders. He was the type of soldier who never followed orders. He wasn't careful enough with that Palestinian he was passing through. Follow orders and you'll do fine."

"How do you know that about the soldier? How do you know he never followed orders?"

"Dahlia told me. This blonde woman I served with. I haven't talked to her in a few years, but she called to ask about what type of jobs exist where we live. Anyway, her daughter served with that boy. She saw him slacking off."

But she had said before. Again and more. The blondes, both of them, had only sons. Sometimes she said things that were impossible and I could think they weren't, until I couldn't.

I used to think my mother lived not for her but for me, but when she told me about Dahlia's call I thought the only part that was true is that she didn't live, even for herself. Even if she did live for herself, she still could not live for me.

And still. I was glad it was just she and I going to the sorting base that day. I was glad that I didn't bring any friends.

"Mom, I am scared," I said. "I am so scared I can't feel my fingertips. I am snapping them under my jaw again. I am scared something could happen."

"Like what, Yaeli?"

"A lot of possibilities."

These were the words of Mom, and me, on the bus that took us to the bus that took me to the sorting base. In time the bus driver joked with us, and even though he said we were loud as a joke, he also truly wanted us to be quiet.

The sandwiches the cook made were kind. Turkey and tomato and mustard. Mom wished she got to see the hostages bite into them.

At the start of that one day, I thought that maybe something would happen and in the end I would get to stay home with Mom, but in the end nothing happened. We spent the morning buying socks and shoe polish. In the afternoon we took the bus to the bus that took me to the sorting base. We fought for a while. Then I said I'd be fine. She kept on brushing my hair, and she kept the hairbrush in her hand after I got on the bus. Through the window of the bus, I saw her dark hands holding it as she stood on the sidewalk. Then the driver pressed the gas and I could not see her anymore. And that was the beginning.

About the Author

SHANI BOIANJIU was born in Jerusalem in 1987. She served in the Israeli Defense Forces for two years. Her fiction has appeared in *Vice, Zoetrope: All Story,* and the *New Yorker.* Shani is a recipient of the National Book Foundation's 5 Under 35, and *The People of Forever Are Not Afraid* is her first novel. She currently lives in Israel.

A Note on the Type

The text of this book was set in Apolline, which was designed by Jean François Porchez in 1993; additional styles were added in 1995. Porchez's goal was to explore the transition from Renaissance handwriting to printed type. The italic cut was influenced by the concepts of master typographers Jan van Krimpen (Dutch, 1892–1958) and Eric Gill (British, 1882–1940), among others. Apolline won the Special Merit Award in 1993 at Japan's Morisawa typeface competition.

The People of Forever
Are Not Afraid

A Reader's Guide for *The People of Forever Are Not Afraid*

When three childhood friends are conscripted into the Israeli Defense Force after high school, they find themselves in a vastly different environment and far from one another—but with all the same angst and ennui of youth. In school, Yael, Avishag, and Lea broke the boredom of their daily lives with the relatively harmless acts of flaunting rules, writing profane words, lying to strangers, flirting with boys; in the army, their flirtations and thrill seeking punctuate a new, darker world with infinitely higher stakes. *The People of Forever Are Not Afraid* follows the coming of age of these three young women in settings as stifling as they are strange. Through their own eyes and in stark, sometimes shocking detail, the three soldiers explore opposing worlds of fantasy and reality, imagination and pure physicality, as they begin to understand who they truly are and who they want to become.

Questions for Discussion

1. The chapters often take a page or more to reveal their narrators by name. Why do you think the author did this?

What clues did you find yourself latching onto to identify each narrator? Do you consider the work required of the reader to be an asset to the novel?

2. Do you identify with Yael, Avishag, or Lea? How much are they the product of their place and time, and how do the small personality traits that distinguish them become significant once they are conscripted into the army?

3. What is the role of the secondary characters (such as Masha, Tom, Hamir, and the Sudanese girl), who feature in temporarily close examinations? Did the passages centered on them further the story or enrich your reading experience?

4. Some more significant secondary characters, such as Dan, Fadi, Hagar, and Emuna, are mainly depicted through the eyes of the main characters. How well do you feel you got to know each of these characters? What role do they play in defining or developing the main characters who know them?

5. How does the realistic and surrealistic nature of the scenes shift throughout the novel?

6. Did you come to the book with knowledge of the Israeli Defense Force? Did you find the book educational? What do you feel you learned from it?

7. Some critics have said that the twenty-five-year-old author's youth shows in her writing. Do you think this is true? What is the commentary of the book about being young today?

8. While still in school, Yael wonders, "When are we going to stop thinking about the things that don't matter and starting thinking about the things that do matter?" What,

to Yael, are the things that "do matter"? What matters to the other main characters?

9. What is the significance of the story of Jonah, repeated at least three times during the girls' schooling? What theme (if any) is the author trying to underscore?

10. Why does Yael keep breaking up and reuniting with her childhood boyfriend, Moshe? Do you think she truly cares for him?

11. Avishag is often depicted as a quiet, introspective character, but through her narration the reader is privy to a craving for communication and resentment for those who don't listen to her. What do you make of Avishag's fear of silence?

12. In Avishag's daydreams, she imagines rewarding an ordinary, unsuspecting girl with recognition for one outstanding talent. Is she imagining herself? Does she think herself worthy of such recognition?

13. Discuss Lea's active role in carrying out her version of justice, from the perceived exactness of avenging the olive tree to her eventual torture of Fadi. Are her actions isolated, or do you see the episodes as signs of an escalating state? Does her experience with the demonstrators at the checkpoint fit into this theme at all?

14. In what ways do the main characters break rules or court danger for their own amusement? Do they seem mindful of the risks they take?

15. How does each of the main characters think about and plan for her future? What drives each toward her activities after the army? Are you surprised by the path any one of them chooses?

16. How do the main characters seem to regard their families, and their family histories before coming to Israel? What influence does the past have on the girls' current lives?

17. At the end of the book, how do you feel about the women's behavior during their imprisonment? How would you want them to react to the boys' assault?

18. While planning their "Lima syndrome" strategy, Yael describes her friends' opposite personas, and later her own: "I have to not make a sound. . . . And pretty soon I may become a song." What does she mean by this? Why is she so upset that her friends did not suggest this on their own?

19. Why does the author include the story of Yael's mother and her time in the army, and Yael's close relationship with her mother prior to boot camp? Does it change the way you think about Yael?

A Conversation with
Shani Boianjiu

Q. You grew up in a small town near the Lebanese border. Can you describe the town? Did your experiences there have an impact on your writing?

A. My town has just a few thousand people, and only one small shopping center. Everyone knows everyone. It is very beautiful; it is up north, so it is very green and every house looks a little different. Most kids are involved in the local Israeli scouts center, a nonpolitical youth movement that builds tree houses and fire banners and tries to instill values like responsibility and good civilianship. The population is secular. We are far from the center of the country and from movie theaters and malls and clubs, and so as a teenager the major weekend night hang-out spot was the park. The library also functioned as the elementary school's underground shelter. During the Second Lebanon War, many missiles fell in my town, and sometimes school was canceled because of this.

I think it helped me as a writer to come from a very small and specific place because it made me so interested in the world. My town is located in a part of Israel that is kind of new (my town is only a few years older than I am), and it is not widely represented in literature. It was great to write about this region, although the town in my book is a lot bleaker and smaller than my town.

Q. **How did you come to write this book?**

A. I started writing what ended up being this book a couple of years after I finished my service, though I actually wrote quite a few stories while I was still in the army; none of them made it into this book. I wrote it for myself, never thinking anyone would ever see what I was writing, certainly not so early in my life, and publishing happened by accident. Some of the chapters in the book started out as separate stories; some events and characters were linked from the beginning. I didn't quite know what I was writing and how the final result would look until I had written many pages.

Q. **Your writing style is unique in that you move back and forth between the present and the past. Was that a conscious choice?**

A. I am not sure if it was a conscious choice, but I don't think I could tell the stories I wanted to tell without moving back and forth in time in the ways that I did. It was more important for me for events and scenes to be revealed to the reader when I thought it was most beneficial for the story I was telling than it was for me to have events unfold in a chronological manner. I guess time is not a very important shaper of experiences for me. An event that happened a year or even four years ago can be much more on my mind on any given day than something that happened that morning.

Q. **Why was it important for you to write a book about female soldiers' experiences in the army?**

A. It wasn't important for me to write a book about female soldiers' experience in the army. I am glad that I was able to give voice to people who are not often represented in fiction: today's young Israelis, female soldiers, northern Israelis, and a whole host of other groups. But I never set out to write a book about female Israeli soldiers. This book is about young Israeli women from the time they are in high school through their twenties. I am an Israeli woman in my twenties, so it was natural that these were the type of characters that I was interested in writing about. I don't think that the book is necessarily only about the army, it is a book whose main characters are young Israeli women.

Q. **All Israeli women are required by law to serve in the army. You were enlisted at eighteen. Were you frightened about being enlisted?**

A. I was not at all scared before I joined the army. In retrospect, I wish I had been more concerned, because the army was quite a shock for me.

Q. **Is there one character in the novel that most closely reflects you or your experience?**

A. Yael, Avishag, and Lea are very unlike one another and very similar at the same time. I wanted to show how little identity an eighteen-year-old girl has when she joins the army, and, at the same time, how crucial the distinguishing bits and pieces that she chooses to hold on to can become in such an environment. Yael's job in the army is most similar to my own, although her stories are most certainly not my own. She is a curious girl who craves human interactions and beautiful things and interesting experiences, sometimes to a fault. I was a bit like her once, though not while I was in the army. Avishag is the saddest of the girls. I think during my army days I was a mix between her and Lea—sad and in my own world like Avishag, and at other times cynical and superior like Lea. What was important for me was to create a friendship between the girls that I didn't have when I was in the army. In many ways I was creating each girl for the sake of the other two.

Q. **You had four- or eight-hour guarding shifts in which you were able to imagine stories. Can you elaborate?**

A. One of the worst and best things about the army was that I had so much time to stand or sit around and be with my own thoughts. I don't think that most people have an opportunity to spend long chunks of time staring into space. It really influenced the way I started to write because I spent very long periods of time with a story in my head. I would see an image or hear a sentence and then I would spend the hours while on guard making up a story in my head and changing it every time I was retelling it to myself. It was awhile before I was able to actually write something down. Even now, I still have to spend a long time holding on to a story in my head before I write it down, although it is harder to find time to just sit and think for hours when you are not forced to do it. Outside of the army there is a lot of pressure to be always reading, watching, or doing something.

Q. **Your native language is Hebrew. What was it like writing this book in English?**

A. I love the English language because it has a lot of words. Writing in English was sort of an accident, but I think it helped me. I had to work harder to find the words I needed. Describing a Hebrew-speaking world in the English language and translating Hebrew idioms and phrases helped me tell stories in a new way, or color a scene in an unfamiliar light.

Q. **What has been the greatest influence on your writing?**

A. Music—I listen to music whenever I am in the first stages of writing to get going. I listen to all types of music. Sometimes I could listen to the same song a thousand times over the course of writing a particular story. Every piece of my writing represents the music it could never quite become.

Reading—I mostly get inspired by reading other people's words, no matter the genre or topic. And learning to sit still and just think for a few hours a day has also influenced me a great deal.

Q. **You portray the novel's characters in an often unsympathetic light. Why?**

A. I am not interested in writing stories about heroes. I am far more interested in the darkest inner corners of my characters' minds. I think a lot of people might feel as though they are the only ones who have terrible thoughts or who have done ugly things, because everyone is so busy portraying such a wholesome image of themselves, young women in particular. I also think human beings in general are not sympathetic. They are beautiful, but not sympathetic.

Q. Is this a surrealistic or a realistic book?

A. I think the book is both surreal and real. I love stories that are only a tiny bit off—some that could have happened but it's difficult to imagine that they did, some that could probably never happen in real life, but it is possible to imagine there's a slight chance they might have happened to someone, somewhere, somehow at some point in time. Readers should choose for themselves how much they have it in them to believe. I think being alive in the real world can sometimes seem more surreal than a surreal scene in a book.

Q. What are you hoping readers will take away from your book?

A. Any scene or sentence from the imagined small lives of girls they don't know.

Recommended Reading:
Shani's Army Reading List

Even though this was not allowed, I often passed the time guarding by reading books. Those were usually the books that were around in the base; a couple of them I brought from home; most were borrowed from the girls in the War Room. I must have read these books hundreds of times, in secret, sentence by sentence.

The Secret History by Donna Tartt
Who Moved My Cheese by Spencer Johnson, MD
Kafka on the Shore by Haruki Murakami
The Time Traveler's Wife by Audrey Niffenegger
The History of Love by Nicole Krauss
And These Are the Years: Fifty Years for the State of Israel
    by Nissim Mishal
Beaufort by Ron Leshem
The Silence of the Lambs by Thomas Harris
Things I Don't Tell by Yael Gadi Taub
Missing Kissinger by Etgar Keret

For additional
Extra Libris content and more
on your favorite authors and books, visit

ReadItForward.com.

Discover fabulous book giveaways,
sneak peeks at great reads, downloadable
reader's guides, and behind-the-scenes
insights from authors, editors,
booksellers & more.